Predators

NICOLE AUSTIN

ELLORA'S CAVE
ROMANTICA PUBLISHING

CAT'S MEOW

Predators, Book One

Micah Lasiter won't let age or physical wear and tear slow him down. Presented with the chance to be stronger than ever before, he doesn't hesitate to join the Predator Project — not that refusing is an option. Too bad nobody warned him about the possible side effects.

Dr. Rebecca Southerby works with cats. Big cats. She's not sure why a scientific research organization wants a zoologist on staff but the great perks make it easy to overlook a few peculiarities. What's shocking is finding her one-night stand at the secret lab and discovering how much he's changed.

Ensnared in a strange new reality, they'll have to work together to bring down the corrupt organization and untangle a web of secrets with the power to either bind them together — or kill them.

EYE OF THE TIGER

Predators, Book Two

Between working as a trauma medic and attending nursing school, Jenny Crosby has more than her share of stress. At least that's what she thought. Then her husband packed a suitcase, withdrew money from their joint bank account and abandoned her. She didn't buy it for a second. Nash wouldn't run. Something horrible happened but the police won't listen. Even her closest friends are encouraging her to get over him and move on.

A few days away from it all is exactly what the doctor ordered. She'll sit in the hot tub, drink hot chocolate and escape her troubles. If only it were that easy.

Nash Crosby is damn good as second-in-command of security. Perhaps too good. Discovering his employer's unethical practices turns him into a liability they can't afford. Nothing will be permitted to stop the Predator Project. Not even a few unwilling test subjects.

Foxy Lady

Predators series, Book Three

For Lance Corporal Renard, her career is everything and she's anxious to tackle the latest training exercise. But the scientists at Nanotech have more in store for Shira than she could've imagined.

Restrained, injected with jacked-up DNA, she's become part of a twisted experiment. Escaping the lab is only the beginning. There can be no return to her old life. No outside knowledge of what she's become. The permanent leash around her neck is more suffocating than a hangman's noose.

Tasked with helping Renard adjust, Army medic Lex McLean had no concept of the challenges Shira faced. Not until he receives a very personal lesson in genetic manipulation.

There's no denying the intense sexual chemistry between them. Not even Lex's hate for Renard has the power to curb his lust. Regardless of a rocky start, survival means joining forces and working together against the true genius behind the Predator Project.

An Ellora's Cave Romantica Publication

www.ellorascave.com

Predators

ISBN 9781419961618
ALL RIGHTS RESERVED.
Cat's Meow Copyright © 2009 Nicole Austin
Eye of the Tiger Copyright © 2009 Nicole Austin
Foxy Lady Copyright © 2010 Nicole Austin
Edited by Shannon Combs.
Cover art by Syneca.

This book printed in the U.S.A. by Jasmine-Jade Enterprises, LLC.

Trade paperback publication July 2010

PREDATORS

∾

CAT'S MEOW

∽

Dedication

ᔥ

To Annmarie McKenna, without whom this story would have crashed and burned.

And to Candy, the first person to read everything I write. Thanks for keeping me from falling into those big fat scary plot holes.

Trademarks Acknowledgement

ᔥ

The author acknowledges the trademarked status and trademark owners of the following wordmarks mentioned in this work of fiction:

Superman: DC Comics

Taser: Taser International, Inc.

Chapter One

ఱ

"We hope to have a table for you in about thirty minutes, Mr. Lasiter."

The perky blonde hostess flashed a bright smile, taking a bit of the sting out of the message, and held out one of those pagers shaped like a drink coaster.

"You're welcome to wait in the lounge if you'd like to have a cocktail."

Micah took a cleansing breath and tried not to take out his frustration on the hostess, who was only doing her job. "Thanks, that sounds good."

He rubbed the stiff muscles in his neck and waited for his vision to adjust before glancing around the dimly lit, jam-packed bar for an empty seat. A long wait to have dinner alone topped off his horrendous day. He'd started with a vigorous predawn workout, followed by one hell of a tedious business meeting and a miserable cross-country flight.

I'm getting too old for this shit!

Thirty-five was hardly ancient, but he'd packed a lot of hard living into those years and had the physical scars to prove it.

A rather intoxicated man vacated a stool toward the end of the long bar and staggered from the room while muttering under his breath. Micah made a beeline for the open chair and sat down next to a tiny brunette, dropping his pager next to hers on the bar. "Mind if I join you?"

The woman studied him for a moment then grabbed his arm in a death grip. "Oh thank goodness, yes! Please." Big moss green eyes sparkled up at him and she sighed in relief.

"How about you keep that drunk away and I'll pay for your dinner? I can't bear another moment of the idiot groping me."

A powerful surge of protectiveness came over him. His spine stiffened and Micah turned, intent on going after the fool. The instinct was ingrained from years in the military and working security, but he didn't view it as doing his duty. He'd always felt protective toward women.

"No! Don't go." She sat straighter, squared her shoulders and lifted her chin. Firm, determined and strong.

Micah's gaze trailed over her petite frame. Narrow shoulders, small breasts and waist, slightly flared hips. She had a delicate, angular face, pert nose. By far, her best features were those beautiful green eyes that missed nothing and her genuine smile. Not the classic definition of a beauty, he thought she was pretty. And there was a certain indefinable quality that drew his interest.

"You look respectable...and sober. I don't think he'll come back, but I'd feel better with you sitting here in case he does."

He swiveled to face her and extended a hand. "Micah Lasiter, barroom white knight at your service."

Her musical laughter sent a shiver of awareness zinging from one nerve ending to the next. She placed her hand within his for a surprisingly firm shake. The instant their skin touched his blood heated, surging through his veins and heading straight for his cock, which jerked to full attention behind his zipper.

What the fuck?

The sudden corporeal response threw him off balance. She wasn't anywhere close to his type—tall, blonde and easy. He didn't go for brainy, complicated women. Too much work. With her hair pulled back in a simple chignon and practical business attire, she appeared prim and proper—a lady.

Ladies never went for him.

"Rebecca Southerby, distressed traveler."

Micah felt dizzy as she turned the full power of that megawatt smile on him. Then he did the most confounding thing. He gave a slight bow, brushed his lips across her knuckles and breathed her in, intoxicated by her warm cinnamon-and-honey scent.

With obvious reluctance, she drew her hand away to trace the rim of her wineglass, gaze downcast, focused on the task. The shy response balanced out her bold strength and was damn sexy.

Signaling the bartender, he ordered a scotch. She enchanted him and Micah wasn't going to watch her slip through his fingers. Not before he investigated this bewildering attraction. He pretended to misunderstand her offer to pay for his meal and took control of the encounter. She was his…for the night. Or part of it anyway. "Would you like a refill while we wait for *our* table, Becca?"

His words had an immediate effect. Honest pleasure lit up her sweet, pixie face, transforming her from stuffy businesswoman into an exquisite beauty. Her eyes sparkled, her lips spread into a dazzling smile and an appealing pink blush spread across her cheeks. When was the last time he'd seen a woman blush? He couldn't remember.

She must see something in him too because she'd put her faith in him, asked for his protection. He sensed a fiery spirit at her core. Intrigued by the enigmatic woman, he was unable to resist the challenge she presented.

* * * * *

"You are a very cunning linguist."

Catching only part of what her unlikely savior said, Rebecca's gaze snapped from the pager, which had started flashing red lights and vibrating, to Micah. She studied his calm expression and shook her head.

He did not just say something about cunnilingus.

No, she had to be mistaken. Or perhaps it was a case of wishful thinking. "You're not so bad yourself."

He'd been a perfect gentleman for the short time they'd been talking, damn him. From the first moment he'd sat down her heart had beat faster. She wanted him, badly. Her ploy of being the timid damsel in distress had worked to keep him close, giving her a chance to be certain he was worth her attention.

Micah rose and extended a hand to help her down from the tall barstool then offered his arm as they walked to the dining room, where he held out the chair and seated her. His good manners impressed her, but he seemed to be holding back. The subtle flirting didn't tell her if he shared the strong, sexual pull exciting her.

She wanted him to feel it. To be turned-on. To want her as much as she wanted him.

Rebecca overlooked the fact that she had not invited him to join her for dinner. All she'd offered was to pay for his meal in exchange for protection from the touchy-feely drunk. At first, anyway. But once they had started talking, she found him to be fascinating and didn't want their time together to end. Not that soon. Not before she got to know him.

Yeah, and it's such a hardship looking at him too! She almost snorted.

There were no words to do him justice. Tall, fit and muscular, more than handsome, but not quite up to the Hollywood standards of gorgeous pretty boys. His long, dark blond hair tied behind his neck added to the severity of harsh features in a face full of character. There was stark menace in brown eyes that missed nothing, implacable resolve in the hard line of his jaw. While his sexy lips were very kissable, she felt certain they could turn vicious under the right conditions.

Beneath the façade of cultivated charm lurked dark shadows he kept hidden from polite society. She sensed an affinity for action and risk. The suit he wore, tailored to his tall, powerful frame, felt wrong. He was no desk jockey.

She had grown up around military men and had no problem spotting one. It was easy to picture him in fatigues, heavily armed, making his way through a jungle. Strong, intense and aggressive. Rambo times ten. Or better yet, in a white billowy shirt, tight pants and boots, brandishing a sword.

"Now what's brought that naughty smile to your pretty lips? Thinking about me?"

Ah ha. There's the bad boy she'd sensed lurking. The kind of arrogant guy who went for shallow beauty and stayed far away from intelligent women like herself.

She decided to test the theory. "Just calculating quadratic equations in my head."

His robust laughter turned her insides to mush. "Need a calculator?"

A sense of humor and not afraid to use it. Nice. She intimidated most men, but Micah was proving to be a delightful exception to the rules. Perhaps there was more beneath the exterior than she'd thought.

Sure, he oozed charisma and sex appeal. Their waitress salivated over him and thrust her fake breasts in his face at every opportunity. Micah remained polite and ignored the blatant flirtation. In fact, she was impressed. Not once had his gaze wandered to the waitress's more than ample cleavage.

"Is there a boyfriend or husband waiting at home?"

For her? That would require having a life outside work. She shook her head.

"What's brought you to Asheville, business? Family?"

"A job interview."

"Really? What do you do?"

"I'm a zoologist. My studies are focused on Felidae — big cats." Her life was boring. She'd much rather talk about him. "What about you?"

"I'm in town for an art show."

Rebecca laughed then coughed, nearly choking on the sip of wine she'd just taken. She didn't buy his answer even before she caught the devilish sparkle in his eyes, belaying the serious expression.

"What, I don't look artsy to you?" He appeared offended.

A crack in the veneer? Interesting. Perhaps even men of steel require reassurance once in a while. "Somehow I can't imagine you having the patience for artistic pursuits."

Micah appeared relaxed as he took a sip of his drink then leaned back in the chair. He didn't fool her. The piercing intensity in his dark eyes told a different story. What she thought of him mattered a great deal to Micah.

"I can be very patient. Want to try me?"

The sexual implication in the simple statement sent tingles racing along her spine.

"How do you see me, Becca?"

His deep, sensual voice flowed over her, heating Rebecca's blood. Their conversation was rife with double entendres, a subtle and skillful mental seduction stimulating her intellect. But the way his hungry gaze devoured her brought new meaning to their playful banter.

The sexual tension that had built between them soared. His expression told her the time for teasing had ended. Awareness spread through her, awakening her body. Her breasts were swollen and heavy. Too bad she'd taken off her suit jacket earlier. Her taut, aching nipples had surely become visible through the thin silk blouse she wore, an indication of her arousal he couldn't miss.

Her head spun and she said the first thing that came to mind. "You're a swashbuckler — a pirate captain."

She wanted to recall the words as soon as they left her mouth. It had to be the wine loosening her tongue since Rebecca did not often imbibe. She had a strong aversion to feeling altered and losing control.

Emboldened when he didn't laugh, she went into vivid detail. "You're supremely confident, larger than life. You buck convention, living by your own rules and code of conduct. Freedom and being in command are your ultimate goals. You're brave, a mysterious renegade with an insatiable lust for life. A total scoundrel, pillaging and plundering women, stealing the hearts of those who are turned-on by the danger you represent."

He remained silent when she stopped speaking and Rebecca bit back a groan. *You idiot. Now he'll make a hasty retreat.*

Micah's unwavering gaze was disconcerting. He made her antsy, but she refused to turn away as he studied her for several long moments.

"Your tone and attitude give the impression you're afraid. That you dislike what I make you feel," Micah stated.

She narrowed her gaze, wondering how he'd come to such an outrageous conclusion. So what if she was leery of the unaccustomed arousal bombarding her. The man made her long for hot, sweaty sex and screaming orgasms. For all the good it would do him. She wasn't a one-night stand kind of woman.

He leaned over the small table, encroaching on her personal space until they were almost nose to nose. Getting way too close for her good intentions to remain intact. She wanted to thread her fingers through his thick hair and feel Micah's lips on hers.

"Your body is sending a very different message."

She figured the weighty, knowing stare was an attempt to intimidate. Her spine stiffened. She would not be the one to avert her eyes or pull back. Not going to happen even though she knew he was baiting her, waiting for a reaction.

"You want me."

Then again, why hold back? She hated games and preferred to make sure people knew where they stood with her. "You're right. I was wrong. You're no pirate. You're an arrogant ass!"

Tossing her napkin on the table, she started to rise. Micah's hand shot out, strong fingers encircled her wrist in a solid but loose grasp, shackling her.

"No, it's my turn and I'm not finished yet."

Oh, great. She couldn't wait to hear more. This should be hilarious. Hurtful words from the past raced through her mind. *Uptight...prudish...cold.*

She settled on the edge of the chair, ready to bolt. Micah didn't release her. His thumb stroked her inner wrist, slow and gentle, making her pulse race. His voice dropped to a low and provocative whisper.

"Nice speech. Too bad it's not how you really feel. Your body tells me you want me." Micah held her securely when she tried to pull away.

"Your eyelids are at half-mast and your pupils are dilated, looking up at me from under those thick lashes. Your cheeks have turned the most enticing shade of pink and are flushed with desire. Even now, your shoulders are pulled back but you're leaning in toward me and restlessly rubbing your legs together."

Rebecca made a conscious effort to still her movements, but she'd given too much away. Micah was right. The light touch of his fingers on her wrist wasn't anywhere near enough. She was desperate for more.

"You're breathing fast and shallow. A blind man wouldn't miss your beaded nipples lit up like headlights, aching to be touched. Those beautiful, pouty lips are parted.

I'm sure you're not even aware of how often the tip of your tongue has slipped out to lick them."

Rebecca worried her bottom lip between her teeth and he sucked in a harsh breath. He read her as if she were an open book, laid bare for his examination.

"Damn, baby. That's so fucking sexy. You've got me so hard. I can't stop picturing your mouth stretched wide around my cock."

Their waitress rudely dropped the check folder near their joined hands. Dismissing Rebecca's presence, the girl addressed Micah in one last-ditch attempt to gain his attention. His gaze never wavered from Rebecca's.

"If you're sure there's nothing else you want, I'll take that to the cashier when you're ready."

He released Rebecca long enough to toss some money on the table then moved around to her chair and held out his hand.

"Are you ready?"

If she passed up a night in his arms, she'd spend the rest of her life kicking herself.

Rebecca tossed caution to the wind and seized the opportunity. One night of hot, reckless abandon before returning to her real life. For one night, she could set aside years of discipline and ironclad control. Give in and experience true passion.

She nodded. "Oh yes."

She was more than ready.

Chapter Two

ഇ

Throughout the evening he had caught glimpses of the fiery passion Rebecca kept locked up tight, covered by the pretense of a prim and serious businesswoman. But the second he kicked the hotel room door closed and they were alone the protective smoke screen surrounding Rebecca Southerby evaporated, along with his plans for a sophisticated seduction.

While she may be a lady in public, it turned out that in private she was every red-blooded man's wet dream—a sexual siren.

She pulled the pins from her dark hair and shook her head, sending a riot of silken waves tumbling to her waist. With her hair down the lights revealed hints of red and gold he hadn't noticed before.

Micah sucked in a harsh breath as in one graceful glide, she dropped to her knees. Watching him from beneath thick lashes, Becca licked her lips and reached for his pants. His belt buckle offered no resistance to deft fingers. A flick of her wrist opened the fastener then she tugged on the zipper.

A feminine hum of appreciation as she dragged the material down his legs made his cock jerk against the confinement of his boxer-briefs. Following her lead, he lifted one foot, then the other, and she slipped off his shoes.

Short, manicured nails scraped a light, tingling path over his legs. When she reached his hips, she paused and leaned forward, pressing soft lips to his cloth-covered erection. The stream of warm air heated his entire body, a fine sheen of sweat breaking out on his skin.

"Jesus, baby!"

The carnal grin that spread across her red lips had his knees shaking. Her fingers slid under the waistband and she pulled the soft cotton over his hips. Eager for more of her attention, his cock bobbed and a slick pearl of cum beaded at the slit. Slender fingers encircled his shaft, rasped over sensitive flesh as she stroked from base to crown, finally breaking eye contact to take a good, long look at his cock.

"I'm so hungry," she whispered.

God yes!

Taking his balls into her other palm, she rolled the taut sac and continued the slow strokes along his shaft. He longed to bury his fists in her hair, directing her mouth to his needy flesh. Through sheer force of will, he held the urge in check, fisting his hands at his sides instead. As her hot tongue trailed along an engorged vein he couldn't prevent the involuntary thrust of his hips. Her soft lips and tongue glided over his length, kissing and licking. Fingers touching. Destroying him.

Perspiration slicked his body, which shook in anticipation as her mobile mouth moved higher, her tongue tracing a scorching path around the sensitive ridge. She lapped at the underside of the crown and he moaned, causing her to focus on the responsive spot. His legs almost gave out as she nipped at the tender spot. Her tongue snaked out to ease the slight pain then delved into his slit.

"Sweet Jesus." His breathing turned rough, choppy.

She had yet to take him into her mouth and the torment was killing him. He certainly hadn't expected she'd be so uninhibited and skilled. Micah didn't know how much more excruciating pleasure he could take. Slickened with her saliva, the cool air in the room added to the amazing sensations. The wicked temptress laughed as he struggled just to breathe. Hungry green eyes watched him as her pouty lips hovered over the tip of his cock. After what was surely an eternity, her lips slowly parted and descended.

Unable to take any more visual stimulus, Micah banged his head against the door and his eyes rolled upward to stare at the plain white ceiling. He found the view safer for his sanity, right up until she sucked him into the silken heat of her mouth.

"Oh Christ, baby."

Unhurried, she suckled the head. Her wicked tongue flicked at the explosive area she'd discovered earlier and Micah came close to detonating. His balls tensed against her palm as a damp finger slid along his perineum. She sucked him deeper and mumbled, creating vibrations that surged through him.

His restraint snapped. Micah's fingers delved into her lustrous hair, flexing and clenching against her scalp. With her firm breasts and torso pressed tight against his thighs, he felt the sensual shivers racking her slender frame.

Good, she was as affected as him.

Her greedy mouth consumed him, tongue lashing his flesh as her lips tightened. Becca sucked hard and took him to the back of her throat.

"Fuck yeah, baby. Take it all." His strained voice sounded raspy.

She didn't fall into a predictable rhythm, keeping him on edge by changing her motions often. One moment she massaged his balls and her lips slowly dragged over his length. The next she plunged fast, swallowing around the head of his cock and twisting her fingers at the base.

He stared down at her, panting and thrusting his hips, concentrating to keep his fingers loose in her hair, following her lead instead of trying to direct her movements.

"Becca—" he warned. "I'm close."

She hollowed her cheeks, sucked his cock with voracious hunger. That damn finger slid farther back, circled his anus. When her fingertip breached the tight pucker he was history. His balls clenched and sizzling-hot jets of cum surged through his cock.

Her throat convulsed, drawing out his climax. She drank him down and then licked him all over, searching out every last drop before finally releasing his spent flesh.

Jesus! She'd sucked the very breath from his lungs. He couldn't breathe, couldn't move. He felt weak as a baby and barely managed to keep himself from sliding down the door.

Wow, now that was hot!

And what an ego boost. It sure explained why some women loved giving blowjobs. Rebecca had never felt more powerful or sure of her sexual prowess. She was almost giddy.

Her previous lovers hadn't brought out this side of her personality. She hadn't even known it existed, regardless of her vivid fantasies. Imagine that, she had an inner porno babe who'd been waiting thirty-two years for someone to set her free.

Ouch! There was a downside though. Her knees ached from kneeling for so long. Probably had indentations from the carpet in her skin too. This inner-slut thing may not be all it's cracked up to be. And she had no idea of proper post-blowjob etiquette. What was she supposed to do now?

She glanced up at Micah. He looked like a sprinter after running a marathon—sweaty and ready to collapse. Although still a rather impressive size, his cock had deflated and hung limp along his leg while her body hummed with sexual want. Her nipples ached, her clit throbbed and slick arousal coated her thighs.

She needed to fuck!

Typical damn man. All that mattered was he'd gotten his rocks off. Now he'd crawl into bed, go to sleep and snore louder than a chain saw, leaving her to her own devices.

What a buzz kill.

Rebecca used a nearby chair to steady herself as she rose. Sure enough, her knees bore an interesting pattern of red depressions from kneeling on the carpet. Lovely!

"Well, umm..." Damn, she had no idea what to say. So much for making a graceful exit. "This was...nice. I should be going. Got an early — "

"Going?" Micah frowned, his expression turned hard and uncompromising. "Nuh-uh, baby. We're just getting started. Don't shut down on me and hide all that fire again. All that passion."

She almost looked around to see who he was talking about. Fire and passion? Certainly he wasn't referring to her. She was a lab geek for crying out loud. But she needed...more.

"I didn't plan this very well. Didn't get my...er, you know...before you got yours. Now you're tired and spent — "

"Becca..."

She waited for him to finish but he hesitated. Perfect. For a minute she had thought things couldn't get any more awkward. She was wrong. Now he'd come up with all kinds of lame excuses she didn't want to hear.

"My name is Rebecca. Nobody calls me Becca." Or any other nickname. She was plain old boring Rebecca. Becca sounded too racy for her. Something a bolder woman would be called.

"Ah, baby." Micah pushed away from the door. "Haven't you figured it out yet?"

Obviously not. Voice stuck in her throat, Rebecca shook her head.

"I'm not like every other man you've known. We're far from finished."

Not finished? She liked the sound of that. A lot.

He moved closer. Really close. Until her breasts flattened against the hard planes of his chest and he cupped the side of her face in his huge hand. Of course, big hands went with a big body. Same as in the animal world with her cats — the bigger the paws, the bigger the kitty. That theory sure applied to other parts of his anatomy. Micah had the biggest, tastiest cock she'd ever had the pleasure of encountering.

Rebecca gave herself a mental shake, trying to clear her rapidly disintegrating train of thought.

"I'm different. I want to be more for you. Special for you. Your own pirate captain."

Oh wow. His eyes had darkened, appearing almost black and smoldering with lust. For her? Men looked at other women that way, but not her. Mousy Rebecca Southerby didn't draw sexual attention.

"You're a combination of Rambo and a pirate. I'm not sure what that would make you. Rambate maybe."

Micah's deep, throaty laughter went right to her core and gave a hard tug. Lord, she could get addicted to his laugh.

"I like that, *Becca*." She didn't miss the emphasis he put on the nickname. "I get to kick some ass Rambo-style and then make off with all the booty."

She returned his smile. This lighter, playful side of the man appealed to her. She doubted let his guard down often.

His arms skated down her side and around her back to grasp her butt. Micah's firm hold had her trembling with desire.

"You won't be left wanting, baby. You see, I plan on making you come." He squeezed her butt suggestively. "Several times." His head lowered and warm breath caressed that amazing spot behind her ear. "Multiple orgasms so strong you'll be hoarse from screaming my name."

He nibbled on her earlobe then bathed the tender flesh with his tongue.

"Again and again."

She shivered as he pressed soft kisses along the column of her throat.

"All night long."

Hell yeah!

She must be dreaming because Micah was too good to be true. A real fantasy come to life, in vivid color even.

Rebecca squealed in surprise as he picked her up and in three quick strides, tossed her onto the bed. Good thing too. His intense expression made her go weak in the knees.

In no time at all he'd divested Rebecca of her clothes. As he stood beside the bed to strip, she drank in the glorious sight.

She'd always thought laws against nudity in public were to protect the innocent from the trauma of seeing potbellies and saggy old people. Now she knew the truth. They were to prevent Micah Lasiter from causing public riots. It had to be illegal for a man to look so good!

The only men she'd ever seen who even came close had been on the pages of magazines. The ultimate in perfection. But Micah wasn't perfect. He'd worked his body hard. Various scars marred the landscape of ripped body covered by tanned skin. In her opinion, they enhanced his rugged sexiness.

His muscles had muscles, and in between were deeply carved indentations. A sensual roadmap Rebecca found she was hungry to explore. She wanted to let her fingers do the walking. To feel the difference in texture from the long mane of dark blond hair framing his face to the darker smattering over his chest, narrowing to a fine trail along his abdomen and becoming a lush nest at the base of his rejuvenated cock.

What the hell was a hunk like him doing in a hotel room with her? He'd climaxed, but he wanted to continue? Wanted to give her screaming orgasms all night long?

Yup, he was unique and should be prohibited for the sanity of womankind.

A rough growl rumbled from his broad chest, reminiscent of her babies. A member of the family Felidae in the genus *Panthera*, also known as one really large, non-domesticated cat. A carnivorous woman-eater. A jaguar or leopard. Perhaps a tiger.

No, those didn't fit.

Rebecca's gaze took in his big golden body and wavy mane of hair again. Micah brought to mind the most fearsome predator, the king of beasts—a lion.

As if proving her conclusion, he pounced on the bed, caging her beneath his larger body.

"I was wrong. You're neither Rambo nor a pirate. You're an animal."

"Mmm…yes." He leaned down and licked a nipple. She arched her back, thrusting the peak closer to his mouth. "A famished animal, hungry for a taste of you."

Micah proceeded to prove just how rapacious his appetite could get. After a long, slow, drugging kiss he attacked her body, emitting animalistic vocalizations as he feasted. Not one inch of skin was passed over. Lips, teeth and tongue tasted. Deft fingers stroked, teased and tweaked. He dominated her, using his weight to anchor her writhing body to the mattress, his strength to bend her to his will.

And she loved every second.

He sampled all except where she wanted him most. Her sex. Shameless, she writhed beneath him. Begged and pleaded with abandon. Micah would not deviate from his planned route.

When he finally settled between her legs, massive shoulders spreading her wide, her heightened level of arousal was almost painful. She nearly came with the first bold sweep of his tongue over her drenched folds but he held her on the edge, pulling back whenever she got close.

"Oh god. Please! I need…"

His tongue circled her entrance then plunged deep, rasping the quivering walls of her pussy. Her hips bucked, reaching for the orgasm that hovered just out of reach. Her channel clenched as he withdrew to circle her clitoris. The bundle of nerves spasmed and pulsed. All it would take was one firm stroke, but again he moved on.

"Fuck," she grumbled, frustrated beyond her normal restraint, reduced to cursing. "You bastard!"

"What, sweet baby?" he teased. "What do you need? Tell me, Becca."

Inhibitions be damned, her need to orgasm was far greater than any sense of propriety. If he wanted specifics, she'd give him explicit, in-your-face instructions.

"Suck my clit. Flick your tongue over it, fast. Fuck me with your fingers, hard. Three of them. And don't stop 'til I come."

Holy shit. Where had that come from? She was a completely different woman with him. Bold and brazen. Daring and free. And damn if she didn't like the new her.

While Micah may be all dominant alpha male, he was pretty damn good at following instructions. He held her clit captive between his teeth, his tongue flicking against the tip and his lips exerting glorious suction. At the same time, two thick fingers powered into her pussy. He twisted his wrist, added a third finger and homed in on the perfect spot where the stroke of his fingertips drove her wild.

Rebecca bucked, fucked his face, muttered incoherent praise. Her entire body tensed to the point only her heels and shoulder blades remained in contact with the mattress. Micah mumbled something, creating amazing vibrations that tore through her pelvis. She strained, grabbed for the prize, screaming his name as overwhelming pleasure exploded, ricocheting from one nerve ending to the next.

He didn't let her down. Micah kept the devastating sensations rolling, building the pressure until all she could do was surrender to the ecstasy. Dazed, she lost count of how many times she came, each peak higher than the last. And when she thought she could take no more, he proved her wrong. Repeatedly.

He gave her no chance to recover. Micah rolled on a condom, aligned his cock with her pussy and slammed forward. He filled her in one great thrust—stretched tender tissues to new limits—reached previously concealed and ignored pleasure centers. She felt full, whole. Blissed out beyond belief.

He took her hard and fast, then slow and deep, constantly changing the tempo. Just barely coming down from one peak he built her back up until she lost all concept of anything other than him. Finally, Micah brought her to one last stunning crest and followed in her wake.

They collapsed in total exhaustion and satiation only to wake a short time later. The slightest touch was all it took to reignite the passion and start all over again. He fucked her from behind then changed position so they both lay on their sides.

The next time she woke up he was carrying her to the bathroom. She'd never had shower sex but soapy bodies sure made for devilish fun. Hands sliding over sensitized skin. Slippery bodies moving in sync. It blew her mind.

For a magnificent finale, she took control and told Micah what she wanted. She got a heady rush from directing their play. She straddled his hips and rode his cock as if she were a rodeo queen, feeling powerful, sexy and beautiful in Micah's arms. He set her free and helped her to fly.

If only the night could last forever and they didn't have to return to their real lives in the morning.

* * * * *

Rebecca woke in the predawn hours held tight against the curve of Micah's body. One heavy arm was slung possessively over her waist, shackling her. Devastating her emotions. The sheets were tangled around them and the room reeked of hot and sweaty sex.

She wanted to stay with him. But she couldn't. Rebecca wasn't stupid. She knew the score. One-night stands did not turn into relationships. Unconscious loving behaviors displayed while asleep didn't equate to true sentiment. He appeared to have laid claim to her, but it wouldn't stand up to the light of day.

The night had been out of character for her. They were opposites and while opposites attract, they also repel. Micah was a man of action, the kind of guy who wouldn't go for long-term relationships. If he did, he would go for beautiful arm candy, not a socially inept science nerd.

She didn't do casual sex, with this night being her one exception to the rule. When she picked a man for the long haul, it would be someone with similar interests. Even though she'd been assertive in bed, she didn't have enough confidence in herself as a woman to believe she could hold the interest of a man like him.

Quiet as a mouse, she slipped from the bed, trying not to moan over all the aches and pains in muscles that had never received such a vigorous workout. He reached out and a pang of regret pierced her heart. If only they could form a lasting bond from their very brief time together.

The realist in Rebecca shook off the destructive thoughts. Lust and mind-blowing sex did not equate to love.

She had to fight not to giggle upon spotting the numerous discarded condom wrappers littering the floor. They'd made some great memories. Ones she'd cherish and hold close on cold nights.

Dressing in the rumpled clothes, feeling sticky and longing for another shower, she brushed a light kiss across his forehead. Then Rebecca did what had to be done. She walked away, closing the door on one of the most exciting chapters in her life.

Chapter Three

∞

"Not yet. Wait for it," Micah instructed.

Rubbing at his temples, he struggled to concentrate on his job and clear the erotic images from his mind. Two weeks had passed since his night in Asheville. Fourteen hellish days of torment. More than twenty-thousand minutes—not one of them free from thoughts of her. She filled his mind every moment while awake and invaded his dreams when he managed to sleep.

Dr. Rebecca Southerby, the one who'd gotten away. Not that he was unable to go after her. Finding her had been child's play. He knew where she lived, worked and spent her free time. He knew lots of facts and figures but longed to know her more intimately. Investigating her background was part of his job since she'd applied for a position at Nanotech Industries, the company where he worked as head of security. Strong work ethics had kept him from using what he'd learned to contact her.

"Hold your positions," Micah ordered. "He has to leave the building or the charges won't stick."

"Suspect's reached the security scanners," Simpson stated. The competent security specialist was on the ball, staying almost a step ahead. "Silence the alarms."

During the break in action, Micah's mind wandered back to Becca. Intimate details haunted him. Facts impossible to know without having slept with her. Facts he couldn't forget once he had. Little things, like how her hair smelled of warm cinnamon, her skin of sweet honey. Amazing details such as the musky, slightly spicy flavor of her arousal. The explosive passion hidden beneath layers of respectability.

Rebecca had shoved her sexuality so deep he doubted she'd known it existed before they met. He'd noticed it from the start. It was in every sensual move she made, the subtle innuendo and veiled meaning in how she phrased things. And soon as he'd gotten her alone, the potency of her innate eroticism had blown him away.

"Suspect's almost to the doors. Ten feet, eight…"

Rawlins' countdown echoed in Micah's earpiece, the security guard's voice cutting through his wayward thoughts. He had to stop thinking about her. Stop fantasizing and replaying every sizzling moment in his mind.

"Five, four—"

"Hang on," Simpson interrupted. "Suspect is stopping."

Damn it! Get your fucking head on straight and in the game before you fuck this up!

"What's happening?" Micah spoke into the microphone concealed by the cuff of his shirtsleeve.

"He's set down the package," Rawlins informed. "Hand's in his pocket. He's pulling out—"

"It's a cell phone." This from Gardner in the security room. "Locking on to the signal. Give me a sec."

After a few tense minutes and several electronic clicks, the ongoing conversation echoed over their com link.

"Stop boring me with the details of your job and answer the question. Do you have it?"

"Yes."

"Good. A black SUV will meet you at the entrance to the parking garage."

"What about the money?"

"Once you hand over the formula, the funds will be transferred to your account. We've already been over this. Stop stalling."

"Fine."

As the conversation ended, Rawlins resumed his countdown. Micah forced his wayward thoughts to the back of his mind and watched for the suspect from across the courtyard. Industrial security didn't offer the same thrill for him as serving a decade of covert ops in the Army had, but he enjoyed his work. Scientific research was a highly competitive field full of spies who would bribe, coerce and steal in order to gain an advantage.

Case in point, the weasel was willing to sell his employer's new technology. A look at his financial records spoke volumes. His wife's lavish spending habits had gotten them deep in debt. Now he risked his career and even his life for money. Micah had no sympathy for the idiot.

What did bother him about the whole thing was the weasel in question had been in daily contact with Dr. Rebecca Southerby. And the organization was in the process of courting her for a top-secret project. Not even Micah knew details of what her job would involve.

He didn't want to believe the sweet and demure woman he'd shared a night with could be wrapped up in theft. The sad truth was she appeared to be in this mess up right up to those big green eyes.

"Suspect is on the move. He's cleared the doors."

"I've got him," Micah said. "Move in."

Either the weasel sensed the impending danger or something tipped him off. Whatever the reason, he started to run.

"Suspect's gone rabbit." Micah began issuing orders rapid-fire, while racing after the target. "Donovan and Moore, seal off all exits. Hendry, isolate all known associates. Don't lose him, Gardner."

"Got him, boss," Gardner replied. "Pick-up vehicle has rolled up to the southwest gate."

"I'm on the suspect. The rest of you converge on the garage. I want whoever is in that vehicle. Lethal force is *not* authorized. Take 'em down, but make sure they'll still be able to answer questions."

Taser in hand, Micah hurtled decorative planters and dodged employees outside enjoying their lunch breaks. He had no trouble closing in on the suspect, a pasty, out-of-shape researcher who spent most of his time working with his mind while neglecting his body.

Seeing the team converge on the SUV, the suspect turned and headed toward the nearby forest surrounding the facility, probably hoping to lose his pursuers in the dense foliage. There wasn't a chance in hell of Micah letting that happen.

"He's headed for the trees."

And Micah was the only one close. Putting on a burst of speed fueled by the adrenaline of the chase, his legs ate up the ground between them, and he gained on the weasel.

Almost there.

He went down, hard. His foot caught in a hole, wrenching his ankle. Micah landed flat on his face and left knee with excruciating darts of pain shooting through his leg.

"Fuck, I'm down. Suspect's in the woods. Call in local law enforcement."

* * * * *

"Where the hell am I?"

"Relax, Mr. Lasiter. We'll be there soon."

Micah got the hazy impression of a face hovering over him then it disappeared before he could focus on the image.

"There"? Where the fuck is "there"?

He tried to reach up and rub his temple but his hands didn't work right. They were sluggish, unresponsive. And what was wrong with his eyes? Everything looked fuzzy and surreal. Detached.

He detected movement, saw flashes of green trees through a dark-tinted window. Heard the hum of tires on asphalt.

The darkness at the edges of his vision closed in. Someone spoke but he didn't understand the garbled words.

* * * * *

Micah's body jerked. His brain struggled to process the information his senses took in. White walls, beeping instruments, numbness in his legs, his left arm freezing cold from the IV fluids.

Oh shit!

They'd operated again. How many surgeries did that make? Three or was it four? He'd lost count. The anesthesia messed him up, and whatever other drugs they pumped into him fragmented his memories. He wasn't sure how much time had gone by since he'd blown out his knee.

"Ah, you're awake. Good!"

He knew that voice. Micah rolled his head to the side to find the head of Nanotech, Gabriel Weltman, sitting in a chair next to the stretcher he lay on.

"You have decisions to make, Micah. With extensive therapy, you may be able to walk again...one day."

He caught some of the words but not all. Stuff about shattered bone and inability to restore function. Enough to understand he was royally screwed.

"There is another way. We've made great strides with our recombinant DNA and gene-manipulation research. There's a procedure our scientists have perfected. The Predator Project."

Weltman rattled off a bunch of scientific stuff that went way over Micah's head.

"We can make you strong again. Stronger than ever. The intended application is military in nature. We believe you are the perfect candidate. Your DNA would be altered, infused with *Panthera leo.*"

Panther what?

Certain words rattled and echoed around in his head. *Stronger than ever. Able to keep working. Top-secret program.*

Micah grasped two important facts. The Predator Project would prevent him from being an invalid. He'd have a second chance. But something wasn't right since he'd never heard of the project before. From the little he knew about research, it sounded as if they'd broken some laws, maybe done things that circumvented moral and ethical standards for experimentation.

And he no longer had an out. Now that Weltman had shared this information, Micah had to either keep quiet and reap the benefits or blow the whistle, which would probably get him killed. Weltman couldn't let him walk—or limp— away. Turning this down would be signing his death certificate. He no longer had a choice.

"Do it!"

* * * * *

What the fuck have I done?

Damn, had they ever done it. They'd infused him with animal DNA, performed more operations to help his body accept the new genetic soup. Stuck him with needles, poked and prodded. Then they became afraid of their own creation, shoved him in a cage, locked up behind steel bars. Security cameras watched him every moment, studying him as though he were an animal in the zoo.

Confused, strapped to an exam table, helpless and in pain, Micah endured the researchers torturing his abusing and battered body. Angry and frightened, he felt something elemental within him begin to shift, an altering of reality.

Glass shattered, pulling Micah from his confused thoughts.

"Oh god."

A nervous female technician had dropped a vial and one of the scientists yelled at her. In his rage, the man lashed out at the woman, striking her face.

"Leave her alone," Micah demanded. The scientist ignored him.

He fought the restraints to no avail as the woman was slammed against the wall and slapped until she dropped to the ground. It brought back vile memories from his childhood.

Rage blasted him, heating Micah's blood. His body jerked, snapped the bindings and changed. In the blink of an eye his world reshaped. Antiseptic scents assaulted his nostrils, creating blinding pain in his head. His vision sharpened, turned to shades of black and white. He felt strong and had a powerful urge to stalk and hunt.

Shrill screams pierced his skull and made his temples ache. He shook his head in an effort to ease the pain, relieved when the horrible sound ended. The rapid pounding of feet brought his attention to the doorway as men rushed into the room. One of the men drew a weapon and Micah dodged behind a table.

A piercing burn slammed into his flank and suddenly his body weakened. His head swam drunkenly, muscles stopped responding. Heavy limbs faltered, causing him to stumble and fall to the floor as his vision dimmed.

* * * * *

"Good, the sedative has worn off."

Weltman's voice jerked him back to the present. Micah glared at his boss, who stood on the other side of steel bars.

"I have to say, Lasiter, you going all feral and shifting into a lion has created quite the stir around here. No one ever suspected the procedure would give subjects the ability to change form. We'd hoped for greater strength but this — Amazing."

Jesus Christ, it's true then. It really happened. I turned into a lion.

Shocked beyond speech, he listened, absorbed. After all, information was power and he needed all he could get.

As he spoke, Weltman motioned for a guard to unlock the door. He moved into the small space, appearing unafraid. Of course, the fact the guard held a tranquilizer gun pointed at Micah's chest would provide a measure of safety.

"We believe your anger brought about the change. Our researchers are currently devising a series of tests to determine what other factors will have the same effect. Thankfully, I had the foresight to hire a specialist in zoology, specifically in large cats. You might remember a bit about her since you performed a rather thorough background check."

Weltman turned to the side, motioned to someone. "I assure you, my dear, it's quite safe. Please join us, Dr. Southerby."

"Becca?" Jesus, how deeply was she involved in this mess? How much did she know?

She stepped into view, sucking all available oxygen from the cell and he forgot why it mattered. His heart and lungs ceased to function, while his cock roared to life. She appeared small and fragile standing next to Weltman.

Dressed in sensible clothes and a white lab coat with wire-rimmed reading glasses perched on the end of her pert nose, Becca was a sight for sore eyes. As before, her chestnut hair had been pulled into a chignon at the back of her head. He longed to release the pins and free the silky mass.

His memories had not done her justice. She was more beautiful than he'd recalled.

Desire shot through him, heated his blood, which sizzled within his veins. Lust arced between them, drew them together. Famished, he drank her in, noticing the signs that Becca was not unaffected by his presence. Her nipples puckered, pressed against the material of her blouse. With trembling hands, she reached for him, only to be stopped short several feet away.

"That's close enough, dear."

"M-Micah. What's going on? What are you doing here? I don't understand."

His gaze was locked on her arm where Weltman's fingers wrapped around the slender muscle, holding her back from him.

"I thought you brought me here to work with a lion?"

Had she not been told what she was getting into? Had she been kept in the dark?

"I did," Weltman responded.

"I-I don't understand."

Seeing Weltman grip her arm so tightly made the anger swell. "Let. Her. Go," he roared.

"Now, now, Lasiter. Don't go getting yourself upset. Remember what happened the last time?"

Too late. There would be no stopping his transformation. Possessive rage grew, urged on by protective instincts. "No one touches her!" The words were spoken in a soft, deadly tone.

Weltman didn't heed the warning. Instead, he pulled Becca tight against his side, held her shackled to him and started dragging her toward the door.

The change hit him fast, altering his body before his mind could object. As before, his senses sharpened. The acrid smell of fear polluted the air, covering the purity of Becca's wonderful scent. Her shocked gasp hit him as hard as a punch to the solar plexus. A heartbeat later, she fainted, slipping to the ground. Weltman let her go.

"Don't shoot," his boss told the guard. Concerned only for his own hide, he made a hasty retreat, slamming the cell door behind him with a resounding clang.

"You're just going to leave her in there," the guard objected, "with that…that animal."

"I'm late for a meeting. And I'm sure as hell not going to fight him for her anyway. She'll be fine. After all, he's the reason she's here."

More likely it served some purpose only Weltman was aware of.

Under the animal's control, Micah followed its instincts. He moved to Becca and stood over her, shielding her body with his. He stood rigid and immovable until the other men left, removing the threat.

Lying down next to her, he licked her face then rested his head on her belly, safeguarding the woman the lion claimed as his mate. Regardless of how much the idea frightened the man, the beast had made its choice. The die had been cast.

There was no going back.

Chapter Four

ഇ

Her body was sore in wonderful places from muscles unaccustomed to such vigorous activity. Rebecca should be satiated and sound asleep but her lover shifted positions and one solid thigh moved between her splayed legs.

She wanted more of him. After all, they had not done everything. There was still a great deal of uncharted territory. This time she wanted to take the lead, be the one in control of their lovemaking.

Careful not to wake him, not before assuring she got what she desired, she rolled Micah to his back. Mmm…what a sight. All that bare male flesh—solid muscle divided by deep chiseled indentations. The difference between his hard masculine sinew and her soft curves were delightful, and deserved thorough investigation.

She started at the thick column of his neck, trailed her tongue over the length, across his clavicle, dipping into the shallow depression at the center before traveling south. The straight line separating his pectorals didn't hold her focus for long. Not once she spotted the darker flesh of his nipples. Rebecca's course veered sharply.

The first wet flick brought the tiny nub to life. The second puckered the areola. On the third, he moaned and shifted. She held her breath and remained still until he settled before resuming her explorations.

She teased and tasted every muscle over his washboard abdomen. Pleased to discover he had an inny, she circled his navel then thrust into the tiny recess. Moving lower, as she sucked the head of his cock past her lips, he woke with a rough groan.

"Damn, baby. That feels so good."

Rebecca took more of his length, bobbed a few times, then released him with a soft pop. "Yes, but I want to ride you."

She attempted to sound bold, but the slight waver in her voice gave her away. Thank goodness he ignored the slight falter.

"Well then, cowgirl, come on up here and take what you want."

His generous nature had her heart jumping for joy as she slid up his body, slow and salacious.

"Lock those pretty thighs on my hips, Becca."

He helped her into position and held his cock upward, never losing patience as she took her time finding the right angle before easing down his shaft. Awkward at first, it took a bit of trial and error to find her rhythm but once she got going…oooh yeah.

Being on top was turning out to be her favorite position. Controlling the pace, depth and angle of each thrust put her in command of her pleasure. His too. And with her on top, the broad head of his cock had a farther reach, tapping against her cervix.

Her orgasm built fast and arrived in a powerful blast, exploding over her body. The long, sustained rapture shook her from head to toe. Micah joined her in ecstasy, the hot splash of his cum washing over her womb extending the earth-shattering elation.

~ ~ ~ ~ ~

Awareness returned in the form of someone lightly smacking her cheek, bringing an abrupt end to memories of a night she held dear.

"Stop that," Rebecca grumbled. "I'm awake."

Even if she didn't know what had happened. Wasn't too sure she wanted to know, either.

"Come on, Becca. Open up those pretty green eyes for me, baby." The deep masculine voice made it past the layers of fog clouding her mind.

Becca? Only one man had ever called her Becca. Someone she left behind more than four weeks ago, sleeping among rumpled sheets that failed to cover miles of sexy, hard muscle and tan skin. A fallen angel who gifted her with one amazing night of pleasure beyond her wildest dreams.

But he couldn't be here, in the mountains. In the top-secret research laboratory she'd been touring with Mr. Weltman, head honcho of Nanotech. She remembered her new boss's brief explanation of the work being conducted. Gene manipulation, a cocktail blending the DNA of humans with that of predatory animals. Surgeries to make it stick.

"Refusing to open your eyes isn't going to change anything."

No, but the delay gave her a chance to gather her composure. She compromised, opened her eyes the barest fraction, just enough to see the gorgeous man who'd invaded her dreams, before slamming them shut again.

She didn't want to face reality. Rebecca would rather be a coward, pretend to be asleep. But the hard, cold surface she lay on was not her bed. The man leaning over her was not her imagination. This was no dream.

And the object of her desire had turned into a lion.

She skittered away from the man she'd once trusted with her body, seeking safety, moving until running into a wall. With her knees tucked up against her chest, she fought to calm her breathing and figure out what on earth was happening.

"W-why am I here? I'm not a genetic scientist. Mr. Weltman said that's what they're doing in this lab." She coughed, choking on the words. "I'm a freakin' zoologist, for crying out loud. I work with—"

The words echoed in her head. *I work with big cats. Tigers, jaguars, leopards—*

And lions. Oh Jesus!

A light bulb snapped on, illuminating the darkness. She'd been hired because Nanotech had been testing their insane genetic concoction on humans —

On Micah.

And he'd turned into a lion.

She slapped a trembling hand over her gaping mouth and stared.

He didn't appear any different. Same dark blond hair bound in a ponytail. Same hard features and observant brown eyes. Same sexy mouth that had done such wonderful things to her body. And the same tall, muscular body she touched in her dreams every night. The same gorgeous man who had brought her to multiple screaming orgasms.

Had they done this to him before the night they'd met? Had she slept with an animal?

Oh my god!

On the heels of that thought came another, more distressing concern as she remembered how her morning had started. With a pregnancy test.

Her cycles had never been regular so being late had not been a concern. Not until her period was two weeks overdue. Last night she picked up a test kit at the local pharmacy. This morning she peed on the stick. When a blue plus sign showed up she raced back to the pharmacy and bough two more kits, different brands to be sure.

One showed two hot pink lines.

The other spelled out the dreaded word "pregnant".

As she toured the facility with Mr. Weltman, Rebecca had barely paid attention. There was so much she had to think about, figure out. Her number one worry, the father. Micah.

Should she try to find him? He deserved to at least know about their child, whether he chose to be a part of either of their lives or not. But how was she supposed to break such

44

life-altering news? She didn't even know if he wanted children or where he lived. She didn't know much about Micah at all.

And what about the child?

Rebecca swallowed hard. Forget wondering if it would be a boy or girl. Concerns about the child's health. If Micah's DNA had been altered before she slept with him—

She didn't want to think it, but would have to get answers. Was it even possible for a human woman to carry an animal fetus? Would the baby be human, lion or able to change form, same as its dad?

She searched her memory for facts on pregnancy in lions. Gestation for lion cubs was around fifteen weeks. And lions birthed litters of one to four cubs.

Could she be carrying more than one fetus?

The room spun, her vision narrowed and Rebecca's consciousness wavered for a few seconds.

Were you? Did they? Before we?

She couldn't bring herself to say the words out loud. She decided to start with the basics. "What's going on, Micah? Please, help me sort this out."

He seemed reluctant, gave a heavy sigh and finally began speaking.

"I worked covert ops in the Army. Got shot and had to retire. When I got out, I took a job as head of security for Nanotech. Figured it was an easy job. Guard some scientists, secure their research."

He paused, rubbed at his temple. Rebecca took a closer look, noting the new lines of fatigue along his brow and bracketing his eyes. Signs of stress.

Hah! Wait until she sprung her news, then he'd know the real meaning of stress.

"I blew out my knee trying to catch an employee stealing information. That may have been weeks ago. I don't know. It's hard to judge time in here."

He extended his arm indicating the caged-in room. She glanced around. No windows or clocks. Just bare walls, narrow cot, exposed sink and toilet, steel bars, and mounted high on each wall, security cameras. Tiny red lights blinked menacingly from the devices.

They'd locked Micah in a cold prison cell, watched his every move, allowed him no privacy. In essence he was a prisoner. In a research laboratory? Good Lord, what was Weltman hoping to achieve?

Hell, she was a prisoner now too. God forbid what would happen if her new employer learned of her pregnancy and who sired the fetus, or fetuses.

She scooted closer, wanting to offer comfort, maybe receive some in return. But she was still very frightened and held back. He continued to talk, telling her about the operations and extent of damage to his knee.

"My body was getting older, weaker. I've put it through a lot over the years. With this latest injury." He shrugged. "I would not have been able to keep working. But I can't even imagine being retired. I need action. I'd go stir-crazy within a week. Give me a month and I'd be climbing the walls. I could take a desk job—"

"But it wouldn't satisfy you."

He nodded and some of the tension eased from his broad shoulders.

"Weltman came to the hospital, told me he could help. Told me they'd perfected a procedure that would make me strong again, stronger than ever before, able to keep doing the kind of physical work I love. Once he gave me details of what they are doing there was no turning back. I knew too much."

And now, so do I.

His story made it sound as if this had all happened since she'd last seen him but she had to be sure. Rebecca kept her gaze averted as she asked the question she dreaded. "So all this happened after we met?"

"Yeah."

Thank goodness! A wave of relief surged through her. There would be no litter of lion cubs, no child able to change its form. A huge weight lifted off her shoulders. She'd still have the normal pregnancy worries, but those were easily manageable in comparison.

She'd edged close enough that when Micah reached out, he touched her arm. Rebecca took the comfort he offered, thinking only of her own bleak situation for a moment. She was trapped in more ways than one.

Tremors assaulted her and she shook uncontrollably. Micah pulled her into the shelter of his strong body, made her feel protected, soothed some of her fears. They were joined now in this and no matter what happened, they'd face it together. Be strong for each other and their child.

"It's called the Predator Project. They started out kidnapping homeless men and women from the streets, people no one would miss."

Rebecca gasped. "But there are safeguards in place, rules governing how research is conducted. You can't leap from conception of an idea to clinical trials on humans. It doesn't work that way."

"Nanotech has circumvented the safeguards, ignored all legalities and moral principles of ethical research practices. The project started out innocent and with good intentions." Micah sighed. "I don't know what motivated the change. Greed, ambition, an external influence—something made them deviate from the initial objective and took the project down a different path.

"I'm their first real success. Weltman himself injected me with the altered DNA. Since then they've done multiple surgical procedures altering my body to accept the changes. No one expected me to turn into an animal. The scientists were almost as shocked as I was when it happened."

A barrage of questions raced through her mind. Was he able to change into the lion at will? If not, what brought the shift on? Was his metabolism higher? When he was the lion did he still have the man's rational thoughts and intelligence? Would he have to fight the natural predatory instincts of the lion? Would he attack her, eat her? Try to mate her? She whimpered.

Micah's warm palm rubbed soothing circles on her back. "Shh, baby. I don't know much about being the lion. It's only happened twice, and both times seem to have been triggered by intense emotion—frustration, anger, fear. We'll figure everything out together. I'll make sure you're safe."

And for the time being, she'd make sure their child remained safe. She decided not to tell Micah. Not until they figured out how to deal with what had been done to him. They would tackle the pregnancy issue later.

The man amazed her. He was the one who'd had his entire existence reshaped and here he was comforting her. She'd been brought here for him, probably to help him adjust since she had a better grasp of felines and their behaviors than she did for people, but she knew one thing for certain. Micah needed her support and knowledge.

She sat up straighter, determined to see him through this bizarre situation. "Tell me, I'm dying to know, what's it like? Does the change hurt? Are your senses different when you're the lion? Are your thoughts still human?"

His smile was tentative, but she sensed his relief over her acceptance.

"I can help you, Micah. We can both get through this, together." Sure, there would be an adjustment period. It would take time for the shock to wear off and for her to come to terms with the overwhelming circumstances. She was certain of one thing, she would not turn her back on him. Rebecca had to come up with a plan and get him out of the lab. This time, there would be no walking away.

Micah had known she was a special lady. Becca's response to this insanity proved it. He shifted their positions, turned so he could see her expressive face. He wanted to give her answers, but he had a few questions of his own. Important questions.

"We'll talk about that later."

His thoughts wandered to the night they'd shared, as they often did. Becca sparked a strong emotional response in him. She made him want things he'd run from in the past. He wanted to wake up holding her every morning. For a man who never spent the entire night with any woman that was a big step. He longed to know everything about her. What made her happy or sad. Her dreams and ambitions. Her heart's desires.

"Why did you walk out on me?"

He didn't have to spell it out. Judging from her body language, she knew what he was talking about. She flinched and lowered her gaze to her hands, which she twisted in her lap. Her response reminded him of how her confidence had faltered after she'd sucked his cock dry. At first, blinded by pleasure, he hadn't recognized the signs. Later, when he'd thought back, he put the pieces together. She didn't put much stock in her sex appeal or prowess. This was the perfect opportunity to give her a boost.

"Becca." With the tips of his fingers, he tilted her chin up, forcing her to make eye contact. "When I woke up alone, I was devastated. I'd thought we really connected, and I wanted more time with you. More *of* you."

"You did?"

Her voice was soft and uncertain. Micah felt the deep primal compulsion to hunt down whatever asshole had shaken her confidence and beat the living hell out of him.

"Damn, woman. You're so hot, sexy and passionate you nearly burned me alive. You're all I've been able to think about since that night. I can't sleep, my concentration has been shot.

When you walked through that door, regardless of this fucked-up mess, I had an instant hard-on."

"Really?"

This time her voice was stronger, and her pouty lips curved up in the stunning smile that had lingered in his mind while they were apart.

"Mmm...if there were no cameras..." He sucked in a hard breath. "Damn, baby. We'd be reenacting that night down to the last, delicious detail. But I'm feeling very possessive. I don't want anyone else to see your gorgeous body. It's mine!"

She snuggled against his side, rested her head on his chest and held him close. "For now, all I need is for you to hold me. Please hold me, Micah."

I'll never let you go! He left that unsaid for the time being.

"I've got you." There was a slight catch in his voice as unfamiliar, tender feelings swamped him. While he wouldn't wish being trapped in the lab on his worst enemy, he was glad to have Becca there. With her by his side, he had a reason to fight and a chance of actually making it out alive.

"We'll get through this together." He didn't make the promise lightly. Regardless of what it took, he intended to make it happen. And he wouldn't let her slip through his fingers again. They'd walk away from this side by side.

Chapter Five

Rebecca figured she spent close to two hours locked up in the cell with Micah before the security guards, casting wary glances in his direction, finally released her. She'd come to the decision that if she was going to be of any help him, she had to gather information. This meant spending at least a little time with Weltman, the crooked jerk. His total lack of morals and ethics disgusted her.

She figured he'd left her in with Micah for a baptism by fire. Let her get over the shock by seeing firsthand what they were dealing with since messing with his DNA. There really was no way to prepare for something no one has ever dealt with before.

"Rebecca…may I call you Rebecca?"

You already have.

She bit back the sarcastic reply and pasted on a phony smile. "Certainly, *Gabe*."

He patted her shoulder and directed her to a steel door with a digital plaque bearing her name. Next to the door was a handprint scanner. She placed her hand on the panel and a few seconds later the door slid open to reveal an ultra-modern workspace.

She shivered, the coldness of the room having a profound effect on her. Front and center sat a crescent-shaped, frosted glass desk with steel legs. At the center of the desk was a thin flat-panel computer monitor, stationed between a sleek phone and an adjustable gooseneck lamp. Everything was shiny silver. The windowless walls and tile floor were pure white. Stainless steel cabinets lined the back wall, several with frosted glass doors. The only bit of color came from a silk bird of paradise placed atop one of the cabinets.

Weltman edged around her to gauge her reaction, anticipation brightening his features. "I hope you like it?"

"I'm stunned," she answered honestly. "It's so..."

"Elegant," he supplied. "I know. I picked it out with you in mind. I think it suits you."

Elegant was not the right description. Cold, sterile — those fit. And he thought it would appeal to her? Not in a million years. She preferred warm colors, living plants and natural wood.

"I...uh, thank you."

She had to fight back a shudder of revulsion as his hand came to rest at the small of her back and he guided her around the desk. He didn't remove his hand or give her any space when they stopped before the computer screen. Instead he moved closer, breaching her personal boundaries.

"The subject's medical files have been uploaded onto your computer. My office, cell and home numbers are programmed into the phone." He handed her a business card with numbers written on the back. "My numbers are on here. You can call me anytime, Rebecca." His voice dropped to a whispery, intimate tone. "Anything you need...or want...I'm here for you. Day or night. I will provide everything you could possibly desire."

Ewww, he's coming on to me.

If she judged correctly by his gray hair and wrinkles the man was old enough to be her father. At least the files being on the computer limited how long she'd have to suffer through his creepy presence.

Desperate to put some distance between them without insulting her new boss, she pulled out the chair and plopped down. She had to tread carefully. She didn't want to piss him off and get fired. Then she'd be separated from Micah, having no idea what was happening to him. That was unacceptable.

"Thank you, Mr. Weltman." Still, she used his last name as a barrier to make the interaction less intimate and bring the conversation back to work.

"I'll require keys to the holding cell." She had to get Micah out of here, and a plan began to take shape. She'd prove the laboratory setting would impede any potential for progress. During her time off she'd find someplace safe to take him. It didn't have to be far away, only private. Not her leased house though. It had to be a place her employer didn't know about.

This delicate balancing act would have to be handled with extreme care. She took a deep breath and plunged ahead, praying it would work. It had to work, for both their sakes. "The files will be helpful, but I'll have to work with the subject one-on-one."

Weltman's face hardened. "The subject is unpredictable and dangerous. Security must remain tight."

She held up a hand, cutting him off. "You hired me because of my expertise with Felidac. Fortunately for Nanotech, I also have a good grasp of human behavior."

In for a penny…

"It is my professional opinion that what you hope to accomplish is not achievable with him under duress." She took a calculated risk, introducing the idea of letting him out of the cell. "For Micah to gain control over the animal, he has to feel comfortable, relaxed. That won't happen with armed guards standing watch. And for the lion to comply, his ingrained need for open spaces must be met."

The color drained from Weltman's face. "You can't be suggesting taking him outside the facility…by yourself."

Rebecca squared her shoulders and lifted her chin. "He will not harm me. I am more than capable of managing both the man and the lion. The security officers gave me a supply of tranquilizers and a Taser should they become necessary, which is doubtful." She held up the business card. "I can also call you at any time I need assistance."

"Yes, the subject seemed very protective toward you, but—"

She held up her hand again. "This is non-negotiable. If you want me to work with him, assist him in adapting, then it's on my terms. Otherwise the whole thing will be a wasted effort."

Weltman rubbed his chin and stared into her eyes, considering what she'd said. Rebecca had to remind herself to breathe. Her heart skipped a beat as she awaited his answer.

"Fine, go into the cell alone. Not outside though. For your own safety, I must insist a minimum of two guards accompany you outside. They will maintain a bit of distance and not intrude unless necessary, but you will stay within sight at all times. I'm not willing to put you at such risk without backup. I'll talk to the techs and have a shock collar put on him for everyone's safety."

She nodded, satisfied with the conditions. She would have agreed to a lot more to get Micah out of the horrible cell. "Thank you."

Weltman raked a hand through his hair and blew out a hard breath. She knew he was readjusting his perception of her. She took a chance by allowing him a glimpse of the iron-clad determination she'd disguised up until that point.

"I'll want written progress reports twice a week."

She bit the inside of her cheek to suppress a triumphant grin. "Agreed."

He watched her for another long moment before moving to the door. "I'll have the security captain bring a set of keys. Let me know when you want to take the subject outside so he can be prepared."

She understood his intention and addressed the situation before it could happen. "I don't want him sedated. Doing so would defeat the purpose."

Weltman stiffened. "Then he doesn't leave the cell." His tone was inexorable.

She opened her mouth to protest but he continued speaking.

"Lasiter has not been outside since the injection and we don't know how he will react or if he'll be able to control the lion. I will not risk the safety of my staff should he be unable to contain the urge to hunt. He won't be knocked out, but he will be given a mild sedative for the first attempt."

She realized he would not budge and conceded the point. "Fine."

In an attempt to soothe his ruffled feathers, Rebecca turned on the charm. She flashed what she hoped was a flirty smile. "Thank you, Gabe. I'm looking forward to working with you on this project."

His smile returned and some of the tension surrounding them eased. "Perhaps you'll join me for dinner one evening?"

Oh, ick!

Her quick nod seemed to seal the deal for him and Weltman hummed as he finally left the office. She hadn't agreed, not really. And Rebecca had no intention of going out with him.

Once alone, she opened the files and began skimming through the ingredients of the DNA cocktail that had been injected into Micah's blood and bone marrow. The advancements Nanotech's scientists had made with the Predator Project were truly amazing. Shame they were done without ethics or morals.

By circumventing standard protocols and restrictions for genetic research they had zoomed far ahead of the competition. Through discoveries made in the quest to find a cure for cancer they had stumbled upon a particular combination of synthetic and animal DNA, along with a reliable method of insertion. The procedure they developed resulted in a binding of the new recombinant DNA in a human subject, successfully modifying genes that would normally reject such an incompatible pairing.

Her hand shook as she clicked the mouse, paging through the information. Her field was not genetics but she felt fairly certain Nanotech had been close to reaching their initial goal— a cure for cancer. That was before Weltman had narrowed the focus to one particular element, which had resulted in going off on a wild tangent. Weltman's notes on his vision of creating a stronger breed of human soldiers had every fine hair on her body standing on end.

To know a man of Weltman's vast resources and greed possessed not only the means but also the key to altering the human race terrified her. The man was certifiable.

Anxious to see Micah, she had a difficult time concentrating. Rebecca shut down the computer and headed for the security office to get the keys. She had to force herself to take it slow and not run down the hallway. Even though she could view the camera aimed at his cell each moment away from him, she worried about how he was being treated.

The outer door of the security room opened with a muted *swish* and her eyes immediately sought out the monitors. Agitated, Micah paced back and forth before the cell bars, looking every inch the restless, caged predator.

"Better get a tranq gun ready if you're going in. Looks like Freak Show's gonna have to be knocked out again."

She couldn't remember the idiot guard's name. He didn't even bother turn around, obviously assuming a coworker had entered the small room.

"That won't be necessary." She spoke in a commanding tone, standing firm and sure, mimicking her father when addressing his troops. "However, it is critical to your future employment that you adjust your attitude, and do it fast!"

"Dr. Southerby." The guard scrambled from the chair and stood at attention. "Ma'am, I didn't see you there."

Micah had told her most of the guards were ex-military. From his attitude and stance there was no doubt this man had served. His military training would prompt his submission to her authority. At least that worked in her favor. "What's your name?"

"Anderson. Tom Anderson."

"I'm going to be watching you, Anderson. If I find even one scratch on Micah Lasiter, you'll be answering to me." She gave him her hardest, most intimidating glare. "Is that clear?"

"Ma'am. Yes ma'am."

"Good." She'd almost expected him to snap off a salute. "Now, my keys?"

He placed a plain metal ring bearing two keys into her open palm.

"Thank you." She glanced around, taking in the state-of-the-art monitoring equipment, somewhat surprised to realize there was no sound. "I take it the cells are not wired for audio surveillance?"

"No, ma'am. We only ever used the cells to secure the unstable subjects before termination." He shivered. "None of us wanted to hear those horrible cries any more than necessary. There wasn't any reason to have sound, but if you think—"

She raised a hand, silencing him. "No, that's fine. I prefer to keep written notes of my work with the subject instead of recordings." Referring to Micah as "the subject" rankled but it was necessary to follow Weltman's example when dealing with his men.

"What about the procedure rooms? Are there disks from the subject's treatments available that I can watch?"

"That depends. The procedure rooms are set up with recording equipment but it does not run continually. There will only be documentation if someone activated the equipment. Any footage on Lasiter will be accessible through his electronic records."

"Thanks for all your help, Anderson. I'll be counting on you to make sure nothing happens to the subject. He's very important to the project. No more tranquilizers unless I give the okay. And no procedures without my expressed approval. Everything concerning the subject now goes through me. Clear?"

"Yes ma'am."

As she left the office and made her way to the cell, Rebecca said a silent thank you to her father. Her mother had died when she was a toddler. She'd grown up surrounded by military men. The general had not only taught her how to hold her own with powerful men, but how to command their respect. The lessons in fighting and tactics that had seemed frivolous were now coming in handy.

Micah stilled when she approached the cell and remained silent as she unlocked the door. The loud clang as it closed behind her echoed around them. She quickly filled him in on what she'd learned so far.

"The security equipment is top-notch. Palm-print readers control most of the doors. From what I saw in the security room the only places not actively monitored are within individual offices. Every hallway, door and window is wired and carefully watched. The other subjects are housed along the same corridor in dormitory-type rooms instead of cells."

"At first, so was I. They moved me here after I shifted the first time."

She nodded. "They do not have the cell wired for sound, so unless a guard is in the immediate area, we're free to talk."

"Good," Micah sighed.

"Getting you out of here is not going to be easy. As much as possible, keep a tight leash on the lion. My plan is simple—prove to Weltman that you are not a danger to me, and that I can control you."

Micah began to pace again and rubbed at his jaw.

"I've made arrangements to get you outside, but you'll be sedated."

He stopped short, his gaze narrowing on her.

"Weltman insisted on a mild sedative because we don't know if you will be able to control the lion's natural instincts once you get out in the open. I had no valid argument for the point. Two guards will be with us, within sight at all times." Reaching the part of her plan where things go dicey, she took care to school her features. "Once it's proven that I can handle you in both forms, I'll convince Weltman the lab setting is detrimental to what he wants to accomplish."

"How the hell are you going to do that?" he barked.

"Simple. We establish a pattern. Right now Weltman believes strong emotion brings on the shift. You have to become unpredictable around everyone other than me. You will gradually decrease your activity, become lethargic when here in the cell and come to life when we go outside. I'll convince Weltman the results he wants are not possible in the lab setting. We get you out of here, I gather the records of what's been done to you, then you disappear."

His penetrating stare turned cold and contemplative. "What do you know about making someone disappear?"

"I'm an Army brat, born and raised. My father made sure I know how to survive no matter the circumstances. Helping you vanish off the radar will be child's play."

He advanced toward her. "Do not touch me, Micah!"

She clenched her teeth and forced herself to appear unaffected. "Don't touch me or show personal interest in me or this won't work."

He came to a dead stop. She could tell it grated on his nerves, but Micah fell into the role she'd set for him. Tense muscles relaxed as he took several deep breaths. He sat on the floor, putting himself in a vulnerable position and under her control.

She squeezed the bridge of her nose, fighting off a stress headache. "This is not going to be easy for either of us." She moved to him, blocked the camera's view and stroked his cheek. "All I can think about is stripping off those clothes, getting my hands and mouth on you. Making love until we're both exhausted and sweaty."

A low, warning growl vibrated through his chest. She clearly saw the same desire reflected in his eyes.

"I know. It's okay," she assured. "We have to be strong. There's so much we have to talk about." So much they had to figure out. She thought about the baby and her natural inclination was to rub her belly where their child rested. Instead, she balled her hands into fists at her sides.

"First we have to get you out of here."

That had to be her top priority. They'd deal with everything else once he was safe.

Chapter Six

ॐ

He kept his eyes closed, breathing even and stayed motionless. He'd been in the facility long enough to figure out the regular pattern and movements of the guards. They'd already made rounds and weren't due for at least another hour. Yet someone moved down the corridor, making no attempt to mask their presence. The light click created by a heel with each footfall made him guess his late-night visitor was female.

The night guard muttered a familiar greeting, which told him it had to be someone on the lab staff. What did they have planned for him now? Micah gritted his teeth in anticipation of more anesthesia drugs and another painful procedure.

Fuck, Becca was right. They had to get him the hell out of here.

His nostrils flared as the delightful scent of cinnamon and honey reached him. What the hell was she doing? There was no way she could have worked out an evac plan this fast.

Keys rattled, metal grated on metal as the cell door swung open. Sheer will and discipline were almost insufficient to keep him from rushing forward. He had to play this out and follow her lead or put both of them at risk.

He'd rather undergo multiple torturous procedures than put her in any more danger than she already faced.

The gentle caress of her fingertips along his jaw was at odds with her abrupt tone. "Wake up, Lasiter. I don't have all night."

"Want me to chain him, Doc?"

"No, thanks. I've got my Taser and we're not going far."

What the hell?

"Come on, Lasiter. Don't make me change my mind and have them sedate you. Let's get this procedure done and over with."

"No more damn procedures." The thought of her performing one of Weltman's horrible procedures on him make Micah's blood run cold.

The guard took a step backward as Micah swung his legs over the cot and sat up. Becca tapped her foot, waiting impatiently, but her sweet face told a different story. The lighting was dim but he had no trouble making out her flushed cheeks and dilated pupils with his enhanced eyesight.

He took a breath, drawing her musky aroma deep into his lungs. She wasn't afraid or agitated. She was wet and aroused.

As he rose to his full height the guard took another step back while Becca latched on to his biceps and guided him out of the cell. They went through the anteroom where another guard watched a bank of monitors displaying the empty cell, and down a short corridor to one of the treatment rooms. The guard shadowed their every step until the door closed behind them and the lock snicked in place.

Becca lifted a finger to her lips. "Get on the exam table, Lasiter. Now that's a good boy." She snapped the wrist restraints shut with a loud click. Once the sound shot through the room a second time, he heard the guard's booted footsteps echo down the corridor.

"We won't have long. An hour at most—"

Micah backed her against the door and sealed his lips to hers. She tasted of coffee and her own unique flavor that had been imprinted on his soul. He'd missed her so much and when they both made it out of this mess, he was never letting go!

Pain bit into his shoulders where her fingernails dug deep. He didn't mind. Especially as her leg rose and hooked over his hip, aligning her warm pussy with his hard and ready to explode cock.

It had been too long since he'd felt the tight clasp of her pussy around his shaft. Too long since he'd been buried balls-deep in paradise. "Becca," he groaned. "This is going to be hard and fast...the first time."

"Yesss. Hard and fast is good. Now is better. Hurry!"

They were on the same page, thank goodness, because he couldn't wait another second. Finesse be damned. Going straight for the tie of her scrub pants, he cursed as it knotted. The hellion just laughed as she released the tie securing his pants with ease then wrapped her slender fingers around his aching cock.

Micah didn't screw around with the knot for long. He simply ripped the drawstring in half. One hard pull tore the crotch from her lacy panties and her slick, warm flesh filled his palm. He sniffed, wondering briefly at the slight difference in her scent but chalking it up to something in the laboratory setting.

"Have you been thinking about me, baby?" Without any preamble, he thrust two fingers between her sodden folds. Wet flesh sucked at his fingers and he came close to finishing before even getting inside her.

"Have you suffered through endless nights, remembering how damn good it was to have this sweet pussy stuffed full of my cock?" Waiting for her answer was torture but he had to know she'd suffered, same as he had.

"Micah," she gasped.

Thrusting his fingers hard, he found the small spot guaranteed to drive her crazy and stroked the area with his fingertips. Becca rose up on her toes, canted her hips and followed the rhythm he set. Her body tightened on his fingers as she neared release but hell if he'd let her get there without him.

Her fingernails dug painfully deep as he withdrew his fingers. He made a point of letting her see the glistening digits before sucking them into his mouth. As her heady flavor burst across his taste buds, Micah dropped his head back.

"Answer me, baby? Did you lie awake every night wishing I was in your bed?"

"Yes, okay. Yes. Now fuck me already, damn it."

He didn't know why it had been so important for him to hear the words. Thankfully, she'd said them. He wasn't sure what he would have done if she'd denied wanting him all those empty nights they'd been apart.

Without another word or further delay, he lifted Becca. As her heels hooked at the small of his back, he slammed her down on his straining cock. He pressed his mouth into the curve of her neck, hoping to muffle the sounds refusing to be held back.

This is where he belonged, buried within his woman's body. Cradled between her thighs. It was so fucking good.

He couldn't breathe, didn't move. The mere idea of withdrawing from her brought the lion closer to the surface. All rational thought fled as Micah gave in to the animal's need for its mate. A roar of possession rumbled up from his chest. He finally had her back where she belonged but they didn't have any protection.

His mouth opened, dangerously sharp teeth closed over her vulnerable throat.

Mine!

"Move, damn you."

Her complaint had his teeth tightening their hold on her neck for a moment before Micah gathered his control. "No condom."

"It's not an issue."

Thank god. He didn't think he could stop. Not with her warm heat surrounding his cock. Micah didn't question her

64

statement. The idea of filling her with his semen was irresistible to both the lion and the man. Of their own volition, his hips began to move in a slow and easy rhythm.

To hell with that, Rebecca thought. Using powerful thigh muscles, she moved in counterpoint, slamming her pelvis against his. Micah took the not so subtle hint and ran with it. He began powering into her, each hard thrust punctuated by the wet slap of their bodies.

It was heaven and hell. She wanted it to last forever but her body screamed for release. The pleasure built quickly, taking her to heights she'd never known existed.

His mouth released her neck long enough to state his claim. "You. Are. Mine."

"Yes!"

"Say it, Becca."

Normally his demanding tone and dominant words would have her spine stiffening. Not with Micah. Hearing the claim on his lips was a total turn-on. She longed to be his.

"Yours. I'm all yours."

His hands spread her legs wider, gripping her thighs tight enough she'd have bruises. Not that she cared. She'd be proud to wear his mark on her skin.

Each forward thrust was harder than the last. Faster. More intense. As if he attempted to get beneath her skin. To lose himself in her body the same way she was losing herself in him.

It was flat-out, balls-to-the-wall sex.

If she had the breath, she would have laughed over that thought. All she managed was to hold on and enjoy the wild roller-coaster ride. As she reached the highest peak her body tensed, preparing for the free fall.

"Now, Becca. Come now."

The command triggered her orgasm and a scream strangled in her throat as mind-numbing pleasure gathered in her core and whiplashed through her body. Micah continued to fuck her through her orgasm then followed her over the edge. He roared again as he climaxed. Hot jets of cum bathed her womb, setting off aftershocks, leaving her limp and shaking in his arms.

Micah collapsed against her, his weight and the wall were all that held them upright. Not until she got her breathing under control and the last tremor ended did she realize his erection still stretched her tender tissues.

"Micah?"

"Not done," he gasped. "Just a second."

It took slightly longer than a second, not that she minded since Micah stayed inside her. Holding on to her ass cheeks, he kept her impaled on his erection and maneuvered them over to the exam table where he rocked her world again. This time they went slower, savored the perfect joining of their bodies. They'd just cleaned up and found a pin to hold her pants up when the guard knocked on the door, bringing an end to the all-too-brief stolen moments.

It was sufficient to renew her motivation to get him the hell out of the lab and hopefully in her bed permanently.

Chapter Seven

ॐ

After three days of working with Becca his control was tenuous at best. Only two thoughts filled Micah's mind each day when as he woke—sex and escape. Both were very high on his list of priorities, but getting Becca to safety had to come first.

It wasn't as if they had not already had sex, several times, in a variety of different positions. But that had been days ago and he wanted more of her. Not sneaking into unmonitored rooms at the lab under the watchful eye of the security staff, though. He wanted her somewhere they didn't have to be afraid or quiet.

So far everything was going as planned. Their trips outside had gone off without a hitch, although the guards seemed disappointed they hadn't gotten the chance to shock him with the collar.

The day-shift guard was making his rounds. Micah had nicknamed him Smiling Jack because the man always wore a cheesy grin.

"Mornin', Lasiter. Sleep well?"

He muttered a banal response, distracted by the sight of Becca headed in his direction. His cock jerked to attention as his gaze swished from side to side following the subtle swaying of her hips.

Jack's attention shot to her lithe body and Micah fisted the edge of the cot, trying to restrain the lion who wanted to claw the bastard's eyes out. He agreed with the cat but had to stay in character. Part of Becca's strategy involved his appearing to be lethargic and depressed. Jumping to his feet, rushing the bars and reaching through to choke the fucking grin off Smiling Jack's face would hamper their cause.

"Jack." Becca gave the man an absent nod of dismissal.

Hah, take that!

If he were less mature, Micah would stick his tongue out and blow raspberries at the other man.

Becca's green eyes narrowed on him while she unlocked the door. He had no problem reading the warning to behave in her tight expression.

"Did you sleep?"

"What the hell else is there to do in here?" he grumbled.

She pulled back and gave him an assessing stare. "I could bring you something to read or perhaps you'd like a pen and notebook."

"What, so I can write down my feelings or some other psychobabble crap?"

Her brow arched. "I'm not staying if you're going to be nasty. Shall I come back later?"

He ignored Jack's snicker and rubbed his aching temples instead. "No, don't go."

With a curt nod to the guard, Becca closed the cell door and dragged a chair—the only other piece of furniture in the cell—closer to his cot. As Jack ambled away, the tension between them changed, becoming charged with sexual energy.

"I know it's been difficult. How are you holding up?"

"Honestly, right now I'd gnaw off my right hand to get you alone. It's taking a supreme effort to stay put when I want to let my claws extend and slice through your clothes. I want to taste every inch of skin that's hidden from view. Then I want to spend several days recreating that night." The sudden flush spreading over her neck and onto her face told Micah she was remembering their one night together. "I've dreamed up with a few new positions for us to try out."

Becca swallowed hard. Perspiration dotted her brow. He didn't want her to suffer, but damn if being close to her wasn't killing him. "I need you."

She nodded and wrote something down in the notepad she always carried. Had it not been for his feline-enhanced hearing he would have missed her whispered words.

"I need you too!"

Lust boiled his blood and his balls ached. The cat roared and tore at the restraints he'd placed on it. Whenever she got him all tied up in knots, which was most of the time, the cat went wild. Over the past few days he'd learned to control the cat's reactions.

He wasn't the only one feeling the heat. Micah's nostrils flared, drinking in the musky scent of Becca's arousal. If he slid a hand under her sensible skirt, he was sure to encounter warm panties dampened with her cream.

"Fuck! Get me the hell out of here. I have to be outside. The lion is going to make an appearance whether we're ready for it or not."

Their eyes met, voracious desires arcing between them. She fumbled the notebook and dropped her pen as she shot to her feet. At the door, she banged the keys against the bar while trying to fit the right one in the lock.

The ruckus drew Jack, no longer smiling, back down the hallway at a fast clip. "You okay, Doc? What'd he do?"

Rebecca glanced at the guard. "Everything's fine. I'm just a bit clumsy this morning. Must have had too much coffee." She shuddered as the cell door shut behind her with an ominous thud.

"We're ready to go outside. Would you please go get one of the other guards? I'll wait here."

Jack shot her a dubious look. "You sure? Fine doesn't mean the same thing to women. At least with my ex it didn't. When she said she was fine, I had to duck and cover 'cause the shit was gonna hit the fan."

"Jack." Becca placed her hand on the guard's forearm then let it drop again as a menacing bark-like sound rose from Micah's throat.

"It's all good for the moment. We've got to get him outside so it stays that way. Understand?"

"You want the drugs?"

"Not today." Their previous outings had all gone well and they hadn't used the medication again after the first time.

Jack spoke into a portable radio and another guard soon joined them. Micah only managed to make it a few steps into the yard before being overtaken by the change. The rapidness of the shift still amazed him. One second he stood tall and human, the next he was a lot closer to the ground with tattered clothes tangled around his legs.

Using sharpened senses, he surveyed the area from his new perspective. He lifted his snout, scenting the crisp mountain air. Fertile land, blooming flora, the distinct saline scent of the guards and Becca's feminine aroma. He homed in on her, filling his lungs.

Acute hearing picked up a soft sound in the underbrush several hundred feet away. Micah sniffed the wind — hare.

He crouched low, pushed off with a flex of powerful muscle and raced across the yard. Long ears poked up from beneath tall grass and twitched. The jackrabbit detected the predator hot on its trail and the chase was on.

Surrendering control to the lion, he simply enjoyed the hunt for the short time it lasted. When it was over, he pranced back to Becca, head held high, feeling proud and dominant. A primal beast providing for its mate. He dropped the limp brown creature at her feet, awaiting praise for a successful hunt.

The anticipated pat on the back didn't come. Instead, she made a soft, sniffling noise. He took in her horrified expression and the twin tracks of tears flowing over her cheeks.

Aw, fuck!

She may be accustomed to the behaviors of fierce cats, but she definitely had a soft side. Irritation prickled over his skin as conflicting emotions vied for supremacy. Micah understood her distress at the senseless taking of a life. The lion, however, didn't appreciate the rejection of his offering and became enraged. Tossing back his head, he released a mighty roar.

Rebecca scrambled to control her instinctive response, but the battle was doomed from the start. Thankfully, no blood marred the brown pelt that lay across the toe of her shoes. She could almost fool herself into believing the rabbit slept if not for the unnatural oblique angle of its neck. At least it had been a clean break and the animal had not suffered.

She squatted down and ran her fingers over its soft fur. The lion paid close attention to her every move, while the guards kept their focus elsewhere.

"Jack—" Her voice came out a weak whisper. She cleared her throat and tried again. "Go get a shovel, Jack. We have to bury it."

Despite the lion's lack of comprehension, the part of his consciousness still occupied by Micah understood. He headbutted her out of the way, knocking her on her ass, gently closed his jaws on the animal then loped away and disappeared into the woods.

The guard's hand tightened on the control to the shock collar and headed out after the lion.

"Jack, no. Wait a minute. I want to see what he does."

"We're not supposed to let him out of our sight."

"I know, but you'll have to trust me. He's not going far."

After a few minutes, Micah returned without the rabbit. Rebecca observed his demeanor. The lion's movements were sluggish and lacked purpose. The internal conflict between man and beast was palpable.

Micah had mentioned his discomfort in making the transition back to human form with the guards watching. Since then she'd had the guards bring along a change of clothes whenever they went outside. She took the bundle from Jack and walked with Micah behind some trees.

Rebecca grinned with the knowledge that Micah didn't have a problem with her witnessing his shift in form. She forced herself not to blink and miss the whole thing. It happened so fast.

She saw no point in wasting the gift she'd been given and drank in the magnificent sight of more than six feet of prime naked male flesh. He was even better than she remembered. With the altering of his DNA, Micah's body had adapted in thrilling ways. He had more body hair. The smattering of baby fine blond hair was almost invisible under the direct sunlight. Her fingers itched, longing to glide over his chest. And his muscles...oh my. His body had been ripped before. Now he was chiseled perfection. Beefy sinew undulated across his broad back as he shrugged into a shirt. She bit her lip to hold back a whimper when the cloth blocked her splendid view. But then he bent to put on the pants and her pussy dampened in appreciation.

Damn, she could orgasm just watching him bend over. The flex of those tight glutes, the tiny dimples above each round cheek... There were no words to do the beautiful sight justice. Her breasts swelled and the soft material of her bra rasped against her hard nipples. Tingles raced to her core with each shallow breath.

Micah turned and Rebecca had to steady herself against a tree trunk as her knees went weak.

His cock had been big before, both thick and long, but now— Damn! She hadn't gotten a clear look at it in the treatment room. Uh-uh. No way could that be the same cock. Full and erect, it hung heavily down his leg. The idea of taking him in her mouth made her lips tingle. Saliva pooled with the memory of his taste. She almost dropped to her knees but she had other, more pressing needs. Her pussy clenched, empty and aching to be filled.

That sure as hell won't fit in me now!

To hell with that. He'd fit perfectly the other night and she'd reveled in every thick inch stretching her wide. She wanted to hold him in her hands, stroke the warm length between her palms. Rebecca started to reach for him then remembered the guards. She had to curl her fingers into the material of her skirt to keep them off Micah. Last thing she wanted was an audience.

"Doc? Everything okay?"

Oh, thank goodness!

She twirled around, latching on to the guard's voice as if it were a lifeline.

"Yes!" The word came out high-pitched, almost shrill. She cleared her throat as she tromped through the brush, racing toward the guards. "We're ready to go back inside now."

Becca tapped her foot impatiently as Micah took his sweet time strolling back into the clearing, arrogant grin firmly in place.

Jack shot her a strange look. "Are you sure you're all right, Dr. Southerby?" He moved closer and whispered so the other guard wouldn't hear. "You're breathing kinda shallow and you face is all flushed."

"I'm *fine*," she gritted out from between clenched teeth. "Now if you're done lollygagging —"

He held up a hand in surrender. "Whoa, okay, Doc. We've already covered that kinda *fine*."

No one spoke on the way back to his cell. Micah covertly watched Becca in his peripheral vision. She was acting strange.

The first time she'd seen him shift, she passed out from shock. That had been days ago. Yesterday her innate curiosity had won out over her reserved demeanor. She had asked tons of questions and developed a few theories. All predictable, expected behavior.

Something was different today. When not being terse with Jack, she'd been quiet and distracted. She'd been impatient with him but he figured it had to do with arousal.

Now he wasn't so sure. Especially since she kept rubbing small circles over her abdomen.

Maybe she didn't feel well.

He loathed going back into the cell while Becca went to her office. Of course, in Weltman's place he'd take the same precautions. Until he had full command of the shift, as well as the lion's reactions, keeping him locked up was the safest course of action.

After the guards left, Becca lingered, still unconsciously rubbing her belly.

"Either you're sick or something has happened. Which is it, baby?"

Her head snapped up. "Huh?"

"What's wrong?"

"Nothing. I, uh…I have lots of work to do." She backed away. "I'll stop by before I head home for the night."

Damn it!

He was so frustrated that he wanted to rip the bars from the wall. She shouldn't be going home alone to deal with whatever was bothering her. How fucking ironic that he finally wanted more than a quick fuck from a woman and he couldn't be with her.

The only woman he'd ever longed to hold in his arms through the night and he was stuck in a cage. They should be lying in bed together, dreaming of the future. Instead he had to moderate every action and put on a show for the guards, while learning to share his body with a cat.

Micah sat on the cot and stared at the ceiling. His shitty fucking karma had finally come back around to bite him in the ass.

Sometimes life sucked!

Chapter Eight

⁊ꙮ

Rebecca hid out in the office she detested, pacing from one end to the other. No doubt about it—the morning outing with Micah shook her up and proved they had to get rid of their supervision. She had to be alone with him, free to touch him. Hold him and be held. Sooner the better.

The time had come to take action.

But what?

How could she get him out of a top-secret facility that they locked down tighter than a duck's butt?

He's the father of my child. I can't just leave him in that cell.

Yeah, and he also turns into a ferocious lion with sharp claws and huge teeth. Oh, and don't forget that enormous cock.

Hah, as if she could forget that!

Tingles raced along her spine, but she refused to contemplate sex with so much at stake. She had to get him out of here first. Last night she'd found a cabin to rent. She had the keys in her purse. Her plans were coming together so what exactly was she waiting for?

By now the security team would have filled Weltman in on the morning's events. Would it be enough to convince him the lab environment was counterproductive to his goals?

Her father's voice flowed through her mind offering a swift kick in the ass. *You'll never find out with your head stuck in the sand, Rebecca. Stand tall and show them what you've made of.*

Yeah, since when did she hide from adversity? The general had taught her to be strong and face challenges head-on. He'd be ashamed of the way she was behaving.

Rebecca squared her shoulders, steeled her spine and stormed out the door. Her heels beat out a steady rhythm as she moved down the hall. She didn't pause or give Weltman's assistant the chance to say a word, she charged right by and into his office.

A guard she had not met shot upright from a chair in front of the desk and turned to face her.

"Rebecca," Weltman gasped, startled by her bold entrance. "That will be all, Martha. Please close the door," he told his assistant.

Weltman stood and extended a hand toward the guard. "Kyle Slater, this is Dr. Rebecca Southerby, the zoologist working with Lasiter." Weltman turned to her. "Rebecca, this is Kyle, head of security here at the lab."

They didn't shake hands, the man merely nodded then followed Weltman's example and returned to his seat. She looked him over and made a quick assessment. Everything about the dark-haired stranger screamed military, from his quick response to the way he held himself.

Instead of sitting, she planted her hands on the desk and leaned in, forcing Weltman to lean back. She would not be able to intimidate him, but the position gave an impression of authority and power. She'd take any advantage she could get.

"This isn't working!"

He sighed heavily. "Kyle and I were just discussing this morning's session."

She kept her focus on Weltman, ignoring the other man. "Then you understand the situation. Being locked up in a cell and under constant guard here at the lab has impeded making any real progress. I'm going to have to take him offsite."

Weltman sprung to his feet and leaned forward, got right in her face. His heated breath washed over her, the smell of onions from his last meal turning her stomach. But she didn't back down and refused to flinch.

"It's too dangerous."

"He won't hurt me, Gabe. He's had plenty of opportunity. If anything, Micah has displayed protective behaviors toward me. The lion is too keyed up here. He won't let Micah take complete control in this atmosphere."

"No. He could turn on you."

She softened her tone and gave the appearance of relaxing her stance. "I know cats, Gabe. That's why you hired me. Working with him here, I won't be able to produce the result you're after. Allow me to work with him from home and I can help Micah get control of the lion."

Weltman dropped back in his chair. He frowned then made brief eye contact with the guard. From the corner of her eye, she saw Slater nod.

"She's right. He won't hurt her."

Holy shit, this is going to work. Because of Slater. She wondered if he knew Micah and was possibly a friend.

"I want results, fast." Weltman rubbed his temple and sighed. "How long?"

She shrugged. "Two weeks for him to fully adapt to the lion and master its instincts. Maybe less. It's hard to predict since I've never worked with anyone like him before."

"He is unique. Our first success." He leaned back in the chair, fingers steepled, and remained silent for several long moments. He seemed to reach a decision and pressed a button on his desk.

"Yes, sir?" The assistant's voice wafted through a hidden speaker.

"Martha, call down to communications and have someone bring a company phone for Dr. Southerby." After disconnecting, he sat back and stared at her. She maintained eye contact and projected an air of competence. Difficult as she found it, she remained silent, waiting him out. She didn't have to wait long.

"Okay, but there will be a few conditions."

She bit her tongue to hold back a triumphant shout. "Of course." She'd agree to anything.

"The phone will be programmed with my numbers, home and work, as well as Kyle's. You will arrange a schedule and check in with him."

"Do not miss a call, Dr. Southerby." Kyle's voice was low with menace. "It will take less than ten minutes for my team to overtake your house."

She'd pegged him as a hard-ass, by-the-book soldier, but he was enabling her to get Micah off the premises. It didn't fit his character and confounded Rebecca. Hell if she'd turn down his assistance, though. And she wasn't about to tell him she had no intention of taking Micah to the house provided for her by Nanotech and make it easy for them to interfere.

Watch yourself with this one, her father's voice warned. *You don't know who he has alliances with or if he's working toward a completely different agenda of his own.*

She played it naïve, the use of his first name intended to portray a relaxed attitude and hide the fear causing her heart to race. "I won't miss a call, Kyle. Lord, your men would give my elderly neighbor a heart attack."

When she glanced back at Weltman, he coughed to cover an evil grin. "We'd hate for that to happen."

Yeah, right! She bet it would just break his shriveled black heart.

"Since we don't know how the subject will respond to leaving the compound, he will be given the same light sedative that worked for his first trip outside." Weltman glanced down at his gold watch. "Give my men an hour to get him ready then pull your vehicle around to the loading dock."

She hated the idea of them sedating Micah again, but had no reason to object without tipping her hand.

"Thank you."

"If all goes well with Lasiter, we have plans for inducting several more subjects into the Predator Project. I have high hopes for a female soldier and plan to try a hybrid DNA cocktail with her. When she's been injected, I want you working with her exclusively."

He planned to alter more unsuspecting victims? A woman? Jesus! The evil bastard was so crooked they'd have to screw him into the ground when he died.

She didn't have the luxury of worrying about other test subjects right now. She had to focus on her immediate goals. Waiting an hour to see Micah again would be hard. There was so much she wanted to tell him. But copying the files from her computer would keep her busy. She'd need every bit of documentation to deal with any medical issues that developed.

After the phone had been delivered and programmed, Slater cautioned her once again.

"Do not miss a call, Doctor."

She didn't need her father's warnings to know Slater represented serious danger and was someone she didn't want to cross swords with.

"Believe me, I won't."

* * * * *

"I'm telling you, the old man has lost it!" Tom stomped down the hallway.

Jack shook his head. "I can't believe Slater agreed to this bullshit. They're going to get the doc killed."

Slater? Micah figured they had to be talking about Kyle Slater, one of the men he'd had handpicked when approached for names to lead security at a new facility. He didn't believe in coincidence.

With Slater working behind the scenes, he might have a prayer of getting out of this alive. He filed the information away for later and continued listening to the two morons talk as if he couldn't hear them.

"Why the hell would the doc take him home with her? The lion could turn on her at any time."

"Fuck if I know. Doesn't make any sense."

"Well, let's get this over with and shoot him up. It will take at least ten minutes for the sedative to take effect."

Jack unlocked the door and warily approached where Micah sat on the cot. The idiot talked to him as if he were mentally slow or something.

"Okay, Lasiter. You're getting sprung so don't give us any trouble."

"Do I look stupid to you?"

Jack stopped and seemed to consider, lowering Micah's opinion of him another notch. Resting his forearm on his thigh, he held his arm still for the injection. Tom swabbed the skin then jabbed the needle into his vein none too gently.

Finally, as the sedative raced through his blood, they left him alone with his fuzzy thoughts.

He'd actually been thankful for the drugs on his first trip outside. The cat had clawed at his skin, fought to be released, yearned to run and hunt. Once he'd shifted, keeping himself in check had been a true test of his mettle. But he'd done it, with Becca's help. She had become his strength, reason and purpose. With her at his side, Micah felt like Superman.

Becca. God, he couldn't wait to get her alone, somewhere private and fuck her senseless.

He vividly remembered the sweet flavor of her arousal. Had dreamed of it often since their night together. The hot, tight grasp of her pussy sucking at his cock. Her soft mewls of pleasure as she rode him to completion.

Jesus, he couldn't get out of the lab soon enough. He had to hold her, skin to skin, without any barriers as he had that night.

He had been sated and sleepy when she'd started a sensual assault on his body with her pouty lips, warm tongue and agile fingers. She'd straddled his hips and slid down his cock, enveloping him in the damp heat of her pussy. She'd felt like heaven. Hot, wet, tight—a damp silken fist with nothing between them.

He'd felt everything. Every flutter of her walls, all the intense heat. Sensation had overwhelmed higher thought. He'd uttered a protest, made a cursory attempt to stop her and get a condom, but he'd been too far gone.

The way she'd moved above him blew his mind. At first tentative and unsure, but once she found her rhythm, she rode him smooth as a barrel racer—hard, fast and with natural grace.

And she'd ridden him bareback.

A shiver of remembered ecstasy raced through his body. His mind floated along on a wave of memories until the guards came back, securing his hands and ankles. There was no fight in him, no motivation to fight, as they all but dragged him through the hallways then waited at a doorway, watching for her car.

* * * * *

Soon as the car pulled up behind to the loading dock a door opened and Micah was led out by Tom and Jack. The idiots had him chained at both the wrist and ankle.

Muttering the vilest curses she knew, Rebecca jumped out of the car and stormed over to confront the guards.

"Take. Them. Off."

Jack glowered at her. "You don't know what he's capable of."

"He's done nothing to deserve being treated like a criminal." She took in Micah's dilated eyes and slack expression. "Besides, you've got him too doped up to be capable of anything."

Nicole Austin

"Lady, you're nuts," Tom said. "It won't come as a surprise when I read in tomorrow's paper that you were mauled to death. I can't believe Weltman is going along with this bullshit."

She refused to back down or be intimidated. Rebecca moved closer, going toe to toe with the man, although the effect was somewhat diminished by having to tilt her head back to make eye contact. "The chains were not your first mistake, but underestimating me just may be the one you most regret."

For his next mistake, Tom put his hands on her, grasped her upper arms and shoved her out of the way. Surprised by the sudden move, she stumbled, twisting her ankle.

Son of a bitch thought he could manhandle her? She hated the testosterone-fueled male belief that just because they were stronger and bigger men could push women around. Well, not her. Nobody shoved her around and got away with it.

Size does matter—one of many lessons she'd learned from her father. Larger opponents required more space to maneuver so she moved in close. The big idiot grabbed her again.

Rebecca allowed her lips to spread into a sultry grin. The distraction worked, drawing his attention to her mouth. That's when she struck, hard and fast. She brought the thick heel of her shoe down on top of his foot. The pain delivered was sufficient to break his grasp and throw him off balance.

Tom wasn't letting it go. He tried to maneuver her into a position where he'd dominate. Then his arm started to cock back.

Oh, hell no!

After years of having sparred with her father's troops, instinct kicked in and she reacted without stopping to consider the consequences. Rebecca grabbed Tom's shoulders. Using momentum and her body weight, she pulled on his shoulders while thrusting her knee into his groin.

He didn't go down and started gathering his strength to strike back. She threw a sharp right jab, clipping the corner of his jaw.

Tom wobbled, and she was tempted to yell timber as he fell to the ground.

Micah growled and pulled at the chains, which rattled but failed to budge. Jack just gaped at his fallen coworker.

She glared pointedly at Jack. "You're not going to be stupid, are you, Jack?"

"No, ma'am," he said, and tossed her a ring of keys. "That's why I'm gonna get out of here before you unlock him." Jack helped Tom up and the two beat feet back inside the building.

What a mess. The unfortunate scene would draw attention, not that she'd have done anything different. When faced with a bully she would always defend herself.

Rebecca sensed the electronic eyes of various security cameras watching, but the immediate threat came from the drugged, angry man left standing before her. Weltman was right, she had no idea how he'd react to different situations. The low, constant growl coming from Micah didn't bode well.

His body trembled as if he fought an internal struggle. She knew the lion yearned to be free. It was clear in the brown eyes staring at the tree line, and the taut muscles rippling beneath his skin as she removed the horrible collar.

She spoke in a soft tone, praying it would soothe him. "You have to keep the lion on a leash, Micah. Shift now and we'll never get out of here. They will shoot you full of more tranquilizers and drag you back to the cell."

She feared it was already too late—the lion too close to the surface. Still, she tried to help. "Breathe through it, Micah. You are strong and can do this. Just a few more minutes." If he shifted, they were both in a heap of trouble. Not that she hadn't already done a good job of screwing things up.

"Look at me," she demanded. When he refused, she cupped his chin and gently turned his face toward hers. His eyes were steady and calm. "Good." She released the breath she'd been holding. "That's good. You have to hold on for a few more minutes. For me. You can do it for me! So I can get you out of here."

He gave a curt nod as she stepped in closer, the warmth of him washing over her. Rebecca worked the lock securing his arms with hands that trembled. Not with fear, but longing. She wanted to be wrapped in his strong embrace, lying beneath his solid mass, taking his cock deep within her body, moving together as one. God, how she'd longed to be with him since the morning she'd foolishly walked away.

Leaving him was her one and only regret.

"Don't be afraid of me. I would never hurt you." He spoke in a gruff tone, having mistaken her desire for fear. "Never, Becca! Neither would the lion."

The chains slid through her hands, landing with a loud clatter at their feet. She stood tall, meeting his hard gaze head-on. She felt like crap for having doubted him even briefly. "I know, but if I don't get your cock in me soon, I'll go insane with the want. So shut up, let me get you out of these shackles and let's get the hell out of here."

His pupils dilated even further and his nostrils flared. Micah held her gaze for a long moment then growled. "Hurry!"

Memories of their night in Asheville flashed through her mind as she sunk to her knees, glancing up at him from beneath her lashes. She made a slow perusal over the rugged planes of his face, along his corded neck and down the roped muscles. Her gaze took in his wide shoulders and chest, narrowing to trim hips sporting a rather large bulge.

"Becca," he barked, "you naughty girl. Stop that or I'll take your right here. Fuck the cameras."

"And that's a bad idea, why?" she teased, thankful to see a bit of the normal spark back in his eyes.

"Don't push me, baby. Weltman would get off on watching."

She shuddered at the reminder of her creepy boss, fumbled the keys and rushed to free his ankles. Before the last chain fell, Micah lifted her to her feet, still strong regardless of the sedation, and got them moving toward the car.

"Where the hell are we going?"

Chapter Nine

&

Micah opened the car window and took a deep breath of crisp, cool mountain air. His first real breath in weeks. A free breath. Man, did it ever feel good to not be watched constantly by the Nanotech guards. He couldn't wait to take a shower without someone observing his every movement.

When Becca went all commando and attacked Tom, Micah's heart had beat against his ribs so hard he thought they might crack. He had been terrified and frustrated because he couldn't help her. Compared to the big security guard she looked so tiny and frail.

Then she kicked Tom's ass and Micah's dick had gone harder than rock. He had never seen anything half as provocative as Becca pounding a man twice her size into the ground.

"Pull over," he snapped.

"What?" Becca shot him a concerned glance before turning her attention back to the road. "What's wrong? Are you going to be sick?"

"Just pull over."

He unfastened the seat belt and waited for her to shift the car into park.

"Micah, what—"

He leaned across the console, fingers spearing into her soft hair, drawing her closer, and claimed her mouth. His tongue slid along the seam of her lips, plunging inside as they parted for him.

Sweet heaven.

It had been too long. She'd called him a pirate captain that first night, and it fit his current mood. He suited savage action to the description. Micah dominated the aggressive kiss, demanded her submission to the forceful thrust of his tongue. With teeth, lips and tongue he plundered her mouth, ruthless in his passion, taking everything she had to give and demanding more.

More of her addictive taste.

More of her sweet warmth.

More of Becca.

The need for oxygen separated them, both gasping for breath. Becca wore a sexy, dazed expression, her lips red and swollen from his kiss. *God, she was beautiful.*

And beyond miraculous, she'd fought for him.

"Okay. Now we can go."

"What?"

"That helped, but we have to get wherever we're going. Fast."

"I...uh..."

Damn, she had no idea of the effect she had on him. Her eyes had gone all glassy and slumberous. Her cheeks held a sexy pink flush. If she didn't get the car moving again, he'd have her stripped bare with his cock driven deep into the tight clasp of her pussy in a matter of seconds.

"Becca." He gave her trembling hand a slight squeeze. "Drive, honey."

Not wanting to delay any longer, Micah studied the scenery before talking again. It was late in the fall season. The trees were shedding leaves, which covered the ground in vibrant shades of gold, orange, red and brown. Considering the chill in the air, once the sun went down they were in for a cold night. He hoped wherever they were going had a fireplace.

"So what happened with Weltman? How'd you get him to agree to let me out of there?"

She shot him a nervous glance. "I went to talk to him about the situation and how the lab setting was detrimental to making any progress. There was a security guy in the office who agreed, but added a condition. I have to call and check in with him. I was given a company phone."

They were traveling a winding mountain road, but she held the steering wheel in an overly tight grip. He knew there had to be a lot more to the story. "And..."

She sighed heavily. "He made it clear that should I miss calling in it would take less than ten minutes for his 'team' to invade my house."

"Fuck!" Sure sounded like Slater. "Where's the phone?" he snarled.

His sudden change in demeanor had her cringing away from him. "In my purse." She gestured toward a handbag Micah hadn't noticed resting between the seats. He grabbed the bag and dug through the various feminine paraphernalia until his fingers connected with a duplicate of the phone he'd used when working for Nanotech. "Damn it!"

"What's wrong?"

"Cell phones can be tracked. The phones are programmed to check for a signal every few seconds, which connects it to any nearby antenna towers and exchanges information. The position of the phone can be pinpointed based on the signal strength. Plus, these particular phones have been fitted with a GPS chip." He dug around in her purse.

"But it's not even turned on."

"Doesn't matter. The company can still track the device." And he would know. Micah had picked out the official communications devices used by Nanotech and installed the chips himself.

He powered up the phone long enough to jot down the stored contact information then located a metal nail file in the bottom of her purse. With great care he pried open the casing and removed the wafer-thin chip, along with the SIM card. Glancing out the window, he spotted a small independent grocery with several cars in the parking lot. "Pull in to the grocery store."

"You can't just ditch the chip."

"Just pull over, baby." He didn't take the time to explain. Once she'd parked the car in a space he said, "Stay here."

She'd pulled in next to the perfect solution—a local vehicle with a trusting owner who didn't lock the doors. A rip in the cloth-covered seat provided a handy hiding spot for the chip. In less than two minutes they were back on the road.

"So Nanotech will be keeping tabs on whoever owns that car now?"

"Yeah." He removed the battery from the phone and dropped both into her bag. "Is there a landline where we're going?"

"Yes."

"Good. Make all of your calls from there or payphones in town. Dial star sixty-seven to block caller id. Keep the calls short. If they try to draw out the conversation come up with a reason to end the call quickly. And don't tell them where you are for any reason." He made a mental note to check her car for tracking devices.

A wicked gleam flashed in Becca's eyes. "Good thing I didn't correct their assumption we'd be going to the house Nanotech provided for my use. They set up the phone service there and probably have a duplicate set of keys to the place."

They'd come full circle to his original question. "So where are we going?"

"I rented a cabin under an assumed name. The physical distance from the lab is only a few miles, but on these mountain roads the drive takes almost an hour to drive it. Cross-country it's much less."

Micah watched her closely, seeing a side of Becca he had been unaware of. He never doubted she was smart, but he looked at his sexy accomplice with new appreciation. Dr. Rebecca Southerby had been endowed with rare, highly valuable qualities found in so few men, much less in women. She had the determined, courageous heart of a warrior and the instincts of someone experienced in battle.

Sure, she'd passed out the first time he'd shifted in her presence. That was a lot for anyone to grasp. In a very short time she'd proven herself to be fearsome, adaptable and fast one her feet in difficult situations.

The woman was damn near perfect...*for him*.

She made him feel things, which was a disturbing prospect. Micah was a soldier, a tough fighting man, not some wimpy guy all in touch with his emotions and shit. What a crock. Real men weren't sensitive and they sure as hell didn't possess some imaginary feminine side they had to get in touch with.

Screw that!

Rebecca glanced at Micah and stifled an inward groan. The man was scowling again.

"What's wrong? You're all pouty again."

"I don't pout," he grumbled.

She couldn't hold back her laughter. "Yeah, right. I'm getting whiplash over here. Your moods swing faster than a menopausal woman. What happened now?"

"Nothing." His voice took on a petulant note.

"Don't have a hissy fit. Sheesh! Forget I said anything."

"That'd be easier if you'd shut up for five minutes and let me think."

"Well," she huffed. "All righty then."

The car filled with thick, almost smothering tension for the rest of what turned into a long drive. At least it cured her pent-up sexual frustration. His current bad attitude had her keeping her distance. Not that she blamed him for the stressed-out reaction. He'd been through hell.

They finally turned onto the private drive and he went into he-man military mode.

Oh joy.

"What kind of security does this place have? How close is the nearest neighbor? And have you taken the time to walk the perimeter?"

She sighed heavily. "Relax, Rambo. There are locks on all the doors and windows, no close neighbors and when exactly do you think I had time to walk the perimeter, even if I was so inclined?"

Muttering something about women — derogatory, no doubt — he jumped out of the car soon as she put it in park and went skulking off into the woods. Well, good, let him go do his alpha he-man routine. She could use a few minutes alone to breathe without him critiquing how she inhaled and exhaled.

Rebecca headed into the cabin alone, locking the door behind her. Let Rambo knock to get in. Served him right.

After hanging her jacket on a coat tree, she glanced around the homey cabin and fell in love with the place all over again. She could easily picture herself living here.

Straight ahead in the sitting area a hunter green, butter-soft leather couch and recliner sat atop braided cotton rugs. The wooden tables appeared handmade. Cute knickknacks were placed through the inviting room.

Off to her right, the kitchen table was covered by a red gingham cloth and the windows bore matching curtains. A large hutch contained stoneware table settings in an apple motif. Throughout the kitchen was a collection of antique teapots in a variety of shapes, sizes and designs.

A doorway to the left led into a bedroom with its huge rustic pine bed covered by a patchwork quilt in warm tones of ivory, rose, sage and cinnamon. Matching pillows were artfully scattered across the top of the bed.

Only one bed.

For the two of them.

And the weather was perfect for snuggling close. If only he wasn't being such a jerk. He'd been through a lot so she cut him some slack but he'd better get over himself soon if he wanted to get lucky tonight.

Rebecca sighed and shook off the wayward thought, instead considering her favorite feature of the cabin. An enclosed porch extended along the back of the building and in one corner stood the hot tub. Images of her and Micah all dripping wet in the hot swirling water drifted through her mind and heated her body.

Oh yeah! She was definitely anticipating some water play.

Her blood had heated up but the air held a distinct chill that made her shiver. She placed a few logs in the fireplace, along with a bundle of dried herbs wrapped in birch bark she'd purchased at a rustic little shop in town. After lighting the fire, she warmed herself before the hearth. Within a few minutes the cabin filled with the scent of bay leaves, sage, rosemary, lavender and cinnamon.

Figuring she might as well get some dinner started, she headed into the kitchen. Busywork should distract her thoughts from Micah and anticipation of the night to come.

She preheated the oven and whipped up some sweet corn muffin batter, which she poured into a pan and put in the oven. While the muffins baked, she opened a large Mason jar of gourmet Southern chili and put it on the stove to heat. With her task completed, Rebecca found herself staring out the window, rubbing her flat tummy, her mind filled with thoughts of the future.

Would Micah be pleased to learn about the baby? Would he want to be a part of their lives? Or would the thought of fatherhood scare the crap out of him? Did she stand a chance in hell of turning them into a family? That's all she ever really wanted—a comfortable home and her own little family.

An arm clasped around her waist from behind and Rebecca screamed. She hadn't heard a sound but someone had gotten into the locked cabin.

She attempted several defensive moves, but her attacker countered them all. Before she knew what was happening, Rebecca found herself turned around, her body flattened against hard masculine planes with arms holding her tighter than steel bands, giving her no room to maneuver. Blood pounded in her ears and her heart rate was through the roof.

"Whoa, baby. Easy. It's just me."

Her head snapped up and she took in Micah's bewildered expression. "H-how did you get in here?" And how the hell had he managed to sneak up on her?

He flashed a sardonic grin. "I specialized in black ops, baby. No cheap door lock is going to slow me down."

Okay, she'd give him that, but she hadn't heard a sound other than the hum of the refrigerator and the crackling fire. He'd been completely silent. She hadn't detected even the lightest footfall on the wooden floor, no squeak of floorboards, not even the brush of clothing as he moved. He must have been one heck of an operative.

"Sorry for being a jerk earlier."

He took her totally off guard. She hadn't expected an apology. And just like that, she melted. "You're forgiven."

His breath warmed that wonderful spot behind her ear as he spoke in a raspy tone. "Something smells good." She shivered as his hot, damp tongue flicked teasingly over her skin.

"Chili and corn muffins." She was proud of how level and calm her voice sounded. "I thought we would sit by the fire and eat."

"I wasn't talking about dinner, baby." Micah chuckled and her knees shook. "Although, I am very hungry," he nibbled her earlobe, "for you."

Chapter Ten

Holding Becca in his arms had Micah tied up in knots. A sense of peace and contentment warred with growing frustration and searing desire. Hands down, the latter won.

He fumbled with the controls to turn off the stove and lifted her. Becca's arms wrapped around his neck as her legs closed over his hips, perfectly aligning her warm pussy with his cock, which jerked to attention. The material of her skirt bunched up, baring the creamy skin of her lean thighs and capturing his gaze.

"I need you, Micah."

"Soon." He tugged at her blouse, pulled it free of her waistband, fingers searching until he found her soft flesh, smoother than the finest silk. "I've been going crazy seeing you but not able to touch."

He suited action to words, divested Becca of her clothes and laid her on a cozy rug before the hearth. Firelight chased shadows over the subtle hills and valleys of her body, teasing him with tantalizing glimpses of the delicate delights he sought.

Starved for the sight of her, Micah's hungry gaze roamed her supple body noting the new glow to her skin, which appeared to shine from within. Her breasts were fuller than he remembered, the rosy nipples a deeper shade of pink. She was the same beautiful woman he desired, yet there were distinct differences.

"Micah."

Her plaintive tone didn't alter his course. She shifted restlessly, reached for him. "I'm not done looking." With one hand, he held her wrists pinned above her head. "I could spend weeks staring at your gorgeous body and never get my fill."

"You will not!" She began to struggle against his restraining grasp in earnest. "If you don't touch me, I'll kill you."

The idle threat, combined with her scrunched-up expression, made him laugh. "Where do you want to be touched?" His free hand glided along the elegant column of her neck, dipping into the hollow of her throat. "How about here?" His fingertips softly traced her prominent collarbone then down the inside of her arm and teased the side of her breast. He circled the mound and decided he was right, it was fuller. "Or maybe here?"

Becca moaned and arched her back, thrusting her breast against his hand, seeking a firmer touch. "Micah," she pleaded.

Giving in to what they both wanted, he cupped her breast, weighed and measured it against his palm. He tweaked her pouty nipple between his thumb and forefinger. She sucked in a hard breath and pulled back slightly, and he made note of her increased sensitivity.

"How about if I taste you too? Would you like that, Becca?"

"Oh yes," she groaned.

As responsive as ever. He loved it.

He trailed the very tip of his tongue around her areola, which puckered tighter. When he blew a stream of warm air over the damp tip, her entire body shuddered and arched higher. He took her taut nipple into his mouth, sucked lightly and pressed the nubbin between his tongue and palate.

Becca went wild, cried out, writhed. Her hips bucked in an instinctive rhythm older than time, rubbing against his hard cock like a cat in heat. One moment she was all soft and fluid motion beneath him, incoherent nonsense spilling from her lips, the next she tensed, stilled and moaned as an orgasm took her by surprise.

Jesus, that was hot. He'd never seen a woman orgasm just from having her nipples sucked. "So responsive."

When the shudders subsided and she calmed, Micah brushed damp strands of hair from her face. "You ready for more?"

"Mmm..." she mumbled. "Yes, more."

While the release had taken the edge off for her, Micah's body was hard and ready. Still, he refused to hurry, wanting to enjoy the time they had together, however limited it might end up being.

"Good." He pressed her wrists to the rug. "Keep your hands there, baby."

"But, Micah," she complained. "I want to touch you."

"Not now, baby. I'm on a short leash. If you touch me this is going to be over before we even get started."

Those big green eyes blinked up at him from beneath thick lashes and he was lost. A warning growl rumbled from his throat. The sound, more animal than human, would frighten most people. But Becca was far from average. The extraordinary woman affected him in ways he couldn't comprehend, awakening needs and emotions he had no idea how to handle.

The only thing he knew for certain, felt with every erratic beat of his heart, Rebecca Southerby was his. She belonged to him, with him, the same way he belonged to her. The very thought scared the hell out of him, but there was no going back. Not now, maybe not ever.

"Micah."

He met her gaze, staggered by the depth of emotions playing across her delicate features. The breath caught in his throat.

"It's okay. I want you to let go." Rebecca hated the idea of him holding anything back from her. She wanted it all. Every ounce of passion and desire. "I want all of you."

Especially your love.

Not knowing how he'd take such a declaration, she kept it to herself.

The future was uncertain, but she wanted to take a chance with him. She didn't want to consider not having Micah in her life, in their child's life. He was theirs, and she'd fight to the death to keep him.

He faltered, appeared wary. She preferred him strong and confident. "I want everything, Micah. Make love to me."

He swallowed, hard, rose to his knees. A protest lingered on her lips, shattering as he pulled the elastic band from his hair and shook out the dark blond strands. With slow, deliberate motions he unbuttoned his shirt and uncovered his strong chest.

Riveted, she stared as he stood to remove his socks and shoes. She held her breath when his long fingers paused at the waistband of his jeans, coming to rest next to the substantial bulge held captive by the denim.

What is he waiting for? Her gaze shot upward, meeting his intense stare. Rebecca melted, her entire body going soft and liquid beneath the heat of his dark eyes.

The rasp of his zipper was loud in the quiet room. She kept her eyes trained on his face, unable to glance away from the sexy determination etched into his solid jaw. He bent to take off his jeans, breaking eye contact, and allowing her gaze to lower.

The man was a masterpiece, carved by a skilled artisan. Tall, broad-shouldered, classic V-shaped torso narrowing down to lean hips and strong legs. His thick cock hung heavily, a pearl of fluid beading at the head. Longing to taste him, she licked her lips, smiling when he groaned, "Later."

"You're no fun."

He shrugged. "I showed you mine. Now it's your turn. Spread your legs, baby. Show me that pretty pussy I've been dreaming about."

Feeling bold and powerful, Rebecca drew her knees up then let them fall to the side. He sucked in a harsh breath, driving her further. She trailed her hands over her body, stopping to shape her breasts and rub aching nipples before continuing on. He followed her movements as her fingers reached the juncture of her thighs.

She circled her slick clit with a fingernail, pressing into her own touch, then dipped lower and spread herself wide while plunging two fingers deep. It was good, but not enough. She wanted more.

"Micah," she gasped. "Make love to me. I need your cock in me." Her fingers moved faster, thrust harder.

"Mine."

The guttural growl struck a chord of fear and excitement within her. Rebecca looked up at Micah, noting his elongated pupils. If she wasn't mistaken, the downy blond hair covering his body had gotten thicker. Her worry about his screwed-up DNA had lingered at the back of her mind and now zoomed to the front. A frisson of unease trickled down her spine as he knelt between her widespread legs, his expression hard and savage.

"Micah."

His gaze didn't rise to meet hers, remaining on her pussy instead.

"I'm up here."

That brought him up short, a sheepish smile gracing the curve of his sexy lips. "Yeah?"

"Umm…that thing I said about letting go," she bit her lip. "I've reconsidered. You change on me, go all hairy and feral while we're making love, and I'll—"

What? What would she do? How the heck could she level a threat that would have any impact on a man more than twice her size?

"You'll do what, baby?" he prompted.

An idea came to her and she went with it even though she didn't have the surgical skills necessary to follow through on the threat. He wouldn't know it to be a blatant lie.

She narrowed her eyes at him, tried for an intimidating look but figured it failed when his smile grew. *Irritating jerk!*

"I'll neuter you." She nodded, satisfied by his frown and furrowed brow. "You keep a tight leash on the lion, Micah. I'm serious!"

He threw back his head and roared with laughter, shaking so hard she thought he might fall over. When he finally recovered, his response angered and embarrassed her. "Bestiality doesn't do it for you?"

She sat up, spine ramrod straight, put both palms on his chest and shoved. "That's not funny!" He didn't budge, but his laughter did end abruptly.

"Whoa, don't get upset, Becca." His ran his hands up and down her arms in a soothing fashion. "I'm sorry. I shouldn't have laughed, but you looked so serious and I wasn't expecting what you said. Created some pretty crazy images in my head."

Oh great. Now she had some wild visuals forming in her mind and had to fight back her own smile.

She didn't resist as he laid her back on the rug. "If I start to shift you can shoot me with the tranq gun, but I'm sure it won't be a problem. Seeing you bare and spread open for me...damn, baby. Drives *me* wild. Not the lion, Becca. Me."

He took her hand, wrapping her fingers around his warm cock, which was harder than steel. She tightened her grip and stroked him from base to crest, his rough groan restoring her confidence. "Come up here. I want to taste you."

"Uh-uh. My sweet tooth is craving you."

She affected an innocent smile and batted her eyelashes at him. "Why can't we both have what we want?"

His eyes darkened, shimmered. The pupils elongating again, but this time she wasn't afraid, realizing it meant she'd turned him on. "I love the way your mind works!" His breathing became more shallow, and she noticed a plump vein in his forehead pulsing.

The obvious signs of his increased arousal stimulated her own. Muscles softened and her blood turned hotter than molten lava, flooding her erogenous zones.

Micah captured her mouth in a scorching-hot kiss that had her toes curling into the rug as she pressed tight against him. He stole her breath, replaced it with his own. Their tongues tangled, tasted, demanded more until the necessity for oxygen broke them apart.

Catching him off guard, putting all her strength into the movement, Rebecca rolled them over. Once on top, she turned, straddled his face and playfully wiggled her ass.

Hell yeah! The position gave Micah a great view of her wet, pink folds. Her puffy little clit peeked out from beneath its hood, a temptation he didn't even try to resist.

He grasped her hips, preparing to settle in for a nice, long feast. Becca, having the same intention, sucked his cock into her mouth, taking him deep. He gasped, swore, struggled not to come as she sucked hard and teased his most sensitive spots with her devilish tongue.

"Jesus, ease up, Becca. I want this to last more than ten seconds."

She mumbled something around his dick and the vibrations nearly did him in. Bolts of fiery lightning seared his spine, and his balls tensed. Micah gritted his teeth, clamped his eyes shut and fought his body's instinctive urge to thrust. He wasn't able to participate until she came up for air.

Pulling her hips, he launched an equally devastating sensual assault on her senses. He followed a simple battle plan—give her as much pleasure as possible. He started off with slow, tender licks, letting her salty-sweet flavor explode over his tongue. Allowing the intensity to build, he followed her direction, paying attention to what elicited the strongest response.

Rebecca gave no quarter, showering him with lavish attention, driving him to an edge he refused to cross. Not before her.

The instant she tensed, the walls of her pussy spasming, her cries rising to the rafters, he let go, following her into ecstasy. She drank down every drop of his release before collapsing, draped over his chest, right where she belonged.

If he could manage not to mess things up and keep her there, he stood a chance at grabbing the brass ring.

Rebecca continued to surprise and delight him with new discoveries. His release took the edge off, but Micah still craved something deeper. Something...more.

She took the lead again, guided him into loose and lazy movements. It started with sweet arousal, made a slow and steady climb to a deep intimacy he'd never known had been lacking. There was no rush to reach the finish line. The ultimate goal wasn't to get off. None of the frantic, wild, pounding sex he'd found so pleasurable in the past.

Becca touched him in ways no other ever had. In her warm embrace he learned the meaning of making love. The strong connection forged with each measured, deliberate joining. The soul-deep sharing of emotions through shared passion. The satisfaction of bringing each other to a pleasurable release.

She taught him what it meant to fall in love.

Hell if that wasn't some scary shit!

After they recovered, Micah reheated their dinner. The chili, which had smelled so good and stirred her appetite an hour before, now made Rebecca's stomach churn. Sitting before a warm fire, naked, wrapped up in a quilt with Micah should have put her in a romantic mood. It would have if her conscience hadn't picked that moment to kick into high gear and start gnawing on her insides.

She gave up the pretense of eating, stopped pushing the food around in the bowl with her spoon and set it aside. Snuggled close to his chest, she basked in his warmth, breathed his scent deep into her lungs. Knowing she'd be content to spend forever just as they were, she dreaded their uncertain future.

"What's wrong? Don't you like the chili?"

Damn it, him being nice only made her guilt grow. "It's fine."

He rested a palm on her forehead. "You're a bit warm. Do you feel all right?"

Realizing she'd been rubbing her tummy, she wrapped her arms around him to still the restless movement. "Yes, just tired. It's been an exhausting week." And wasn't that the understatement of the century.

Micah had a right to know about the baby. She wanted to tell him, but how? Such weighty, life-altering news couldn't be blurted out. *Oh, by the way, I'm pregnant.* Lessening the impact would take finesse.

She yelped, startled when Micah rose suddenly with her in his arms. "Then it's past time that I tucked you into bed."

"Mmm," she purred as all sorts of lascivious images involving the two of them locked in a variety of positions on the big bed flooded her mind.

Micah laughed softly. "Not for sex. To sleep. You need to rest."

Rest? Hah! She could think of many much more interesting ways to share a bed with Micah than sleeping.

Dismissing her guilty conscience, she let her fingers do the talking by tangling them in his downy chest hair. "I'd rather play."

"Becca," he grumbled. "Relax. Let me take care of you."

"Oh, yes. Please do. I have this itch that needs to be scratched—"

She laughed as he tossed her onto the bed. Rebecca bounced once and came to a sudden stop as he landed on top of her. Damn, she loved this playful side of him.

"An itch, huh? Where?"

He flashed a rare, lopsided grin and all her worries evaporated. When the right time arrived, she'd find the words to share her news—later. But not now, when she had him back in her arms. Rebecca indulged her greedy, selfish urges to keep him to herself for one night and not permit anything to come between them.

She reveled in who she was with Micah. He banished the nerdy and shy zoologist, releasing the inner vixen she normally kept under tight control.

Slipping a hand between their bodies, she thrust a finger between her legs. "Down here," she said, hardly recognizing her own sultry voice. "It's a deep itch I can't reach." She lifted her hand to his lips, tracing the curves with her damp fingertip.

His lips parted and Micah sucked her finger into his warm mouth. Fierce heat blazed through her body, raced from one nerve ending to the next, making her feel as if she'd burst into flames. His eyes sparkled with mischief when he released her finger.

"Well, I happen to have this handy scratching post you can use to take care of your itch."

Rebecca's heart stuttered, seized for a moment, then pounded against her breastbone. Micah looked at her with pure adoration and something else softening his hard features.

Dare she even think it? Could he be feeling what she did? Had he fallen in love with her? Panic tightened her chest with the realization. She'd really gone and done it—fallen in love with Micah. *Holy crap!*

His smile, so rare and precious, returned to his lips. "I don't offer to demonstrate often, but you're special." He cupped her chin and stared deep into her eyes. "How about it, baby? Wanna give it a spin? Every test drive comes with a satisfaction guarantee." The charming rake winked at her. "I'll keep scratching 'til that itch is taken care of."

She had no idea how long she stared at him, not saying a word.

"Becca?" His brow wrinkled with concern and he started to pull away. "I'm sorry. You're tired and here I am fooling around."

"No," she gasped, reaching out for him. "Micah, please." At the sound of her emotion-choked voice, his gaze snapped back to hers. "Make love to me."

The corner of his lips twitched then his mouth spread into a huge grin. He looked happier than a kid set free in the toy store on Christmas morning. She prayed her secret, when revealed, wouldn't destroy the fragile bond they'd forged.

Chapter Eleven

❧

"You have to work with the cat. Don't fight its natural instincts, Micah."

He yowled in frustration. For two days Becca had lectured him on lions and their behaviors. She might be an expert on big cats but she had no clue about the lion within *him*.

His lion had a single thought permeating his one-track mind—fucking.

Micah waged a constant war against the lion's biological imperative to mount and mate Becca, over and over, again and again. He had to fuck her until his seed penetrated an egg and her belly swelled with his cub or, better yet, cubs. Wanted nothing more than to pounce on her and fuck until he was too exhausted to continue.

"Micah." She touched his flank and before he could stop it, the lion snapped at her hand. He jerked the lion back, wickedly sharp teeth missing her vulnerable flesh by a narrow margin. Too narrow for his sanity.

The change overcame him fast. In the blink of an eye his senses dulled, fur receded and his body altered. Each time it happened he anticipated pain but it never came. The experience sapped his energy and left him starving to replenish the massive calories he'd used.

"Jesus, you know better! Never try to touch the lion when he can't see it coming," he barked.

When she didn't respond, Micah lifted his heavy head and met her frightened gaze, instantly regretting his harsh tone.

Aw, fuck! Good job, asshole.

He'd scared the hell out of Becca. She held a hand over her throat, her entire body trembling as she fought back tears. Ignoring his state of undress, he pulled her into his arms, stifling an inward groan as she brushed against his painfully hard cock.

"Shh," he soothed. "I'm sorry, baby. I'll work harder and get the lion to behave."

"I don't know how to help you," she sobbed. "I feel like a total failure."

"We'll figure it out, together. Right now all I'm worried about is keeping you safe. If I hurt you..." he shivered, horrified by the very idea. "I'd never forgive myself."

Becca rubbed at her eyes with balled-up fists. "I have to go to the lab—"

"Absolutely not," he roared.

She jerked back, afraid of him again, making him want to punch something. He hated causing her to fear him. "I would never intentionally hurt you." The words were low, spoken almost in a whisper.

"I know you wouldn't."

Did she? He doubted it was possible considering his actions.

"Micah," she implored. "Neither one of us knows exactly what's been done to you. I only skimmed some of the scientific notes on the procedure, but didn't have a chance to read the specifics on your case."

He didn't have to read the specifics, he lived with them. And he had done his own homework online while Becca slept. The more he learned, the more he realized how drastically what he felt as a man conflicted with the lion.

Micah's feelings toward Becca were possessive and protective. He longed to bind her to him permanently. The lion's primary goals were to dominate and procreate.

According to the information he'd found, the female went into heat for several days and would fuck any available lion, even forgoing food to have sex up to forty times a day. No way could he get it up forty times a day, not that he wasn't willing to try.

Something Becca said broke off his internal musings and drew him back into the conversation. "What?"

"Haven't you been listening?" she huffed. "Kyle has been acting odd when I call to check in. I feel like he's trying to tell me something, but I've been following your advice and keeping the calls short. By going into the lab, I can reassure Weltman we're making progress and also try to get Kyle alone, see if I can find out what's going on."

Micah scratched at his jaw, wondering what Slater was up to. The other man wouldn't do anything without a deliberate plan. And what Becca said had merit. They needed move info from his medical records—something was missing. The opportunity to determine Slater's intentions would be a bonus. It would be good to know who he had in his corner when, not if, the shit hit the fan. He had no doubt it would, because he had no intention of ever being under Weltman's thumb again.

"All right, but we do this my way, Becca. I won't risk anything happening to you."

She didn't quite manage to hold back a triumphant grin. "What could possibly happen to me at the lab?"

Anger surged through him as he remembered Tom's hands on his woman. The lion's rage added to his own had Micah primed for a good knock-down-drag-out fight. "Have you forgotten a rather physical run-in with one of the guards when you were busting me out of there?"

"That was nothing," she shrugged off his concern. "A minor misunderstanding, which proved I can take care of myself."

"The guards won't underestimate you again, and you won't walk away from another confrontation unscathed."

"Fine, I'll be careful and do what you say, but we've got to have those files, Micah."

They settled on a plan, even though he didn't like it. Since he couldn't risk setting foot in the lab, Becca had to go in alone. She'd come up with an idea for transporting his clothes while in lion form. They loaded everything into a duffle bag and put the strap around his neck before he shifted.

"Oh shit! Shift back, Micah. Hurry!" Becca cried.

If the rapid change from man to beast and back again within the span of several moments hadn't been enough to steal his breath, the expandable strap tightening around the lion's thick neck certainly had been. Micah cursed, ripping at the bag even once he could breathe again. "Jesus Christ. I won't have to worry about Nanotech anymore if I succeed at strangling myself."

"Oh my god! Are you okay?" She grabbed the bag and began working the buckle to lengthen the strap. "You scared the hell out of me."

"Scared you?" He shook his head. "Took about ten years off my life."

After she had the strap extended as far as it would go, she placed it around his neck again. Micah rubbed at his jaw, trying to decide whether stupidity or desperation compelled him to give it another try.

He focused on the image of the lion in his mind, pleased to still be breathing when his body reshaped itself. Unfortunately his relief was short-lived. Becca threw herself at him, wrapping her arms around his neck and hugging him tight enough to cut off his air supply. His deep growl had her stepping back, a sheepish grin on her flushed face.

"Please be careful. I'll kick your ass later if you do anything stupid."

Hah! He was more worried about her impetuous streak getting Becca into a boatload of trouble. With him stuck outside, he wouldn't be able to help her. At least with his technical skills he'd been able to fashion a listening device from materials he'd had her pick up in town. Regardless of the safety measures in place, his heart clenched as she got in the SUV and headed down the private drive.

The lion's powerful legs ate up the distance across the mountain terrain between the cabin and the lab. From his vantage point high on a tree limb, hidden behind the colorful leaves, he had a great view of the grounds surrounding the facility.

Waiting didn't bother him under normal circumstances. He had the patience and calm of a great hunter. Too bad these weren't normal circumstances and he was anything but calm. The lion's keen hearing picked up the sound of Becca's vehicle before she drove into view. Once she made it past the gates, he jumped down from the tree, shifted and got dressed.

He turned on the receiver and heard her take a deep breath, followed by a metallic bang as she closed the car door. No sooner had the she made it through the front doors than the hair on the back of his neck stood on end and all his instincts screamed that she was in trouble.

* * * * *

Approaching the main entrance of the top-secret laboratory, Rebecca rubbed her sweaty palms on her slacks, held her breath and placed her hand on the scanner plate. Blue light glowed around the edges of her hand, which grew warm from the sensors. She didn't breathe again until the door issued a series of electronic clicks and slid open.

Cool as a cucumber, her father's voice coached as she walked down the hall to the echo of her heels clacking on the tile floor. She nodded to a white-coated technician, turned the corner, almost making it to her office before being intercepted by Kyle Slater.

"Hello, Dr. Southerby," he greeted. Kyle wrapped his long fingers, firm yet gentle, around her biceps and guided her down a connecting corridor toward the examination rooms. "We weren't expecting you today." His voice sounded tight as if he were stressed. "You're alone?"

Keep your answer short and sweet. Don't give him anything.

She nodded. "Yes. I just stopped by to go over some files."

When he didn't say anything else, butterflies took flight in her stomach. Her hands itched to rub her abdomen, but she didn't give in to the impulse.

"Where are we headed, Mr. Slater? I have a great deal of work waiting back in my office."

"This will only take a moment. Weltman wants an update on your progress with Lasiter. He will also want to know where Lasiter is and why he's not with you."

Then why were they headed in the opposite direction of Weltman's office?

Kyle stopped before a steel door, swiped his identity card and placed his palm on the scanner. When the door slid open, he drew her into a small room with a table and two chairs at the center. The far wall held a large mirror she presumed to be a one-way window.

"What's going on? This looks like one of those interrogation rooms from a TV cop show."

He didn't answer the question. "Please have a seat. Mr. Weltman will be with us in a moment." Kyle positioned himself next to the entrance, back against the wall, staring blankly toward the mirrored glass.

Rebecca sat straight, hands folded in her lap, schooled features not reflecting the jumbled thoughts racing through her mind.

Did they suspect something? Had she somehow given herself away? Had they discovered Micah was on the property?

She didn't have to wait long for answers. The door whooshed open and her red-faced boss stepped into the room.

Don't panic. Hold your tongue.

"Well, if it isn't our missing zoologist. We've been searching everywhere for you, Dr. Southerby. Imagine our surprise when you strolled through the front door."

She bit her tongue, remained silent.

"Would you mind telling me where you've taken my test subject?"

"I—"

Weltman held up a hand, cutting off her response. "Don't say he's at the house I provided for you. We've already checked."

Don't say anything, her father's voice advised.

Weltman glanced at the guard then nodded toward the door. "Let's introduce the doctor to our latest success, Slater."

Turning on his heel, he didn't wait to see if they followed. Kyle once again latched on to her arm and led her to one of the exam rooms. She knew Micah heard every word, and prayed he didn't do anything rash.

She blinked a few times as her eyes adjusted to the bright lights of the room. Then Weltman moved to the side.

"Oh. My. God!" Her hand flew up to cover her throat as horror filled her.

A tall, dark-haired man struggled against the restraints holding his naked body to the examination table. Freshly sutured surgical incisions riddle his tan skin. "What have you done to him?"

"Dr. Southerby, this is Crosby, our latest subject in the Predator Project. He's been injected with *Panthera tigris*."

Sweet Jesus, they'd screwed with another man's DNA. And he didn't appear to have volunteered for the project. First a lion, now a tiger. What will they do next, create a bear? The whole thing was turning into some surreal, screwed-up fairytale.

The man's wild gaze shot around the room. Perspiration broke out on his brow. "No! No more doctors. No more drugs.

No more procedures," he cried. "I can't take any more, you sick fuckers."

"We've discussed this before, Crosby," Weltman said in a cold tone. "If you don't calm down, we'll have to sedate you."

His gaze locked on Weltman and the man's struggles immediately stopped.

Weltman nodded. "Good." He turned to face her. "Crosby has not yet managed to shift. We don't know what the problem is, but you will begin working with him today..."

His dramatic pause had her heart rising into her throat as panic tightened her chest. She knew whatever he said next wasn't going to be good.

"Soon as you return Lasiter to his cell. Slater will escort you to retrieve my shifter."

Nope, not good at all.

She opened her mouth to say...something, she wasn't sure what, but the words died on her lips as shrill alarms began shrieking and red lights flashed in warning. "Security breach, sector four," an electronic voice repeated several times.

"Ah," Weltman exclaimed. "My guess is that would be Lasiter arriving to rescue the fair damsel."

No, Micah. Don't put yourself at risk for me.

Kyle spoke into a handheld communicator, issuing orders rapid-fire. A few moments later the alarms were silenced.

"Slater, bring Rebecca to my office. We'll wait for Lasiter there. I don't want him to meet our newest creation yet."

Kyle reached for her arm and Rebecca bristled. "Don't touch me," she muttered. "I'm perfectly capable of walking on my own."

Chapter Twelve

ဢ

Kyle shot her a wicked grin and Rebecca's hope rose. Could he be an ally?

"Are you wearing a transmitter?"

Caution, she reminded herself. "Why would I admit it to you if I was?"

"Because I'm trying to help. I served with Micah. He pulled my ass out of the fire more times than I can count. I'm finally getting a chance to return the favor."

There was something reassuring in his eyes. An indefinable quality that had her trusting him. Wary of his intentions, she nodded. "Yes, Micah can hear everything so if you're setting me up, he'll come after you."

"Where is it?"

"Left lapel."

His smile grew. "I almost feel sorry for him. You're gonna give him a run for his money. You're absolutely perfect for the lucky bastard."

"Umm..." she hesitated. "I'm going to take that as a compliment and let it slide."

Kyle laughed. "Priceless." He drew her into the hall but turned down a side corridor she was unfamiliar with.

"Where are we going?"

"Security breach was sector four, the loading docks. Micah will be long gone from that area by now. I suspect we'll find him near the security control room."

He held her shoulders, leaned forward, moist lips parted, and for one startling moment Rebecca thought he intended to kiss her. Instead, he spoke into her collar. "I hope you got that, Lasiter. I cleared the control room. We'll meet you there."

He'd barely finished speaking and lifted his head when white smoke billowed through the corridor and Micah's deep voice echoed around them.

"You're slipping, Slater. I already hit the control room, armed myself and tripped the alarms from there to throw off the hounds."

Rebecca shivered. His voice sounded different—cold and detached.

Kyle laughed and raised his hands, palms outward. "You sneaky spook. Always were a step ahead of everyone else."

"Step away from her, Slater."

Kyle took two measured and deliberate steps backward, but his sharp gaze remained locked in the direction of Micah's voice.

Her knees wobbled as he suddenly materialized from within the dense smoke looking every inch the hardened warrior she'd first pegged him as. His body vibrated with a dark menace she felt rolling over her, paralyzing her with fear that snaked along her spine. She didn't dare take a breath or make even the slightest movement.

She detested her reaction, but the man before her was not the sweet lover she'd fallen head over heels in love with. He'd gone into full Rambo mode, promising violent retribution for anyone who dared to cross his path.

"Micah?" He didn't acknowledge having heard her.

"Unfasten your weapons belt, Slater."

Kyle took his time working the clasp with one hand then let it dangle from his fingers.

"Drop it and kick it over here."

"You're wasting time," he protested while following Micah's instructions.

The belt skittered across the floor, zooming past her, holding her focus until Weltman's nasally voice cut through the tension-filled silence.

"Dr. Southerby's not going anywhere, Lasiter. Not until I test the fetus."

"Oh shit," she gasped. How had he found out about the baby?

No one uttered a word for what was surely only a few seconds, but the silence seemed endless to her. When Micah spoke, his voice was colder than solid ice.

"I won't buy into your mind games so hurry up and spill whatever toxic swill you're trying to sell."

His maniacal laughter rang out, constricting her chest and making it difficult for Rebecca to breathe.

"She didn't tell you." He nodded. "Venomous bitch, just like all the others."

Others? What on earth was he talking about? Had the man lost his mind?

"We were watching her house. When she didn't show up with you, I sent a team in to search the place. Found not one but three positive pregnancy tests in the bathroom trash can."

Rebecca had no problem visualizing her movements. Crumpling up the boxes, tossing in the instructions, staring at the three test sticks lined up on the counter. Picking them up with numb fingers and dropping them into the wicker basket, intending to carry the trash outside but her scrambled thoughts had distracted her from completing the task.

"Is it yours?"

Weltman's wretched voice broke the images. Her gaze shot to Micah, who appeared unaffected by the news. She looked only at him, pleaded with her eyes for understanding. "I only found out the day they brought me to see you. The day I found out…" *that you turn into a lion.* She kept the last part to herself.

There was no way to justify not telling him about the baby.

To her horror and disbelief, he never even blinked or spared a glance in her direction.

"Slater," Micah growled, "don't even think about it."

Other than making sure his open hands could be seen, Kyle remained still.

"Rebecca," Micah said in that lifeless tone. "Pick up the weapons belt and bring it here."

She did as he commanded, moved to his side, placing the belt into his hand. His arm wrapped around her waist and jerked her against his side. His fingers dug painfully deep into her hip and she flinched. Rebecca prayed he hadn't noticed, but when she met his hard glare she knew he'd seen the involuntary reaction.

The same eyes that had showed such warmth and emotion for her a mere hour before were now empty and lifeless. He looked at her as if she meant less than nothing.

Her heartbeat pounded in her ears and she stumbled along as he dragged her down the hallway. Arrogant, macho jerk, issuing orders to her as if she were some green Army recruit incapable of figuring out anything for herself. Passing judgment on her actions and treating her like crap.

She kept her mouth shut, bided her time. Let the impervious idiot think he had all the power and control over her. He'd learn the truth soon enough.

The baby didn't need him. She didn't need him.

Want him, yes.

Love him, absolutely.

Need his holier than thou attitude, hell no!

"Give me your keys."

Becca didn't say a word as they exited the facility, which surprised and relieved Micah. He did a quick scan of the surrounding area and stripped some branches from a nearby shrub, using them to jam the entry door shut. It wouldn't stop the security team but should buy him a few precious minutes.

All his concentration narrowed down to the task at hand, getting them both out alive. He'd sort everything else out when they were safe. Or better yet, when he could breathe again and the vise grip clamped tight over his chest eased up.

In all his years working covert operations and high-level security he had no trouble keeping his mind on the job until it was completed. He had not suffered heart palpitations or sheer terror when under heavy fire or when things went to shit. Not until he heard Becca describe the room she'd been taken to as an interrogation room.

The lion roared in frustration, demanding to be set free to protect its mate. The sight of Slater holding Becca close, his head leaned into the curve of her neck—

Murderous rage beyond anything he'd ever felt almost had him releasing the lion. He had longed to shift and then slowly rip Slater and Weltman apart, piece by bloody piece.

Reaching the SUV, Micah yanked the passenger door open. "Get in. I'm driving."

Becca did so without a peep, her expression unreadable. He was tempted to lock her in the car and go back inside but knew he wouldn't feel better while she remained on the premises.

Once they cleared the main gate, his thoughts turned to the confrontation with Weltman.

Dr. Southerby's not going anywhere, Lasiter. Not until I test the fetus.

Rebecca's reaction had given the words validity. All the color had drained from her face. Their gazes had met and he'd seen the truth in her eyes.

Becca was pregnant.

Weltman had radiated maniacal glee at having spoiled her secret. *She didn't tell you. Venomous bitch, just like all the others.*

He had hoped it was some screwed-up fantasy from the man's delusional mind. Then Weltman dropped a bomb that had torn through Micah's heart.

We were watching her house. When she didn't show up with you, I sent a team in to search the place. Found not one but three positive pregnancy tests in the bathroom trash can.

Is it yours?

His mind had reeled with the possibility and he'd almost let down his guard, catching Kyle's slight movement just in time.

Becca's frantic words had ripped out the remaining pieces of his heart.

I only found out the day they brought me to see you. The day I found out…

The day she'd found out he now shared his body with a lion.

I'm going to be a father.

The very idea sucked the air right out of his lungs. He took his hand from the steering wheel long enough to rub the ache building in his temples.

He glanced at her from the corner of his eye. Becca sat rigid and quiet, staring out the windshield. She looked like a cold stone statue—distant and immovable.

Fuck!

He really couldn't blame her for not telling him. What woman in her right mind would want some fucked-up science experiment to be the father of their child?

His life was such a mess. During their night in Asheville, he'd walked on air, thinking he'd found what he had not even know he'd been missing in Becca. Then she'd left him.

For a second time his life had taken a stunning new turn — fatherhood. The woman of his dreams, pregnant with their child.

Her habit of rubbing her flat tummy, the changes in her body, all the pieces fell into place. He imagined the cute little house with a white picket fence, a couple of bicycles lying in the yard.

But an unemployed lion shape-shifter didn't fit in the picture.

Some people just weren't meant to be happy.

Micah checked the mirrors. So far nobody was on their tail, but he needed reinforcements. He had one goal now, get Becca and their baby out of this mess. Once he knew they were safe, he could start thinking about taking down Weltman.

On one of her trips to town he'd had Becca pick up a pay-as-you-go cell phone, which he'd stashed in the glove box for precisely this situation.

"Hand me the disposable phone," he ordered.

Micah cussed himself. His tone had come out harsher than he'd intended and she visibly bristled. Damn it, he had to keep his emotions out of this or he wouldn't be able to function. He didn't have the luxury of falling apart even though the woman he loved beyond reason — the family he'd never dreamed of — was slipping through his fingers.

Wanting reassurance that both Becca and the baby were all right, his first call went to a medic he'd worked with and trusted, Lex McLean. Two other names came to mind. Nash Crosby, who he'd served with in the Army, and his second-in-command at Nanotech. When unable to reach Nash, Micah called a secured, private satellite number.

"Talk to me, man," Kyle Slater said as he answered the call.

"What the fuck's going on?" Micah demanded.

Slater laughed. Then Micah heard footsteps and a door slammed.

"I was wondering how long it would take you to call me."

"Hopefully doing so wasn't a huge mistake." Micah prayed he'd made the right decision.

Slater remained silent for several long seconds. "This is a fucking job, nothing more. You, I owe my life to."

Some of Micah's tension lifted. He wasn't stupid. He wouldn't give Slater his full trust. Not yet. "Is anyone on my tail?"

"No. I have the boys here tied up chasing their dicks at the moment, but they won't be distracted for long. I'm sure you've already ditched the doc's company phone and house. Nanotech hasn't discovered your hidey-hole. The doc did a good job of covering her tracks on that front, but I wouldn't advise staying close for long. The time has come to tap into your emergency resources and become a ghost, my friend."

"Not quite," he corrected. "Consider the doc long gone, but I have a score to settle first."

"I was hoping you'd say that."

He easily pictured the devious anticipatory smile flashing across Slater's otherwise hard face. The man lived for the thrill of a good fight. Thankfully, he was on Micah's side. He'd hate to go up against the mean bastard.

Chapter Thirteen

✵

"When did your life go so far off track?" Rebecca asked her reflection in the bathroom mirror.

On the drive back to the cabin, Micah had busied himself making his plans. He spoke to her for the first time when he turned onto the private drive.

Stay in the car while I check the cabin.

He had searched the cabin then waved her inside with orders to stay there and gone off to do his Rambo routine.

All night.

She'd gone to bed alone and woken up alone.

There were subtle signs of his presence. A mug he'd rinsed out and left in the sink. The scent of bacon lingering in the air. A plate of food kept warm in the oven for her. She'd almost wept over the full pot of coffee.

A firm knocking on the door had her pulse rate soaring as she wondered what he was up to now.

Rebecca took a calming breath and opened the door, stunned silent by the gorgeous man on the other side, smiling at her. A blond Adonis—tall, lean and sexy as hell. And his smile—absolute sin. His smile brought to mind carnal visions of long sleepless nights rolling around between the sheets. That seductive smile was sure to have kept him from ever being lonely.

"Hey, Doc!" He held out a steady hand toward her. "Name's Lex. I'm a medic. Spent some time in the military with the big guy. He asked me to check on you and the bambino, make sure everything's okay."

She shook his hand, but instead of letting go, Lex flashed that provocative grin and led her to the bed, then pressed on her shoulder until she sat down.

"Any cramping or spotting going on that we have to be worried about?"

She shook her head as he unhooked a stethoscope from around his neck and blew on the end to warm it.

"Good!"

He kept up a constant, one-sided conversation and before she realized his intentions, Lex had the first two buttons of her blouse undone. He was quiet as he listened to her heart and measured her respirations.

She didn't even have a chance to protest as the lethal rake laid her back on the bed, placed a pillow beneath her head, pulled up her shirt and unfastened her jeans with nimble fingers. She tried to relax as he listened at several spots over her abdomen, his expression thoughtful.

But when he started to palpate an area above her pubic bone, she came to her senses and shoved him away. "Whoa!"

Rebecca refused to think about her instant reaction to his warm, questing fingers. Nope, some things were better left alone.

"Look, no offense, Lex, I appreciate the concern. I'm fine. The baby's fine. You coming in here, undressing and touching me — not so fine."

His grin turned carnal but his expression appeared sad. "Aw, come on, Becca. We didn't even get to the good part yet."

She fastened her jeans and started buttoning her blouse, proud to see the shaking in her hands was almost imperceptible. "I probably don't want to know what you consider the 'good part' to be."

"Well, the pelvic exam, of course."

"Micah," she hollered at the top of her lungs.

The rake tossed back his head and laughed.

Lex continued to laugh right up until he got an eyeful of Micah's furious expression as he charged into the room, shoved the medic against the wall and held him by the throat.

"Since I like you, Lex, I'll make your death quick but it's going to hurt. Bad!"

Rebecca smacked the back of Micah's head, fighting to hide her grin as his head snapped forward and the two morons' foreheads cracked together. She enjoyed this caveman protective side of him a bit too much. "Give the rabid feline routine a break already. Jesus, Micah, you sent him in here."

She shrugged. "The man has no concept of personal space."

With obvious reluctance he released Lex and took a step back. Because she was sick and tired of the dominant-alpha-in-charge routine, she smacked the back of his head again. He was ready for it this time and didn't budge.

"You could have asked me if everything was okay or at least warned me you'd called a medic."

Becca turned and walked out gracefully with her head held high. But Micah didn't miss the slur against his masculinity muttered under her breath. Witnessing the return of her fiery passion took his cock from flaccid to rock-hard in less than four seconds flat. God, she was gorgeous when worked up. Not angry, she just wouldn't put up with any crap. It was one of the many things he loved about her.

"Damn, buddy. You said she was beautiful, but you failed to mention the feisty part. I like her." Lex clapped him on the shoulder. "She's gonna keep you on your toes."

She would, if he had a chance in hell at holding on to her or figured out how to tell her he loved her.

He kept his gaze trained on Becca until he couldn't see her anymore, then turned and got right in his friend's face. "Whatever the hell you did, don't even think about doing it again. I'll kill you if you touch her."

"Stand down, sir. I wouldn't have a chance of trying anything. Go figure, but that hellcat is fixated on your ugly mug."

"What did she say?" he huffed.

Lex flashed his patented cat-that-ate-the-canary grin. "She didn't have to say. Hell, a man would have to be blind not to see she's all yours."

Micah bit his cheek to keep his smile under wraps. "And don't you forget it. I catch you cozying up to Becca and I'll rip you a new one."

"Yeah, whatever." He slung an arm around Micah's shoulders as they headed out to the kitchen. "So who else is coming out here to the boonies to play? I can't think of many guys who like you enough to hump it all the way out here."

He stopped Lex before they got within range of Becca. "Right now it's just you. I've got several things in the works, but you've got the most important duty."

Any humor that had lingered in Lex's expression disappeared and he had his game face on. "Which is?"

"Against my better judgment—Becca. You're going to get my emergency cash and take her to my safe house."

Lex studied his eyes for several long moments. "And you haven't told her yet." He scrubbed at his jaw. "Great!"

"There's more. I told you the basics of what they're doing...what they did to me. Now they have Crosby."

"Aw, Jesus! Have they experimented on him yet?"

Micah sighed. "Yes—Becca saw him."

"What about Slater? You trust him?"

"I don't have much choice."

Lex squeezed his shoulder. "All right, man. I'm in. Whatever you need."

The unconditional support humbled him to the point he could hardly speak. Micah muttered out a thank you that didn't come close to touching the gratitude he felt. He had no doubt Lex would forfeit his own life to protect hers.

Once all three of them were in the kitchen, they worked together to prepare dinner. In an attempt to make some point Micah wasn't getting — probably because he lacked estrogen — Becca became very friendly with Lex. She touched the condemned man often and gifted him with flirty smiles, which served to feed the flames of Micah's temper. Lex, the ass, ate up the attention, no matter how many daggers Micah shot at him with his eyes.

After dinner Becca sat down before the hearth and the slick operator dropped down next to her, making every breath burn in Micah's lungs. Hell, he was bound to be breathing fire in a matter of minutes.

"We'll take turns watching the perimeter. Four-hour shifts. You're up first," he growled at the medic.

Lex sighed and took one last stab at Micah, speaking in a soft tone but ensured his voice carried. "I better go or He-man will blow a gasket."

Micah didn't try to prevent the growl from escaping when Becca leaned over and placed a butterfly-soft kiss on the other man's cheek. "I think they messed up and used grizzly bear DNA instead of lion."

He stomped over to the door, held it open, and giving in to the childish impulse, slammed it shut once Lex stepped outside.

Without a word, Becca made her way into the bedroom, locking the door behind her. Hah! She knew that wouldn't keep him out.

He counted to five and strolled into the room as she was shutting the bathroom door. Micah stripped and lay down on the center of the bed to wait. She didn't make him wait long.

She strolled out wearing a simple cotton nightshirt, no makeup, hair in a braid, and stole his breath. "You're so damn beautiful it hurts."

Becca crossed her arms beneath her breasts, which only made her rosy nipples visible through the thin material.

"We need to talk," he stated.

"Talk? Yeah, that's why you're stretched out on the bed nude and sporting an erection, to talk." Her bottom lip pressed out in a sexy pout. "There's only one thing I want to know."

"What's that?"

"You haven't said a word about the baby. I have to know your intentions concerning our child —"

Rebecca didn't have time to finish what she'd been saying. In the blink of an eye, Micah was out of the bed and kneeling at her feet. His arms wrapped around her in a possessive hold and his lips fluttered over her belly in the sweetest of kisses.

"Oh god, Becca. I'm stunned, awed and scared shitless."

His reaction startled her and did bizarre things to her heart. She closed her eyes, praying this meant he wanted their baby.

Micah rose, kissed the tip of her nose, both eyelids, drew her into his embrace, tucking her head under his chin. It felt so right being in his arms. They fit together perfectly. Did they have any chance of making a go of it?

"I never imagined myself as a father, teaching my son to ride a bike, or intimidating my daughter's dates."

He stumbled over the words, his voice tight with emotion, prompting Rebecca to lean back. She stared into his dark eyes and her fears melted away. Her pirate was back. The corner of her lips inched upward even as fat tears streamed over her face.

"Aw, baby. Don't cry. It tears me up!"

His shaky hand wiped at her tears, which had her smiling brighter and crying harder.

"Becca, damn it? You're killing me here. Are you happy or sad?"

"Happy," she choked out. "Relieved. I was so worried when I first realized. Didn't know if I should track you down, how you'd feel about a baby? When you shifted...well, we had to deal with that first. Then Weltman—"

His growl rumbled over her words and that protective streak made her smile stretch even wider. "Down, boy." She patted his cheek. "When he found out and used it against you," she scowled. "I wanted to kick his ass."

"I'm getting you out of here. Somewhere safe." Micah leaned forward, gave up on wiping the tears away and instead began planting loud, sloppy kisses all over her face. "Tomorrow. Lex is taking you—"

"No," she objected. "I'm not leaving without you."

"Becca, I have to know you and the baby are safe. Then I can figure out my next move. The man you saw in the lab, Crosby, I served with him. He's my second-in-command at Nanotech. I can't leave him in there."

She nodded in understanding, had expected he'd go in but had selfishly hoped otherwise. She hated it, but knew the soldiers' code he lived by. Micah couldn't walk away and leave a man behind. "I'll hate it, but I'll go with Lex tomorrow. I'll keep our baby safe, but you have to promise me something."

"What is it, baby?"

"I want you to promise me that you'll come back to us. That you'll be there for our child as he or she grows up."

Then she added the clincher. A soldier would never go back on a promise made on his honor. Once given, he'd do everything and anything to fulfill his vow. "On your honor, as a soldier, promise me, Micah."

His eyes narrowed as he considered her words, likely wondering how she knew exactly how to get an unbreakable promise. Staring into her eyes, wearing his heart on his sleeve, Micah made the vow she prayed would bring him back to her.

"I love you."

"Oh, Becca. I love you too."

Hearing the words made her heart soar. She locked them into her heart, seared the moment into her memory, tried not to think that this could be their last night together. Micah loved her. She didn't need anything other than him.

"Make love to me, Micah. I want you."

"You too. So much, Becca."

She stood on tiptoe and her lips melted over his. The kiss started tender and warm, a display of affection. Soon sparks ignited and Micah's big body wrapped around her— protective, possessive and potent. The kiss changed as he took control, nibbling on her lips, thrusting his tongue deep into her mouth, his addictive taste swamping her senses.

There were certain instances when she didn't the mind him going all dominant alpha male on her.

Her clothes disappeared beneath his persistent fingers. His hands stroked and heat blasted through her bloodstream, melted her muscles, turning her soft and pliable. She pressed closer but couldn't get close enough.

"Micah," she pleaded.

"Get on the bed."

The growled words had shivers racing down her spine. She loved it when he got primal. Still, she teased and taunted, drawing the beast closer to the surface by crawling over the mattress on her hands and knees, wiggling her ass, enticing her man.

He hit the mattress hard enough to make her bounce. She giggled until his hands seized her hips, his knees pushing her legs wide apart, and in one fluid movement his cock slammed forward, completing her.

"Oh yes!"

He became unpredictable, thrusting hard and fast then slow and deep. She yelped as his teeth clamped down on her shoulder, holding her in place. Rebecca took everything he had to give, met each movement, demanded more, which he gladly provided.

His cock slid from her and she whimpered. Micah flipped her over, moved between her legs, filling her as she wrapped her legs around him, holding him tight. Their lips collided in a fierce kiss. He stole her breath, replaced it with his own.

More than their bodies joined. She felt his heart and soul reach out, entwine with hers, binding them together. Pleasure built, intensified.

He rolled, putting her on top. Rebecca didn't miss a beat as she moved on top of him, the position making her feel him even deeper. He cupped her breasts, tweaked her nipples, bucked his hips to meet her every plunge.

She flew, soared to the heavens then felt herself falling, crying out his name.

"I've got you, Becca. Let go. Give it all to me, baby."

His fingers pressed her clit, shattering her, taking her orgasm even higher. Finally he roared, swelled within her and bathed her womb with hot blasts of cum.

She collapsed on top of him, listening as his breathing calmed then deepened with sleep. He made soft snuffling noises that brought a smile to her face.

When she should have fallen dead asleep her mind churned. In the morning she'd have to be strong for Micah. No tears. She knew the drill—kiss your soldier goodbye, smile and wave. Remain certain of his abilities while praying for his quick and safe return.

"You better come back to me in one piece, Lasiter, or else."

Chapter Fourteen

∞

You promised – on your honor – so you damn well better come and get me. And you better be in one piece or I'll kick your ass.

Becca had punctuated each threat by poking him in the chest. The three weeks they'd been apart felt like forever. Micah indulged in a smile over the memory. His woman was strong and feisty. That knowledge had been his lifeline, something to cling to when he had to send her away with a trusted friend.

"Lex." He growled the other man's name. If the handsome, cocky bastard had touched Becca he was living on borrowed time.

He took a deep breath, struggled for patience. He was dying to see her, touch her, breathe her in, drink from her lips…

Deep in the heart of the African jungle, he took shelter from the drizzling rain beneath large green leaves and observed the small house. His safe house. Restless energy had him amped up. Drawing on years of discipline, he stayed put. He wouldn't let his impatience put everything that mattered most in the world to him in jeopardy.

Once he was sure his tail was clear, that he wasn't leading danger straight to her, only then he would go to Becca.

If he had been followed, the person was highly skilled as Micah found no evidence of another presence. And the house he watched appeared secure.

The front door burst open and anticipation almost had him jumping from his covered position, racing across the distance. Musical laughter reached out, wrapped around his chest, squeezed. Hands fisted at his sides, he rocked forward on the balls of his feet for what felt like an eternity.

And then there she was, dancing in the rain. Too far away to see her eyes, he knew the smile on her sultry lips would extend to their moss green depths.

She stepped out of the door looking happy and healthy. A riot of dark silken hair flowed over slender shoulders to sway around her tiny waist. Rain quickly plastered the thin material of her tank top and shorts to her skin.

Damn, she was a beautiful sight for weary eyes.

His heart stopped and a huge lump clogged his throat.

"Becca." He whispered her name in a broken voice. Many times over the long weeks he had feared failure and worried what would happen to her if he didn't come for her.

A large form slipped from the door way, sharp eyes scanning the surroundings, lips returning her smile. Micah's hackles rose and insidious rage soared. The fact he had sent Lex with her, asked the other man to protect his woman, did not penetrate the red haze of anger clouding his mind.

Mine!

As he watched, Lex drew Becca into his arms and began dancing with her, holding her wet body close to his much larger frame.

Without conscious thought or direction, his body began the familiar process of change. Muscles, bone and tendon reshaped. Short tan fur covered his body while around his face a lush mane appeared.

Before the man could protest the lion's powerful legs drove him forward with single-minded purpose—reclaiming his mate.

* * * * *

Rebecca knew Lex didn't buy her false smile, still she forced her expression to reflect happiness instead of worry and longing. She felt as if a heavy weight pressed down on her chest. Not even the thrill of studying all the various species of animals surrounding the safe house eased the ache.

A desperate compulsion filled her, drew her outside. She didn't question the why of it.

She said yet another silent prayer, plastered on another happy face and danced out into the nearly constant rain. Since the Congo area of Africa where they'd hidden out got upward of eighty inches of rain a year there were only two options — sit inside and mope or get wet.

Lex was one step behind her leaving the house. He'd been so understanding and kind. The two of them had formed a strong friendship during their forced confinement. She thought of him as the big brother she'd always wished to have. At the thought, she flashed him a real smile.

He joined her, humming a tune as he twirled her around the clearing, lightening her mood.

The anguished roar of a big cat thundered through the jungle. Rebecca didn't have to see him to know.

Micah had come for her.

At last!

Her spine went rigid as Lex tensed, his gaze frantically searching the area, and a gun appeared in his hand.

She didn't get a chance to identify Micah or tell Lex not to shoot. One second she was scanning the immediate area, the next Micah hurtled through the air. Five-hundred pounds of pissed-off lion pinned Lex to the ground with his wrist held tight between all those sharp teeth. She didn't know what had happened to the gun.

In different circumstances she would have had a good laugh over the remnants of shredded clothing clinging to the lion.

"Lex," she spoke in the most soothing tone she could manage in the current life-or-death situation. "Don't move unless you want to pull away a bloody stump."

She slowly moved in closer, shushing Lex as he mumbled urgent warnings. The man was scared as hell, not that she blamed him. "Shut. Up. Micah won't hurt me. You might warrant a second thought, but friendship isn't going to save your ass now."

Rebecca put her face right in front of the lion's, staring into familiar eyes and stroking his luxurious mane. "Micah...honey." She considered scolding him but wanted to keep his focus away from Lex. "I missed you so damn much."

She kept speaking in a tone meant to soothe and words intended to coax him away from their friend. "You bite him and get all bloody and I'm not going to want to kiss you."

He watched her for a moment before dropping Lex's wrist. A brief glance had her sighing in relief. "That's a good boy." He'd left the imprint of his teeth in the soft flesh but had not clamped down hard enough to break through skin.

With her fingers buried deep in his thick mane, she began moving to one side, tugging him along. "Come back to me, Micah. Shift for me. I've missed being in your arms. I need you to hold me."

Once they'd moved several paces from Lex, she knelt and threw herself against him. She wrapped her arms tightly around his neck, her face cushioned by his mane. "Please don't make me wait any longer," she implored. "I love you, Micah."

She fell back as he shifted but didn't release her hold on him. In the blink of an eye her body was covered with by solid male muscle. In particular, she noticed one extra-hard muscle as it nestled against the soft curve of her belly.

"I'll, ah...just make myself scarce while you two catch up."

Neither one of them acknowledged Lex's soft whisper. Micah figured his friend was smart enough to know when to get good and scarce.

Rebecca's busy hands were everywhere, touching every inch of skin she could reach, further arousing him. Tears gathered at the corners of her eyes, making his heart turn over in his chest.

"You're not hurt anywhere, are you?" Her brow furrowed with concern. "If you've come back to me hurt there's going to be hell to pay."

He couldn't help smiling over her threat. So small and delicate beneath him, but his woman was no softie. Her strong spirit more than made up for what she lacked in stature.

God, the way she made him feel. This was home—she was home. Being in her arms brought him a sense of joy he'd never known possible.

"I'm fine, baby. Not a scratch on me."

She stilled, stared into his eyes. "What about the lab? Did you get Nash out?" He felt a shudder run through her. "Hurry up and tell me so we can make love."

He raced through a very brief explanation between planting loud, smacking kisses all over her sweet face. "Everything is handled. Crosby's fine. Found another 'subject'—a woman. She'll be okay." He paused, hovering above her lips. "We'll talk more later. Need you now, Becca!"

"Yes," she sobbed. "Here. Now."

Clothes tore, were tossed to the side. Becca spread her sexy legs in welcome. He traced two fingers along her slit, growling when he found her wet and ready. With one measured thrust he filled her balls-deep, covered her body and learned the meaning of ecstasy.

He didn't so much as breathe—just soaked in the glorious feeling of being held in the hot, velvet clasp of his woman's body.

Having other ideas, Becca sunk her teeth into his shoulder and writhed against him, spurring Micah into action. He reared back then plunged deep, taking her hard and fast, the way he knew she enjoyed.

"Yes, Micah," she cried. "Hard. Good. So good."

He loosened the lion's leash, gave in to his animal side knowing she'd accept all of him. Strong arms and legs held him tight, not allowing him much room to move. And it was beyond good. Everything he'd never known he wanted and more.

The gentle rain washed over them, rolled down his back. He ignored everything but her. Powerful sensations built, gathered at the base of his spine but didn't slow him down. Not until Becca's entire body tensed then spasmed, taking him soaring with her.

As they settled back to earth, Micah rolled to his side and rested his palm over her belly, imagining her growing large with their child. His world, his future. Nothing else mattered.

"Where should we go?" He stared into her bright green eyes. "We'll make a home and raise the baby anywhere you want."

"I don't care where we go, Micah, as long as we're together."

"There has to be someplace you'd like to go."

"Hmm. Well, I have always wanted to see Paris, Madrid, Rome, Athens…"

"Then Europe it is, baby."

"Are you two done yet? Is it safe to come out?" Lex bellowed from somewhere off in the jungle, sending them both into gales of laughter. "There's a seriously huge python smacking its lips at me."

"No," Becca giggled.

"Come back later," Micah added.

Much later.

He still had a lot of catching up to do. At least they'd have a lot of years together in which to do so.

He knew they'd have their ups and downs. There would be hard times to balance the good. Difficulties to overcome because of his ability to shift. But Micah sensed there would be more laughter than tears and he felt sure, all the way down to the marrow of his bones, they'd always face life's challenges together.

"How are we going to get rid of him?"

"Don't worry, baby. I've got plans for Lex. He's going to be very busy."

Rolling to his back, he kept their bodies joined.

"I've been waiting forever for you to ride me again. Don't keep me waiting."

Her sultry smile filled his heart with joy and had him looking forward to many years with this amazing woman.

"I love you," she gasped and began rocking her hips. "Do that meow thing for me."

Unable to deny her anything he let loose a joy-filled roar that had the native wildlife, along with a human medic, running for cover.

EYE OF THE TIGER

&

Dedication

ℬℭ

To Rachel, whose heart is even blacker than mine. Thanks, creampuff!

Trademarks Acknowledgement

ℬℭ

The author acknowledges the trademarked status and trademark owners of the following wordmarks mentioned in this work of fiction:

Formica: Formica Corporation

OnStar: General Motors Corporation

Oreo: Kraft Food Holdings, Inc.

Tony the Tiger: Kellogg North American Company

Chapter One

🔊

"Make illegal u-turn. What the fuck?"

Jenny Crosby shook her head in disgust. "Look, you crazy GPS bitch. I'm not about to try something so incredibly stupid in the middle-of-nowhere North Carolina on a curvy mountain road with no streetlights during a moonless night. Sheesh!"

Okay, so the GPS unit in her SUV wouldn't even hear her argument, but Jenny was sick of dealing with the damn thing. "I've seen nothing but trees and dark, winding roads for hours now. No other cars. No houses or hotels. Not even a lousy fast food joint. *Nada!*" In frustration, her fist slammed down on the console. "Just lots of 'sharp curve ahead' signs. If you made me take a wrong turn, I'm going to fry your little electronic brain. Ha! That would sure teach you who's boss."

Jenny shivered. "If I don't find the cabin soon, I'm gonna be screwed. And not in a good way." Hell, at this rate she'd be sleeping in the car and it was way too cold for that nonsense.

Whenever nerves got the better of her, Jenny ended up talking to herself. The random thoughts rushing through her mind flowed from her lips in all their unedited glory. Her husband claimed it was an endearing quality. She figured he probably said that just to bring her diarrhea of the mouth to an end.

She took another quick glance at the map displayed on the screen. "You and I need to come to some sort of understanding, find a way to communicate. Oh, and another thing —"

Her diatribe was cut off by a ding as the GPS alerted her she'd reached the point where it wanted her to turn.

"Make a legal u-turn." The modulated female voice remained calm and emotionless.

"A legal u-turn? That's a little better, but where the hell am I supposed to make a u-turn?" She slowed the car to a crawl and peered through the windshield. One side was mountain, the other a cliff with no guardrail. The road itself was only two narrow lanes with a solid yellow line dividing it in half. "There isn't even a freakin' shoulder along the side of this road. Only a long drop and a sudden stop, you dumb bitch." And another sign warning of a sharp turn.

A one-hundred-eighty degree hairpin turn.

"Infernal damn machine! That's not a u-turn." After coming out of the curve, the road straightened for a brief stretch, allowing her to go a bit faster. She hated driving in the dark and had been warned to watch for black ice on the road. Of course, since she was from Florida, she had no idea what that meant.

Jenny glanced down at the small square screen showing a map and her current position. "What now, genius?"

With her attention divided between the monitor and the road, she studied the details. The picture was very sharp, and a bit too detailed. It looked like she'd driven right off the map into uncharted territory, which is exactly how she felt. Yet according to the know-it-all device, she was within five miles of reaching the rental cabin.

"Wahoo! I am so ready to stretch my legs." She'd been traveling all day and late into the night. Her leg muscles were cramped, her rear end numb and molded to the seat. It would be a major relief to get out and walk around.

She had found the cabin rental notice through an e-mail posting at work advertising things other employees had for sale. An image of the rustic living room flashed through Jenny's mind. A fire burned in a large, flagstone hearth. This glorious amenity, along with the hot tub, had sold her on renting the place. "Damn, I can't wait to take a long soak in that baby." If her hands had been free she would have rubbed them together in anticipation.

For several days she'd dreamed about lying before the fire, sipping a glass of wine and reading a good book. She'd stocked up on supplies before leaving home and was ready to veg. "Mmm...some hot chocolate with marshmallows would go down real good right about now." The perfect vacation from her stressful job at the trauma hospital, plus much needed time to lick her wounds and let her broken heart heal.

Her demanding job as a trauma tech and simultaneously attending classes toward getting a nursing degree was tough, but she loved it. The drama, excitement and adrenaline rush of saving a life kept Jenny motivated. She'd learned a heck of a lot, made some great contacts, and was sure the hospital would hire her on as an ER nurse once she graduated.

Working evening shift kind of sucked, not allowing any opportunity to have a social life, but she still had a good time. Many times after work her co-workers would all get together at the sports bar down the street to relieve the strain of a difficult shift. She loved hanging out with the medics who also worked at the firehouse. They were a great group of guys and a ton of fun. She would miss her co-workers, but needed this time off to prevent herself from burning out.

It was also time to accept the unsolicited advice everyone kept giving her. *"Time to face facts and move on. He left you in the dust, Jenny."* Her broken heart wouldn't heal until she came to terms with reality.

She would never forget arriving home in the early morning hours to an empty apartment. The red light on the answering machine winked at her from the darkness. When she pushed the button, it had not been a message from her husband. Instead she heard her own voice letting him know she'd be late. Jenny had gone to bed alone, not really worrying about her husband until she woke the next day ready to rip him a new one.

She'd walked through the apartment searching for a note and cussing him but found nothing. On further inspection, she'd discovered some of his clothes and a suitcase missing. The idea he'd gone on a business trip without a word made her even madder. The first twinge of unease had surfaced when she'd called his office at Nanotech.

"I'm sorry, Mrs. Crosby. We haven't heard from him since yesterday morning." The department clerk had acted as if the whole thing put her out.

Jenny had tried calling his supervisor but the man was out on medical leave. At the police station a bored detective informed her nothing could be done until her husband had been missing for forty-eight hours. She'd been checking their bank balance online when she discovered the large withdrawal that had been made the day before.

The policeman who helped her fill out the missing persons report had been helpful but offered no hope. Every day she called the station, at least twice, to see if they'd discovered anything. Every day the overworked officer assigned to the case told her the same thing. "Mrs. Crosby, your husband left you. He packed his bags, took some cash, and drove away. He may come back or contact you at some point, but that's doubtful. There's nothing else we can do for you."

Friends and co-workers had been supportive...for awhile. She knew what they believed. She was beginning to wonder if they might be right, even though she still had faith in her husband. With so much time gone by doubt plagued Jenny, tearing her apart. "Maybe I have been dumped and I'm just too stupid to admit it. Abandoned by the love of my life. The man who vowed we'd have a lifetime together." The idea took away some of the shock and numbness, allowing anger to creep in.

"Son of a bitch took off. Probably with another woman. Typical rat-bastard man!"

A glance at the small navigation screen showed she was getting closer to the cabin. "Almost there," she sighed in relief.

Jenny shivered a bit and shifted in her seat. She was anxious to sit before a roaring fire and warm up. The cold night air had long ago seeped into her bones, but she kept the window partly opened and the heater off. The drive from Florida had left her fatigued and sleepy and the chilly winter air helped her stay awake and focused. The last thing she wanted was to wreck her car on this lonely mountain road.

She glanced up through the windshield and a shill scream rose from her suddenly tight chest. Her heart stopped beating and everything moved into slow motion. She held the steering wheel in a white-knuckled grip and reacted on sheer adrenaline.

Some suicidal maniac stood in the middle of the dark street not fifty feet ahead. Jenny did everything possible to avoid hitting the person, but her options were limited. Turning right meant crashing into a solid wall of rock. Probability of survival—slim to none. In a split-second decision she yanked the wheel to the left. Crashing into the trees or a drop down the side of the rolling mountain seemed the better choice.

She stood on the brakes, hard. The tires began to squeal then slide. Jenny said a quick prayer the heavy SUV wouldn't roll and stared in horror at the thick tree trunk illuminated by the headlights and coming closer by the second.

"This is so not going to turn out good," she said to the GPS bitch, who all of a sudden had nothing to say. Then everything went black.

Adrenaline pumped through his system, keeping Nash going. He didn't know where he was and it didn't matter as long as he kept moving. If he stopped, he'd be a dead man.

He considered shifting into his tiger form. The newly acquired ability to alter his physical shape frightened him. He hadn't mastered the phenomenon and wasn't sure he could control the animal. And a tiger would scare any rational person. They'd run rather than offer assistance. Not to mention tigers didn't have thumbs and there'd be no way of hitching a ride. He would have laughed at the thought if he wasn't running for his life.

Things were dire. No ifs, ands or buts about it. When the bastards from the lab caught up with him, they'd kill him, drag his dead carcass back to their diabolical hellhole and continue to experiment on his decomposing remains.

Normally, he had a great sense of direction. Too bad it seemed to have failed him now, when he needed it most. He was having a hard time determining which way was up, much less north from south. For several precious moments, he leaned against a tree praying for his head to stop spinning. A rustling sound somewhere nearby got him moving again.

He might stand a chance if he could reach a town, or even a house. If not…

He shuddered, not wanting to consider what would happen.

He had no clue where he was. His captors had been too careful. All he remembered was being yanked from his car, blindfolded, drugged and taken God only knows where. He didn't know what state he was in, or even what country for that matter.

He was well and truly lost, not just his body. His mind had taken a hike too. He didn't remember anything prior to being snatched. It was as if his memory had been wiped clean leaving no trace of the past. Erased as easily as a chalkboard and left blank.

At least he was out of the lab. He had bided his time, watched and waited for a lapse in security, and then took matters into his own hands.

When he found the road, Nash wanted to weep with relief. Instead, he held his emotions in check. A road was good, but he wasn't home free yet. Not by a long shot. He didn't know where to go, where his home was or even if there was anyone he could trust.

He stumbled out onto the blacktop, struggling to stay upright as violent shivers assaulted his body. The temperature must be somewhere below freezing, and the thin medical scrubs he wore were soaked from a tumble into a frigid stream. He had no feeling in his fingers or toes, and his lungs burned with each wheezing breath. Shifting into his feline form would help with the cold, but there were other risks he wouldn't take. Like the possibility that once he became the tiger he might not be able to change back. He was terrified of becoming trapped within the animal.

Bent over, gasping for air, he figured things couldn't get much worse.

"Aw shit!" He was so fucking wrong. Things can always get worse!

Bright headlights cut through the inky darkness from around a curve and there wasn't enough time to avoid being run down. It might even be the goons from the lab. If so, they wouldn't slow down anyway. In fact, they'd probably run right over him to eliminate the threat to their insane project.

His thoughts scattered in a million different directions, and time did that funky thing. It slowed, moving through thick molasses. The vehicle raced forward, and Nash stared into the shocked face of the most beautiful woman he'd ever seen. It was like watching a sports instant replay. Imminent death or not, nothing seemed more important than drinking her in, memorizing her features.

Golden blonde hair framed an oval face. Her mouth opened to form a perfect O, and her big brown eyes widened in surprise. At the last second, she seemed to pull herself together and wrenched the wheel.

He wanted to clamp his eyes shut but stared in stunned fascination, frozen in place, as the car came closer. Too close for comfort. A blast of glacial air hit him as it skidded past with mere inches separating them.

Jesus!

Wasn't your life supposed to flash before your eyes when you came close to dying? He didn't see the past, only the frightened expression on the woman's face.

Unable to maintain traction the tires locked up and the woman lost control of the SUV. He watched in horror as the driver's door slammed into a huge tree and the vehicle came to a shuddering halt. At least it had saved her from going over the side of the steep mountain and plunging to certain death.

"Holy shit!"

He wanted to check on her, make sure the woman was all right, but he couldn't breathe. Nash clutched at his chest, felt his heart thudding against his sternum. If the woman had been hurt it was his fault. "Please let her be okay!"

If she survived the crash, this could be the answer to his prayers. It would be warm inside the vehicle, and since it hadn't been going too fast or taken the tree head-on, it might still be drivable. He tamped down the hope. Better to not get excited before investigating and making a thorough assessment of the situation.

Instinct and training kicked in and he went to work. His first priority, assure the safety of the innocent woman. Only then would he start revising his impromptu escape plan according to the new circumstances. He hated the idea of drawing her into his troubles but she was his best chance at making it out alive.

Nash entered through the passenger door and was engulfed by a fog of white powder hanging thick in the enclosed space. The airbags had deployed making it difficult to see. He found the woman crumpled against the driver's door, her body cushioned by the side-impact airbag. She appeared to have been knocked unconscious. He placed two fingers on her neck, relieved to find a steady pulse. He watched the even rise and fall of her chest, relieved she had no trouble breathing. Bruised and battered for sure but she should be all right.

After several minutes of careful maneuvering, he got her settled into the passenger seat, fought the airbags into submission, and slid behind the steering wheel. He shifted into park and turned the key in the ignition. The engine turned, but didn't catch.

"Shit!"

They both desperately needed the SUV to work. Neither one of them would make it through a night exposed to freezing temperatures.

Nash resorted to sweet talk. Hey, it worked with temperamental women. At least he thought so but what the heck did he know. "Come on, baby. Turn over and I'll get you a nice oil change as soon as possible."

This time when he turned the key, Nash lightly pumped the gas pedal. The engine coughed, sputtered then roared to life.

"Yeah, baby!" In triumph, he punched his fist into the air then turned the heater to full blast wondering why the hell it hadn't been running.

It took infinite patience and agonizing time they didn't have to slowly work the car off the tree. He put the SUV in reverse and moved a few inches, switched to drive and gained a few more. Finally, with a sharp squeal, the twisted metal peeled away from the tree.

Now the remaining issue was to find adequate shelter.

The map on the glowing LCD screen caught his attention. The unit had been programmed for a destination within a few miles' drive. After a bit of snooping in the center console, he discovered a rental contract, keys and pictures of a cabin.

"Good a place as any," he muttered, glancing over at the unconscious woman.

He drove slow and easy, not wanting to push the mangled vehicle too hard. Almost a half-hour later, following the computer's directions and limping along, they arrived at a cozy A-frame cabin tucked away on a private dirt road. Nash hoped it would prove to be a safe haven for the night. Some rest would do his tired and battered body a world of good.

Chapter Two

ဢ

The firm, insistent slap of something solid against her cheek was starting to piss Jenny off. Her head ached, feeling as if it was being split in two by a dull axe. Must have had one too many B-52's at The Dugout last night after her shift. She batted ineffectually at the irritant, but that only seemed to make the annoying person more determined.

"Wakey, wakey. Time to rise and shine."

Oh, hell no!

The masculine voice increased the pain slicing through her throbbing head. He needed to back off before she got really mad.

"Come on, honey. I'm too tired to carry you into the house."

Say what?

What the heck was going on? Must have been one doozy of a night.

Jenny cracked open one heavy eyelid enough to see his handsome, rugged face hovering only inches away. Too bad she couldn't see him clearly, but her eyes refused to focus. Must have really tied one on to have ended up crashed out in some strange place and not know what had happened. This was bad and entirely out of character for her. Jenny always remained in control and never drank to the point of passing out.

Her interest piqued, she let her eye open a bit more then slammed it shut, but it was too late. Images of Nash filled her splintering head.

She'd seen enough to get her blood pumping and generate a sexual ache, which spread through her faster than an out-of-control forest fire. Mentally, she catalogued his sensual features. Rumpled, wavy black hair and dark complexion lending him a dangerous air. Square jaw sporting a few days beard stubble. Add in the most stunning blue eyes and it added up to her husband being one gorgeous hunk.

Dayum, she was one hell of a lucky woman!

Everything about him was strong and masculine, but his eyes stirred her the most. She would gladly lose herself within the fathomless blue pools. Something she'd seen in the brief glimpse had been off, though. He appeared to be a bit agitated and almost seemed lost.

She was confused. Her fuzzy brain seemed to be playing tricks on her. The man sure looked like her husband, but how could he be here? He was long gone. The victim of foul play. Someone had killed him or he would have come back to her.

"Oh my God. If you're here that can only mean one thing. I-I'm dead. Killed in the car crash."

And doesn't that just bite the big one?

"You're not dead, but you probably have a concussion. Let's go inside where it's warm, beautiful."

A concussion? That would explained why she was seeing a handsome ghost of the past. As delusions went, this one was pretty nice though. He spoke in the sexy voice she loved, creating an instant sexual response.

Jenny creamed her panties.

Okay, so maybe she wasn't dead, but how could he be real? Where did he come from?

Confusion and fear made her head pound harder. Did she dare risk believing he was real when finding out this was all from a concussion would crush her spirit?

Maybe it's all some crazy dream and in the morning everything will be back to normal. The last few months will have melted away and I'll be tucked into Nash's arms, at home, in our own bed.

Eh, not likely but a girl could hope.

It grew blessedly quiet and he no longer slapped her cheek. Thank goodness. He must have given up the futile idea of waking her up and left her alone when all Jenny wanted to do was hold onto the dream as long as possible.

She must have lost consciousness again because she was startled when a strong arm slid beneath her legs and another behind her back as he lifted her not insubstantial weight. Being a tall and voluptuous size sixteen made carrying her a difficult task for the strongest of men. If the hallucination carrying her was indeed her husband, he had more than enough strength to pull off the feat. Nash had a definite romantic side and had carried her to bed on numerous occasions.

A wet blast of cold seeped right through the layers of clothes she wore. Jenny snuggled closer. Holding her tight against his chest, his heart beat in a soothing rhythm beneath her ear, and she began to relax.

He staggered a bit as they went through a doorway, seemed to lose control of his hands then lowered her to her own shaky legs, which resisted standing. Her rescuer made it several more stumbling steps before dropping onto the wood floor.

"Ouch!" *Oh great! Okay, Jenny. This is serious. Time to snap out of it and figure out what the deal is.*

With great effort, she forced the horrific headache into submission long enough to take stock of the situation. A quick glance around and she discovered the rental cabin. She had stared longingly at the pictures of the place and had no trouble recognizing her surroundings.

Jenny shivered as a gust of wind shot through the cabin and twined around her like a lover, delving into every susceptible crevice. She shut and bolted the door, locking the cold air outside.

Pushing emotion aside, she used her trauma training to evaluate the gorgeous apparition sprawled on the floor. Just the sight of him had her trembling and on the verge of breaking down. She couldn't be weak and selfish. Jenny had to be strong for him. If this turned out to be real and not some dream, she'd celebrate later. With Nash.

"Come on, Jenny. Get your head straight and assess the patient. Medics can't afford to be distracted, no matter the circumstances."

Because this was her husband she had to be twice as strong about focusing on her patient. If she lost control, panicked, she wouldn't be able to do either of them any good.

Taking a deep breath, she set out to do her job.

Nash had lost consciousness. She touched his arm. The icy coldness of his skin had her yanking back her hand. He breathing was quick and shallow. His skin, which had gone pale, was covered in goose bumps and he shivered uncontrollably. His lips and fingertips held the blue tint of cyanosis.

Diagnosis — hypothermia.

She raced around the cabin, hands shaking, struggling to remain cool, calm and collected. In the small bedroom she found several thick blankets. Jenny peeled away his clothes, growing more concerned because his shivering had decreased. That wasn't a good sign.

"Damn it, Nash. Come on. Don't do this to me."

If he wasn't a ghost she had to work fast to save his life. Still, her fingers lingered, tracing various white and pink lines that hadn't been there before, wondering who had created the surgical scars and why.

Her mind spun as hope surged no matter how hard she'd fought to concentrate. Jenny tried to sort out the situation, prayed this was really happening. She had somehow managed to stumble upon her missing husband two states away from home in the mountains.

"That sounds insane. Next thing they'll be taking me to my very own padded room."

But the man she touched felt real. And her raging emotions were certainly genuine. She bit her lip and went back to work. Once she had him wrapped up snug, she moved to the hearth, thankful someone had set out tinder and wood. She found a box of matches on the mantle, struck a long taper over flint and lit the fire.

The hot tub would be wonderful but wasn't about to happen. He was five inches taller and outweighed her by about forty pounds. Plus, warming him too rapidly would not help their cause.

There was only one remaining option—body heat.

Kicking off her shoes, she stripped down to bra and panties, and climbed under the blankets with him.

"Come on, Nash. You've got to fight for me. For us! I can't do this alone."

His skin was freezing but she gritted her teeth and lay down on top of him, sharing her warmth. Jenny rubbed her hands up and down his arms in an attempt to get his blood moving. She wouldn't lose him now that she'd found him again. That idea was unacceptable.

The changes were gradual. His body temperature began to rise and she started to relax as they made it past the critical point. Somehow she'd make him well and figure this tangled mess out.

It grew warmer beneath the mound of blankets and her energy ebbed as fatigue settled in. They fit together so well, and his chest made a comfortable pillow. She'd missed the simple pleasure of lying with him.

Her emotions ran the gamut from elation to anger and doubt to contentment. Her heart surged with joy that he was alive and in her arms. She was mad at him for having deserted her without a word. A brief doubt of his love and commitment surfaced. Finally, a surge happiness she hadn't felt in months allowed her to rest and breathe easier. Now that the crisis had passed, exhaustion seized control, still she held him tight.

"I'll never let go again," she vowed as sleep claimed her.

Something hard ground against his sternum bringing back the nightmare of captivity in vivid detail. The small cell, cold steel bars and constant observation. He was being held down and subjected to more painful torture at the hands of the insane scientists.

Needles, catheters and excruciating surgeries without anesthesia.

The lab.

Nash woke with a gasp and sprung into action. He grabbed hold and flipped over, pinning his tormentor beneath him. Only it wasn't one of the scientists but the startled face of a beautiful woman looking up at him.

Long golden hair fanned out around her face. Light brown eyes flecked with amber crinkled at the corners and seemed to smile at him. Her body was curvy and warm, generous breasts flattened against his chest. Long, smooth legs rested between his, and his cock nestled comfortably against the warmth of her sex. Half-naked, wearing only a satin bra and panties, miles of soft skin brought his every nerve ending to life. His cock jerked, happy to be pressed to such a lush woman.

The huge shift in circumstances made his head spin. He'd gone from being held captive and subjected to horrendous medical procedures to running through the woods, freezing his ass off and finally found himself in the arms of a goddess. The sudden change gave him mental whiplash but his body had no trouble in making the leap. He went from flaccid to rock-hard arousal faster than ever before.

There was something about her that drew him in like iron to a magnet—potent and irresistible. He felt as though he knew this woman, had known her forever, yet they were strangers. How could that be possible? He cautioned himself to be careful while unraveling the mystery.

The minx had his number. A wicked grin crossed sensual pink lips and her fingernails slid down his back, scoring the skin and heating his blood. She didn't stop until the bare cheeks of his ass were held firmly within small hands.

His luck sure had changed in a hurry.

"Don't start something you aren't planning to finish, Sunshine."

The endearment was perfect for her. From her golden hair to bright eyes filled with desire. All the way down her luscious body burned hot under his and her brilliant smile certainly outshined the sun.

"I always finish what I start. You know that."

The saucy reply, spoken in breathless whisper, turned Nash on even more. She pressed closer, wiggled along his cock and he nearly rocketed past the point of no return. He wanted nothing more than to sink into her body and stay there forever, but something nagged at the edges of his mind. She seemed so familiar.

"I'm having this major sense of déjà vu. I don't even know your name. Yet at the same time, I feel like we've always known each other. It doesn't make any sense."

She remained quiet for a few seconds, cupped his cheek in her hand and stared into his eyes. God, how he'd love to lose himself in her soulful gaze, but her words shocked him down to the tips of his toes and affected him as if he'd been doused with ice water.

"Don't act as if you don't know me, Nash Stephen Crosby."

Uh-oh! He may not know much, but he knew whenever someone used your full name it meant you were in big trouble. And how did she know his full name anyway?

"You've always known me better than I know myself. What the hell happened to you? What are you doing out here in the mountains? You've been missing for weeks."

He stared into her tawny eyes, willing himself to put the pieces of this bizarre puzzle together but no matter how hard he tried, he wasn't able to make things fit.

The woman began to shake. Looking down, Nash followed the trail of tears flowing from her eyes as she struggled to keep the intense emotions bottled up inside. Her tears created a tension that fisted tight around his heart. An ache worse than any pain he'd suffered at the hands of the scientists. She affected him in ways beyond comprehension.

A name flittered around the edges of his consciousness and he fought to capture the elusive word. His heart screamed in agony. This woman was important to him. He felt it down to the marrow of his bones. The answers were right there, just out of reach, teasing his memory.

"God, Nash. Whatever it is we'll deal with it…together. Stay with me. Don't run away again. I love you!" She stared up at him, eyes begging for understanding. "Please. I need you."

The panic in her eyes and the strain in her sweet voice tore at his soul. Something shifted in Nash. Like the massive impact of a wrecking ball crashing through a brick wall, the barrier keeping his memories hidden crumbled and fell. Pain sliced through his skull, seared his brain and blinding white light filled his vision. He felt as if a red-hot poker had pierced his eye and been shoved deep into his head.

All at once he was bombarded by flashes of the past racing through his mind. A pattern developed and one constant emerged—the woman he loved beyond anything else.

Chapter Three

ഇ

"Jenny!" he breathed. "Sunshine? Is it really you?"

He knew her name but still seemed confused, which irritated the hell out of her. "Of course it's me. What other woman would you be sleeping with?"

Why the hell did he keep acting like he didn't completely recognize her? But her anger fled as fast as it had arrived, replaced by need. The most important thing was the fact she held her husband, alive and well, in her arms. Wherever he'd been, whatever had happened, they'd deal with it later. Together.

She'd been without him for too long. He was where he belonged and she had a strong desire to reconnect with him. Affirm he was alive. Reestablish their bond. Feel him everywhere. Hold him inside her, tight and intimate.

"I need you, Nash! Please. I've missed you so much."

She wiggled seductively, pressing her damp panties against his hard length. Jenny was desperate for him fill her. To share their bodies, be as close as possible. Tangling her fingers in his hair, she pulled his face down to hers. With the first brush of his lips the fear and desolation of the past months washed away on a tidal wave of euphoria. She traced the familiar curves of his mouth with her tongue and surged into the warm cavern when his lips parted. His somewhat spicy, masculine flavor flooded her senses, breathing life back into the shattered shell she'd become, cleansing away the grief.

Only Nash was not quite as she remembered him.

There was something she couldn't put her finger on. Some essential change in him. For the time being she let that go. All she cared about at the moment was holding him, loving him.

Their tongues tangled, caressed and explored as her heart pounded against her ribs. He tasted incredible. The power of their kiss had her trembling with desire. She didn't need or want foreplay. All Jenny needed was to hold Nash as close as possible, take the man she loved deep within her body.

Desperate for his cock, she lifted her legs, wrapping them around his waist. The hard length settled against her folds but remained separated by the thin barrier of her panties.

"Nash. I need you. Now…please!"

He shifted his hips and the head of his cock bumped into her engorged clit, sending shock waves through her entire body. His hands clenched, took hold of her panties and made quick work of ripping the material. Whether his mind recognized her or not, instinct guided Nash's body in tempting and teasing her in all the ways she enjoyed. The wicked devil made shallow thrusts along her slit, coating his shaft in her slick response, stoking the burning need without giving her what she wanted. What she needed.

"You want my cock, Sunshine?"

Jenny's heart surged, logging in her throat as the cherished endearment passed his lips. She'd always loved it when he called her by the pet name.

"Yes, Nash. Give it to me. Give me all of it."

On the next downward sweep of his cock the broad tip lined up with her entrance. Jenny held her breath as he stared into her eyes. In one long slow stroke, Nash filled her—heart, body and soul. They held still for several heartbeats, absorbing the rightness of the moment.

"Damn," he gasped. "Feels like home."

They fell into a natural rhythm of give and take, reacquainting their bodies. With each driving thrust his cock head tapped against her cervix. On the withdrawal it dragged along her G-spot creating the sweetest friction. His girth stretched her delicate tissues, which closed in around him, fighting to hold him deep within her grasping body.

Jenny held on tight, enjoying the flex and play of his firm muscles beneath her hands as they moved together. Passion mounted and tension coiled in preparation of a stunning release. Their hands were busy touching every inch of flesh they could reach.

Nash was right there with her, matching thrust for thrust, taking her higher than ever before, giving her mind-blowing pleasure. His musky scent enveloped her, the slap of sweat-slicked skin a sensual music for this erotic dance.

The sudden tensing of her body stunned Jenny, arriving faster than she wanted, hurtling her into ecstasy beyond compare. Nash jerked once then thrust hard twice and filled her with hot jets of cum. His shout of completion guided her back down to earth. Tender fingertips smoothed the damp hair away from her face.

"My Sunshine!"

The words were filled with heart-wrenching sentiment. She watched in amazement as it happened. Like a bolt of lightning piercing a dark, cloudy night, Nash's face cleared and he began to tremble. Myriad complex emotions passed through his dark eyes—recognition, grief, tenderness and bewilderment.

None of it could top the jumbled feelings assailing her. Seeing the flash of memories burst through the fog clouding his mind made her heart soar and lifted some of the horror of his disappearance. The past weeks melted away.

She had met Nash through mutual friends. They became lovers, fell for each other hard and fast, gotten married within months of meeting. They'd shared a great life in a beautiful beach bungalow on the Gulf of Mexico. Everything had been wonderful right up until Nash got out of the military and joined a company conducting scientific research. The work was so hush-hush he had not been allowed to tell her anything about what he did. And with each day she'd watched as he become more withdrawn and distant, until the day he vanished.

In the intervening weeks Jenny had talked to anyone who would listen, and hounded many others who refused to hear her out. She'd known there was no way he had left her without a word, no matter what the evidence showed.

The police had been sympathetic at first while laying out the obvious facts. Nash had made a large withdrawal from their joint savings account. A suitcase and some of his clothes were missing from the closet. His car was gone and there had been no signs of foul play. It appeared to everyone as if he'd left her, but she'd known better. He would never willingly leave her behind.

"Why did you leave? Where'd you go? Where have you been all this time?" In her urgency, the questions spilled from her, one blending into another. She glanced at the white circle of skin on the fourth finger of his left hand. "And where is your wedding ring, Nash? God, what happened to you?"

Nash rolled to his side, gasping as even more vivid memories rushed through his mind. He wanted to answer all her questions, but wasn't sure how to explain it all or what to say.

"It's complicated. I'm still trying to catch up and don't know where to start."

"Why don't you just start at the beginning? There's no need to rush."

What a mess! He'd gotten too close, discovered too many company secrets, and seen what the scientists were doing. "Actually, there is a big need to rush. We don't have much time."

They were looking for him. And no matter how much he longed to tell Jenny everything, doing so would put her in danger. Nash wasn't willing to put her at risk.

"It's better that you don't know most of it. There's a laboratory somewhere not far from here. The scientists are messing with recombinant DNA, stem cells and gene-splicing. The test subjects are not there on a voluntary basis." He paused, stared down at her confused expression. "I saw too much, Sunshine. They'll be coming after me."

Nanotech's plan was genius. Abduct homeless people from the streets, men and women who won't be missed. Take them to a containment lab in the mountains and play with their DNA to see if a race of powerful soldiers was producible. By skipping years of testing and not applying for government approval, Nanotech stood to make a quick and tidy fortune.

He'd been assistant supervisor in charge of security and had not even known about the laboratory facilities. Finding out what his employer was doing sent him into a panic and Nash had gotten sloppy. The bastards had easily caught him and then taken precautions to make it appear as if he'd left Jenny. They inducted him in their diabolical project, adding tiger DNA to his own.

Hell, it sounded insane in his mind and he'd lived it. Jenny would never believe him.

He gazed down into her sweet, beloved face. His wife. The love of his life. Somehow, the bastards had managed to expunge her from his mind. A chill raced along his spine at the idea of never having remembered her and the love they shared.

Erased wasn't the right explanation for what had happened because his memories were back. It would be more accurate to say they'd locked his memories away behind a thick barricade. She was the key that had unlocked the door.

Being back with her was wonderful, but she wasn't getting back the man she'd known. They'd altered him, turned him into a bizarre freak of science. Making her understand was not going to be easy.

Nash vividly recalled the shock of shifting into an animal for the first time by accident. One second he'd been a man standing in the holding cell, the next he'd morphed into a new form, falling down onto four paws. His hearing had sharpened, distinguishing the lowest levels of sound. Colors had dulled from his widened field of vision, which sharpened into contrasting shades of gray. The tests had revealed incredible night vision better than with any enhancement goggles he'd worn as a man.

The lab had been taxing on the animal's acute senses. Strong antiseptic smells wreaked havoc with his nasal passages and created intense headaches. On the trips they'd taken into the mountains, the carnivore had come alive. The urge to hunt had been irresistible. Nash had stalked smaller animals, captured his prey with an innate skill and ripped apart the carcasses with sharpened claws, devouring the warm meat with pointed teeth.

As a tiger, he moved with grace and stealth, able to get close to the scientists without them detecting his presence. Put him in a rocky area and he became almost impossible to locate due to the uncanny ability to blend into his surroundings. His captors never had any problem keeping up with his whereabouts though. The bastards had implanted a tracking device beneath his skin and used a shock collar to control him. To get away, after removing the collar, he'd shifted and chewed through his thick pelt in order to remove the chip, which now rested at the bottom of a steep ravine.

No way would Jenny believe any of the insane events of the past weeks. She'd figure it was paranoia, a conspiracy theory or that he'd lost his mind. Until he got to the right people and found a way to shut down the lab they were both in extreme danger. He had to keep his mouth shut. Without the details, she didn't present a threat to his former employer.

Jenny's trembling hand fluttered over her mouth, holding back her horror.

"The scars? Wh-What did they do to you?"

This would be really hard. Would she turn away from him when he'd just found her again? Hell, would she even trust him or believe anything he said if he told the truth?

He made a mental note to figure out how they had ended up in the same place. It was too big a coincidence to ignore.

"I don't know much about the science, but they did things to make me...stronger. And they messed with my memories. While I was in the lab, I didn't remember you, my job or our home. I was kept heavily drugged to make me pliable for their experiments and testing."

Nash didn't want to think about the things they'd done to him, much less tell Jenny. Eventually, he'd have to reveal the beast hidden beneath the exterior of the man, but he'd have to figure out the best way to ease her into this new, altered reality.

"I managed to escape when someone messed up." Another odd occurrence he'd have to think about. He left out the fact that the tiger had gutted a man and left him for dead, too. "I ran all night through the woods trying to figure out where I was and how to get help." There were still big questions he needed to answer for himself.

"Where are we and what are you doing here?"

"I-I had to have a break. Between the stress of school, work and you... No one would listen to me. They all said you'd left me and I needed to accept it, to move on. I needed to get away from...everything."

Her words were cut off on a sob. Nash offered comfort, wiping her tears and holding his wife until she once again calmed.

"It's going to be all right now, Sunshine. I'm here and I won't let anything hurt you." Nash prayed he could live up to that promise.

He had to get in touch with the one man in the company he trusted. Micah Lasiter would help him sort this mess out.

As long as they hadn't gotten to Micah he still had hope. If they had—

He shook his head to clear away that unthinkable idea.

It was urgent he make contact, but not as important as reassuring Jenny. The rest of the world melted away when he was in her arms. For this one precious night, which could be their last night together, he would focus on her. Live a lifetime in a few short hours.

How she'd ended up here didn't matter. They'd figure everything out in the light of day. Right now, he needed to hold on to his wife and bask in the warm glow of her love.

His cock jerked to attention as she brushed against his hip. Nash had a lot of lost time to make up for, and he planned on starting right here and now. The romantic setting couldn't be any more perfect—a cozy cabin in the mountains, lying on a bearskin rug before a roaring fire. They had both been in a desperate rush earlier. He intended to slow things down and make love to his wife.

"Want to fool around, Sunshine?"

Chapter Four

❧

Jenny took in her husband's come-fuck-me expression and melted. His heavy-lidded eyes had darkened with lust and his sensual lips sported a naughty grin. The rapid recovery surprised her since in the past he'd required a few hours to be ready again.

A little alarm bell rang in the back of her mind, insisting this was important and had something to do with the changes in Nash. She ignored the warning.

"Already?"

His smile broadened. "Mmm-hmm," he purred.

"There's a hot tub on the back porch. I've been daydreaming about it since I signed the rental contract." Her thoughts scattered as she pictured water glistening on Nash's body in the moonlight. She imagined licking each drop of water from his tanned skin.

"Come on." Nash helped her stand. "You go climb into the hot tub. I'll fix us a snack and join you in a few minutes."

He leaned forward and took her lips in a slow, seductive kiss with none of the previous urgency. His tongue made a lazy exploration, delving into every recess of her mouth, teeth nipping lightly. Jenny leaned into his strong frame, enjoying the slight abrasion of his chest hair over her beaded nipples. Tingles started in her breasts and spread outward, bringing every sensitive nerve ending to life. Liquid heat gushed from her core and her renewed arousal dampened her thighs. By the time he broke the kiss they were both gasping for air.

"Go, woman." Nash turned her with a gentle push to get her moving in the right direction. "Get moving or I'll be fucking you against the wall."

She failed to see anything wrong with the idea.

His hand came down on her ass cheek and she yelped, more from being startled than the small sting created in the fleshy globe. She put extra sway in her hips then paused to give him a salacious grin before opening the door. "Don't take too long. It's cold out there."

Nash's eyes twinkled with mischief. "Don't worry, Sunshine. When I join you in the hot tub, I'll have you heated up again in no time."

Once outside, Jenny wrestled the cover from the tub and figured out the controls for the jets. Her nipples tightened almost to the point of pain in the chilly air of the enclosed porch. She dropped into the warm churning water with a blissful sigh and leaned back, resting her head on the padded edge. "Damn, now this is worth every penny of the rental fee."

The tub had more than adequate room for her to stretch out and float on the surface. Languishing in the hot water, her body and mind relaxed. Tense muscles eased and her thoughts drifted, for once not fretting over every little thing.

"I am one hell of a lucky man!" Reverence and honesty rang clear in Nash's husky voice.

"If you'd get that fine ass in here you'd be getting lucky."

Nash laughed and the happy, throaty sound soothed her battered soul.

"Yes, ma'am. But no funny stuff until you've eaten. It's gonna be a long night. You'll need your strength."

"Yeah, right. After round two you'll be sawing logs until well after sunrise." Two go-rounds had always been his limit.

He set a large tray laden with food on a nearby table, dragged it closer to the tub then slipped into the water with a hiss. "Damn, that's hot."

"Which is the whole idea, honey."

Large hands grasped her hips and tugged, drawing Jenny closer. Nash cradled her in his lap, one arm supporting her back. She closed her eyes and rested her head on his shoulder.

"Open," he commanded as something cool and smooth brushed her lips, which parted for him. Her teeth pierced the fleshy piece of fruit. The rich sweetness of the red grape burst over her tongue.

Jenny's jaw dropped when she glanced over at the tray to see what other treats he'd prepared for them. Grapes, strawberries and banana slices overflowed a large bowl. Thick ham and cheese sandwiches were stacked high on a plate. He'd opened her stash of Oreo cookies and next to the package sat a jar of peanut butter. The fact he remembered her favorite treat touched her heart and made her tummy gurgle in hunger.

"Jesus, Nash. That's about three days worth of the food I brought. You've got enough there for six people."

He gave a sheepish grin and shrugged. "I'm starving!"

They took turns feeding each other bites of food. As their bellies became full other appetites arose and eating became teasing foreplay. Nash dug his index finger deep into the peanut butter then held it out to her. Knowing how it would affect him, she tipped her chin down and held his heated gaze from beneath her eyelashes. She licked down one side of his finger, up the other and circled the tip with her tongue.

"Suck it, Sunshine." His rough groan set off tremors low in her belly.

Nash basked in the glow of his wife's innate sensuality. Jenny's lips parted and she nibbled on the tip of his finger, driving him to distraction before slowly sucking the digit into the warmth of her mouth. Her busy tongue twirled around the length until she reached his last knuckle. As she reversed direction, she sucked hard, hollowing her cheeks. He pictured her taking his cock between her lips and the rock-hard organ jerked against her hip. It had been too long since he'd felt her talented mouth suck him to the back of her throat.

Surging to his feet, he sat on the cushioned edge and placed Jenny between his spread legs. Dipping two fingers into the jar, he painted his cock from root to tip with the salty treat.

Jenny didn't need any further enticement. She enjoyed her ability to bring him to his knees by pleasuring him with her sexy mouth. The fingers of one hand circled the base of his cock while the other cradled his balls. Her wet tongue lapped at him, devouring every last drop of the peanut butter before drawing the crown past her lips.

"Damn, that's good."

Sharp teeth nipped at the sensitive rim sending sparks shooting straight to his balls, which drew taut. She flicked her tongue into the slit, hummed while tasting his pre-cum. Nash's head fell back between his shoulders as her tongue circled the head then probed the most amazing spot on the underside.

During their years together she'd learned how to take him right to the edge and keep him teetering there. Putting her skills to good use, Jenny used every trick she knew. Nimble fingers rimmed his anus, stroked his perineum and massaged his balls. She used her lips, tongue and teeth—sucked, licked and nibbled. Even the noises she made were a tool of pleasure, loud slurps stoking his arousal higher, and her hummed moans vibrating through his flesh.

When his climax would be held back no longer, Nash didn't bother to warn Jenny. She knew how to read his body and was be prepared for the hot jets of cum hitting the back of her throat. Her convulsive swallowing drew out his pleasure. He couldn't prevent the loud roar from rolling through his chest any more than he could stop the release of his semen.

The tiger pulled at its leash. Nash gave in to the untamed instincts and acted on the impulses bombarding his body. He didn't pause to catch his breath. One fast sweep of his arm cleared the remnants of their feast from the small table. Plates shattered and the tray landed with a resounding thunk on the wooden deck.

"Nash!"

Jenny quivered as he turned toward her. His wild and hungry eyes had become so dark they appeared black. His jaw looked more prominent, his expression savage. A jolt of panic shot through her, but she pushed it aside and focused on her excitement.

This was Nash, her tender and loving husband, not someone to be feared. The whole beasty routine started having a very different effect on her. She found this new primal edginess was a major turn-on.

He lifted her out of the water as if she were lighter than a feather and laid her on the table with her bottom resting at the very edge. The primitive intensity radiating from him in waves made her think of a cartoon animal putting on a bib and sharpening a knife as it prepared to dine. That image failed to lighten the impact of his carnal stare.

Hands that trembled parted her knees and he barked a warning. "Stay!"

Yeah, not a problem. She was pinned to the spot as effectively as a deer caught by headlights.

And damn if he didn't look sexy as hell with his dark hair wet and rumpled, clinging to his face. Beads of water glistened in the moonlight, streamed over ripped muscles, and raced along delineated indentations. One fat drop quivered where it clung to his taut nipple. Jenny longed to capture it on the tip of her tongue then lick away all the remaining water from every inch of skin.

She screamed as he fed on her pussy as if starved. Broad shoulders forced her legs wider, almost to the point of pain. There was no slow buildup or finesse, Nash ravished her. Eager slurps and moans filled the air as he consumed the cream from her slick folds. His tongue felt rough, abrading tender tissues, creating the most delightful friction. The wet appendage thrust deep into her grasping pussy. Jenny swore it almost hit the back of her throat before the tip curved upward to stroke her sweet spot as it retracted.

Her fingers wound through his hair and held him in place as her hips bucked, her pussy fucking his face. The dominant behavior and rough treatment, so uncharacteristic of Nash, drove her into a wild frenzy. Unfathomable pleasure gathered in her core as he took her to incredible heights.

"Nash," she gasped. "Oh God. Please." Overwhelmed, she wasn't sure if she begging him to stop or keep going. Uncontrollable spasms shook her entire body and all she could do was to hang on tight.

Her orgasm hit with the force of a tsunami. Wave after wave swelled then crashed over her, bombarding her with endless ecstasy. He stayed with her, sucked her engorged clit, riding out the storm until her body calmed, lapping at her folds until he'd devoured every drop of pleasure.

Aftershocks still burst through her body as he gently lifted her, dried them both, and carried her to bed. She lost count of how many times throughout the night they made love, always in a different position.

He'd become a tireless sex fiend.

If this was a side effect of what they'd done to him in the lab, she might have to volunteer for the program just to be able to keep up with him. She'd definitely have to order some mega vitamins.

Not that she was complaining. Nope, so far she was very satisfied with her new-and-improved husband.

Chapter Five

ဆ

Jenny yawned and rubbed her eyes. She had not managed to get much sleep. She would doze off then wake up in a panic, reaching out for Nash. Each time she did they made love again, reestablishing their strong connection.

Nash prepared a huge breakfast feast and wolfed down massive proportions, but she had little appetite. Finally, she stopped pushing food around the plate and set it aside. Nash had shared small pieces of the horrible information he'd discovered while held captive at the lab. She'd taken time to think about it and was ready to talk.

She'd been proud of his job as the second-in-command providing security for a research company committed to developing a cure for cancer. Never would she have suspected the scientists' discoveries had lead them on a very different path. One that paved the way for unconscionable actions and a frightening goal—creating genetically enhanced humans.

"Let's see if I've got this right. The company is kidnapping innocent people and fucking around with their DNA. They're going against all ethical and legal regulations governing research. Their morals are corrupted, bent to suit their own purposes. When you found out, they abducted you and turned you into one of their guinea pigs."

He rolled his neck then stared at the ceiling for a minute. "Yeah, that's pretty much the issue in a nutshell. The military took interest in the concept and gave them funding. I don't think they realize the company has taken the idea past the research stage and are experimenting on humans."

He reached across the table and picked up her hand, giving it a reassuring squeeze before releasing it again. She stared into his eyes, seeing the awful truth in his steady gaze.

"Nash, what the hell did they do to you?"

With a heavy sigh, he scrubbed a hand over this face in a telling gesture. She knew he was trying to find a way to sugarcoat what he had to say. That was the last thing she needed or wanted. She decided to steer the conversation in a different direction, ask some of the other questions bothering her.

"Okay, so this secret lab of theirs, with all this fancy, state-of-the art security in place. Yet you somehow managed to escape after weeks of not finding any point of weakness." Jenny drummed her fingers on the table. "Don't you find it suspicious that their tight security became lax at the opportune moment, allowing you to get away?"

"Was that a rhetorical question?"

She nodded. He seemed to know where her line of reasoning was headed. "So how do we, working on our own, bring down a major organization with strong government connections?"

His expression hardened. "*We* don't. I need to get in touch with Micah Lasiter. He'll help me sort this out. Get me in touch with the right people."

"Your boss?" she gasped, certain her skepticism showed in her expression. "But he's one of them."

"I trust Micah. He's not just my boss. You know we're old friends. He wouldn't condone illegal research. Once he knows what's going on, he'll help me."

Yeah, and leave her completely out of everything. "I'm in this now, Nash, so don't even think of trying to shut me out."

They had brought her luggage into the cabin earlier. She went to her purse, got her cell phone, and pushed it across the table. "Here. If you trust this friend then call him."

Nash shook his head. "I can't, Sunshine. Cell activity is too easy to monitor and intercept. I need a secure, untraceable way to contact him."

Frustrated, she dropped down into her chair. Okay, no cell phone. The cabin had a landline but caller ID ruled out that as an option. Considering their location, finding a payphone was a long shot.

"Oh, I know. We could send up a smoke signal." She wanted to bite back the sarcastic comment as soon as it left her mouth.

He merely snickered.

"Do you think they could have followed you here?" Jenny cast a nervous glance around the cabin.

"No!" His tone was firm and confident. "I took care of the tracking mechanism." Pausing, he seemed to reconsider. "They might be able to use another...altered subject to follow my trail, but I don't think it would work. The training process has not progressed that far. I doubt they've had time to teach the others how to track or hunt."

"Oh, oh, oh." Jenny shot up from the chair as if her ass were on fire. "I know. The SUV has that OnStar satellite thingy. You can use it to call Micah."

Nash rubbed his chin. It was an old habit she knew well. It meant his very analytical mind was busy picking her idea apart, determining potential problems and probabilities of success. Without warning, he grabbed her, spinning Jenny around in circles.

"You are amazing!" He stopped twirling, but her head continued to whirl for a few seconds. She stared into his eyes, delighting in the enlarged pupils and darker blue color reflecting heated desire.

Lowering his head, he drew her into a slow kiss. Nash traced her lips with the tip of his tongue before delving inside to tease and tantalize. He nibbled and sipped, tasted and explored.

Jenny's body softened, melted into her husband. Her hands traced the planes and angles along his chest, noting changes in him. During his captivity his body had become leaner and more defined, roped with muscle. His kiss tasted different too, the sweetness now seasoned with a spicier flavor and boldness. When they'd made love he'd been insatiable and aggressive. Almost primal. Animalistic.

She pulled back, needing to catch her breath. One kiss and she was ready for him. Her body hot and wet. But now was not the time. They had to sort through this tangled web of deceit first. After exposing the lab and ensuring Nash would be safe they could fuck like rabbits.

"I doubt the security team has thought about monitoring satellite communications." He considered their situation for a moment. "Have you noticed anything strange lately? Seen anyone watching the bungalow or taking an unusual interest in your schedule?"

Jenny thought about it. Working evening shift, paying extra attention to her surroundings when driving home late at night had become habit. When Nash had disappeared, she'd experienced the creepy crawly feeling of being watched those first few weeks.

"For a while, I would have sworn someone was watching me, but it all figured in with your disappearance. I told the police. They brushed off my concerns, said I was imagining things because of you leaving." Tears stung the back of her eyes. "The detective made me out to be a hysterical and hormonal woman scorned. He made me feel as if I was losing my mind.

"Anyway—" She shook off the useless anger and frustration. "There was a van, one of the windowless deals used by plumbers and other businesses. I noticed it sitting several houses down the block for the first week. But I decided someone was having work done on their house and shrugged it off as strung-out nerves. I haven't seen anything odd since then."

His grip on her shoulder's tightened and his expression turned hard, taking on a dangerous glare. "Fucking bastards. My guess is they were watching you to see if the police gave any credence to your belief something had happened to me. God, Jenny—" His eyes closed briefly before he stared down at her. "If they'd hurt you..."

Nash didn't need to complete the statement. His anger over any potential harm she'd faced was evident in his clenched jaw and pained expression.

"How many people knew you were coming here?"

She considered his question for a moment. "Only my mother and I didn't tell her specifics. Nobody at work knows what I planned for vacation other than to get out of town."

He brushed the tip of her nose with a tender kiss. "Good! Even if the organization checks up on you they shouldn't realize you're gone yet. We'll have to risk it and hope Nanotech isn't monitoring satellite communications."

"Make sure you get Micah to bring you some clothes." Jenny gaze swept his body clad in only the thin medical scrubs and grinned. "Not that I mind you being naked or going commando."

❈ ❈ ❈ ❈ ❈

"I want to know more about this lab and what they did to you? And why haven't I heard about Micah before if you're such good friends?"

They sat before the fireplace, sipping hot chocolate. It was early afternoon and would still be a few hours before help reached them. Nash had known the hard questions were coming, seen them in her eyes, but wasn't eager to discuss the particulars. He'd didn't want Jenny to be in danger but she deserved to know details.

"I'll start with Micah. The only contact I've had with him since you and I met revolves around work. You know that I signed a confidentiality agreement so I can't get too into Nanotech business."

He settled with his back propped against the couch, legs stretched out toward the hearth, casually crossed at the ankle. "I met Micah in the Army when both of us were green recruits. Micah excelled in espionage. My marksman skills took me in a different direction, although we did work together at times it wasn't often. Our paths crossed again when I applied for the security job with the company. Micah had already been with them and was one of the reasons I took the job. He's a good guy. Fiercely loyal.

"Even though he's my supervisor, he works in another part of the country. We don't see much of each other. I started hearing rumors about top-secret research and experimentation, which I didn't give much attention. Not at first. When one of the scientists went missing after stating ethical concerns to higher-ups, I began to investigate on my own." He glanced at Jenny. She watched him close, hung on every word.

"I discovered things. About the lab, and what they were doing. Word got back to the wrong people. I intended to get Micah involved but didn't reach him in time since he'd gone on medical leave. Someone found out I was asking questions so they sent a cleaner after me."

Confusion clouded her eyes. Nash changed course for a moment to explain. "A cleaner is similar to a hit man. When the situation goes FUBAR the cleaner is called in to purge any trace of the organization—scrub the scene. This can include destroying evidence and eliminating witnesses. I became an unacceptable risk, but they still had certain uses for me."

Jenny gasped. He took hold of her freezing cold hands, rubbing them between his own in an attempt to warm her up. Her brown eyes were wide with shock and fear. "I'm okay, Sunshine," he reassured. "Do you want me to continue?"

Jenny nodded.

"I got sloppy, panicked. The cleaner got the drop on me, knocked me out with an electroshock weapon. I was drugged and bound for transport, taken to the lab, and woke up strapped to an exam table. The scientists explained their project. It was quite brilliant really. Abduct the unwanted dregs of society for testing no subject would willingly submit to. The initial goal of altering DNA to remove cancer changed when other potentials became clear. The new government sponsored goal, create an unbeatable team of enhanced soldiers. Combine the DNA of the world's strongest, fiercest hunters with that of the test subjects. I doubt the government knows how far the scientists took things."

He rubbed his chin. "The results weren't quite what they'd expected. A dozen or so people were altered that I'm aware of. They received DNA from wolves, bears, big cats, sharks...you name it. When the human's bodies revealed weakness, operations were performed to alter organs, muscles and bones. Some didn't survive. A few had to be terminated."

Fat tears streamed down her cheeks, but Jenny didn't make a sound. Nash pulled her into his arms, offering what comfort he could. She remained stiff and on edge. Tremors rocked her body.

"Oh my God. What...how...Jesus..." Her voice trailed off as she buried her face against his chest.

Anticipating her next questions, Nash prepared to plunge ahead. Jenny surprised him by leaping to her feet.

"I need to take a break." The words were spoken softly. She appeared weak, her complexion pale from shock. "I'm going to take a walk."

He moved to join her, but Jenny held out a hand to stop him.

"Alone!"

Nodding, Nash gave her the space she needed to sort through everything he'd said. It was a lot. Hell, he still had a difficult time coming to terms with everything that had happened. For Jenny, it was all new territory.

Chapter Six

ഌ

Restless and needing to move, she paced the dirt driveway, afraid to go very far while sorting through what Nash had told her, along with her conflicted emotions. Anger, betrayal, shock, disbelief and joy all warred for dominance.

In the weeks since he'd disappeared, she had spent a lot of sleepless nights watching late night television. Her mind latched onto episodes of *Science Fiction Theater*. The whole situation, everything that had happened, made it seem as if she'd been tossed into the middle of a bizarre movie starring mad scientists and brutal killers.

It was a lot to stomach, requiring a huge leap of faith. She wanted to believe in him, but Lord, talk about far-out craziness.

Maybe the drugs they'd given Nash had caused vivid dreams. Dreams so real his mind had been tricked into thinking those mental trips had been real. Or he could have suffered a head injury. Yeah, it was something to consider.

Hell, maybe he'd been abducted by aliens.

Anything was better than his employer having screwed around with his DNA. That horrifying nightmare was unthinkable.

Then there was the matter of him never telling her anything. Sure, Nanotech required silence and he'd signed a confidentiality agreement, but she was his wife. For that matter, why had she never asked more questions about his work? Until his disappearance, she'd been happy with her ignorance.

Frustration overwhelmed her and Jenny took it out on a tree, kicking the hard trunk. The soft sneakers she wore provided no protection against the blow. "Ow! Smart, Jen. Real smart." She hopped around on the good foot, rubbing her injured toes through her shoes.

At the end of the drive, she turned and headed back toward the cabin. "This was supposed to have been a stress-free vacation. Rest and relaxation. Ha!" While she rejoiced at having found Nash, she wanted to rail over the injustice of how their lives had been pitched into total chaos.

Jenny came to an abrupt halt. What had happened didn't matter. She would stand by her man no matter what trouble came their way and get him whatever help he needed.

Something he'd said raced to the forefront of her mind. *"They received DNA from wolves, bears, big cats, sharks…you name it. When the human's bodies revealed weakness, operations were performed to alter organs, muscles and bones."*

What the hell had the whacked-out scientists done to her husband? He'd only given her sketchy information. Jenny had no clue. But she sure as hell was going to find out. Armed with medical knowledge she could combat any ill effects.

Fixated on her immediate goal, she started off once again, ready to get some answers. A low, resonating rumble filtered through the trees, making her gut clench. It was a menacing, animalistic growl. A warning.

A twig snapped, branches rustled and the growling grew in both volume and nearness.

Well, didn't this new predicament just make her damn day. Here she was out walking in the wilderness, by herself, being stalked by what sounded like a very large animal.

When you step in it, you really step in it.

RUN!

Her entire body froze to the spot, regardless of what her head screamed the message wasn't getting through. Fear paralyzed her muscles. Instinct told her to get far away from whatever it was, but she knew predators were enticed by the chase.

Too late!

The biggest cat she'd ever seen strolled from the forest, blocking her path. Lions in the zoo had nothing on this enormous creature. Walking on all fours it was only about a foot shorter than her. If the beast rose on its hind legs —

I'm going to be eaten alive.

"Nice, Simba," she crooned in what she hoped to be a soothing tone. "Easy now. Holy shit, you're one hell of a big kitty."

He had a huge head and intelligent golden-brown eyes that seemed to study her. A thick mane covered his chest almost down to the knees and flowed more than halfway across a very muscular back. His coloring ranged from light buff on his torso to a dark cocoa brown at the tip of his tail. The lion's proud stance gave him a regal quality.

The cat yawned, revealing a sharp set of immense teeth, and he flicked the brown puffed end of his tail in her direction. His lazy demeanor didn't fool Jenny. The animal was on high alert, waiting and watching.

"Getting sleepy? That's good. You go take a nice long nap and I'll catch ya later."

She had no way to warn Nash. Eventually, he'd come looking for her and the lion would get him too. Well, unless the lion got filled up on her first and took a nap.

What a delightful thought.

"People don't taste very good, you know. Not one of those cases where they say it tastes like chicken." As she spoke, Jenny took slow steps away from the animal. "Nope, we taste horrible. Meat's all tough and gamey. You'd be much happier with a nice filet of venison."

Prepared to take another step back, she was stopped by the sharp cry of what sounded to be another large cat.

"Oh great. This just gets better and better!" She quivered, made a snap decision and stepped to the left, pivoting to get a look at the new arrival while moving from between the two animals.

Let them fight over her. She was okay with that. Maybe they'd kill each other and she could make a break for it.

A large tiger stepped into the open. Jenny blinked a couple of times, trying to clear her vision. Nothing changed. There were still two big jungle cats eying each other warily.

"A lion and a tiger. Oh my! Now all we need is a bear." Her voice came out squeaky, pitched high, bordering on hysteria.

The two animals facing off made a very surreal sight. She fought down the hysterical laughter threatening to burst free. God, if only she could chalk this up to a hallucination.

Talking softly, Jenny continued to take tiny steps away from the building confrontation. "Play nice, kitties. Ignore the silly human. You'll have a better time chasing each other."

With her back to the trees, careful of making sudden movements, she eyed both animals. Somehow, a tiger showing up made perfect sense to her spiraling-out-of-control mind. The tiger's stocky body stood tense and on edge, prepared for action. Shiny fur, ranging from almost white to reddish-orange, was overlaid by a pattern of dark stripes. While not as large as the lion, the tiger was still a force to be reckoned with.

The beast turned his intense blue gaze on her. Jenny felt her legs wobble. She backed into a tree. Unable to remain upright any longer, she slid down onto her bottom.

Blue eyes?

Those eyes, they looked so similar to Na —

"Oh my God. No. Please, no."

All thoughts of slinking off evaporated as her brain struggled with what she was seeing. Her mind raced as she put two and two together, not liking the result, grasping for alternate answers.

Nash had told her Nanotech's scientists were playing with crazy shit but what she imagined couldn't be possible. Over the years, amazing leaps had been made with genetic research. More than ten years ago they'd cloned that damn sheep.

What the hell was its name?

"Either Molly or Dolly? Fuck, I don't know the stupid sheep's name," she mumbled, knowing the animal's name didn't matter. Not with the two cats preparing to fight. But the scars on Nash's body—those mattered. The sick fucks had done things to him, enhanced his strength, operated. What if they—

Dammit, no.

If you wanted to perform illegal groundbreaking research, you'd set up a secured lab in the middle of nowhere. Do whatever it took to protect your secret. Especially if the potential return on your investment was huge. Men with the ability to change into animals was beyond huge.

Military agencies, foreign interests, terrorists— They'd all shell out big bucks for technology that advanced the strength of their soldiers. Make regular soldiers stronger, turn them into some of the fiercest hunters in the world and the superpowers would hand over a fortune.

The tiger moved to position himself between her and the lion. He seemed protective or maybe possessive. Shit! She had a hard time figuring out men. Animals were a whole different story.

Each step the tiger took was matched by the lion and the cats began an odd dance of advance and withdraw.

"There's no sense in having a catfight over me." She glanced into the stunning blue eyes of the tiger again, and her heart beat so fast she was afraid it would burst.

If he is...

That means...

Then who the hell is the lion?

Bits and pieces clicked into place from her earlier conversation with Nash and her mind made a huge leap. Panic bubbled up in her chest, strangling anything she would have said as she scrambled around the tree trunk, keeping her eye on the animals.

Good Lord. She had to be wrong.

The two cats growled and roared, each taking the other's measure. Jenny hoped to fade into the background and miss the fight.

No such luck.

The lion crouched down, ready to spring at the tiger. No, at Nash. He'd be torn to shreds. She trembled, her mind raced, searched for a way out of this nightmare.

Should she run? Scream? There was no one to hear her cries or offer aid. The cabin's isolation was one of the reasons she'd rented it for her vacation.

Fuck! She couldn't run. She had to reach her husband. He was in there…somewhere. And he was her only hope. That's why he was here, to protect her, right? But how much of Nash's intellect did the tiger share? Would he even know her?

A ferocious growl vibrated from the lion's broad chest as he leapt, nearly scaring the piss out of her.

"Nash!" His name erupted from her lips in an anguished scream as the cats attacked. Growls, roars and shrill cries of pain rang out from the tumbling, churning mass of fur. Claws ripped at tender flesh. Teeth sunk into a vulnerable throat. An endless, dark river of blood flowed over the dirt.

Jenny had to do something to help Nash, but what? How the hell did a human break up a fight between two bloodthirsty predators?

No, one of them was her husband. Something about the way the lion moved made her believe this animal also shared a human's intelligence.

Considering what she believed to be the reality of the situation, she saw only one sure-fire way to bring an end to the skirmish. She had to react, fast. There was no time to think about it.

Pushing past her fears, Jenny squared her shoulders and waited for an opening. Where she found the courage, she had no idea but a gap appeared between the two cats. She hollered the first thing that came to mind and stepped right into the middle of the fight.

"Hey! You two morons, please stop this nonsense. I'm not going to watch you kill each other."

Oh, please let there be human men under all that fur and muscle!

A trail of fire burned down the back of her right calf as a powerful paw and unsheathed claws met with denim covered skin and muscle. No doubt the strike was intended to land on the other cat. That knowledge didn't ease the excruciating pain. Air exited her lungs in a rush leaving her breathless. She glanced over her shoulder to get a look at the damage. Ragged, blood-coated strips of denim covered her lower leg. A pool of blood soaked into the ground around her foot.

Cold sweat slicked her body and her field of vision narrowed. Funny, the sight of blood had never bothered her before at work. Of course, that was always someone else's blood, not her own. Damn if it didn't hurt too.

"I don't feel so good." Her voice dropped to a weak whisper as she plunged face-first toward the ground. The last thing she heard was Nash calling her name in a harsh tone full of fear.

Chapter Seven

ଛଠ

Nash's claws sliced through fabric and flesh easy as a hot knife through butter.

Spending the rest of his life in the deepest, darkest, most vile pit in hell would not atone for hurting Jenny. There was too much force behind his movement to stop the momentum when she stepped between him and the lion.

She swayed and he shifted. Leaping forward, he wrapping her in the protection of his arms. Nash rolled as they fell, allowing his body to take the brunt of their impact against the hard-packed dirt road and keeping the lion in sight.

"Jenny? Talk to me, Sunshine."

As he rose, holding Jenny in his arms, the lion shifted form. He'd never seen anyone else make the change before, but Nash sure knew how it felt. The sudden flash of bright lights as the senses and body altered. The momentary disorientation created by such a drastic change in perspective.

Observing the shift was mesmerizing. If he'd blinked, he would have missed it. But the naked man covered in bite marks, gashes and abrasions now standing where the lion had shocked the hell out of him. A heavy sense of dread settled in his gut.

"Oh God. They got to you, too."

Micah Lasiter nodded. "Let's get her inside and take care of that wound. Then we'll talk."

Nash paced the confines of the small cabin. Thanks to his new super DNA, his wounds had already started to heal. He'd cleaned the gashes in Jenny's leg and covered it in bandages, but she required more advanced care. While Micah had placed a call to someone he trusted, Nash located the first-aid kit Jenny kept in the car and coaxed her into taking a couple of pain pills. The medicine had done its job and knocked her out.

"Talk to me, man. Make me understand."

Micah raked his fingers through shoulder-length dark blond hair. "While thirty-five may not be old, my body has taken a beating over the years. Hiding my physical limitations became harder after taking that bullet last year. Then I blew out my knee. That's why I was on medical leave." He rubbed at the damaged muscles.

"They came to me with a proposition to join the Predator Project. I became the first non-civilian their new and perfected procedure was tested on."

Micah sighed. "I had few options. Once they told me what they were doing, I knew too much. It was either become their test subject or be eliminated. It all sounded so simple and amazing. Inject me with some souped-up lion DNA and I'd be stronger than ever before." He laughed but the sound held no humor. "They left out a few minor details, such as the fact that I'd turn into a lion."

Nash couldn't believe what he was hearing. Micah had gone into this as a willing volunteer?

"They kept me isolated, hired a zoologist to help me through the transition and teach me how to handle my new abilities. I didn't find out about your disappearance until after everything had gone down and Dr. Southerby met you at the lab."

Nash remembered Weltman bringing in a woman to meet him right before things got crazy and alarms started going off.

"Weltman confronted Becca and I had to get her out of there. I didn't know about you until later or I would have pulled you out too."

"Wait a minute," Nash interrupted. "The head of the organization is in on this? I got the impression a few of the scientists had taken it upon themselves to circumvent the standards for research and experimentation."

The lines of strain furrowing Micah's brow grew deeper. He closed his eyes and took several calming breaths. "The project has Weltman's full backing and support. It's his baby. Upon discovering a solution for binding the DNA and delivering it into the subject's bloodstream the plan was to begin testing on disposable subjects. After perfecting the process they'd go for a few specific trials on individuals with previous military training. Strong men capable of handling the alterations. That's when I was recruited. Weltman himself plans to undergo the procedure once proven safe.

"From what I've learned, the project has been in place for more than a year. All the previous test subjects either died during the transformation or their bodies rejected the DNA cocktail. A few went insane. I was the first success."

Stress and exhaustion had taken an obvious toll on his friend. His thick hair now had a sprinkling of gray. Deep lines bracketed the corners of his eyes where before the golden skin had appeared youthful and smooth.

"All those poor unsuspecting people." Nash muttered some creative curses and rubbed at his aching temples.

Micah nodded. "How'd you wind up in this mess?"

Nash continued to pace, wearing a groove in the wooden floor. "A tech arrived at headquarters to find out what was being done about a scientist who had gone missing. Took me by surprise because I hadn't heard about anyone being missing. Hell, I didn't even know about the facility until the tech gave me details.

"He also wanted to report ethics concerns over how things were being done at a lab. Since you were out on medical, I conducted his first interview. Never heard much though. We were being monitored. As soon as he started talking about unwilling subjects and taking homeless people from the street, Jennings busted in and took over."

Steve Jennings, head of operations, was the man to whom both he and Micah answered. Nash remembered the older man storming into the room and directing him to forget about everything he'd heard. He'd been told the issue was top-secret and would be handled personally by Jennings.

"They left me out of the loop, but I refused to let go. There were too many unanswered questions, especially about the secret facility. Many of the things the tech had said bothered me. Two days later, I heard about his disappearance and began checking into the matter on my own." He rubbed at the beard stubble covering his jaw.

"I screwed up, got too close, and learned things they didn't want me to know. Got busted by Jennings while talking to the wrong person."

In his panic, he'd attempted to contact Weltman, certain the man had no idea about the immoral practices being carried out right under his nose. The mistake had cost him.

"I got careless, overestimated myself. They snatched me right out of my car." He glanced at Jenny's motionless form on the couch. "Made it look like I'd bailed on Jenny. They kept me prisoner in the lab until yesterday when security got lax and I escaped."

Micah chuckled. "Yeah. I recommended everyone on the lab's security force. When I learned where you were, I arranged for the breach in procedure and waited in the woods to get you out of there. Ran into a bit of trouble myself with Jennings." A look of regret crossed his face. "He's no longer a concern."

Nash held up his hand. "And how is it that my wife wound up here on the very same night security became lazy and I escaped? That's too much coincidence for me!"

"I purchased this cabin. Posted notices on e-mail bulletins at the hospital where Jenny works offering it up as a very affordable vacation rental. She e-mailed back and set up the rental dates." Micah gave a negligent shrug.

"Anyway, that's how I was able to get here so quick. I've been here for weeks. Just had to clean things up and cover my tracks." He drummed his fingers on a thigh that vibrated with nervous energy. "Speaking of which, it won't take them long to find this place. We've been lucky so far but it's not a safe location."

He'd already known they couldn't stay here much longer, but what now? His conscience wouldn't allow him to walk away. There were still innocent people in the lab, suffering as he had. He also had to consider the frightening consequences of the military gaining access to the procedure or the altered subjects.

"We've got to take them down."

Micah raked his hand through his hair and nodded. "Doing the right thing won't be easy or come without significant risk."

Nash glanced at Jenny again. Even if his conscience had let him turn his back, his love for Jenny gave him determination. She was such a good, caring and compassionate person. She would never walk away from innocent people in need of help. If she knew the details, she would want him to do whatever he could to save them.

"Make some calls," he growled. "Assemble a team. We'll need electronics, computer and explosive specialists. We go in, get the subjects out, fry their records then blow the place sky-high."

"Good. I already have a team. Sorry, but I had to find out where you stood on things before bringing you in."

Micah being a step ahead didn't surprise Nash. His friend had an uncanny ability to analyze a situation and find all the possible pitfalls with deadly efficiency.

"We have to consider our status, Nash. They've turned us into animals with the ability to reason and walk among humans. The public will be frightened and can never find out or there'd be nowhere we could ever live in peace. This will have to be a silent mission. None of the team has full disclosure. Any subjects we pull out will have to be handled with kid gloves."

Shit. There was no way of just letting the subjects walk out of there. They'd have to be isolated, taught to deal with their new status.

"I want to get General Hughes involved, keep everything hush-hush. The subjects can be trained under his guidance and protection."

Nash nodded. Hughes had been their mentor in the Army. Next to Micah, he couldn't think of anyone else he'd trust with something so critical. "The General will be a powerful asset to have on our side."

"We also have to consider the chance they've established a failsafe. If the records have been stored elsewhere then taking out the lab doesn't mean we've cancelled the project. We have to take out the entire Nanotech network."

"This has to go down without any mistakes..." Nash let his words trail off. Micah knew the consequences of failure as well as he did.

Remaining silent and still was a struggle for Jenny. The horrors being perpetrated in the lab made her blood run cold. Hearing Nash recount what had been done to him, how they'd turned him into a shapeshifter with DNA from a tiger, boggled her mind.

It all felt too strange to be real. Yet this was now her life. Her husband had a tiger lurking beneath his skin. His best friend was a lion. And people who'd been turned into God only knew what were still being held in the lab, kept in what amounted to cages, while horrible tests were conducted on them.

Pride was an emotion she'd become familiar with in regard to her husband, but never to the extent she felt now. Nash was a good man. He wouldn't let this injustice continue and he'd make sure the others got whatever support they would need to cope with what had been done to them. From the brief exposure to Micah, she felt certain he also had a good heart and would make sure the right thing was done.

Their lives had been thrown into turmoil. Nothing would ever be the same again. Not only would they both have to adjust to Nash's new abilities, there would be the necessity of hiding what he was from the rest of the world. Other scientists would want to study him, figure out how the procedure worked and try to replicate the result. The general populous would be afraid, while the government and military would want to use him for their own purposes.

She wondered what would happen to her education and career. Moving, changing schools and jobs all seemed to loom on the horizon.

No sooner had the thoughts entered her mind than Jenny chastised herself for being selfish. This wasn't about her. She had to protect Nash, regardless of what personal sacrifice was required. She loved him and would do anything for him.

Including follow him back inside the lab to make sure he made it out alive.

Two more men arrived at the cabin and the team of four discussed their plans never suspecting she listened to every word. Jenny kept a tight rein on her emotions, schooling her features into a blank mask and controlling her breathing so they'd think she remained asleep.

Chapter Eight

ഇ

An entire day came and went in a blur of activity. Kyle Slater gave Jenny an antibiotic injection, irrigated the lacerations and closed the wounds with a special compound—one of the good things to have come from Nanotech—that eliminated the need for stitches.

Nash scowled as he watched Jenny limp around the kitchen, preparing sandwiches for everyone. She'd been too quiet and subdued. Without her running dialogue, he felt at a loss, unable to get an accurate fix on her emotional state. He tried to convince her to take it easy but understood her need to stay busy.

Layouts and maps were scattered across an old wooden table. The team had gone over every step of their plan until the details were second nature. They were as ready for tonight's raid as they were going to get. Tensions ran high and they all needed a little down time. Nash knew exactly how he wanted to spend the next few hours. First he needed some privacy.

"Someone should check the perimeter to make sure they haven't discovered our location."

Micah nodded. "Sam, Kyle and I have got it covered. We'll be back in two hours."

Jenny ignored their departure and continued to clean the same stretch of countertop she'd been working on for more than ten minutes.

"Come on, Sunshine. Let's take a break."

"I'm fine," she insisted.

He put on an exaggerated hangdog expression, which wasn't very hard to do since his ass was all but dragging. "Good, then you can keep me company while I get some rest."

She hung the cloth over the faucet then rinsed and dried her hands. Her anxiety made his heart clench. They both dreaded the dangerous night to come and needed some alone time to talk before the team headed out. He knew there were many things weighing on her mind.

Nash moved in behind Jenny, sliding his arms around her waist and brushed tender kisses along her neck. "I need you." She leaned back into him, and he settled his erection between the lush curves of her ass. "Let's spend the afternoon making love."

The shiver of arousal that raced through her body was more than enough encouragement for him. He guided her to the bedroom, kicking the door shut behind them.

Jenny wanted to make love but not yet. She needed more answers first. Nash had left out a lot of specifics and made it clear he didn't want to discuss it. That was too bad. She needed to know.

"Exactly what did they do to you in the lab?"

He didn't seem surprised by the question even though his body did tense. Jenny sat on the edge of the bed and watched him closely. He stance was rigid, legs shoulder width apart, hands behind his ramrod straight back. The strain he felt showed in his drawn features. While she wanted to lessen his burdens before he went and risked his life, the white elephant in the room had to be addressed first.

"I need to hear the rest of it."

His body clenched tighter and his eyes narrowed on her. She wouldn't back down.

"Tell me, Nash. What are the end results of everything they did?"

"This is going to sound insane." He sighed and rubbed at his temples. His voice started out quiet, gaining strength as she nodded in encouragement.

"They changed me, infused my body with DNA taken from tigers and altered my organs to accept the foreign genetic code."

He stared somewhere in the vicinity of her knees, not telling her anything she hadn't already learned when she wanted concrete information. She knew a lot from when the guys had talked while thinking she was sleeping. It wasn't enough.

"In the driveway—the tiger and lion. That was you and Micah?"

Startled that she'd made the connection, his gaze snapped to hers. He nodded, confirming her suspicions, and dropped to his knees. Nash took her hands into his larger ones, his fingers absently stroking over her knuckles.

"It's hard to explain, Jenny. The first time it happened, I thought I was having a drug-induced hallucination. Then they taught me how to shift at will. I picture the tiger in my head and my body transforms. All my senses sharpen. It's awe-inspiring and terrible all at once."

"You didn't know about Micah?"

"No. It came as a shock to find out he'd allowed them to screw around with his genes."

She scooted back on the bed, away from his touch. Putting distance between them didn't help settle her frazzled nerves. Thinking she'd seen him in the eyes of a tiger and hearing random bits of conversation between the men had not made it real. This, the seriousness in his expression and tone of voice, gave all the rest substance and legitimacy. Her husband, the man she loved, had a wild animal living inside of him. It didn't get any scarier than that, yet her curiosity refused to be shelved.

"I want to see." Maybe if she witnessed his change with her own eyes she could better understand.

Blue eyes narrowed on her as Nash searched her face. "See what?"

"Why are you being obtuse?" She folded her arms over her chest and glared at him. "You know what I'm talking about. Show me, Nash. I need to see it happen."

He rubbed his temples again, but rose and began to strip until his clothes lay scattered around his feet, talking to her the whole time. "I know you, Sunshine. You're going to have lots of questions. I haven't lived with the tiger very long so I don't have a lot of answers. We'll have to figure things out together."

She nodded, distracted by the sight of tanned skin stretched taut over rippling muscles. Jenny's gaze wandered over broad shoulders, defined pecs and six-pack abs. She longed to run her fingers through the sprinkling of dark hair, trace every dip and swell of masculine flesh. She glanced lower, drinking in the sight of trim hips and delineated sinew. Even flaccid, his thick cock was impressive. The base of his long shaft surrounded by a nest of black hair, and his weighty sac hung between powerful legs. She loved everything about him, from the new scars adding to his rugged appearance, to the shimmering awareness in his gorgeous eyes.

This was Nash, her handsome husband, the man she loved regardless of any changes wrought by a bunch of quack scientists. She didn't see any wounds from his fight with the lion—with Micah. She wondered if they'd be visible on the tiger and found she was anxious to see his other form. With a slight nod, she indicated her readiness for him to continue.

Transfixed, Jenny watched as the transformation began to take place. A shiny pelt sprouted from his skin as his legs shortened, his body compacted while simultaneously his nose and mouth elongated into a snout. The whole process took mere seconds before he'd dropped down onto padded paws, Nash's steady gaze observing her from a tiger's face.

If she'd blinked, she would have missed the whole thing.

"Holy fucking hell!" She was shut up in a small room with a huge tiger and unlike at the zoo, there were no bars between them.

Jenny scrambled farther over the bed until her back hit the headboard. Her vision blurred as she squinted then slammed her eyes closed.

Okay, I didn't see that. When I look again, Nash will be there, not a tiger.

She took a deep breath, opened her eyes and blinked, hoping to see something less frightening.

Nope, still a tiger.

Rubbing her eyes didn't make any difference either. That old saying about seeing being believing ran through her mind. What a major understatement. She didn't want to trust her eyes or believe but the terrifying truth stared her right in the face.

Nash had turned into a humungous living, breathing tiger.

If he'd confessed to having an affair, that would be hard to overcome but they would survive. If he'd lost his job and they wound up homeless, Jenny figured she could handle that too. But this was something she had no way to combat. She had no real-life frame of reference to deal with such a shocking event.

Yes, she had seen the tiger before, even registered the fact that its eyes looked very similar to her husband's. But she had not seen Nash turn into an animal. One whose tongue lolled out from between a sharp set of teeth and dripped saliva onto the floor.

Any minute now she'd pass out then wake up to find out it had all been some wacked out dream.

Wait for it. It'll happen.

Only it didn't.

She never lost consciousness. And the big feline's stare didn't waver. He remained motionless with the exception of a rapid twitching of his tail.

A strange rush of excitement swelled. The amazing feat awed Jenny and her curious nature got the better of her. She wanted to see it happen again. Wanted to reach out and explore the animal, feel the changes in his body.

"Does it hurt? It happened so fast." The cat didn't move and she smacked her forehead. "Yeah, like you can answer questions now."

Her entire body vibrated with a combination of excitement and stunned disbelief. She had a powerful urge to stroke his fur but without knowing who was in control, Nash or the tiger, she held back.

What the hell was she supposed to do now?

The overload of conflicting emotions wrung her out and sapped her energy. Drained, she dropped onto the bed, curled her arms over her face and plunged her fingers into her hair. A slight tug resulted in sharp pain along her scalp, which helped center her frenzied thoughts. She wavered back and forth between shock and awe.

"This is so not happening. My husband didn't just turn into a cat and I'm not carrying on a one-sided conversation with Tony the Tiger."

Something cold and wet pressed against her forearm. With slow, measured movements, she lowered her arms. There wasn't even a full inch in between his flaring nostrils and the tip of her nose.

"Jesus, you've got a huge mouth. You could probably remove my head from my shoulders in one bite." Every fiber of her being longed to reach out and touch him but a strong survival instinct stayed her hands.

One corner of his mouth curved upward in a feline parody of a devious smile. That extra long tongue rolled over parted lips.

"You look hungry, but please don't eat me."

The catty grin expanded.

"Ha, a catty grin. That's a good one. Don't go getting any frisky ideas, mister. You can wipe away that foolish smile. I don't care about the rules of the jungle. There will be no interspecies sex happening so get those lascivious thoughts out of your head. A girl has to draw the line somewhere and that's a biggie for me. No bestiality." She glared at him. "I mean it, Nash."

Once again, saliva dripped from his pink tongue.

"Gross. Since you're new to being a cat, I'll give you credit for not knowing this." Her voice dropped to a conspiratorial whisper. "Only dogs drool. Cats are supposed to be more sophisticated and higher class. They don't fetch, lick their balls in public or come when called. You really do need to study up on this stuff if you're going to put on a cat suit."

Tilting his head to one side the tiger seemed to consider her words.

"So." Jenny fisted fingers that itched to explore. "You're in there somewhere, aren't you, Nash? You understand everything I'm saying and are in control of the beasty, right? 'Cause I'm dying to touch you, but I'd be really upset to pull back a bloody stump."

His warm tongue rasped over her knuckles. Jenny smiled at her husband, taking the action as encouragement. Under all those layers of fur lurked the man she loved, and he would never hurt her.

"Okay, I'm going to pet you now. Remember, no biting." Jenny didn't give herself time to think about the insanity of her actions. She thrust out a hand, sinking her fingers into his soft pelt, enjoying the teasing caress of the silky strands along the sensitive skin between each digit. Her hand came away with excess hair clinging to her skin.

"See that." She held her hand before his face. "You're shedding. Guess who won't be sleeping in bed with me when we get home? Not that you'd last five minutes in Florida wearing that heavy fur coat. All the humidity will make you a frizzed-out mess. That is if the subtropical temperatures don't give you heat stroke first." She snorted over the visual that popped into her head.

"I guess we'll be relocating. I'm setting you straight right now though. I don't care what kind of tiger you are, no way am I moving to Siberia." Just thinking about snow made her shiver. "We'll have to figure out a way around the grooming issues. No matter how much I love you, I won't be able to deal with you hocking up hairballs."

Her mind raced. "I have so many questions that I'm betting you don't have answers for. I guess we'll have to learn about all this together."

Jenny let her hands wander over the powerful creature, learning every roped mass of muscle. She luxuriated in the sensation of his beautiful fur beneath her hands, knowing it would feel glorious to rub her naked body against him.

Tracing each stripe, she took her time getting to know this new part of her husband. She placed a palm flat on the floor and compared the size of his paws to her hands. "You've got some big feet, buddy. Any muddy pawprints on the floor will be your job to clean up."

A sudden stream of tears took her by surprise. She hadn't realized she was crying. Giving in to the irresistible impulse, Jenny wrapped her arms around his big neck and hugged Nash close, seeking comfort. Her emotions were all over the place. While she was thrilled to be holding him in her arms, she wept for the ordeal he'd gone through. And she longed to feel his arms wrapped around her while they made love.

Sitting back on her heels, she stared into his eyes for several long moments, laughing as he licked the tears from her face. "Okay, I like the kitty but it's time to switch back."

Blue eyes tracked her every movement as Jenny rose and flicked open the buttons of her blouse. Her voice dropped to a husky, seductive tone as her fingers skimmed over her bared belly and went to work on her jeans. "I need you, Nash."

He watched as she shrugged off the shirt then shimmied her hips while smoothing the denim over her legs. Soon, her bra and panties joined the growing pile of clothes on the floor. As she crawled onto the bed, he had yet to move. Once settled in the center of the bed, she cast him a questioning glance.

Finally the tiger walked to the foot of the bed, crouched down then launched his body into the air, landing on all fours directly over her. A brief flash of fear caused her muscles to tense. Being pinned beneath a fierce tiger had her heart pounding against her ribs. But then she looked into her husband's eyes and relaxed, if only slightly.

Fiery fingers of desire spread through her. Man, beast or a combination of both—they were all Nash. And she needed to feel him held tight within her body.

Her legs rubbed together restlessly. "Nash, I want you. Make love to me."

Extending her hand, she held her breath and waited to see what he would do. There was no hesitation. He rubbed against her outstretched hand, a gravelly purr rumbling up from his chest.

The tiger playfully licking her wrist was gorgeous, but the urge to hold the man within her arms became too powerful to deny. Jenny scratched behind his ears, basking in the cat's enjoyment, before trying to tempt him again.

"Don't you want me?"

He remained in the same position—head cradled in her hand—and allowed his body to change form. In the space of time between one stuttered heartbeat and the next, her husband took the place of the cat. The bristle of a few days' beard stubble rasping against the tender skin of her palm.

"I know it's a major adjustment and a lot to take in. If you need time…"

Maybe it was all the crazy movies she watched that made Nash's changes exciting for Jenny. Could be her endless hope there were other life forms in the universe and to one day meet one. Possibly her love of animals. She didn't know or care why. He was still Nash, and she still wanted and needed him. For better or worse.

"Jesus, Nash. Would you get with the program and fuck me already."

Jenny's other hand shot forward, fingers trembling against his sensual lips. Acceptance and love and need all crashed over her. "I don't need time, Nash. Just you. All of you."

Chapter Nine

ॐ

How he'd ever managed to find and marry such an amazing woman never ceased to blow his mind. From the first time their eyes had met across the yard at a mutual friend's barbeque, Nash had known Jenny was special.

Her irreverent hard-ass attitude and flippant wisecracks were an attempt to disguise the truth. One only had to look past the surface to see great depths of compassion and love. Over the years, life had taught her to hide that soft, vulnerable underbelly. Otherwise people took advantage of her abundant generosity and walked all over her.

There was no mistaking the love and acceptance he saw in her warm brown eyes. Acceptance for all of him. He knew coming to this point had not been easy on her. He loved her all the more for her steadfast faith and trust in him.

He hated that they didn't have much time. There was so much he wanted to say. In a few hours he would go back to the lab, put his life on the line to bring an end to their immoral practices, save others from suffering as he had. Their plan was dangerous and he might not make it back out alive.

Nash was a master at hiding his emotions. He had learned to keep his inner thoughts off his face, but he let the mask slip now so Jenny would see everything he didn't know how to say. In response, her body tensed and she shook her head.

"No! You wipe that look off your face, Nash. This isn't goodbye." Her breath hitched. "You're coming back to me. In one piece! Anything else is unacceptable." In desperation she grabbed his shoulders and tried to shake him. "You hear me, Nash? I will not lose you a second time. I can't!"

Previously, he hadn't felt the need to tell Jenny about the precautions he'd taken. His current work had not been extremely dangerous, but he'd learned in the military to take steps in protecting those things precious to you in case of the unthinkable. He never imagined they'd actually have use for the safeguards he had put in place, but in light of recent events he knew the time had come to prepare her.

He took a deep breath and forged ahead. "The jewelry box I gave you on our wedding day has a false bottom."

She kept shaking her head, refusing to listen. Nash held her face in his hands. Stubborn to a fault, Jenny clamped her eyes shut.

"Sunshine, you have to listen. This is our insurance policy. I took these precautions for you but never thought they'd be needed before this mess."

When she looked at him, Nash felt as if the weight of sadness in her eyes would crush his heart, but he had to continue. "If you can't figure out how to get the panel open then smash the box."

"Nash," she gasped. "I can't destroy my wedding present."

"Jenny, if something goes wrong tonight you will do what I tell you. Get the key from the jewelry box and go to the airport. The bank is in the Bahamas." Nash gave her detailed instructions, all the while praying she would never need to access the contents held within the bank box—a new life. He'd always worried about his old life and enemies catching up with him. Not only had he obtained new passports and IDs for them, he'd also stashed away funds in an untraceable account. Enough to support her in comfort for the rest of her life. "You go find yourself a villa in Spain or Italy, anywhere far away, and never look back."

"Fine, I'll get out of the States and go somewhere no one knows me." She gave him the words but her dark eyes were defiant.

"Whatever crazy plan you have running through that pretty head of yours—forget it! I need to know that you're safe or I'll be distracted. The only way I have a chance tonight is if I have my head on straight and focus on what I'm doing. I can't do that if I'm worrying about you."

She tried to turn away but he held her steady. "Promise me, Jenny." Her word was a bond she didn't take lightly and wouldn't go back on. "Promise me that if things don't go as planned you'll do as I said."

"Fine." She all but spat the word at him. "If anything goes wrong, after I kill Micah for not bringing you back, I'll get out. But that's not going to happen, Nash. You're coming back here. Back to me. So don't tell me that you'd want me to continue living and find a new love. No way would you leave me alone to lie on some sultry Mediterranean beach in a bikini with slick foreigners circling me like sharks."

A possessive rage swelled in his chest and rumbled from his throat as the threatening growl of a fearsome animal.

"There, keep that image in your mind for motivation. The last thing you want to do is leave me alone, brokenhearted and vulnerable. The perfect affluent and susceptible target for Rico Suave, the gigolo anxious to find a meal ticket."

The sassy witch had the nerve to flash a triumphant smile at him. "Not gonna happen, Sunshine. You're mine!"

"That's right, you big, bad beasty. I'm all yours. Always!"

Jenny intended to keep her promise, but she never specified exactly what part she agreed to. Should the unthinkable happen, she'd empty out the safety deposit box and get lost. That she'd do for him. But she could not, would not, stay hidden in the cabin while Nash risked his life to do the right thing.

Hell no!

This would not be their last time together. They'd have a tomorrow, a future together. She intended to make sure of it.

She took a long hard look at her husband, no longer seeing the man he'd been but the one he had become. A dichotomy—part man, part tiger. An intelligent human with high moral values, a protector of life, combined with one of the world's largest and most powerful alpha predators, a true carnivore that must kill to thrive.

God help her, but the idea of unleashing the beast thrilled Jenny. She wanted him, all of him. Not the restrained Nash or the slow and tender lovemaking they usually shared. She wanted him wild, crazed with need. Feral.

He brushed a soft kiss across her lips and while she found it to be sweet, it was the last thing she wanted...so she bit him. Hard. A crimson bead formed where she'd punctured his lip.

Momentary shock dilated his pupils, crowding out the blue and darkening his eyes. "Sunshine, I'm hanging on by a thread here, trying to be gentle."

"Don't you dare hide from me, Nash. I don't want nice, polite sex." To emphasize her words, she dug her fingernails into the thick muscles of his shoulders. A brief flash of pain narrowed his gaze before heat spread across his handsome face.

"You don't know what you're asking for," he growled.

"Yes I do. I want all of you. Everything. Man and beast. I want savage fucking. Raw, untamed hunger. Carnal mating. Take me, Nash. Claim me. Mark me as yours."

Stunned, she stared as he tossed back his head with a violent roar. Muscles swelled, rippled beneath his skin. When he grinned down at her, Nash and the beast had truly become one. His pupils were elongated slits and his teeth— Holy shit! His canines had turned into wickedly sharp fangs.

Icy tendrils of fear skated through Jenny but didn't have time to take root. He moved with inhuman strength and speed, flipping her over onto her hands and knees. Not giving her a chance to steady herself, Nash lifted her hips, holding her right where he wanted, and shoved her legs apart, creating a space for himself.

His rough tongue rasped a heated path along her spine from the crease of her ass to the nape of her neck, firing Jenny's blood. Her dangling breasts felt swollen and heavy, her nipples ached, needing to be touched. His teeth raked over the sensitive curve where neck met shoulder and she trembled in anticipation. Would his teeth pierce her skin? She didn't want to consider why the mere idea caused her pussy to clench, a hot gush of arousal readying her.

She nearly wept with joy as the broad head of his cock probed between her legs, parted her folds. He stroked over her slit once, twice.

Quivering in need, Jenny moaned, "Nash. Now! I need—"

Anything else she would have said was lost as the full length of his cock slammed into her, hard and demanding. Without pause he withdrew, leaving her empty. Her body convulsed, belatedly struggled to keep him inside her.

Her cry of dismay cut off on an abrupt thrust, the force of which would have driven her forward had he not kept a secure hold around her waist.

She'd done it. Jenny had freed the beast within the man. On each forward thrust he slammed against her womb and his balls slapped her clit. Each withdrawal was a complete retreat. The rapid pace kept her from catching her breath. Her fingers dug into the linens, scrambled for purchase. Nash never slowed. His movements were fluid as waves crashing into the shore, in and out, fast and relentless. Like a machine—tireless, precise and devastating. All she managed was to hang on and enjoy the incredible ride.

Pleasure coiled in her core, winding tighter and tighter, building to mammoth proportions. She wanted to slow down the orgasm hurtling toward her at a breakneck speed, but lacked the strength to resist. The violent pounding made her breasts swing. Her nipples dragged across the sheet, sparking embers that shot straight to her pussy. The flames burned hot, enveloping both of them.

The weight of Nash's sweaty chest pressed her torso farther into the mattress. His teeth scraped her flesh then pierced the skin, animalistic and possessive. The bright flare of pain fanned the fire, igniting her orgasm.

Consumed by the conflagration, Jenny soared. Coiled tension burst, showering her in ecstasy. It was too much for her body to contain. Her back bowed and she was assaulted by brutal spasms. She felt as if she exploded, shattered into a million pieces.

A tremendous roar echoed around the room as scalding jets of semen filled her, driving her even higher until her body, unable to withstand any more pleasure, gave out. She collapsed with Nash covering her like a damp electric blanket.

At some point the pieces floated back to Earth and reformed. She came back to herself—sated, exhausted and happy—held within the shelter of her husband's strong arms.

The room dimmed as day turned into night and still they clung to each other.

With all her might, Jenny prayed the sex had scrambled Nash's brain enough that he'd forget all about saving the world. She was weak. Neither her heart nor soul would survive losing him a second time.

As if hearing her thoughts, Nash spoke the four words she dreaded.

"I have to go."

Jenny wanted to be childish and greedy, throw a tantrum, demand he stay. Instead she kissed him, putting all her emotions into the soft mating of their lips. "I know."

She slipped from his embrace, pulled on her robe and gathered his clothes. "I'll make some coffee while you get ready."

The forced smile was meant to be supportive, but if the worry lines etched into his face were any indication, had missed its mark.

Chapter Ten

❧

Strapping on weapons reminded Nash of gearing up for a military mission. The familiar rush of adrenaline surged through his blood and kicked up his heart rate. He knew the other three men were skilled and had confidence in their abilities. That didn't stop him from worrying. Not about the others, they would remain focused and do their part. But what about him?

In his peripheral vision, he observed Jenny as she fiddled with her coffee cup. Her hands shook and she shifted about on the chair, unable to sit still.

She looks more nervous than a whore in church. He almost laughed over the irreverent thought, spoken in Jenny's voice, playing through his head.

He hated the idea of leaving her there alone and knew she'd have a hard time keeping her promise, but taking her with them wasn't an option. He considered having one of the men stay to protect her. There were too many reasons that wouldn't work. Jenny would throw a fit over having someone stand guard. Plus the team already had too little firepower and couldn't afford to leave any of their limited resources behind.

He moved in behind her and stroked a hand over silky blonde hair. She startled and would have jumped out of her own skin had he not firmly placed a hand on her shoulder.

"It's just me, Sunshine." Nash massaged her tensed shoulders. "Relax. Everything's going to be fine." At least he hoped so.

"I-I should go with you. As a lookout—"

"Jenny!" His tone was harsher than he'd intended. Nash took a breath and made a conscious effort to soften his voice.

"We've been through this. If you're out there, I'll be distracted. I need you here, safe and sound, waiting for me. I need you to be patient. Just a little while longer. Then I'll take you home."

Vivid images formed in his mind. Him and Jenny, strolling along the beach holding hands as they'd done on many occasions. This time they silently observed the antics of the two children frolicking at the water's edge. A family.

The scene felt right. Good. So good he decided to do whatever it took to make it reality. Jenny had always wanted kids but he'd asked her to wait, give him a few more years before fully settling down. Life was short. He didn't want to delay anymore. In fact, he experienced a sudden yearning to take that final step with his wife.

He leaned over, brushed her hair away from the slender column of her elegant neck. Unable to resist the temptation of her smooth skin, he placed a tender kiss on the sensitive spot behind Jenny's ear before speaking in a soft tone so only she would hear. "I've been thinking. Scary, I know. But isn't it past time we start making some babies."

She gasped as he breathed the words against her ear. "It's time for me to grow up, find a less risky career. Hell, maybe I'll even stay home with the kids while you're out nursing the world back to health."

Jenny turned to face him, her big brown eyes full of hope and longing. She reached out to trace the line of his jaw while searching his expression. "Do you mean it, Nash? You're finally ready?"

"Yeah, Sunshine. I mean it. If you still want to have kids—" Her fingertips pressed against his lips and cut off the words.

"Of course I do! I know what you're thinking. I'm not afraid of what you are…what you've become. I love all of you, which now includes the tiger." She shrugged. "If you pass the ability on to the kids, we'll deal with it—together."

There was no mistaking the resolve in her steady gaze or assured voice. And no denying the end result or its affect on him. His chest grew tight as his pulse soared and his breathing turned erratic. He had not thought it possible to love Jenny more than he already did but he'd been wrong.

"I love you too, Sunshine. You stay here…safe. One last time, Jenny. Then I'm done saving the world. Someone else can take a turn."

A lone tear rolled down her cheek. Nash kissed away the salty drop.

Without another word, Jenny walked the men to the door and wished them luck. The pounding of booted feet stopped until the lock clicked into place, then resumed. Feeling suddenly weak, she leaned on the heavy barrier and whispered a prayer for her husband's safe return.

Busy—she had to stay busy. She needed the distraction. Otherwise, she'd drive herself crazy with worry and never be able to keep her word.

A glance around the small cabin didn't offer any ideas. She'd cleaned the kitchen, almost scrubbed the Formica right off the countertop. The table had been put to rights with a red gingham cloth in place. Nash had stoked the fire before he left.

Her lip quivered and she clutched at her tight chest.

Don't dwell on him, she chastised. Nash is fine. He's well trained and knows what he's doing!

Jenny moved around the room, straightened the pile of magazines on the coffee table and fussed with the crocheted blanket hanging over the back of the couch. She shifted a few knickknacks on the mantle, brushing away imaginary dust. When she ran out of tasks in the living room, she headed for the bedroom.

Her gaze landed on the rumpled bed where such a short time ago, Nash had fucked her. Hard and wild. More like the animal than the man. God, how she'd loved every hot and glorious touch. Every frantic second of their coming together.

The air still reeked of sex. Jenny took a breath, drawing the seductive scent deep into her lungs.

She rubbed her flat belly, remembering the words she'd waited so long to hear. *"Isn't it past time we start making some babies?"*

Perhaps they had already gotten a start on their family. The seeds of their future could even now be growing in her womb. At the mere thought, heat spread through Jenny.

The waiting was going to drive her insane. They'd only arrived at the cabin two days ago, but for lack of anything else to do, she stripped the sheets from the bed and found a fresh set in the cedar chest. Making the bed only took a few minutes. Since she had yet to even unpack, the room was as tidy as it had been the night before.

In the bathroom, she gathered the towels they'd used then took all the linens to the small laundry room off the kitchen. Jenny added some detergent to the washer and turned it on. Back in the main room, she glanced at the door then to the clock on a side table.

"Twenty minutes," she huffed. "Stupid clock must not be working. No way has it only been twenty minutes." With exaggerated stomping she made her way over to the table, grabbed the clock and shook it a few times. Then she held it to her ear, irritated by the sure and steady ticking sounds.

"I can't do this!" She set down the clock with a decisive *thunk.*

"Sorry, Nash. I tried. Really I did! But if I stay in this cabin for another minute, I'll pull my hair out."

Nash had left a loaded pistol in the nightstand—just in case. She made sure the safety was on and tucked it into the side of her fur-lined boot. Her jacket hung on a coat tree by the door. Jenny pulled the warm down-filled garment over her arms and drew the zipper all the way to her throat.

"I'm just going to check the perimeter." The lie didn't relieve her anxiety.

After locking up, she pocketed the key. It didn't take her long to make a complete circuit around the property. The crisp night air and open space eased the sense of claustrophobia she'd felt while inside.

Without the cloaking haze of city lights and pollution, millions of stars were visible in a sky that appeared endless. She wasn't much of a nature girl, but enjoyed the musical sound of crickets chirping.

"What a beautiful night." The peace and serenity made it hard to believe violence would be shattering the calm a few short miles away. "It'll be safe to take a short walk."

Sometime later, God only knows how long she'd been tromping around in the woods, Jenny had to face facts. She was well and truly lost. "I'd give twenty bucks to have the damn GPS bitch talking to me in that unflappable monotone of hers right about now."

"Fuck!" A root hidden beneath some crumpled leaves caught the toe of her boot and she almost face-planted. "The things I do for that man. Ugh!"

Perhaps a strenuous walk in the dark over rough terrain after having wild-monkey-sex with her shapeshifter husband had not been one of Jenny's brightest ideas. Sore muscles protested the activity and the wound on her calf ached something fierce. The cold had long ago penetrated her warm clothing to settle deep in the marrow of her bones.

"I could be sitting in front of a roaring fire, sipping hot chocolate laced with brandy, but nooooooo. What fun would there be in that? I'd much rather be lost, freezing my ass off in the middle of a scary forest on a pitch-black night."

Having arrived in a clearing, she plopped down on a fallen tree for a good pout. "All right, smartass. Find yourself a way out of this one." With her elbows propped on her thighs, Jenny hid her face in her hands.

Rustling sounds in nearby foliage ended her self-disparaging train of thought and she snapped to full attention.

Tentative yet curious, a brown-and-white rabbit hopped out of the safety of its hiding place. They studied each other for several moments. The animal's eyes appeared intelligent. She wondered if it might be a shifter like Nash and Micah.

"Hey there, Thumper. I bet you know the way back to the cabin, don't ya."

The rabbit cocked its head to the side as if considering what she said.

"How about you do that presto-magico thing Nash does and turn into a human?"

They continued to observe each other. "No? That's okay. I don't mind. How about if you hop on over to my cabin then and I'll follow you?"

The bunny merely twitched his whiskers at her in a rather suggestive manner. "Don't be getting any frisky ideas there, Thumper. I'm married to a tiger, and to him, you're nothing more than a light snack."

She looked around the quiet clearing. "No, huh? Well maybe there are some frogs around here somewhere. I wonder how many I'd have to kiss before finding a handsome prince who will take me to a land far, far way."

All of a sudden the rabbit went on high alert. Its tall ears twitched and moved this way and that, picking up the faintest sounds. If she wasn't so frightened, Jenny would have laughed as the image of an old rabbit-ear T.V. antenna being moved around to find the best reception popped into her head. But this was no laughing matter. The small animal sensed danger nearby and without sparing her another glance, it darted off through the underbrush to safety.

"Hey, wait. Where are you off to in such a hurry?" Jenny could remember no other time in her life when she had felt so alone and vulnerable as she did in that moment. "Thanks a lot, pal."

The night had become devoid of all sound and movement except for the gentle breeze flirting with tree branches high above. Nothing else moved as the entire forest held its breath along with her, waiting in keen anticipation.

Something stirred off to her left, made no attempt to cover its passage. She considered attempting to hide, but her body froze to the spot and wouldn't follow orders. "M-maybe it's a hiker or a forest ranger?" Not that either would be wandering around in the dark. "Only deranged serial killers and horror movie starlets would be that stupid." How had she managed to sink so low as to join such dismal ranks?

The man who entered the clearing, definitely no hiker, wore a tailored business suit. If that had failed to clue her in to his importance, his posture, the very way he held himself, projected confidence and superiority. There were a few things out of place screwing up the image though. His gray hair was in a state of utter disarray, decreasing the impact of his expensive haircut. A dark red stain had been absorbed into the fibers of his otherwise impeccable clothing. And then there was the gun held in his right hand and pointed directly at Jenny. Not a chance in hell he hadn't seen her either. The man's angry gaze was locked in on her.

"Well, I'm just fucked six ways to Sunday now, aren't I," she mumbled. The verbal banter usually had a way of easing her tension and drawing a secret smile from Nash. Too bad he wasn't there to smile and ease her stress.

Oh boy!

When Nash found out she had not stayed in the cabin…shit. He was going to be one hell of a pissed off beast. She'd hate to be in this guy's shoes when her husband caught up with him.

He moved closer and she just couldn't keep her mouth shut. "Didn't your mother teach you it's not polite to point?"

Chapter Eleven

ℬ

Nash sighed in relief as the facility's alarms were silenced. The harsh sound was hell on his sensitive hearing. And being back in the building made his skin feel too tight. He had to get out of there...soon.

The team had made quick work of neutralizing the security force and clearing the building. While Kyle and Sam were checking another area, Nash and Micah came to the last exam room along the corridor. He shivered in revulsion. The whole place brought back memories he'd rather forget.

A glance through an observation window stopped his heart. Weltman and two of his white-coat lab rats were busy hovering over a woman, who was restrained to an exam table.

Micah swiped a card taken from one of the security agents through the access panel. The door opened with a soft *whoosh* into a scene straight out of his worst nightmares.

The woman muttered incoherently and made sluggish attempts at breaking free of the restraints. Nash knew how strong the sedatives favored by the facility were and was shocked she wasn't unconscious.

Weltman turned to face them, blocking their view of what was being done to the woman. "Ah, if it isn't my two wayward shifters. Welcome back, gentlemen. You're just in time to meet our latest subject."

"Step away from her," Micah ordered.

They both held guns leveled on him but Weltman didn't appear to be concerned in the least. In fact, he shrugged off the threat. "Wouldn't be a smart move to harm me." He tapped the side of his head. "I'm the only one with the details you need."

"Step back from the woman." Nash growled, taking a step closer. "We already downloaded everything we need from the computers."

The lab techs turned, hands raised, and moved to the side.

"You're a little too late. I decided to take a different approach with Ms. Renard, since my feline expert turned out to be such a disappointment." He glanced toward the doorway. "Will Dr. Southerby be joining us?"

A loud growl rumbled from Micah's throat. Nash glanced at the other man to see his eyes had changed. The lion was very close to the surface, barely restrained. Nash wondered what exactly the zoologist was to his friend.

Ignoring the question, his attention moved to the techs. "Has she been injected?"

The man simply held up an empty syringe in answer to the question.

"With what?"

"She's a hybrid." Weltman puffed up his chest with pride. "A combination of red fox and wolf."

"Damn it! Get her untied. She's coming with us."

He glanced at Micah, concerned over the way the other man remained silent, except for the occasional growl, while staring at Weltman. Something must have happened between the two men that Micah hadn't felt the need to share.

"None of you are leaving." Weltman's calm statement should have given him pause, but the man had obviously lost his marbles. Nash stayed focused on his mission objective—getting out alive.

The techs helped the woman to stand. He admired her strength as she pushed them away, standing on her own two feet, even if she was rather wobbly. "Are you okay? Can you walk?"

Her head whipped in his direction, a curtain of thick black hair with crimson highlights flaring out over her shoulder. Her ice blue gaze locked onto him with piercing intensity as she took his measure. Clear eyes, unaffected by the drugs they'd pumped into her system. "I'll walk out of this loony bin on my own two feet, thanks."

A shot rang out, the sound almost deafening in the small space. Weltman cried out in pain and grabbed his side where blood darkened the fine material of his suit.

"Jesus, Micah. What the fuck are you doing?"

"He was reaching into his pocket."

"Whether I use the device to summon security or not, my team is going to take you two down. You'll never step foot outside the facility."

Micah tossed back his head and laughed. "It's over, old man. Your team has been taken out. No one will be coming to save you from paying for what you've done."

The woman took a lurching step forward, steadied herself, and moved closer to Nash. "Mind telling me who the hell you are?"

Nash gave her a quick rundown of both his and Micah's involvement with the lab and their plans. When he finished speaking, she nodded. "Lance Corporal Shira Renard. Second Division out of Camp LeJeune."

A Marine. Good. It explained her fortitude and unwillingness to take assistance.

"I was selected for this special detail. The first of several dozen scheduled to arrive here over the next few months. We were told this would involve specialized fitness testing and training for battle."

A side door they hadn't noticed opened and Kyle Slater stuck his head into the room. "Locked down and secured. Charges are set." He nodded toward Shira. "She a subject?"

The door behind them swished. Nash and Micah turned in time to see Weltman slip out of the room while they'd been distracted.

"Son of a bitch!" Nash moved to follow, but Micah held him back.

"Stick to our objectives." He pointed to a blood trail on the white tile floor. "Weltman won't be hard to find. We have to get everyone out and blow this place. Then we can worry about tracking him down."

Against his better judgment, Nash relented. "Fine, let's move."

The rest of the mission went smooth as silk. Itchy to get back to Jenny, he glanced at the assembled group. Slater was the explosives expert and because of his previous job working security for the facility, he knew the place inside and out. Micah was on a call with the General making arrangements for a meeting with the woman. There was nothing left for Nash to do and his instincts were screaming that he needed to get back to Jenny. And he had to go after Weltman. He wasn't letting that bastard get away.

Perceptive as ever, Micah seemed to read his mind. "Are you headed back to Florida after this?"

Nash shrugged. "Briefly." He and Jenny would have to relocate. Make a start somewhere no one knew their names.

"If you need anything…"

Micah didn't need to finish. Nash knew what he was saying. The sentiment went both ways. "Same here."

"Get out of here then. Go take care of your wife. We'll wrap this up and be on our way soon."

Nash said his goodbyes and left the conventional weapons behind. Everything he needed lie inside him. Rather ironic that the weapon Weltman had created would be the means to his own destruction.

Once he moved out of the open and into the shelter of the dense woods, he shifted. The tiger had no problem sniffing out the blood trail. Silent and deadly, he stalked through the forest. In no time at all, he'd caught up with his prey.

Each minute away from Jenny was like a thorn in his side. Soon he realized that she had left the safety of the cabin. He could smell her scent lingering in the air. His hackles rose.

In a hurry, Nash didn't waste time circling Weltman or surveying the area. Never slowing in his rapid stride, he crouched low and sprung forward in a powerful leap, landing a short distance from his target. He would have pounced, attacked Weltman from behind, but not with Jenny in danger. He roared a warning to the other man. If he hurt Jenny —

Nash's heart froze when Weltman spun around, holding a gun to his wife's temple. Tucked tight against his side, she was undeterred by the weapon. The spitfire fought his hold — kicking, biting and cussing. From the smug expression on Weltman's face, the bastard knew exactly who he'd captured. Hell, Nash himself had placed her picture in his personnel profile while instructing subordinates on Nanotech's stringent requirements for background checks.

"Ah, there you are, Crosby. I figured you'd be along eventually. Imagine my surprise at finding this hellcat out here alone." Weltman flashed a truly evil smile. "You really are slipping. Don't you know better than to leave a woman wandering about unprotected? She is a rather pretty liability though. And feisty. I like them feisty!"

"Let me go and I'll show you feisty, you warped motherfucker."

"Your woman has a rather foul mouth, Crosby, but that's okay. I'll teach her discipline and respect before I'm finished with her." The sick bastard suggestively rubbed his crotch against her ass. "After we have some fun first, of course."

Weltman stroked her temple with the gun. "Not quite adequate compensation for all the grief you've caused me, but I'll make do."

"Aww, do you expect us to feel bad for you? If you're looking for sympathy, it's in the dictionary between shit and syphilis."

The bastard pulled back his arm and hit her with the gun. It didn't knock her out, but Jenny sagged against him, forcing Weltman to support her weight. She almost succeeded in pulling him off balance.

Nash didn't blink as he watched, waiting for the perfect opening. The slightest slip from Weltman was all he'd need to make his move. No matter what else happened in the small clearing, he would not allow Weltman to leave with Jenny.

Her physical assault got nowhere, and Weltman simply ignored her verbal attack. He spoke of his big plans in an almost wistful tone that raked on Nash's nerves worse than fingernails scratching on a chalkboard.

"You and your friends have only succeeded in delaying the inevitable. Do you really think I'd be so stupid as to keep everything in one place? Thanks to you, I know better than that. All you've managed to do is slow my plans marginally. Before winter's end, the Marine Corps will have an elite unit of powerful shape-shifting soldiers. But that won't be the end."

Nash didn't blink and his attention didn't waver. He remained crouched low to the ground, ready to spring into action at the opportune moment. Hearing Weltman's plans made him sick and sealed the man's fate. When he struck, it would be a fatal blow.

"Once word gets around, as it always does, the technology of the Predator Project will be in great demand. Can you imagine the bidding wars between foreign nations, each desperate for what only I can provide."

Between the blow and listening to his diabolical plot, Jenny appeared stunned. She hung limp over Weltman's arm as he continued. He spoke loud and sure as if lecturing before a captivated audience.

"I will have all the power. I will control nations, decide who will be the strongest, who will survive. I alone will rule the world and have control over its armies."

Weltman shifted his weight and Jenny dropped to the ground as he made a sweeping gesture with his right hand. She rolled, pulling a pistol from her boot, but before his arm completed the movement or she took aim, Nash sprung.

Weltman landed on his back with more than four hundred pounds of enraged tiger coming down on his chest, knocking the breath from his lungs.

Nash didn't hesitate. He followed the beast's instincts, went right for the man's throat, sharp teeth tearing at vulnerable flesh and bone. He bit, clawed and growled, blinded by the bloodthirsty predator's anger over the threat to its mate. Only Jenny's soft voice brought him back from the edge.

"Stop, Nash! Come on, honey. I doubt he tastes very good. Too much piss and vinegar." She moved to his side, placed her hand on his head and stroked behind his ears. She showed no fear, secure in the knowledge that he would never hurt her.

"Come on, hot stuff. Take me home and I'll let you eat me instead."

She took a firm hold of the scruff of his neck and he immediately became passive. He stared down at Weltman, morbidly fascinated by the blood gurgling from the open wound and soaking into the ground.

Jenny dropped to her knees beside him. Grabbing his fleshy jowls, careful to avoid the blood on his fur, she turned his face toward her and away from the grizzly remains of his former employer.

"It's over, Nash. Let's go home. I need you!"

Jenny expected him to shift, but Nash remained in tiger form. At least he'd stay warm with all that fur covering him, even after taking a dunk in the stream to wash away the blood. If he shifted back and walked the distance naked, he'd probably freeze to death. The temperature had dropped drastically since she'd left the cabin.

223

She laughed aloud over the idea of Nash walking through the woods, bare-assed and shivering, his limp dick slapping against his thigh with each step.

The tiger's big head swung in her direction and he glared at her. That only got her laughing harder. "That new fur coat of your comes in pretty handy."

He continued to walk at her side and she began to wonder if he'd be able to shift back again. She sure hoped so. Shifting into a tiger was a handy trick, but she wanted a man sleeping next to her in bed at night.

"You can change back, right?" She eyed the big beast warily. "You're now unemployed and I'm only working part-time. I sure as hell can't afford to keep your big butt supplied with raw meat."

She got the distinct impression he was doing his best to ignore her. "Cat got your tongue?" That one got her laughing so hard she had to stop walking and catch her breath.

By the time they reached the cabin her fingers were numb and her entire body ached. She looked forward to a long soak in the hot tub. Still a tiger, Nash walked the perimeter before letting her unlock the door. "Just 'cause you're paranoid doesn't mean they're not out to get you, right?"

He growled a warning and head-butted Jenny's thigh. She stumbled into the room, cursing him until she caught what appeared to be a feline smile on his big mouth. "All right, catman." She licked her lips, noting how his blue gaze followed the movement, and peeled off her jacket. "You're gonna have to switch back if you want to get laid. Otherwise, I'll have to unpack my vibrator."

She headed for the bedroom, peeling off her clothes and left a trail in her wake. She was reaching for the suitcase when strong arms wrapped around her, drawing her into the shelter of Nash's warm body.

His nude and very aroused body.

"There's no need to unpack your rabbit when you've got a tiger by the tail, Sunshine."

Epilogue
Six Months Later

೪೨

Nash stepped out onto the wraparound porch and drew the clean mountain air deep into his lungs. Out of habit, his gaze swept the landscape for any potential threat. Spring had arrived in their little corner of the world almost overnight. Bright wildflowers and green grass swayed in the gentle breeze.

They had made a cross-country move—left crowded beaches of Florida behind for a rural home near the Continental Divide. He still didn't feel completely safe.

Over the past few months he'd learned to utilize the tiger's sharp senses while in human form. That's how he heard the SUV rambling along the dirt road toward the house long before it became visible. The vehicle parked beneath the shade of a huge cottonwood tree. Jenny climbed out, swung a backpack over her shoulder and shot him a bright smile.

He toyed with the gold wedding band she'd placed on his finger the day they married. It had only ever left his hand once, when taken by the wacked-out Nanotech scientists. Nobody would ever take it from him again.

Her bag hit the floor with a loud thump as Jenny's arms wrapped around his waist and her body pressed close.

"I take it the test went well?" Never once had he doubted her, but she'd been nervous about the series of written tests to become a nurse. Not that she had to work. The money he'd stashed away over the years would last a lifetime if they were careful about their spending. But Jenny needed to be busy taking care of people. She thrived while helping others.

"They're actually going to hand me a license to torment sick people. Can you believe it?"

"Congratulations, Sunshine. You worked hard and earned it. I'm very proud of you."

She held him tight, her tongue sneaking out to create a hot trail along his neck. His body hardened as she nibbled at the corner of his jaw.

"Mmm..." she purred. The vibration of her lips heated his blood. "I learned some interesting things in that anatomy class." She feathered kisses over his jaw until their lips met.

Taking full advantage of what she offered, he fastened his mouth on hers, their tongues tangled, devoured. Never losing contact, he walked backward, taking her inside, moving together through the house until the mattress hit the back of his thighs.

He needed to be inside her, a part of her. They pulled at clothes, both eager for each other. He had planned an evening of romance, but it would have to wait.

They fell onto the bed, a tangle of limbs with Jenny on top. Her eyes were heavy-lidded and filled with desire. He knew that look, what it meant—she wanted to take control, which suited him fine. For the moment.

"Show me what you learned."

Jenny wanted to show Nash how much she loved and appreciated him. She told him, often, but words couldn't express the depth of her emotions.

Their life wasn't perfect. She didn't expect it to be. But Nash made her truly happy. She spent more time laughing than crying. With each passing day, her love for him grew even stronger. They had no idea what the future would hold or the long-term effects of what the Nanotech scientists had done to Nash, but they'd face it together.

"I'm going to make you come so hard, Sunshine."

One of the benefits of his altered DNA was his amazing recuperative abilities. He could go all night, his body ready for her again only minutes after climaxing. They would make love over and over until she finally collapsed in exhaustion. The man was killing her with sex. *Oh, but what a way to go.*

"You always do!"

He moaned as she moved down his body, tasting and arousing him with lips, teeth and tongue. She knelt between his legs and watched his pulse beating in the thick veins snaking around his long cock. Without hesitation, she fisted his shaft, fingers failing to meet, and took the velvety crown into her mouth. She sucked him deep, found each of his sensitive spots with her tongue. Reaching lower, she took his weighty sac in her hand and began the gentle clenching she knew he enjoyed.

His fingers tangled in her hair, massaged her scalp, touching her in the only way available to him. "Yes, Sunshine. Take it all. You love sucking my big cock."

Yeah, she did. But she had a surprise for him. She watched him from under her eyelashes, knew he was close from the tension in his jaw and the way his balls had drawn tight. Never breaking eye contact, she released his cock and sucked a finger into her mouth, taking care to get it nice and damp with her saliva.

"Oh shit," he groaned. "What have they been teaching you in those classes?"

She pulled the finger from her mouth and laughed over his worried expression. "You're gonna love this."

Jenny took his cock back into her mouth, lavishing his soft skin with attention. Applying strong suction, she drew him to the back of her throat, distracting him from the damp finger rimming the tight pucker of his anus. Finally delving inside, she fingered his ass, searching out that magical spot guaranteed to blow his mind. When she found it, Nash tossed back his head and roared. The sound was much more animal than human.

She launched an all-out attack on his senses, sucking his cock in a steady rhythm while fucking his ass with one finger, another stroking the shallow groove behind his balls, massaging his P-spot from the outside.

The combination had a powerful effect. Nash bucked his hips, matching the pace she set. His sac, cradled in her palm, spasmed. Jenny swallowed convulsively as hot jets of cum hit the back of her throat. His climax seemed endless, continuing until he begged her to stop.

She curled up next to him, pillowed her head on his chest. His heart pounded frantically beneath her ear as he struggled to breathe.

"Jesus, woman. I think you sucked the life right out of me. I can't move."

"Oh, I don't know about that, tiger." She took his still semi-hard cock into her hand, grinning when it immediately responded, swelling and lengthening. She'd woken the beast, felt it prowling, pulling at its chains.

That wasn't good enough. Jenny wanted him unleashed. "Maybe some more mouth-to-mouth resuscitation will fix you right up," she taunted.

Nash moved—fast. Before she knew what had happened, Jenny found herself flat on her back. His knee nudged her legs apart and he settled his pelvis in the cradle of her thighs.

"You wanted the animal, Sunshine. Well, you've got him." With one commanding thrust, he hilted inside her.

She asked for no quarter and he gave none. Nash fucked her, wild and untamed. Wrapping her legs around his hips and digging her fingernails into his back, she held on tight, riding out his passion. She would never get enough of this side of him, when he became more animal than man, driving her to amazing heights of pleasure.

Nash pulled out suddenly, flipped her over onto her stomach. He lifted her hips, putting her on her hands and knees, their favorite position. One hard thrust and she came apart.

As she orgasmed — each of the many times he propelled her over the precipice — Jenny screamed his name.

Life with her shape-shifting husband would never be dull. She wouldn't have it any other way.

FOXY LADY

 જી

Dedication

ɷ

To Chad, Mike, Ryan and Daniel. You never fail to inspire me.

Trademarks Acknowledgement

ɷ

The author acknowledges the trademarked status and trademark owners of the following wordmarks mentioned in this work of fiction:

Band-Aid: Johnson & Johnson Corporation

Girl Scouts: Girl Scouts of the United States of America

Humvee: AM General Corporation

Jeep: DaimlerChrysler Corporation

Prologue

ഇ

"You are one seriously sick fuck!"

And that was putting it mildly.

Shira Renard was well and truly screwed. Thick leather restraints bound her wrists and ankles to a cold metal examination table. The quack scientists had also secured leather straps across her chest, pelvis and thighs.

She'd considered Gabriel Weltman a bit quirky, but weren't all the geeky science types a bit touched? With his gray hair and expensive suits he looked the part of a seasoned businessman. Now she knew different. His appearance had deceived her. The kook had gone way beyond weird and shot right to the top of the totally-out-of-his-freaking-mind category.

While only half listening to his screwy plan for world domination, she searched for a way out of this mess.

"Through my diligent work, Nanotech is decades ahead of any other scientific research organization. What we've accomplished is better than curing cancer—more important. Not only have we discovered how to splice human DNA and combine it with that of the world's fiercest predators, we have perfected a procedure to successfully bind the manipulated DNA in a human subject, modifying genes that would normally reject such an incompatible pairing."

She glanced at the ceiling and although she didn't see any security cameras the doors were air-locked, requiring the swipe of a magnetic card. Of course, first she had to get out of the restraints before worrying about the door or any security personnel.

As Weltman continued blathering on, he picked an imaginary piece of lint from his expensive suit. "Just picture an army of soldiers more powerful than any other. Trained fighters with the strength and instincts of the world's most dangerous animals. Extreme predators. Imagine how much governments would pay to possess such an unstoppable force."

Interesting, but she had no desire to become one of his freaky experiments.

"Sure," he shrugged, "we've had our share of failures. Some of the early subjects didn't survive the procedure. Others didn't maintain their human intellect. They were reduced to savage beasts intent only on hunting prey and had to be put down."

Put down? Jesus! He was talking about the human beings he'd screwed up as if they were insignificant, of no real consequence. The man was a psychopath with delusional fantasies of power and wealth—a total megalomaniac. And she'd landed right in his clutches.

"We have had two major successes, both felines. A lion and a tiger."

Oh my!

"And let me guess, next will be a bear."

Ignoring her flippant remark, Weltman continued as if she hadn't spoken.

"In your case, I have created something a bit different."

In her case? Oh hell no!

"A hybrid, so to speak. The combination of DNA from two animals— *Vulpes vulpes* and *canis lupus*."

"Huh?" Shira had no clue what *vulpes* meant but didn't *canis* refer to canines? No way was he turning her into a dog! Not in this lifetime. She'd kill him first.

"You, Lance Corporal Renard, will receive the DNA of the crafty red fox and vicious gray wolf."

"No. Fucking. Way!" Shira spit out the words while struggling against the restraints, frantic to break free. "I didn't sign up for any hokey genetic crap."

Weltman merely smiled and that cocky grin was by far the most frightening thing she'd ever seen. The man had gone completely off his rocker.

"You won't get away with this, Weltman. You can't go and fuck around with my DNA without my consent. I'm a Marine. You'll have the entire Corps on your ass."

The old bastard tossed his head back and laughed with such maniacal glee icy tendrils of dread skated along her spine.

"You are priceless, Renard. Where do you think I got the funding for the Predator Project?"

No! No fucking way! She didn't want to hear any more. If her hands had been free she would have stuck her fingers in her ears and chanted "lalalalala" to drown out his words.

"I have the full backing of the United States Marines, and you volunteered for this detail."

"No!" she hollered. "I didn't sign on for your insane Predator Project. I'm here for fitness evaluation and training."

"So very naïve for a soldier." With an absent gesture, he made some notes on a clipboard.

"There are twenty-two ways to kill a man with no weapon other than bare hands." Shira spoke calm and clear. Her statement had the desired effect, drawing his attention to her. "I am trained in each and every one of those ways. But before I kill you, Weltman, I'm going to make you suffer. You see, I have also perfected the most painful interrogation techniques known to man. It's my specialty. I can draw out the process, make it nice and slow. Excruciatingly slow."

"Hmm." He considered what she'd said for a moment. Good, maybe he'd see the light and stop this insanity before it went too far.

"Those skills will come in handy once we start your predator training." He scratched down more information on the papers then tossed the clipboard onto the counter.

She flexed corded muscles, yanked at the restraints, creating a metal squeal of protest from the table but getting no closer to freedom. Jesus, this was like some bizarre nightmare or late night movie. How the hell could it be happening to a Marine in the United States?

"Give her the sedative."

One of Weltman's assistants stepped forward and ran an alcohol swab over the bulging vein in her forearm then shot her up with a clear fluid. The effects were almost instant. Lethargy stole through her body, zapping both her strength and will to fight. Her vision wavered and her mind grew sluggish. Shira screamed long and loud. All that came out was a pathetic whimper.

"Now, my dear, we make history."

She fought against the drugs, focused on survival. Regardless of the medication, her heart slammed into her rib cage as the techs approached with a much larger syringe. The liquid it contained swirled and various colors shimmered like some kind of psychedelic light show at a rock concert. Weltman's voice distorted, slowed and stretched, making no sense to her muddled brain.

The pinch of the needle drew her attention back to the tech. A silver needle attached to the syringe disappeared beneath her skin. The man smiled at her as he pushed the plunger. "Don't fight it."

Easy for him to say.

Fire raced up her arm and Shira screamed in her head, the sound never made it past the lump of fear clogging her throat. She felt the liquid burning through her veins, slamming into arteries. Organs shriveled, contorted in agony. Her back arched as her entire body fought against the foreign substance, the leather straps cut into her skin. She prayed for the sweet escape of death from the misery spreading through her, altering more than flesh and blood, warping her brain functions.

The door swished open and two men entered the room—strangers. Weltman turned, stood in front of her, blocking her view of the newcomers.

"Ah, if it isn't my two wayward shifters. Welcome back, gentlemen. You're just in time to meet our latest subject."

Shifters, were these men the ones he'd turned into cats?

Oddly, the stuff changing the very fiber of her being helped to clear her thoughts as she caught a glimpse of the two hunks. Both men were tall and rugged, probably in their mid-thirties, military background obvious in the way they held themselves and handled their weapons.

One man had wavy dark blond hair pulled back in a tail. His dark brown gaze swept the room and zeroed in on Weltman. The other had straight black hair, a bit long and rumpled, and laser-sharp blue eyes that missed nothing.

"Step away from her," the blond ordered. He seemed to be in charge.

"Wouldn't be a smart move to harm me," Weltman taunted, and tapped the side of his head. "I'm the only one with the details you need."

"Step back from the woman." The dark one actually growled, moved closer. "We already downloaded everything we need from the computers."

The lab techs moved to the side, giving her a clear view of the soldiers. No, Weltman had called them shifters, whatever the hell that meant.

Weltman rambled on about some expert feline doctor. Shira tuned out the useless information and reassessed her body. The fires eating her alive from the inside began to lessen and she was able to take a breath that didn't singe her lungs.

Another growl registered and her gaze snapped to the blond. Maybe the drugs were still screwing with her vision because his eyes were doing something funky. They glowed and his pupils warped, stretched.

"Has she been injected?" This from the dark one.

The bastard lab tech held up the empty syringe.

"With what?"

Good question! She'd like to know a hell of a lot more about what had just burned through her body.

"She's a hybrid—red fox and gray wolf." Weltman spouted the same line of crap he'd given her. "That is, if she survives the conversion."

"Damn it! Get her untied. She's coming with us."

Surprisingly, the techs moved to follow the blond's orders and began untying the restraints.

"None of you are leaving."

Weltman really was bonkers if he believed that. The two guys had guns trained on him. How the hell did he think he'd stop them from doing whatever they wanted?

The idiots in the lab coats grasped her arms as Shira struggled to make her legs work. Not wanting their slimy hands on her, she shoved them away.

"Are you okay? Can you walk?"

She whipped around to face the dark-haired guy. Genuine concern shadowed his eyes. Could she trust him enough to go with him?

Did she have any other choice?

"I'll walk out of this loony bin on my own two feet—"

Her words were cut off as a shot rang out. Weltman squealed and grabbed his side. Blood seeped between his fingers, darkening the suit material.

"Jesus, Micah. What the fuck are you doing?" the dark one asked.

"He was reaching into his pocket."

Weltman interrupted the argument. "Whether I use the device to summon security or not, my team is going to take you two down. You'll never step foot outside the facility."

The blond, Micah, threw back his head and laughed. "It's over. Your team has been taken out. No one will be coming to save you from paying for your crimes."

Shira pitched forward, fought to remain upright, and stepped closer to her would-be saviors. "Mind telling me who the hell you are?"

Nash Crosby introduced himself and gave her a few down-and-dirty details, including the fact that both men had worked security for Nanotech before being brought into the Predator Project. Micah had actually agreed to the injection — crazy bastard. Nash had been jacked, taken into the project by force.

Her gut instinct told her these two men were on her side.

"Lance Corporal Shira Renard. Second Division out of Camp LeJeune. I was selected for this special detail. The first of several dozen scheduled to arrive here over the next few months. We were told this would involve specialized fitness testing and training for battle."

The side door opened and another dark-haired hunk stuck his head into the room. Damn, all these gorgeous guys were from the deep end of the gene pool. Shame she was in no shape to really appreciate her handsome rescuers.

"Locked down and secured. Charges are set." The new guy nodded toward her. "She get injected?"

The door behind them swished before anyone could answer. They all turned in time to see Weltman slip out of the room, taking advantage of the distraction.

"Son of a bitch!" Nash moved to follow, but Micah held him back.

"Stick to our objectives." Micah pointed to a blood trail on the white tile floor. "Weltman won't be hard to find. We have to get everyone out and blow this place. You can track him down after the lab's destroyed."

For a moment, Nash looked ready to argue before he nodded. "Fine, let's move."

"You good to go?" The new arrival, Kyle Slater, flashed a penlight into her eyes, checking her pupils.

"I'm fine. Let's get the fuck out of here." She'd figure out what to do about the shit they'd jacked her up with later. These men were now her best chance of making it out of Weltman's fun house alive.

They hit the hall running. Slater tossed her a gun. Shira checked the chamber and clip then thumbed off the safety.

The place had seemed pretty normal before. Now, with only the illumination of backup strobe lights and the staff gone, it was eerie as hell. They'd already cleared out the lab employees and gotten what they needed from the computers. God, she hoped that meant they knew how to fix what had been done to her.

Once outside they moved across the yard at a rapid clip and gathered near two SUVs while Slater prepared to blow the place. Micah got on the phone, setting up a meeting with a general he thought would be able to help her.

She already noticed differences in herself. Everything ached but she felt stronger and all her senses were on high alert. Her vision was sharper, better in the dark. And her nose was on overload with all the different scents of first the lab and now the wilderness.

"Renard," Micah called. "Come on, you're with me."

She climbed into the back of an SUV. The driver wasted no time getting out of there. The vehicle barreled down the private road.

"So what now?"

Micah raked his hands through his hair, pulling the long strands free of the elastic band, and turned to look back at her over the top of his seat. "Sam and Kyle—"

They were almost at the main road when Slater detonated the facility. The multiple explosions were followed by an impressive fireworks show. She sighed as debris and flames shot up into the sky.

The lab may be out of commission but she had a feeling the nightmare was just beginning for her.

Needing answers, Shira brought Micah back to the conversation. "Who are Sam and Kyle?"

"This is Sam Atherton," he clapped the driver on the shoulder. "You already met Kyle Slater, who just blew up the lab. They're going to take you to General Hughes. He's a good man. He'll figure out how to handle your status with your unit after the dust settles.

"I have to make a stop in Africa but I'm not deserting you. I'm picking up Dr. Southerby, who helped me after I'd been injected. I'll be sending a medic to work with you until we can make it there. His name's Lex McLean. Lex will have access to all the Predator Project files."

Micah sighed, scrubbed at the beard stubble covering his jaw. The man looked prepared to drop some heavy info on her. Shira sat up straighter, listened carefully.

"Look, I'm not going to sugarcoat it. The next few weeks are going to be hell. The human body isn't designed to accept animal DNA. You're facing several surgeries to help your body adjust. Then we'll have to see if you've gained the ability to shift—"

"Shift? Weltman called you and Nash his wayward shifters. What exactly does that mean?"

"This part is going to be hard to believe. If we had more time, I'd show you but for now you'll just have to take me at my word." He searched her expression, she wasn't sure what he was looking for but he must have found it because he kept talking. "Nash and I were injected with feline DNA. Both of us can change forms or shift into our animal counterpart. For Nash that's a tiger. I shift into a lion."

She came real close to laughing but something in his dark eyes stopped her cold. Whether it was true or not, Micah believed what he said.

Oh Christ!

"So that means…" She couldn't say it. Didn't even want to think it.

"I'm not sure what it will mean for you. Weltman said he did something different with you, injected you with a combination of—"

"Red fox and gray wolf," she finished for him. "Yeah, I know."

"So in a couple of weeks…"

Shira forced down her rising terror. "In a couple of weeks, I may or may not turn into a furry beast."

Great!

Let the games begin.

Chapter One

ဆ

What day is it?

Hell, he wasn't even sure what time zone he was in.

Lex McLean had made a rough drive out of the Congo and hopped on a tiny puddle jumper that bounced around the sky, threatening to crash at any moment. Next had been the long flight over the Atlantic to New York crammed like a sardine into an uncomfortable seat with no leg room. The final insult of the endless journey had been a seemingly endless drive upstate into the Adirondacks.

He was tired, cranky and hungry as hell. Standing at the door to the infirmary, he sniffed the air and realized the rank scent assaulting his nose was coming from him. Great, he could add stinky to his list of complaints. He desperately needed a shower, a good meal, a firm bed and at least eight uninterrupted hours of sleep, not necessarily in that order.

Since he was running on pure caffeine, the smart thing to do would be putting off meeting the Marine he'd been sent to help until tomorrow. With his curiosity running so high, Lex knew he'd never shut it down long enough to sleep.

Might as well get this over with.

He'd read the file on Lance Corporal Renard from cover to cover. Her rise through the ranks had been marked with commendations and praise from her commanding officers. Renard pushed herself hard, took on the toughest assignments and every available training opportunity. Water survival, evasion and resistance, jungle warfare, interrogation, escape training—you name it and Renard had not only mastered the skill but excelled while doing so.

On paper she was one badass bitch. He wondered how well she'd coped with the physical changes and new reality since becoming part of the Predator Project. Red fox and gray wolf—a wicked combination. The first and only hybrid.

The woman he watched through the observation window lying on a hospital bed took his breath away. Midnight black hair followed the graceful column of her throat to brush the top of her shoulders. Tempting golden skin covered toned flesh. In repose, she appeared so soft and sweet it was hard to imagine her facing combat situations, regardless of what her file said.

Of course, he also had a difficult time picturing her turning into an animal. Never would have believed it possible until he'd seen two of his friends shift right before his eyes. One second Micah Lasiter and Nash Crosby had stood before him as men. In the blink of an eye he'd been looking at a lion and a tiger. He'd also got a real up close and personal glimpse of the lion's sharp teeth.

Lex had seen a lot of things during his time in the military but nothing had prepared him for watching his buddies turn into animals.

How the hell he was supposed to help Renard deal with her new reality was beyond him. Other than the information he'd gathered from Micah, he had no concept of what she faced. Plus, she didn't know him from Jack so why the hell would she trust him?

In the same situation, after having already been tricked and genetically altered, he'd go on the offensive. Fight to take back his life, no matter how fucked up it had become.

Lex moved into the room quietly, not wanting to disturb Renard's sleep, but the desire to get closer wouldn't be denied. Her chest rose and fell with each deep, even breath. Thick black lashes fanned out over her cheeks and her eyes moved rapidly beneath her eyelids. He wondered where her dreams had taken her, what her fantasies were.

God, she was beautiful.

His cock swelled and stood stiffly at attention as Lex pictured her naked body caged beneath him, the two of them moving together. He'd capture the sweet sounds of her pleasure, take them into himself. Fuck her all night long.

He added getting laid to the top of his growing list of needs.

Jesus, McLean. Get your shit together.

He had to be professional, detached, stop thinking of her as a woman and remember the lance corporal was an assignment.

Yeah, and the erection tenting his scrub pants was real professional.

Lex took a calming breath and fought to get his own racing heart under control as he placed two fingers against the firm pulse beating in her slender neck. The immediate electrical charge racing up his arm almost made him jerk away from her.

Holy shit! What the hell just happened?

Felt as if she'd electrocuted him. Damn, he must be more tired than he'd thought.

* * * * *

Finely honed instincts had Shira playing possum. She kept her breathing even, forced her body to relax. Not one muscle twitched as she lay perfectly still and assessed the situation.

Her arms and legs felt heavy, weighed down but thankfully not restrained. Whatever they'd drugged her with had affected her vision. Indistinct shapes surrounded her, giving the impression of a hospital room. She closed her eyes, relying on her other senses. The astringent smell of antiseptic filled her lungs and various equipment beeped. Sure seemed to be a hospital but she knew better.

She'd been here before, visited often in her nightmares since being rescued. Funny thing was she didn't remember returning to the Middle East or being captured. Must be the drugs fucking with her memories.

Then there were the really bizarre visions racing around in her head, wreaking havoc on her nerves. Vivid dreams that felt so real. Her, racing through the forest, jumping over downed trees, splashing across a stream, digging her claws into damp peat moss, tail whipping out behind her like a flag. Yup, in her sleep she had fur and a tail. Damn drugs had her mind convinced she'd turned into a fox. Now all she needed was a henhouse to raid.

Thank goodness her sense of humor remained intact. Shira had a feeling she was going to need it.

The air-locked door opened with a whoosh. Someone wearing blue scrubs took a syringe from a med box and injected fluid into the IV line connected to her left hand. Her head swam but the moment she was alone again, Shira rose and stumbled drunkenly across the room, leaning heavily on the IV pole. Her hip banged into a metal table as she reached the drug box and pulled out two pre-filled syringes that had needles attached. With her blurry vision she couldn't read the labels and had to hope it was something powerful.

She made it back to the stretcher and struggled to heave her leaden body onto the thin mattress. Sweat coated her skin and she was out of breath by the time she got settled with the syringes secreted beneath her thigh.

Consciousness came and went, along with fleeting impressions. For a while, Shira swore she heard the incessant plink of water dripping. At one point the fluids entering her vein burned a path along her arm and into her chest. And she heard the Arabic bastard's taunting comments ringing in her head.

This time she'd take out as many of them as she could before making good on her escape.

The door swished open again. She bit the inside of her cheek, the pain helping to clear muddied thought processes. Someone moved into the room. The pungent scent of sweat and male musk moved in on her right side. As two thick fingers came to rest against her neck she heard a masculine gasp.

Shira struck out at her adversary. Her right arm came up under his, fingers grasping firm triceps. Caught off guard, she was able to pull him closer. Her left hand came out from under her hip, swung across her body. She slammed both needles deep into his shoulder and depressed the plungers, holding on tight as his large body bucked.

Having no idea what she'd injected or how it would affect her captor, Shira gritted her teeth and held on tight. He cursed and thrashed, dragging them both to the hard tile floor. Darkness closed in, fading her vision until everything went black.

* * * * *

Jerking awake, Shira shoved at the heavy body sprawled against her side, weighing her down. The crisp scent of pine and musky outdoors still filled her senses from her latest romp through the forest. For a minute her head spun before settling in the present. Her vision cleared and she gasped, shocked to her core.

The sexy blond was not at all what she expected to see. Sun-kissed skin covered lean muscle and gave the impression of a California surfer. A fox but not the furred kind. And definitely not Arabic. Either the man had turned traitor or she wasn't in Afghanistan...

But then where the fuck was she?

Surely she wasn't being held prisoner by her own people. Her mind refused to wrap around that horrible idea. No it had to be something else, but the last assignment she remembered had to do with physical assessment and training.

Fuck it. She'd figure out this mess later. Right now she wasn't going to squander what might be her only chance to make a break for it.

She ripped off a strip of tape securing the IV line in her arm. Grabbing the blond's ID badge, she quickly patted him down for any weapons. Finding nothing, Shira used the bed rail to pull herself up and staggered to the door. She swiped his badge through the card reader and watched as the light turned from red to green.

Too easy!

She smelled a trap but there was no choice other than play out the hand she'd been dealt.

Her left leg wasn't working well, forcing her to lean heavily on the wall as she lurched down a hallway lined with rooms similar to the one she'd just escaped. Turning a corner, she spotted a portable x-ray machine and other devices that convinced her she wasn't back in the Middle East. They didn't have such advanced medical equipment.

She spotted the security camera at the same time a shrill alarm pierced her aching head. A cold draft on her rear end told her all she needed to know about the flimsy hospital gown. Barefoot, the left half of her body refusing to function, she didn't stand a chance of taking down the two burly soldiers headed straight for her.

They were Army. American Army.

Aw, fuck. This was really bad.

Refusing to go down easy, Shira fought with everything she had until they got her pinned to the ground and a sharp needle pierced her thigh. Whatever they pumped into her hit as they dragged her back into the room with surfer boy. As the darkness closed in again, she stared at his handsome face, memorizing his features and plotting his downfall.

* * * * *

With his last memory one of being attacked, Lex came up swinging. His fist made a satisfying connection with someone's jaw before General Hughes' booming voice brought him up short.

"Sergeant McLean — at ease, son."

Memories flooded into his mind as he rubbed at gritty eyes. He'd been checking on Renard, feeling for her pulse when she'd stabbed him with a needle. Whatever she'd shot him up with had burned through his body. While the drug had left him groggy, he also felt strong. Stronger than ever before.

"What's the damage, sir?"

He watched the general's expression turn grim and steeled his spine in preparation for bad news.

The general appeared fit and commanding as always, but Lex noted new streaks of gray in Hughes' brown hair, along with deeper lines and obvious signs of fatigue marring his hard features.

Waiting the other man out, Lex glanced around his surroundings. He was still in Renard's exam room, lying on a second stretcher someone had brought in for him. She'd been returned to the room and this time leather restraints secured her at the wrists and ankles. He pushed away images of her nude and erotically bound, and focused on the general.

"When Nanotech was hit, Lasiter's team confiscated copies of their records and procedures. We've been going over everything with a fine-toothed comb, looking for ways to combat the altered DNA."

Shit! This was worse than he'd thought. The general never stalled or wasted time sharing well-known facts. Usually the man got right to the point. That meant bad news for Lex. He fisted his hands at his sides and struggled to remain calm as he listened to Hughes talk.

"Slater grabbed a drug box on his way out, which has been helpful with treating Renard. Poor girl had a bad reaction to medications and her last surgery did not go well." Hughes paused to clear his throat. "Our doctors believe the hybrid combination of fox and wolf she received to be the problem.

"She'd passed the point of no return and the only way to help was to choose one of the animal's genes over the other. Following Weltman's procedure notes, she was injected with red fox genes this morning. She's had some adverse effects from the anesthesia but had otherwise been doing well."

Lex didn't like what he was hearing. The general resorting to following Weltman's procedures meant everything had gone FUBAR. Tired of waiting for the other shoe to drop, he interrupted. "With all due respect, Sir, just tell me. What the fuck did Renard shoot me up with?"

Hughes sighed, scrubbed at the day-old stubble covering his jaw. "One syringe contained Haldol."

Okay, a large dose of the antipsychotic drug explained why he'd dropped like a rock. Still, Lex sensed there was more to it than that. "And?"

"The second syringe contained one of Weltman's genetic cocktails."

Christ, no!

His heart palpated and his chest tightened as if trapped in the jaws of a powerful vise. One second he experienced a heat wave and with the next erratic heartbeat he broke out in a cold sweat. His hands went numb and breathing became a chore as Lex was hit with the overwhelming desire to escape. He shoved away the oxygen mask a nurse tried to fit over his mouth and nose.

"What?" he panted. "What was it? What the fuck am I?"

"Wolf."

With one word the general changed his entire life. All the information Micah had shared with him filled his head. He faced multiple surgeries to help his body adjust. Then at some point in the not-so-distant future it would happen—he'd sprout fur, claws and fangs. He'd shift into a wolf.

A freakin' werewolf.

Life as he'd known it was over. His career shot to hell.

Lex glanced over at the restrained Marine and silently vowed to get his revenge. When she least expected it the bitch was going down.

Hard. Slow. Painfully.

Chapter Two

For the first time in—had it been weeks?—he felt human, which was a joke because part of his humanity had been stolen from him. Lex had been living in hell since that first night on base, when the spitfire Marine had attacked him. After too many surgical procedures to count the doctors deemed him adjusted.

Physically—sure. Mentally was a whole different ballgame.

And later today they expected him to shift.

Christ. He didn't know if he could go through with it. Sure, they'd told him the basics of how it worked and what to expect. But the idea of turning into a wolf still freaked him the fuck out. Considering the things he'd seen and done, for fear to grab hold of him, twisting his insides in knots, took some seriously bad shit.

He felt good—stronger than ever. And he knew making it through this day would require all the strength he could muster.

"Mornin', Sir." He paused to acknowledge a lieutenant he met in the hallway before entering the security office. Something was up. As the door opened he was hit by a high level of chatter and excitement buzzed in the air. His entrance had gone unnoticed by the security personnel who had gathered around a monitor, debating over a black and white image.

"What the fuck is it?"

"All three components are wired into the base, which controls the device."

One of the guys tapped the screen. "Here's the power source."

Moving in closer, Lex studied the oddly shaped device unlike anything he'd ever seen in the field. Three prongs from a central base, each vastly different. He didn't see any components of an explosive or communications device. There were also two sets of batteries, something he presumed to be a power charger, and a tube containing a liquid or gel-like substance.

Short and thin, the first probe curved inward. The second was thick and long, phallic in appearance. The third consisted of four balls of increasing circumference connected by a thin shaft.

He had definite suspicions as to what the image represented. Listening to the men's conversation confirmed his thoughts.

"We need to open the box."

"Renard will throw a fit. I'm not crossing that bitch."

Renard? The package was the Marine's?

"So you're just going to hand it over to her not knowing what the hell that is?"

"Oh come on, it's some fancy vibrator. What else could it be?"

"Who the fuck knows. You haven't taken the time to find out."

"Captain will be pissed if we don't open it."

"The captain will never know unless one of you dumbasses tells him."

"I'm going to offer to do the job for her."

Lex almost laughed aloud as he imagined what the kick-ass-and-take-names-later Marine's response would be. Would almost be worth it to hang around and watch.

Unseen, Lex slipped back out into the hallway, turning over what he'd learned in his mind. Renard had ordered one hell of a sophisticated sex toy and had it delivered to the base. Ballsy move. Knowing it would get scanned, pretty desperate too. Must be damn important to her.

Exactly what he'd been looking for — a weakness.

His lips curved up into a twisted grin. Poor little Renard, all jacked up and in need of sexual release. Probably spent a fortune on the toy. She'd sure miss it if something happened to her new best friend.

She'd just made it easy for him to hit her where it hurt most. Take away the toy and he'd be taking away her fun. The bitch deserved that and more for what she had done to him.

And he intended to make sure she got exactly what was coming to her.

* * * * *

Standing naked before the mirror in her quarters, Shira chewed on her bottom lip and struggled to still the slight trembling in her hands. This wasn't her first attempt at shifting from human to animal — far from it — but it would be her first glimpse of the red fox that now shared her body, mind and soul.

Not separate entities sharing a body, the woman and the fox were a combination of each other. And the ability to shift came with many benefits — increased strength, sharper senses and the keen instincts of a predator.

"Yeah, so why the hell are you so afraid to see the fox?" she asked her reflection.

She had no answer other than the old adage that seeing is believing. Witnessing her shift would make this craziness all too real.

The process of shifting was neither difficult nor painful. It happened fast. Blink and she'd miss the whole thing. Yet somehow being able to alter her form and watching it happen were two vastly different prospects.

"Stop being such a baby. Just get it over with already, Renard."

Shira took a couple of calming breaths then reached out for the animal. The shift took over and she rolled with it. Familiar disorientation briefly stole her focus. When she looked at her reflected image once again, the fox sat on its hindquarters, tongue lolling out of a mouth full of wickedly sharp teeth.

The kooks at Nanotech had injected her with a hybrid combination of gray wolf and red fox, which fucked her up. She'd been reinjected with only fox but the lingering wolf DNA made her larger than the average red fox. The reddish-brown fur was lightest at her snout and grew darker along her flanks. Her tail, legs and ears were black and brown. Covering her jaw and trailing down her breast and belly was a patch of soft-looking white fur Shira longed to run her fingers through.

Preening before the mirror, she decided that she made one heck of an exquisite fox. She turned around and looked over her shoulder at her bushy tail swishing around in the air. *How freakin' cool!*

Like a kid before a funhouse mirror, she tried out different expressions and found she could manage a rather comical parody of a smile. Then she scrunched up her snout, pressed back her ears and let a low growl rumble up from her chest. With a sharp yip she jumped back a few feet, startled by the ferocious image.

Holy crap! She wasn't just a pretty face.

Ha! Take that, Lex.

The medic was such a grump. So she'd attacked him while in the grips of some wild hallucinations, shot him up with wolf. She'd apologized. What more did he want? He should be thanking her for the enhancements he'd gained with the animal DNA.

Micah Lasiter—the guy who'd gotten her out of Nanotech's insane asylum—had sent Lex to help her adjust.

Well, she had screwed that all to hell. Now he was in the same boat as she, adjusting to the animal sharing his body.

Mmm...and what a body it is.

Tall, muscular and sexy as all get out—Lexilicious was one fine hunk of man. Shame he was such an aggravating, cocky dickhead.

And he was scheduled to go outside and shift for the first time today. If she wanted to get in a peaceful run without the grump along, she had to shake her tail.

Another quick shift—paws and doorknobs were a no go—she shrugged into a robe and headed for the security desk. She saw no sense in getting fully dressed since she'd be shucking her clothes again in a few minutes.

The pre-run ritual was one she despised. A general announcement went out on the security communication band. Those not involved with the Predator Project were told they were working on training animals. Then a special collar—for tracking and control—was fitted around her neck.

Understanding the need for the device didn't mean she had to like the intrusion on her freedom. And if one of the supervising soldiers thought she was out of control they could shock her with almost a million volts.

Shira shivered. As part of her training she'd been tased. It was an experience she never wanted to repeat.

In its remote location, untamed mountain lands surrounded the base. A huge chain-link fence kept civilians and large wildlife out. It also kept her from going too far while in animal form.

Once out of sight from the populated section of the base, Shira stripped off her robe and set it on a tree stump, along with her flip-flops. Picturing the fox allowed the change to sweep over her.

The scent of a hare hit her snout and she scampered off into the underbrush for an exhilarating game of chase.

* * * * *

Picture the wolf. Don't fight the change. Let it happen.

Micah's words echoed through his head on a continuous loop. Years of training helped Lex remain calm, keep his breathing even and his thoughts focused.

There's nothing to it. Just let go.

Yeah, easier said than done. Micah's first change had been effortless. He'd been angered by a perceived threat to Becca. The change had taken him by surprise. Lex had to work to make it happen. He stood outside—cold, naked and vulnerable—with a shock collar around his neck.

He took a calming breath and allowed the pictures of gray wolves the scientists had showed him to fill his mind. Some of the wolves he'd seen were gray and white, others had mostly brown fur and a few had been shades of black. He tried not to think about the color variations and instead trained his thoughts to their form. Wolves were pretty similar in structure to large dog breeds. Tapered snout, narrow chest, powerful back and legs—they were built for stamina and ideal for covering long distances quickly.

How the hell was he supposed to get his human body to change into a wolf? Especially when he experienced an odd sense of disorientation.

Tossing back his head, he groaned in frustration. Only what escaped him was a long, mournful howl. Lex shivered as he looked down to find a furry chest, lean forelegs and big black paws.

Holy shit, he'd done it. A yip left his throat and the wolf's body took a quick sidestep. Glancing around, he realized that everything looked sharper. Most colors washed away to crisp variations of black, white and gray. And the smells...wow.

Run!

The word had barely entered his brain before the animal took over and he zoomed through the woods, hurtling downed trees with ease, sniffing the crisp air. He felt wild and free. Powerful. On top of the world.

Instincts kicked in as he explored the landscape, pausing to leave his own scent in various locations. He called out, searching for others of his kind, but got no response.

Lex ran for miles, avoiding areas occupied by the soldiers. He played in a stream, chasing fish, and eventually lay down in the shelter of some shrubs to rest. He must have dozed off at some point because he jolted to awareness as the most glorious scent teased his nostrils. His entire body went on high alert as he crouched in the bushes, patiently waiting to catch a glimpse of his prey.

His nostrils flared as a rustling nearby captured his intense focus. He remained still and in place until the most amazing creature appeared. The female bounded, twisting in the air, snapping at the butterfly it tried to capture.

Drinking in her heady scent had his groin tightening as his cock swelled and his balls tingled. He had to have her. Yet Lex continued to wait.

Eventually, the butterfly flittered away and something else caught the female's attention. She shot off through the brush. In an instant, Lex was on her, giving chase. Peat moss cushioned his paws as he ate up the distance, closing in on her flank. When the female noticed she had company, she put on a burst of speed.

Over, under and around obstacles, the pair raced through the woods, across the stream and along the fence line. Faster and stronger, he could have taken her to the ground at will but found the game too much fun to cut short. He enjoyed the way her lithe body quivered when she felt his hot breath across her backside. And if he didn't know better, Lex thought the canine grin shot in his direction had come-and-get-me written all over it.

The female enjoyed the game as much as he did.

But running with his painfully hard cock flapping against his belly and his balls bouncing was not fun. Putting on a burst of speed, he overtook the female. Sharp teeth grasped the soft, vulnerable flesh of her neck as his bigger body drove her to the ground beneath him.

She whined and barked a sharp reprimand. Lex didn't let go. He'd won and she belonged to him. He had every intention of ramming his cock deep inside her warm body and filling her with his seed.

Sudden jolts of electricity slammed into him, driving his shaking body from the female. He rolled to his side with a sharp yelp. Muscles contracted involuntarily, the pain leaving him breathless and incapacitated. He watched in shock and disbelief as the female rose and raced away.

Damn it!

Then he saw them. Half a dozen soldiers surrounded him, moving forward with caution. One held a black box. Human intellect warred with animal instincts. He wanted to rip the soldiers to shreds and go after that sweet piece of tail. But he'd been taken down because what he'd been doing was wrong.

God, he hadn't cared if the female had been willing or not. He would have taken her either way.

There was a lot more to being a shifter than he'd considered. Not the least of which being that when his intellect won over and he changed back, Lex lay nude on the ground surrounded by a military team.

Off to the side, holding a robe wrapped tightly around her, witnessing his humiliation—his nemesis. Renard.

Jesus, the female his wolf had been so desperate to fuck was Renard.

Could this day get any worse?

* * * * *

Shira counted her lucky stars as she made her way back inside. One minute she'd been happily playing in the forest. The next she'd been trying to outrun a wolf. A very aroused male wolf.

When he'd covered her, caging her beneath his powerful form, she'd been so wet and ready to fuck. The wolf's shaft had been long and hard and she'd wanted every firm inch slamming into her dripping folds.

Then the soldiers had arrived, just in time, and she'd realized the wolf had to be Lex. The bastard.

Jesus, and she'd almost let him fuck her in their animal forms.

There may be tons of sexual tension between them but their mutual hatred kept their lust in check.

Until today.

The animals didn't give a shit if they liked each other.

She needed to get off in a big, bad way. It was the only way to ease the need to fuck her sworn enemy.

Lex was such a baby, holding her hallucination-induced attack against her. Sheesh! When the hell would he get over it and move on? Then they could get it on.

First things first. A stop at the security office would get rid of the hateful collar.

"Hey, Renard. I was just headed to your quarters. You got a package." The security officer, Jake Hampton, held a plain box bearing a generic shipping label just out of her reach.

Thank you, Jesus. Her prayers had been answered.

It was about time. She'd called her favorite toy store and placed a rush order— paying extra for express shipping—and waited impatiently for it to arrive. Sweet relief from the constant ache Lex inspired was almost within her grasp.

Jake shot her a sultry grin as he rubbed his fingertips over the white cardboard. "Of course, we had to scan it..."

That stopped her short for only a moment. But with the tension and frustration riding her hard, she didn't care if the whole base knew she'd ordered a vibrator.

"You could have the real thing, darlin'," one of the other guards taunted and crudely grabbed his crotch. "All you had to do was ask."

Another joined in the game. "Or maybe begged a little."

"Not if you were the last man on earth, Chavez," she huffed.

"If the lights start to dim..." Jake teased.

"Well then you'll have all sorts of yummy visions dancing around in your head."

"Hell, I already have those," he muttered under his breath.

With that, Shira snatched the box out of his hands, turned and dashed down the hallway, anticipation putting extra pep in her step. Her own fingers had never been enough. She required extra stimulation to find release. And the bad boy in her hands was guaranteed to send her soaring.

Halfway through the door she had the box ripped open then upturned it over her narrow bed, shivering in delight as each item hit the mattress. Grabbing scissors off the desk, she set to work on the air-tight plastic imprisoning her new playmate.

Her hands shook as she traced her fingertips over the most wonderful device ever created by man, the Ultimate Pleasure Wand. Damn, was it gorgeous and worth every penny she'd paid.

The first articulation was short, thin and covered with little bumps, perfect for pleasuring the clitoris. The second was what every woman dreamed to find in a man. Eight inches long, perfectly curved to hit the G-spot, thick as her wrist, and riddled with simulated veins to create the most delightful friction.

But that wasn't all. Oh no. The final wicked appendage consisted of four balls of increasing diameter connected together by a thin shaft for anal play.

The entire device was covered by the latest compound that felt like human skin and contained six vibrating bullets to ensure maximum enjoyment. And it heated up too. *Oh hell yeah!*

Damn thing did everything but take you out to dinner, practically rendering men obsolete. The only drawback she could see were batteries losing their juice but she'd purchased both regular and rechargeable ones. A tube of tingling mint lube completed her order. Shira figured she was better prepared than a Girl Scout.

She twisted off the base, grabbed the first battery, considered which way it was supposed to go in and dropped it into the chamber. When both batteries were in place she screwed on the bottom and hit the power button.

Nothing happened.

Okay, so she'd probably put the batteries in upside down. Fixable. Shira opened the bottom again and upturned the vibe. Only one battery plopped out onto the mattress.

"What the fuck?"

She peered into the guts of the vibe and saw the other battery nestled in place. Firmly in place.

"No. Don't do this to me," she pleaded. The battery wouldn't budge no matter how much she shook and jostled the toy. Damn thing was stuck, wedged in tight.

"Noooooooooooooooooo! This can't be happening. No fucking way."

All right, she had to be calm and rational. How the hell could she get the battery out?

She glanced around the small room, looking for an answer. Her gaze landed on the large wooden wardrobe. Taking slow, easy breaths, she walked across the room, placed the vibe against the side of the cabinet and proceeded to bang the hell out of the damn thing.

Breathing heavy now, Shira again peered inside and there was the battery, still lodged firmly in place.

"Son of a bitch."

Possessing better-than-average intelligence, she should be able to figure this out. It couldn't be that hard to get a battery out of the confines of the blasted device. She just needed to think.

She glowered at the battery and tapped her fingers on her chin. Obviously it was a tight fit between the walls of the compartment and the battery. She needed something to grasp the end and drag it out.

Inspiration struck. Tweezers.

Shira raced into the bathroom, grabbed her tweezers and set to work, quickly discovering that the job required something much longer. Shaking with frustration, she pulled on her robe and secured the belt in place before racing out into the hall. Her destination—the lab. They had lots of implements in there. Surely they'd have something that would reach the battery.

When she arrived at the locked glass door, Shira pounded as if the hounds of hell were on her heels. She imagined how she would appear to the technicians inside, wearing a silk robe, mussed hair framing her face, eyes wide and wild. Her entire body shook with frustration.

The startled lab geek who came to the door appeared frightened. Instead of opening the door, he pressed a button and talked through the intercom. "W-what is it, Corporal?"

"Let me in, Sims." Even she heard the desperation in her voice. Shira fought for calm control. "I need to borrow some tweezers to fix a very important, top-secret device."

"Umm...Ma'am. You're out of uniform."

No shit, Sherlock!

Irritation boiled and she pounded her fist against the barrier. The tech trembled as she spoke through tightly clenched teeth. "I know. Just give me what I need and you can get back to work."

He reached toward the lock, hesitated. *Jesus, what a wimp.* He was enlisted Army for crying out loud.

"Private," she growled, using her most commanding tone. "Open the damn door or you'll be running bunk drills for the next sixteen hours."

That did it. The geek must be well versed in the torture of bunk drills because without second thought he opened the door and stood out of her way.

She knew what she wanted, and where it was kept. Had seen the techs using the long-limbed tweezers in their work. In less than five seconds she had what she'd come for and was running down the hall.

Back in her room, she fought to steady her hands. The first few tries resulted in scraping against the end of the battery but failed to dislodge it. Finally—on the tenth attempt—she grabbed hold of the cylinder and began rocking it loose. It seemed to take forever but finally she had the damn thing free and in anger, threw it across the room. The battery hit the wall with a loud thunk, leaving a mark, then fell to the floor and rolled under the wardrobe.

Shira took the time to read the instructions and successfully loaded fresh batteries into the wand. As she screwed on the base and depressed the power button, she held her breath.

The toy came to life in her hands, buzzing and gyrating. She let out a whoop of pure joy and triumph. Disaster had been adverted and now she was going to have some fun. Blow off some steam.

Get off.

Oh hell yeah!

Chapter Three

ൟ

As painful as it would be for him, Lex needed to apologize. For the past few days Renard managed to avoid him. Not that he could blame her after what had happened during his first shift. He looked for her everywhere to no avail. That's how he wound up standing at the door to her quarters — completely innocent in his intentions.

Hey, technically his intentions were good. At least when ignoring his ulterior motives.

And as luck would have it, Renard presented him with an opportunity Lex could not resist when he knocked on the door. An unsecured door that swung open, granting him entry.

"Hey, Renard. Anybody home?" he called out as he peeked through the opening.

No answer.

Nudging the door wider, he glanced around her personal space. He shouldn't go in. Should respect a fellow soldier's privacy.

Good one. He almost laughed. Unsecured possessions were fair game.

Neat as a pin, the room could have come straight out of a Marine SOP handbook. Nothing personal on display, everything in its place. Even the blanket on her bed was stretched taut and tucked in precisely. Hell, a quarter would probably bounce off the damn thing.

Unable to resist, Lex pulled a coin from his pocket to test the theory. Sure enough, the quarter rebounded.

Holy shit! Talk about a buttoned-down-tight soldier.

He glanced into the wardrobe, not surprised to find her gear folded and displayed with precision. If he had a ruler, no doubt the distance between each item and its placement on the shelf would be within a fraction of an inch of what regulations required.

Far from the state of his room, that's for sure. He followed SOP—for the most part. Just not to such an anal-retentive extreme.

Sliding open the desk drawers revealed only the most basic supplies and manuals, nothing personal or of interest. He moved to the nightstand, hesitating for a moment as his conscience nagged. Recalling a certain image on the security scanner, he brushed aside those pesky morals, pulled open the drawer and struck pay dirt.

"Well, well, well...look what we have here." The perfect means to exact his revenge. Not that a vibrator could measure up to a life-altering event.

As he plucked the flesh-toned, rather intimidating vibrator from its resting place, Lex's blood pressure went through the roof. While he walked around horny and in serious need of relief, the sneaky little fox was busy satisfying herself with an electronic marvel.

Well her good times were about to come to an abrupt end. No way in hell would he walk away and leave the toy there. Not happening. If he had to suffer then so did she.

"So think fast and get out of here before she comes back."

He couldn't walk down the hallway of a military unit carrying the three-shafted vibrator. The ribbing would never end. Why the hell hadn't he brought something to conceal the contraband sex toy?

Because then he would have had to admit premeditation. At least to himself.

Moving to the wardrobe, he grabbed a white towel and spread it open on her bed. He tossed the vibe on top, along with the lube, battery charger and spare batteries. Rolling everything up in the towel, Lex paused. An image of the Grinch slinging a sack of stolen Christmas presents over his shoulder came to mind, which he ruthlessly ignored. Renard deserved to have her joy snatched out from under her.

With the towel tucked under his arm, he wasted no time heading for his own room at the opposite end of the building. Although it wouldn't be a good idea to keep the contraband. God forbid if they had an inspection and someone discovered the sex toy. There would be no explaining that away.

Fuck! He had to figure something out. Moving quickly through the halls, careful not to draw unwanted attention, he barely breathed until the door to his quarters closed behind him. Now he just needed a temporary hiding place while he figured out a better solution.

Lex's gaze scanned his room, landing on the locked briefcase containing the Predator Project files as someone knocked on the door.

"Sergeant McLean?"

"Yeah. Uh...just a minute." Shoving the bundle into the front compartment, he closed the flap. "Enter."

The door swung open to reveal one of the security team. "General Hughes wants you in briefing room A."

"When?"

"Now." The man's expression let him know the situation was serious. "Everyone's waiting."

Fuck!

Lex grabbed his case and double-timed it toward the briefing room.

* * * * *

General Hughes sat at the head of the big polished oak table. Beneath his drumming fingertips rested a file labeled Predator Project with Top Secret stamped across the front in red.

Shira hadn't known the general long, but the highly controlled man did not make careless gestures. His obvious agitation filled her with dread. Shit was going down and she was determined not to be left out of whatever happened.

Masculine voices drew her attention to the doorway as Micah Lasiter stepped into the room with Lex right behind him. Lex dropped his bag on the table and saluted the general.

"Sir," Micah greeted and offered his hand.

"Daddy!" A petite brunette squealed from the doorway and raced toward the general, who jumped up and caught her in his arms.

Micah raked a hand through his hair and mumbled, "Daddy? Oh shit!"

The general's gaze never left Micah as he addressed the woman. "Princess? What are you doing here?"

"Holy shit. This is priceless," Lex said and sputtered in a valiant effort to contain his laughter.

Shira's gaze darted from one tense man to the other. The general's eyes shot daggers at Lasiter who looked as if his balls had shriveled up and were attempting to crawl into his body to hide.

Damn, this was going to be good. An ex-soldier from the general's unit somehow involved with his daughter. She sat taller in her seat, hungrily drinking in every nuance of the unfolding drama.

"Micah and I just got in from Africa. We're here for a meeting about a project I was involved in at work that went bad."

"You were at Nanotech?" the general growled.

"Not now, Daddy. We're going to be late."

He turned and finally looked at his daughter. "You told me that you were working with lions somewhere in the South."

"I was. A lion and a tiger—"

"Then why the blazes are you with him?"

"But your last name's Southerby." Micah scrubbed at the stubble on his chin. The poor man appeared to be thoroughly confused.

On pins and needles, Shira waited to hear the rest. Her gaze bounced back and forth between the players as if watching a tennis match.

"It is," Becca shrugged. "Mom and Dad weren't married when I was born."

"Shut up, Lasiter." The general shoved Lex's bag out of the way and pulled out a chair. "Rebecca, sit down."

All attention in the room turned to the leather satchel that started to hum and thud against the wooden surface. Lex made a lunge for it but Hughes got to the bag first.

"What the hell. Who does this belong to?" Hughes opened the flap, which had been left unlocked, and rooted around. The rolled-up towel he dropped on the table buzzed and skittered about.

Oh no he didn't!

Lex started to protest. Hughes just held up his hand, signaling for silence, then unrolled the towel. Shira's brand new vibrator danced across the table. Batteries rolled this way and that. Hughes stared for a moment before gingerly picking the toy up by its base. "Who belongs to this?"

The general made eye contact with each person in the room. Heat crept up Shira's neck and into her cheeks. As his stern gaze landed on her, Shira swallowed hard and the bottom dropped out of her stomach.

Busted!

What the hell was she supposed to say?

"It's my bag," Lex confessed. "I...umm—"

Every eye in the room focused on him. Somehow he still managed to stand tall and appear unruffled.

"Son, I don't even want to know." Hughes shook his head, tossed everything back into the bag and slammed it against Lex's chest.

Numb, shocked to the core, Shira didn't move or breathe as she struggled to process what had happened. The sadistic dickhead sacrificed his dignity to save her? She couldn't believe it. The jerk hated her. Why the hell would he protect her?

Then a different kind of heat blasted through Shira. The bastard had been in her room, gone through her private things. Stole her fucking vibrator.

She held the edge of the table in a white-knuckled grasp as her entire body vibrated, demanding action. A red haze clouded her vision as she watched Lex fumble around. The vibrator stilled and the sudden silence in the room was almost deafening. Contemplating all the pain she would inflict, Shira began to rise as she fought back her body's urgent need to shift.

"Everyone sit down," General Hughes commanded.

Reluctantly dropping back into her chair, she tuned out the conversation as Lasiter briefed the general on his daughter's involvement in the highly classified project.

Shira debated the slowest, most painful methods of killing a man. Nothing quick or painless for the bane of her existence. No, Lex would suffer.

She watched him from the corner of her eye. He didn't appear to have any weaknesses. Tall, packed with solid muscle. Sexy as all get out. Would be a shame to ruin his devilish smile by knocking out some of those perfect white teeth. And marking up all that taut, tanned skin—criminal.

Maybe she'd fuck him first. Hell, the way she saw it since he took her toy Lex owed her orgasms. Multiples. The explosive kind that left her boneless and put a satisfied grin on her face.

Mmm...she'd love to have that hard body of his beneath her. And if his cock was in proportion to the rest of him, she'd have one hell of a sweet ride. She'd taste him before fucking herself on his shaft. Dip her tongue into every groove, sink her teeth into meaty flesh.

Shift and find out if a fox and wolf going at it would be half as amazing as she'd imagined.

Ever since the guards had interrupted them in the woods thoughts of wild bestial fucking had teased and tormented her vivid imagination. The idea of leaving human worries and niceties behind and engaging in raw, primitive sex thrilled her to no end.

The large, powerful wolf forcing her to the ground and thrusting his huge shaft between her slick pussy from behind. Sharp teeth piercing her thick pelt, holding her captive for the savage pounding of his cock.

Her breasts swelled and grew achy. The rough material of her shirt abraded diamond-hard nipples with each deep breath. Her belly quivered and hot cream rained from her folds, soaking her panties.

Shifting in her seat, she clamped her thighs together. The slight pressure wasn't enough. She needed more.

"Renard," the general barked.

Lex watched Shira closely. Startled when the general called her name, her head snapped up and wide, crystalline blue eyes locked right on him. There was a plea in her gaze.

Poor thing. She'd missed the entire conversation.

He could relate. For a moment he considered taking pity on her and restating the general's question. Almost. He enjoyed seeing her flounder too much to help her out. Instead, he leaned back in his chair, folded his hands and let her squirm.

Hmm...on closer inspection he reconsidered the cause of her distress. Dilated pupils were surrounded by only a thin circle of blue. Her hungry gaze devoured him. That cute nose of hers flared and her cheeks were suffused with a pink flush. The pulse point in her neck pounded and her breathing came too fast.

Renard wasn't displaying signs of anger over the vibrator incident. Nowhere close. The naughty fox was fighting some serious arousal.

For him.

Now that was something he'd be glad to help her out with. At a more appropriate time and place.

Shit, he couldn't believe what he was about to do.

"What do you think, Renard? A team of four to go after the scientist trying to reestablish the Predator Project should be sufficient."

Relief and gratitude flashed in her eyes for a split second before she went into serious soldier mode.

She nodded. "A small team can get in and out quicker, be more efficient."

Feeling the general's assessing stare, Lex turned his attention back to the head of the table and nodded. "Lasiter on point, Slater for demo—"

"Both civilians," Hughes interjected.

"Who you've included in this briefing, have knowledge of the unique situation, and military training under your command. The less people who learn about the existence of shifters the better."

"Fine. Who else?"

Lex sighed inwardly at the general's capitulation. "Renard on search and rescue, and me." He rushed on to head off any potential argument. "You've gotta have a medic who understands shifters in case the bastard has injected anyone."

"No." Hughes' hard tone made Lex's hackles rise. "I understand your desire to be involved, McLean. Problem is you've only shifted a handful of times over the past few days and you don't have control over—"

"I'll help him," Shira piped in.

Stunned speechless, Lex marveled at her confident expression.

"Daddy." Becca placed her hand on the general's arm. "I'll work with Lex. Give me two days and he'll be ready."

"Princess, this is a military matter. You're not getting involved."

Becca laughed. "I'm already involved. I worked with Micah and helped him gain control of his lion. I can certainly handle a wolf. Where else are you going to find a zoologist trained in animal behavior who won't freak when a human shifts form right in front of them?"

"She has a point, Sir."

"Shut up, Lasiter. You got her into this mess, which we will discuss later."

Becca slapped her palm on the table. "Oh no you won't. Micah had nothing to do with Weltman recruiting me to work on the Predator Project."

"But he has everything to do with your continued involvement," the general growled.

This was headed south fast. Time to bring the focus of the meeting back to the mission.

"I know the doc and trust her skills. Give me two days to work with her and Renard. At the end of that time if you're not completely satisfied that I've got the wolf under control, I'll stand down."

"Fine," Hughes grumbled. "Two days. Get the animal under control and come up with a detailed mission plan. Then I'll consider giving the team a green light."

The general rose and dismissed those under his command and placed a restraining hand on Becca's shoulder. "Not you two." He glared at Micah. "We have a lot more to discuss."

As they left the room, Renard brushed against his side and Lex's skin tingled.

"I'd love to be a fly on the wall for that conversation." Her husky whisper heated his blood and made his cock ache.

Fuck! He needed to get her under him but they had to work closely together. Fucking would only complicate the situation.

The next two days were going to be pure hell.

"Oh, and another thing!"

Taking advantage of his distraction, Renard shoved him against the wall and fisted his balls. "If my vibrator is not back where it belongs within the hour—" She applied enough pressure to ensure she had his complete attention. "These will be hanging from the rear bumper of my truck."

Chapter Four

൭

Private showers — what a luxury.

The unit's digs must have been housing for officers at some point because regular enlisted grunts had to share communal bunkrooms and showers. Being assigned to General Hughes' unit sure had benefits. Hot water that didn't run out and high-pressure showers were on top of the list.

Shira stood under the pounding spray, let the tension slowly melt away. Each time she shifted and the fox had a vigorous workout the aftereffects were the same — ravenous hunger, sore muscles and an insatiable desire for sex.

Before the meeting she'd pigged out. This glorious shower would take care of the aches and pains. And next, if the jerk-off had returned her vibrator, she would go for the Big O. Several of them.

Shira squeezed some lavender-mint gel into her palm, worked up a thick lather and let her fingers wander as she thought about the meeting. And Lex. Taking her toy had been a ballsy move. On the other hand, walking around with it in his satchel — stupid.

God, the look on his face when the general had accidently tripped the power button. Of course, her expression would have been pretty damn comical too. Then Lex had gone and turned into Mr. Gallant, claiming ownership and saving her from total humiliation.

Now she owed him. And he'd expect payback. The question was what he'd want?

Maybe sex.

Nah, he hated her, right?

Mmm…what she wouldn't give to go a few rounds with the sexy medic. Her body heated as she pictured dropping to her knees and taking his cock deep into her mouth. Flicking her tongue in the slit to get a taste of him. Wrapping her lips around the silk-over-steel shaft. She'd bet her life savings he'd taste smooth and rich.

Taking her aching breasts into her hands, she tweaked diamond-hard nipples as she imagined lightly scraping her teeth over the sweet spot beneath his ridge. Sucking him hard and teasing the sensitive strip of flesh behind his balls. Hearing his moans and watching him come apart. Swallowing around the head as hot jets of cum shot down her throat.

Hell yeah!

She pinched her nipples harder and moaned as the tug shot through her belly to echo in her clit. Soapy fingers glided over slick folds. As she circled a fingernail around the distended bundle of nerves, her head fell back between her shoulders. Wanting more, she thrust two fingers into her pussy and located that amazing spot so few men were capable of finding. She rode her hand hard, fucking her fingers deep and scraping her nail over the head of her clit.

So good.

With her free hand, Shira lifted her breast, dropped her chin to her chest and sucked her nipple between hungry lips. The sharp edge of her teeth nipped at the turgid peak as she fucked her hand, reaching for the orgasm hovering just out of reach.

So close.

And yet so far.

No matter what she tried satisfaction evaded her grasp.

Her mournful cry reverberated around the tiled stall. Disgusted by the failure to push herself over the edge, she rushed through the rest of the disappointing shower that had become more routine task than special indulgence.

"Damn you, Lex!"

Shaking out her hair, she finger-combed the short strands, rubbed lotion into still-damp skin then headed straight for the nightstand.

"My toy better be in that drawer or —"

Shira stalked into the room and nearly swallowed her tongue. Stretched out on her bed was more than six feet of hard male flesh. Nude flesh. Miles of bronzed skin covering rippling muscle. A big hand fisted the most gorgeous cock she'd ever seen. Mesmerized, she couldn't take her eyes away from the hand making lazy strokes from base to tip, a pause for his thumb to swipe over the crown, gathering the fluid beaded there, before descending.

"Or what? I could make a few suggestions."

Thick fingers tensed, gripped the shaft hard, increasing the pace. Shira licked suddenly dry lips. His masculine moan sounded distant as she stared at the living, breathing wet dream. She wanted to trip and fall right on top of that long, thick cock.

"Come closer, little red fox. This big bad wolf won't bite…hard."

His fairytale come-on snapped her out of her sexual stupor. Until then she'd almost forgotten about the pain in the ass who inhabited that incredible body. She didn't even want to consider the fact they were both naked, aroused and all alone in her private room.

Crossing her arms under her breasts, she glared at him. "What do you think you're doing?"

"Offering my assistance. From the sound of it your shower didn't provide any relief."

Shira groaned inwardly. "Just return my vibrator and no one will get hurt."

Undeterred by her attitude and ignoring her demand, he continued to stroke his cock. "Tell me, Renard, does shifting leave you hot and bothered too? Aching to fuck? 'Cause it drives me crazy." His gaze dropped and she couldn't help following suit to watch his fist work his cock. "And my hand isn't enough."

She understood all too well. While the toy helped, she craved more. The warm friction of a real cock sliding along the sensitive walls of her pussy. Fingers and a mouth—other than her own—sucking her tender nipples. Gaining mutual satisfaction with someone who shared the same burning needs.

"I know what you need, Shira. I need it too. We're both unattached adults with clean bills of health. Why not indulge."

All valid points. And birth control wasn't an issue since she had an implant in her arm. Why was she having such a hard time remembering the reasons she shouldn't fuck him?

Lex watched Shira as she watched him, taking in all the signs of her arousal. Keeping his ass on the bed severely tested his restraint. He was dying to suck on those ripe pink nipples. Couldn't wait to gather the cream glistening on her slender thighs and spread it over his throbbing cock. Thrust his tongue between the bare lips of her beautiful pussy.

He groaned as her hands cupped full breasts and pinched her nipples. She wanted him as much as he wanted her. "Come on, honey. I guarantee it will be better than that fancy fake cock. Take what you need."

Shira stood at the foot of the bed, her gaze skated over his body like a hot caress.

"Lex." His name rolling off her tongue in that husky tone had his fist tightening on his cock.

"Yeah, baby?"

"Shut up!" She took a step closer. Then another. "You talk too much."

Shira crawled onto the bed and he couldn't take his eyes off her. She moved over his body, a hungry predator locked onto its next meal. Him.

Fuck yeah!

Pushing his legs apart, she made a place for herself. With her lips hovering above his erection for the space of several heartbeats all she did was stare. As if that wasn't enough to drive him insane, the tip of her tongue traced a path over her lips, moistening the plump curves.

Elegant fingers pushed his lax hand out of the way and covered his dick, drawing a harsh moan from him. Then her dark head dipped toward his groin and Lex knew he wouldn't last long.

Shira didn't tease or play games—she went right for the brass ring. Warm breath washed over his tense balls and then they were engulfed in the damp heat of her mouth.

"Oh yeah, baby. Suck 'em. Use your tongue."

She hummed around his sac, creating a wicked vibration that blasted straight through his cock and his hips bucked. "Damn that's good."

Sucking him hard, her talented tongue lashed at his tender flesh. She hummed again then opened her mouth. His wet balls slapped against his perineum and another fiery jolt raced through his shaft.

Far from finished, she fisted the base and proceeded to lick his cock as if it were her favorite treat. Watching her pouty lips part and swallow him whole was the most seductive thing he'd ever seen. Shira nosily slurped and sucked, consuming him with a voracious appetite that took his turbulent lust to a whole new level. Needing an anchor in the violent storm, Lex speared his fingers into her silky hair.

Taking him to the back of her throat, she swallowed and strong muscles pulled at his crown. Damn, that quick he was close to exploding. But he didn't want to come this way. He desperately wanted to feel her pussy tighten around him as his seed bathed her womb.

"Christ," he gasped. "Stop, baby. I don't want to come yet."

Heavy-lidded eyes gazed up at him from beneath thick lashes and he knew he was in trouble. Her fist tightened on the base of his cock while her other hand moved between his legs to roll his balls gently in her palm.

"Too good, baby," he warned. "Can't hold back."

Eyes sparkling with glee never left his. But her fingers, they slid from his balls, danced along his perineum and circled his anus.

She wouldn't dare.

Renard did more than dare. As she slurped and sucked hard on his cock, swallowing against the head, her finger breached the tight ring of muscle and plunged deep. Back and forth that devious finger thrust until she stroked the small protrusion that ended his fight.

"So fucking good. Keep going, baby," he gasped. "Here it comes."

Each shallow stab of his hips made his tight balls thud against his perineum. Every stroke of her finger whipped up lightning that gathered in his sac before shooting through his shaft.

His entire body tensed and his eyes slammed shut. Pure bliss detonated in his groin, streaked outward and practically blew his head off. He was vaguely aware of powerful sucking drawing every last drop of cum from his balls.

Lex floated for a while. When he came back down it was to find Renard licking the remaining semen from his still semi-hard shaft.

Crawling her way up his body, she placed small kisses and playful nips of sharp teeth along his torso. "There's an advantage to being a shifter you probably haven't learned yet." Her husky voice rasped over his nipple and his cock jerked to attention.

"Micah filled me in before sending me here," she purred.

Hearing his friend's name on her lips while she was in bed with him stirred unexpected anger in Lex. Foreign emotions tightened his chest but he ruthlessly pushed them aside. He would not allow himself to get wrapped up in this woman.

The witch who turned me into a shifter, he reminded himself.

He'd take her body, fuck her every way possible. Use her for sex. There would never be more than sex. Really good sex. Mutual satisfaction.

"Shifters have an abbreviated recovery time and can go for hours."

A knife plunged into his heart and twisted as he wondered how Micah had imparted this information. Had he told Renard or shown her?

From out of nowhere, a low rumble rolled up through his chest. The menacing growl was a clear warning. She just grinned and straddled his hips, nestling his hard cock against her slick pussy.

Something in him snapped and the animal's instincts took over. Before he realized what he was doing, Lex grabbed her hips, reversed their positions and flipped her onto her belly.

Stunned and more than a little turned on by Lex's sudden aggression, Shira didn't fight — at first.

A firm hand between her shoulders shoved — none too gently — thrusting her chest and face into the pillow. She took a deep breath and her lungs were flooded with Lex's unique masculine scent. His other arm slid under her belly, yanking Shira to her knees.

The same heady rush she'd experienced when the wolf had run her to ground and prepared to mount her had Shira's fox fighting to be set free. Barely restraining the urge to shift, she burst into action.

She kicked out at his legs and groin and Lex pushed her knees apart. He moved into the opening, his muscular thighs preventing her from clamping her legs shut. Shira went wild beneath him. She bucked, trying to dislodge him until sharp teeth closed on her vulnerable throat. Shira went completely still. Her heart beat wildly and her breathing came in harsh pants.

In the wild, weaker animals were subjugated by those who were stronger. Although she didn't have a submissive bone in her body, the fox reveled in being dominated by the powerful wolf. Had she shifted, the fox would have rolled over and bared her belly.

He didn't wait or give her time to refuse. The fat head of his cock swept along her folds, notched at her entrance and in one swift thrust, hilted inside her. Tossing back her head, she howled, the sound more animal than human, as Lex pounded into her at a punishing pace.

Wet and ready for him, she slammed her hips back, meeting each hard thrust. The sound of flesh slapping against flesh joined with their primal grunts of pleasure, creating a music all their own. Each glorious time his cock plowed through the quivering walls of her pussy ended with his balls striking her clit.

Pushing her ass higher made him go deeper. His crown tapped on her cervix and the tension coiled in her belly.

"Yes," she hissed. "Fuck me. Harder. Faster."

He met her impossible demands, taking their frenzied fucking further, driving her to the brink. Suddenly the coil sprung. Immense waves washed over her, threatening to drown Shira. It went on and on, stealing the breath from her lungs. Smothering her face in the pillow, she sank her teeth into it as her pussy clamped down on his cock, which swelled impossibly larger, stretching Shira to her limits. Hot spurts of cum filled her. His teeth let go of her neck and he shouted.

Lex collapsed against her, his big body covering her back. He somehow managed to roll them onto their sides.

As she struggled to gain control of her breathing, Shira realized the sweaty skin touching hers didn't have her racing for the shower. And the heavy arm draped possessively over her abdomen didn't bother her in the least.

Strange.

She yawned in contentment and brushed off the odd thoughts, deciding to think about them later.

Much later.

Maybe after another fantastic round…or six.

* * * * *

While the phone pressed to his ear rang, Lex stared out his office window into the quad and waited for the line to be answered. He shifted on the chair, sitting gingerly on his sore ass and wounded pride, his thoughts circling back to the woman who had him so wound up in knots.

Shocked the hell out of him but when he sparred with Renard, she'd slipped beneath his defenses and taken him down. Several times. The woman had serious skills in hand-to-hand combat. She kept her body in amazing shape, earning his grudging respect. And he had carnal knowledge of every sexy inch of her body. He'd tested her flexibility and strength in a variety of ways. She never failed to please and impress.

Respecting someone you hate shouldn't be possible. Caring about them — no fucking way. And yet somehow, she'd gotten to him, no matter how ridiculous he found the idea.

Renard had a great military record but reading a file didn't give you the whole picture. You had to talk to others who knew the person and observe their actions. Every single person he'd called couldn't speak highly enough about her.

As if on cue, Renard stepped out into the quad. She stopped in a shaft of sunlight and her head dropped back between her shoulders. Undertones of blue glistened from within the glossy strands of black hair. She took a deep breath, causing her breasts to lift toward the sky as if in offering to the gods. A tingling awareness skittered through Lex's body.

He may not like her, but he wanted her. Bad!

"Yo."

"Hey, Gunny. This is Sergeant McLean."

"McLean, hey man. Been a long time. How're you doing?"

"Good, thanks. Listen, I need some information on a jarhead you worked with a while back."

"Anything you need."

Lex knew he'd be able to get an honest assessment of Renard from Gunnery Sergeant Ramirez. They'd met while serving in Iraq, the Sunni Triangle. After pulling a wounded Ramirez out of the line of fire, Lex had delivered treatment doctors later insisted had saved his leg from amputation. It was those kinds of bonds, forged in battle, a man could trust.

He continued to watch Renard as she neared a PFC working in the hot sun, struggling with his task of dismantling a section of broken sidewalk. She didn't continue walking and ignore the grunt or his menial task as everyone else did. Not Renard. She stopped, studied his efforts and using simple body mechanics, showed him an easier, more effective way to complete his job.

And this wasn't the first time. He'd seen her commit multiple acts of random kindness, making it increasingly harder for Lex to hate her.

"You were in Afghanistan, the Kunar province, with Lance Corporal Renard—"

"Hell yes, I was," Ramirez interrupted. "There's no one else I'd rather have at my side going into bad shit. Not even you...no offense. You won't find a stronger, more honorable or skilled soldier out there, male or female.

"Our team got blindsided. Renard ran right into it, drew the insurgents' fire, allowing everyone to get out. Except Renard, she got pinned down and captured. I was part of the extraction team that went in after her. She was in bad shape after being held for several days and still she managed to hump out a wounded soldier — one who'd been sent to rescue her."

Ramirez's version of the incident confirmed what he'd already heard and explained Renard's long list of commendations and medals. What impressed him the most was the loyalty she inspired in other hardened soldiers.

"You get the chance to work with Shira, don't pass it up. And when you see her, give her a big juicy kiss and tell her Rico says hi."

Lex wasn't aware of the snarl rumbling through his chest until Ramirez started laughing.

"Ah, so you've already gotten a taste of sweet Shira. I owe you, McLean, but hurt her and there's nowhere you can run that I won't find you. And when I do, I'll reach down your throat, grab your balls and yank them out. Then I'll teach you the real meaning of pain. *Comprende, amigo?*"

Oh he understood all right. And he had no doubt the Gunny would follow through.

"I hear you, Gunny, loud and clear."

"Good, then you won't fuck this up."

That still remained to be seen.

Chapter Five

ഔ

Forty-nine. Fifty.

Falling back, Shira dangled upside down, knees hooked over a horizontal bar. The taxed muscles of her abdomen quivered after the brutal set of vertical crunches but her workout was far from over. She pulled herself up, grabbed the chin-up bar, untangled her legs and dropped to the floor. After downing some water, she picked up a jump rope to get her lower body warmed up before starting on lunges and squats.

As distraction techniques went, some hard exercise was usually all it took to clear her mind. But even the tried-and-true method failed under the pressure and her thoughts kept circling straight back to Lexilicious.

For two days they'd been almost inseparable. They ate together, planned the mission, fucked, sparred, worked with Becca, fucked some more. He even intruded upon her showers. In theory, she should be enjoying this peaceful time alone instead of working her body past the point of exhaustion in a lame attempt to ease her restless anxiety.

So much for theories.

No matter how hard she pushed her body her mind still raced, hitting her with over a thousand thoughts of Lex per minute. She worried how things were going with the general. Had he passed the test? Remained in control of the wolf? Would he be permitted to go on the mission?

What about after the mission? Would he drop her faster than a bad habit? Was it just convenient sex to him or did it mean more? And when the hell has it started meaning more to her?

All questions she refused to voice aloud.

God, what had happened to her? All of this was so not her. In the past, she'd run from intimacy. When the sex was over, she was the first one in the shower then out the door. Not with Lex. The sticky, messy aftermath of sex didn't bother her when he lay by her side. Neither did the lack of privacy or personal space. Quite the opposite. She slept better when he passed out in her bed, his loud snores ringing in her ears. Even his gruff attitude turned her on.

Lex had gotten under her thick skin, become an addiction. One she didn't know how she would survive without.

The gym door burst open and hit the wall with a resounding bang. Startled, Shira lost track of the rope, which got tangled up in her feet. Last thing she saw on the way down—before she face planted onto the blue mat—was Lex's feral grin.

The truth pounded her harder than the floor, knocking the breath right out of her. Didn't matter the blond surfer dude wasn't anywhere close to her type. Contradictory to how the jerk annoyed the hell out of her. Not even the awareness that he fundamentally hated her made a difference. She'd gone and done the unthinkable and fallen for the jerk.

Aw shit! Idiot!

Big hands grabbed her under the arms and pulled Shira onto unsteady legs, holding her up as she wobbled.

"What the hell, Renard? You overdid it, didn't you?"

He muttered several choice curses under his breath. Gathering the last of her strength, she flattened both hands on his chest and shoved. When he didn't budge it pissed her off.

"How are you going to hold up your end of things on this mission when you can't even fucking stand up?"

Her? He worried about her fitness to complete the mission? Ha! Funny when it was Lex the general had doubts about. Why the hell couldn't she hate him? Sure would make her life simpler, not that she ever took the easy route.

"I'll be fine after a soak in the hot tub. You just worry about yourself and keeping the wolf in check."

Ooh, score. Direct hit!

His forehead furrowed and his gaze narrowed. She noticed his jaw had clenched tight as the hands holding her up fisted the material of her sports bra. Lex shoved her toward the locker room and followed right on her heels.

"We're gonna have to rub those muscles down or you'll be useless to the team."

He wanted to do a lot more than rub her down. As usual, shifting had left Lex with the profound need to fuck Renard senseless.

Thinking about rubbing all that lean sinew, oiled fingers sliding over petal-soft skin, gave him an instant hard-on. He was helpless to do anything other than fuck her…again.

God, his head was messed up. He hated her, wanted payback for what she'd done to him. And yet he fucked her every chance he got. Justified using her because this situation was all her fault. If she hadn't injected him none of this would've happened.

Keep repeating 'em and you might start to believe those lame-ass reasons.

Directing Renard to one of the massage tables, he growled, "Lie down."

She crawled up onto her belly and the sight froze him in place. So much bare skin. The sports bra and jersey shorts barely covered anything, and the way the material clung to the full curves of her perfect ass—

Fuck, no panty line. She probably had on one of those lethal thongs she liked to wear.

His sly little fox was trouble with a capital T.

Lex shook his head. No, not his. No matter how badly the wolf wanted to claim her, mark her. Mate her.

My bitch.

"Something wrong?"

Oh, if you only knew, baby.

"Nope, not a thing."

After sliding off her running shoes and socks, he grabbed a bottle of massage oil and started with her feet. She purred when the pad of his thumb slid along her arch, which had him groaning. This was going to be pure torture.

"Oh damn. That feels so good."

Lex ground his teeth and continued to work her muscles, blocking out the smooth glide of sinew beneath his fingers.

Think about something else. You can't jump her bones every other minute.

Why the fuck not? He had no answer for that one.

Her breathing slowed and she made the sexiest noises as he worked her thigh muscles. His erection pressed against his zipper, aching to sink into the tight, hot, wet clasp of her pussy. Or better yet, her ass. He'd wanted to get inside her gorgeous ass since the first time he saw her.

Think about something else. Anything else.

They could be walked in on at any moment so he had to stay in check. Deciding to avoid temptation, he skipped over that lush ass and moved on to massage her arms, shoulders and back.

He still needed more answers about Renard and the best way to get them would be to ask. "The general told me the anesthesia they used gave you hallucinations." Her entire body tensed. "What did you hallucinate?"

Rolling to her back, Shira searched Lex's light brown eyes. All the wonderful gooey arousal his talented fingers had stirred went right out the window. She had known the questions would come sooner or later. Clearing the air between them would be a relief.

"Medications have always hit me hard but the anesthesia...shit. The stuff fucked with my head. When I woke up, every instinct—everything I saw, heard and smelled—told me I was back in Afghanistan." There was no controlling the shudders that raced through her. She didn't even try.

Shira met his hard gaze head on, not flinching from the anger tightening his expression. "I heard the insurgents' voices and had no doubt I'd been recaptured, even though it didn't make sense because I had no memory of going back to the Middle East. But it was so real and everything was exactly the same." She shrugged. "I did what I've been trained to do."

For several minutes he didn't speak. Then he surprised the hell out of her by pushing her upper body back down on the table and resuming his massage of her arms.

"Did you know what was in the syringes?" His voice had deepened, turned raspy.

"I assumed I'd been drugged because I didn't feel right and my vision was fuzzy. Figured the syringes held more of the drug. And the needles were the closest thing to a weapon I found. Lex—"

She sat up and grabbed his hand. "I would never intentionally go after a U.S. soldier. And after everything I've been through since Weltman injected me, I wouldn't deliberately inflict the same misery on my worst enemy."

God, I'm so sorry. I love you. Please…forgive me.

For now, those sentiments, no matter how heartfelt, were better left unsaid.

When he turned away her heart shattered and her lungs burned. She wanted to reach out to him, hold him close. Comfort him. She was afraid to move, barely breathed.

Without a word, Lex's calloused fingers began to work on her quads. Lying back again, she tried to relax. She knew acceptance would take time and forgiveness may never be possible.

Damn, even with their serious conversation, his touch had a profound effect. Especially when his fingers were a mere inch or two from her soaking wet pussy. She hissed as his knuckles brushed against her swollen lips.

Had to be accidental.

"You're wet, baby."

Without warning, he grabbed her shorts and whipped them and her panties down her legs, shoving her knees apart in the process.

"I love that you keep this pretty pussy bare. Such a fucking turn-on."

Two fingers slid along her slit and slammed deep into her core. His palm rubbed against her clit as he finger-fucked her, fast and hard. Her hips began to move of their own volition and she grabbed onto the table frame. Those wonderful fingers unerringly found her G-spot, stroking the bundle of nerves so sweetly. Intense waves of pleasure rocketed through her.

"As much as I love fucking your pussy there's something else I've been dying to try."

"Anything," she gasped then squealed in shock as he flipped her over and positioned her on her hands and knees. Fat drops of oil landed on her lower back and rolled down her crack. His wet fingertips returned to circle her pucker. Moaning, she pushed back, shivering in delight when he breached the first ring of muscle.

"Ever since I saw that toy of yours, I've wanted to get inside this ass."

Far from a considerate lover, Lex didn't ask if she wanted it. Didn't attempt to convince her. He simply took what he needed, leaving no room for her to think, control or direct. All she could do was accept what he gave.

Fuck if she didn't love that about him.

His fingers thrust and scissored, stretching her sensitive tissues, making room for his big cock. Briefly she panicked, gasped for breath. His cock was huge—long and thick. She'd only ever taken slender toys in her ass. He would split her in half.

"So fucking hot and tight."

Lex's palm slapped her ass and she yelped, startled by the loud sound and heated sting. He dragged her down the table and spread her legs wide until they split open to dangle over the sides — good thing she was flexible — and her pussy rested on the padded frame.

His oiled crown pressed against her opening, which clenched tight. Her instinct for self-preservation was strong.

"Relax," he demanded.

Shira fought to breathe and made a conscious effort to loosen her muscles. His fat crown entered slowly, stretching, burning. She cried out at the pleasure-pain ripping through her.

"Let me in, baby. I need in." A plea entered his tone, making Shira's heart flip-flop. Determination filled her. She would refuse him nothing.

The second ring of muscle loosened and in one firm stroke, he hilted deep in her ass.

Sweet Jesus.

It was too much. Afraid to even breathe, Shira held statue-still as her body slowly began to adjust and what had been overwhelming mere moments ago was no longer enough.

"More," she gasped. "Move."

Flexing her muscles, she tightened around him, which must have been the signal he'd been waiting for.

"So tight. Hot. Good."

Lex pulled all the way out before slamming back in, stretching Renard without mercy. His balls slapped against her pussy and the hellion went wild beneath him. Her hips thrust to meet him. Her narrow, hot channel fluttered around him, milking his cock, sucking him deeper.

He rammed into her ass over and over, the loud slapping of flesh on flesh fracturing his mind, sending him spiraling out of control.

"Jesus, Lex. You're a fucking animal."

The wolf. His animal was close to the surface, fighting its leash. His fingers dug into soft curves, hips pistoning, the loud echo of flesh slapping on flesh. Rutting like a wolf.

How the hell had he forgotten the wolf? The beast hadn't left his mind, not for a second since she'd first inject him. It had influenced his thoughts and actions, shared his body. Hell, he'd even dismissed where they were, ignoring the high chance of discovery and potential consequences.

He faltered, lost his rhythm.

"You're stopping?" Shira shrieked and hammered back against him. "Don't you dare stop."

Lex dug down into the well of hatred that had driven him and found it nearly empty. God, how he wanted — needed — to hate her.

How could she do this to him? Make him forget, lift the weight of the world from his shoulders and make his problems disappear?

He called on the wolf, gave it some freedom. Reveled in its fierce howl. The wolf recognized its bitch and had no issues holding him back from taking what belonged to him.

Mine. The single word roared in his mind.

Hard and relentless, he savagely drove into his fox. Her body tensed, strong muscles clamped down. She met him thrust for punishing thrust but he sensed her holding back. Not that he'd allow it.

Lex changed his angle, rocking her pelvis against the table. Her fingernails scrabbled for purchase to no avail. He was in complete control. Powering into her, wanting her to feel every inch of his cock plowing through her spasming tissues.

When she gave in and the orgasm broke, her entire body shook. He continued to fuck her, drawing out the pleasure, losing track of how many times she orgasmed for him.

Finally, with a ferocious howl, he joined her. The heated flood of his cum pumping into her ass induced a barrage of aftershocks. The small spasms milked every last drop of seed from his balls.

Collapsing over her back, he panted, starving for air. For more of her heady scent. God, how good she felt beneath him. Hot, vital, strong. Perfect.

His mate!

No. Lex shook his head to clear the insane idea. There would be no permanence or tender emotions with this woman. He had to get away from Renard before he did something really stupid like cuddle up close, fall asleep with her cradled in his arms, and never let her go.

He had his cock zipped into his pants and made it out the door before the passion began to cool from their sweaty bodies.

Chapter Six

∞

Eight steps, about face, eight more steps. Over and over again, Shira repeated the same endless loop. Pacing like a caged animal, changing her mind with each change in direction.

Go talk to the general, explain the situation.

No, her military career was already in doubt.

Go to Micah Lasiter, another shifter.

No, he's a civilian.

Maybe Kyle Slater, a human.

Even worse, a human civilian male.

Maybe the doc, Becca Southerby, soon to be Lasiter. Army brat, zoologist, female.

And the general's daughter. No, not even the doc would understand.

Damn it, do something other than pace!

Her last encounter with Lex made it clear she could not go on this mission with him. Not with the tumultuous undercurrents running between them. Too much of a distraction.

She still didn't understand what had happened. The man was all over the place. He went from pissed off to caring concern, normal conversation to the silent treatment, gentle seducer to crazed animal.

Jesus, the way he'd taken her—raw and savage. More beast than man. She'd loved it while he was on top of her but once the bastard got his rocks off he'd zipped up and then couldn't get away from her fast enough. And in the process, he'd torn her heart out.

After such intense sex, popping her anal cherry, she had needed more. To be held—treated as if she mattered. Really stupid because she knew the score. They weren't friends or even lovers. She was nothing more to him than a convenient outlet for the sexual aftermath of shifting. A means to scratch the itch.

"Fuck this!"

Lance Corporal Shira Renard being wishy-washy instead of taking charge of a situation—hell no! Squaring her shoulders, she moved swiftly down the hallway, head held high. At her destination she didn't hesitate. Shira lifted her fist and delivered three solid raps to the door.

"Enter."

She moved into the office and stood at rest, feet shoulder-width apart, hands clasped behind her back. "Sir, do you have a minute?"

General Hughes kept his nose buried in the paperwork that held his attention. "Barely. What is it, Renard?"

"I need to discuss a personal conflict concerning tonight's mission."

His head popped up and she was subjected to Hughes' assessing gaze for several long, uncomfortable seconds during which he seemed to look straight down into her soul. She may have bought more of his attention than she wanted.

Finally, he nodded. "What's on your mind, Corporal?"

Similar to ripping off a Band-Aid, she got right to the point. "I don't believe McLean and I can put aside our personal issues and work together."

Hughes leaned back in his leather chair and rubbed at his temple. "I had shared similar concerns. Especially with the way McLean came to be injected and his initial animosity toward you. But watching you and McLean work together this week allayed my fears." He sighed heavily. "What's changed? Has McLean done something I haven't been made aware of?"

Other than fuck me blind? She quickly shook off that train of thought.

Shit, now the general thought Lex was the problem. "No," she rushed to assure. "It's me. I don't feel that I can keep my focus and properly execute my duties."

"McLean would be a distraction to you in the field," he nodded. "Fine. He's cut. I'll take care of it."

No! Not Lex. She needed to be cut. It couldn't go down like this. Lex would think she'd set him up, made Hughes doubt his fitness. Fuck, she had to fix this.

"With all due respect, Sir, I should be cut. Not McLean."

Hughes braced his forearms on the desk and gave her a hard stare Shira found difficult to meet.

"Your opinion is noted, Corporal, but my mind is made up. McLean may have done well today but I have more faith in your ability to control the animal. Fact of the matter is you've had longer to work with the fox and prove your mastery. Now I suggest you go prepare to head out, unless there's anything else?" His brow arched quizzically.

The general stating his decision meant he would entertain no arguments from her. She bit back a defeated sigh. "No Sir."

"Good. You're dismissed, Renard."

"Thank you, Sir."

Closing the door behind her, Shira realized she should have anticipated this move, more carefully considered the possible outcome. Put in the same position as the general, her decisions would have mirrored his. Unfortunately, Lex would view getting cut because she'd expressed concerns to the general as outright betrayal.

What a colossal disaster.

* * * * *

Cut from the mission because General Hughes didn't think he'd be able to control his wolf. What a crock of shit. He had more than proven his capacity to keep the wolf on a tight leash. Something about this stunk to high heavens and he intended to find out exactly what. At least he still remained on the team in a support position so he wasn't completely out of the loop.

Using every last ounce of his discipline and training, Lex hid his anger deep and turned on the charisma. With his patented charm-their-panties-off grin in place, he approached the general's admin. He'd caught several longing stares coming from the specialist and figured she'd be his best shot at information.

"Specialist Kamachi?" He sat on the edge of her desk and gave her a long, heated once-over. "What's different, darlin'? There's something…can't quite put my finger on what, but it's driving me crazy." Taking her hand in his, Lex nuzzled her inner wrist. "New perfume?"

Kamachi shook her head, her big brown doe eyes never leaving his.

"Hmm…have you done something different with your hair?"

"No, Sergeant." She fluffed her curls. "I haven't."

Lex laid it on thick until the petite brunette practically purred. Then he went in for the information he sought. "I'm sorry, honey. I'm such a mess today. I just can't believe what's happened."

"Oh no." She held gripped his hand tighter, scooted closer. "Is there anything I can do to help? What happened?"

So sincere and concerned for him. Damn. His conscience nagged, told him it was wrong to play her. His need to know had him pushing aside shame and carrying out his own agenda.

"Hughes bumped me down to support on a special mission. If I just knew who or what convinced him to do so…" He sighed dramatically and put on a hangdog expression.

"Well, maybe I'd be able to fix things, get back on the mission, save my career."

"Y-your career could s-suffer because of being bumped?"

At his nod she chewed her lower lip, leaned in closer and spoke in a low, conspiratorial tone. "Well, a Marine came to see the general right before he had me send for you. Lance Corporal Renard."

That miserable bitch.

He'd hoped it had been anything or anyone else. She'd already fucked up his life by altering his DNA but now she'd gone too far. Sabotaging his military career. Making the general doubt him. *Not gonna happen but nice try, Renard.*

"Sergeant," Kamachi whimpered. "Please, y-you're hurting my hand."

Aw fuck!

He had to get his rage under control before this situation went from bad to worse. "Sorry, sugar!" He placed a chaste kiss on each angry red fingerprint then stepped back. "And thank you. This conversation will be our little secret." He winked on his way out.

As he stormed down the hallway, Lex imagined all the ways he'd make Renard pay. The devious fox had fucked him over for the last time.

Musical feminine laughter caught his attention when he approached briefing room D, the room the team had been using to plan the mission due to be launched within the next hour. A husky, teasing voice he'd become intimately familiar with froze him in his tracks.

"You are such a big baby. It's just a little paper cut."

"You suck, Renard."

"Swallow too," she retorted.

"Oooh, baby. Soon as we're done here."

"In your dreams. I don't do civilians."

"Will you at least kiss it and make it better?"

From his position outside the open door, Lex ground his teeth. If Slater and Renard continued to flirt he'd be spending a lot of time in the dentist's chair getting his teeth fixed. Sure, harmless banter often helped relieve stress before going into a potentially dangerous situation. He'd indulged in it himself at times. But that was *his* fox Slater was talking up, damn it.

His fox?

Lex shook his head. The woman had him so screwed in the head that even when she made him furious he still wanted her.

"All right," Renard said. "We're go at 1630. Grab your gear."

Lex took that as his cue to get moving. He had to come up with a plan, find a way to convince Hughes they needed him on this mission.

His lucky break arrived a short time after the team had deployed in the form of critical new intel. The identity of the scientist attempting to resurrect the Predator Project would have a profound effect on the team and their mission. It sure as hell was blowing his mind.

"Why the hell didn't we know this sooner? Christ, we have copies of the death certificate." General Hughes reread the classified document then balled it up in his fist.

"The death certificate is genuine. Probably paid someone off." Lex shrugged. "Because of their history with Nanotech and Gabriel Weltman, that team can't proceed with this mission, Sir."

"And how the hell do you propose I stop them, Sergeant? We have no contact with the team to protect us all. This is not a sanctioned op. It won't show up in any file or record, no matter how highly classified. If anyone outside the team caught wind of this we'd all be stripped of rank and dishonorably discharged." He raked his hand through his hair. "Good Lord, if anyone found out I've been harboring genetically altered soldiers who can shift into animals, I'd be tried for treason and live out my days in Gitmo."

He was well aware of everything Hughes said but remained silent as the general vented. When his CO ran out of steam, Lex seized the opportunity. "There is a way to save us all, Sir."

The general tensed and his sharp gaze locked in on Lex. "Go on."

"I helped plan this op, know the details better than anyone else. When they arrive on the scene, the team will do their own recon, which will take time. Time I can use to get there before they go in. If I leave right now, I can stop them. Then I'll put together a team of soldiers who know not to ask questions and we'll take down the target."

"We haven't tested you in the field. What if the stress brings out your wolf?"

"Oh, I completely intend to use the wolf, Sir."

"You what!" Hughes' hands slammed down on the desk with a thunderous bang.

Lex took a slow breath. Everything rode on him remaining calm and convincing the general. "A human would draw the team's fire, alerting the target to our presence. The wolf can get in undetected."

Hughes rubbed his brow, pinched the bridge of his nose then moved in close. Lex stood toe to toe with his mentor, refusing to back down.

"Son, you pull this off without all of us getting thrown under the bus and not only will your career be guaranteed, I'll owe you my life."

Lex vehemently shook his head. He would never be able to repay the general for all he'd done for him and the other members of the Predator Project. Hughes had his unconditional loyalty and respect. "No Sir. It's the other way around. I will forever be in your debt for making sure Lasiter, Crosby, Renard and I didn't become caged lab rats. We all know what would have happened to us if anyone learned about the existence of shifters."

Just the thought chilled Lex down to the very marrow in his bones. Scientists would want to study them, the military would want to use them and the general public would want them locked away or destroyed. All equally frightening prospects.

Hughes clasped his shoulder, neither requiring further words. They both were well aware of how much rested on this mission coming off without a hitch.

* * * * *

Crickets chirped, small animals scurried through the underbrush and something splashed in dark water that strikingly resembled a moat. The big splash was a little too close for comfort. Shira prayed it wasn't an alligator. Or a snake.

Jesus, she didn't even want to contemplate the snakes. Their intel on the area had cautioned about poisonous water snakes and pythons big enough to eat a full-grown gator. She shuddered and eased a bit farther away from the water's edge, swatting away yet another house-sized mosquito.

This damn swamp sucked big fat hairy donkey balls. Perfect place for a mad scientist to set up shop though.

In the light of day, the area was probably pretty with its dense growth of oak and palm trees. Even the saw palmettos were appealing until getting too close and the sharp spines covering the stalk bit into tender flesh. Not even her thick swamp boots provided adequate protection.

In the dark of night, the place gave her the fucking creeps.

A low, throaty bark-like noise arouse from somewhere behind her. Fuck, she really didn't like that sound. Even her fox recoiled as she wondered what kind of animal gave such an ominous call and what it meant.

Keying her earpiece, Shira spoke softly. "Simba, being stalked. Gotta move. Now."

Simba. She laughed inwardly over Micah Lasiter's code name on this mission. Of course, hers wasn't much better.

"Negative, Foxy Lady. Hold your position."

"Can't. It's getting closer."

"What is?" Slater asked.

"Not sure but it's big."

"Hold position until I take out the perimeter guard," Lasiter ordered.

Following a civilian's orders irked. So what if he'd put more years in and had been some big shot at Nanotech? Taking a backseat didn't sit well with her. She thrived when in charge with one exception—sex with Lex.

No, don't think about Lex now. Stay focused.

When word came down to move in, she wasted no time putting distance between her and the swamp thing. She went through the door low, quickly scanning the anteroom before heading deeper inside. Adrenaline pounded through her veins as she headed down a narrow hallway toward the main workroom.

From intel, heat signature readings and their own scouting, they knew four people were in the lab and two guards were stationed outside. Lasiter had already taken down the two outside. He and Slater would come in from the back, secure the four remaining targets and take them back to the base for questioning. The medic, Wilson, would stay with the Humvee and only be called on if someone required immediate medical attention. Since he wasn't in the know, the farther they kept him from the action the better.

Her job was to destroy all evidence, including any DNA, so no one else could carry on with Weltman's sick vision.

Clearing the doorway, Shira could only stare open-mouthed at the bizarre laboratory that made her think of old late-night horror flicks. The entire left wall of shelves housed large jars containing various organs and body parts floating in a brownish liquid. At the back of the room a long table held a series of interconnected fluid-filled containers. An old-fashioned green chalkboard dominated the right wall, covered with symbols and scribbled notes. On a table at the center of the room were stacks of notes, a microscope, slides and vials of blood. Strange lighting cast a green glow over everything.

Approaching the table, she scanned the labels on several vials. *Carcharodon carcharias, ursus arctos horribilis, crotalus…* All Greek to her.

She picked up a stack of drawings revealing strange sci-fi creatures. A frog with bats ears, wings and fangs. An owl with a cat's head and front legs. A shark with armored scales. A toucan with an alligator's snout. Holy shit! She holstered her weapon, removed a compact camera from her pocket and began snapping pictures.

Strange sounds emanated from a birdcage that sat on one corner of the desk. Curious, she pulled off the cover.

"Sweet Jesus." Taking a quick step back, she covered her mouth and stared at the strange creature. It had the body of a large bird, possibly a vulture, with a long monkey tail and the head of a wolf. The abomination stared at her, black forked tongue lolling out of a snout full of sharp teeth.

Hands grabbed her from behind, taking full advantage of her momentary shock. One arm held Shira's back against a flat chest and the other held a sharp instrument at her throat. In her peripheral vision she saw the large syringe held in a masculine hand.

Not again!

Slater's warning over the comm device in her ear came a few seconds too late. "Heads up. Three secured, one remains unaccounted for."

Thanks a lot, slick.

"You don't like my creation? Shame! Egor was my first success. He can't shift but is a great companion. I wouldn't recommend trying to pet him though. Those teeth are very sharp."

That voice. She'd recognize his evil tone anywhere. Heard it in her nightmares. Gabriel Weltman.

No. Couldn't be. Nash Crosby, the man Weltman had turned into a tiger, had chewed him up and spit him out. No fucking way had Weltman survived.

She ignored the shouts coming through her earpiece — something about an intruder — different words from a long-ago conversation echoing in her head.

"Just picture an army of soldiers more powerful than any other. Trained fighters with the strength and instincts of the world's most dangerous animals. Extreme predators. Imagine how much governments would pay to possess such an unstoppable force.

"We've had our share of failures. Some of the early subjects didn't survive the procedure. Others didn't maintain their human intellect. They were reduced to animals intent only on hunting prey and had to be put down.

"We have had two major successes, both felines. A lion and a tiger.

"In your case, I have created something a bit different. A hybrid, so to speak. The combination of DNA from two animals — vulpes vulpes and canis lupus. You, Lance Corporal Renard, will receive the DNA of the crafty red fox and vicious gray wolf."

Catching movement in her peripheral vision, Shira glanced toward a shiny silver container on a nearby shelf. In its reflective surface she glimpsed a vision from her worst nightmares. Gabriel Weltman, gray hair a bit longer and unkempt, same cruel eyes though. And he once again held a syringe, prepared to inject her with another of his fucked-up concoctions.

To hell with that. She'd fight to the death. And this time, she'd kill him herself to make sure it got done right.

But something was very wrong. Her knees trembled, threatened to buckle. Her chest hurt, making it hard to draw enough air into aching lungs. A wave of warmth flashed over her and she broke out in a cold sweat. Bile churned in her stomach and her bowels weren't feeling very stable either.

"I-I don't feel so good."

Talk about an understatement.

Absently she wondered if that weak whisper had really been her voice. It sounded so distant. Detached.

Something skittered across the tile floor and she glanced down to see a big gray wolf staring up at her, sharp teeth bared and growling low in its throat. There was a camo bag hanging from its neck.

The wolf didn't scare her, although she wasn't sure why. Her brain seemed to be shorting out but she experienced a moment of clarity.

"Lexilicious?"

Chapter Seven
❧

A sense of déjà vu washed over him as Lex stared out over the boggy sawgrass marsh. He'd taken a Jeep, then a plane, and a harrowing airboat ride through the swamp to help Lance Corporal Shira Renard. He was tired, cranky, hungry and smelled bad. He had desperate need of a shower, food and a firm bed.

The difference—this time he didn't want the bed for sleeping. He wanted Renard in that bed with him, naked and wet, his cock sunk balls-deep inside the velvet clench of her pussy.

When had fucking her stopped being a predictable result of the shift and turned into a constant desire?

Shaking his head, he concentrated on the mission. He stripped, stowed his clothes and gun in a small duffle and looped the strap around his neck. The shift came over him quick and within moments he raced across the sawgrass on four paws. Other wildlife gave him a wide berth. The medic sitting on the hood of the team's Humvee didn't even see him pass by.

Soon as the laboratory came into sight, Lex sensed an unnatural stillness in the air. Finding two downed guards confirmed his suspicions. He was too late. The team had already gone in.

Damn it!

Forgetting stealth, he rushed around the structure. At the back corner he found Micah Lasiter and Kyle Slater busy securing zip cuffs on three more suspects. That left one more out there. Renard was nowhere in sight.

Slater, first to notice the wolf, drew his gun. "Holy shit. What's a wolf doing in the fucking swamp?"

Lasiter shoved the other man's arm, throwing off his aim. "That's gotta be McLean."

Lex didn't stop to confirm his identity. He ran straight through the open door and into the building. Maintaining traction on the tile floor was nearly impossible. His nails clicked as he scrabbled across the slick surface.

Lifting his snout, he found Shira's soft scent and followed, only peripherally checking other rooms as he passed. A kitchen that stank of garlic and tomatoes, a rec room with the television playing the theme song of a popular sitcom, shared sleeping and bathing quarters.

Turning a corner, he heard voices.

"You don't like my creation? Shame! Egor was my first success. He can't shift but is a great companion. I wouldn't recommend trying to pet him though. Those teeth are very sharp."

That had to be Michael Weltman, Gabriel's twin. The true genius behind the science of the Predator Project.

"I-I don't feel so good." Renard's voice sounded odd— weak and slurred.

Putting on a burst of speed, he charged into the room. What he found nearly dropped him flat on the floor. Weltman held Renard against him, a human shield. Glassy gray eyes shifted wildly from one place to another, never settling anywhere for long.

Michael didn't seem surprised to be facing a wolf in his remote facility. The info they'd gathered on him revealed a long history with various mental facilities until his twin had take over care of his brilliant yet insane sibling.

"Lexilicious?"

He made a quick assessment of Renard, who appeared to be in shock. Dilated pupils, shallow breathing, diaphoretic, dazed, slurred speech. Weltman held a large syringe with his

Foxy Lady

thumb on the plunger. The needle had pierced Renard's skin and a thin trickle of blood rolled down her neck.

Lex dropped his head, letting the bag slide to his feet. As he shifted, he crouched over the bag, blocking his actions from view as he drew his weapon. In one fluid motion, he stood and took aim at the quack's temple. The other man's gleeful grin sent chills racing along his spine.

"*Canis lupus,*" Michael breathed. "And able to shift. How delightful."

"Put down the syringe and I'll tell you all about it. Nice and slow now."

Michael's maniacal laughter flooded the room and turned Lex's stomach to rock.

"Shift again. Show me."

"Soon as you put down the syringe."

"No." His hold on the syringe tightened, depressing the plunger, shooting some of the fluid into Renard's pulsing vein.

Take the shot, she mouthed.

Lex caressed the trigger, focused on the target frighteningly close to her head. If his aim was off by the tiniest fraction, he could inadvertently shoot her. Statistics and probability factors echoed around in his mind while the threat to Shira brought everything into proper perspective. His reluctance to shoot boiled down to one startling fact.

Had it been anyone else held by the loony bin reject, he wouldn't have hesitated. Not for a second. But that wasn't just anyone.

That was the wolf's mate. His woman. He would not risk hurting her.

A vise closed around his heart and the truth hit Lex like a sucker punch to the solar plexus, knocking the air from his lungs. At some point he'd learned to rely on the wolf's strengths and instincts, stopped seeing the ability to shift as a curse. He'd even quit blaming Renard for injecting him and gotten over her part in changing him. He'd used hate as a shield, a way to maintain distance and hide from the frightening feelings Shira stirred in him. And the wily fox had managed to sneak in under his defenses anyway.

Take the fucking shot, Renard mouthed. He ignored her demand and focused on her captor.

"What's in the syringe?" That information would be crucial to counteracting whatever circulated through her bloodstream.

Michael's deranged grin grew even more disconcerting and he was all too happy to share his twisted deeds. "Metaxalone and succinylcholine."

Christ!

Anesthesia drugs. Lex had no idea which medications had resulted in Shira's violent hallucinations. Metaxalone would sedate her brain stem, inhibiting normal body functions such as spontaneous respiration. Succinylcholine, typically used in emergencies to intubate a patient, would paralyze her. If given enough, Shira would be conscious, aware of what happened, yet unable to lift a finger in her defense.

Fighting to control the shaking in his hand, Lex lowered the gun to his side. "Come on, Michael. Put down the syringe. We don't need her. We'll go outside and I'll show you the wolf. The shift is amazing, it happens so fast."

For a brief moment, Lex thought he'd gotten through to Weltman, whose fingers relaxed their tight grip on the syringe. Then understanding passed through his stormy eyes and his thumb slammed down on the plunger.

Shira muttered something unintelligible. Lex had no trouble reading her intention to take down Weltman in her turbulent expression. When her body refused to respond, going lax in the psycho's arms, her eyes widened in sheer terror. The mental anguish in those blue pools was nearly his undoing.

Seeing his chance at escape, Weltman shoved her at Lex and ran.

He caught her limp body, struggling with her dead weight, and moved Shira as gently as possible to the floor, adjusting her neck to keep her airway open. "I've got you, baby."

The wolf paced beneath his skin, howling in outrage, demanding he go after the man who had dared harm their woman. Ingrained training as a medic fought against the predator's instincts. He couldn't leave Shira in her vulnerable state.

Making a quick search of the room, he found basic first-aid supplies, including an oxygen tank, bag and mask. After gathering what he'd need, Lex returned to her side and assessed her vitals. Shira's panic drove her pulse rate through the roof while her breast barely rose as her body attempted to draw in oxygen. Her frantic blue eyes constricted his chest, limiting his own ability to breathe.

A grayish cast crept over her skin and her fingernail beds turned white. "You're not getting enough oxygen. I'm going to put a mask over your face and breathe for you." He continued to speak, hoping his voice would help ease her anxiety. Holding the mask sealed over her mouth and nose, he turned on the oxygen and squeezed the bag.

Terrified, fighting for her life, Shira latched onto the lifeline Lex provided. His voice helped soothe her and his constant presence assured her she wouldn't face this nightmare alone.

"Lasiter and Slater are right outside the door. They won't let him get away. Weltman's the whole reason I'm here. New intel came in after you left. That wasn't Gabriel Weltman. It was his brother, Michael." He chuckled. "Pretty ironic their mother named those two evil bastards after archangels.

"Michael has a long psychiatric history. Regardless of his mental issues, he's a brilliant scientist. Gabriel had the business smarts. Together they made a frightening team. They faked Michael's suicide to get him out of the institutions. We figure he's been hiding out here fucking around with DNA for the past twenty years, staying below the radar. Everything he discovered, Gabriel took to Nanotech."

She tried to express understanding in her eyes since she couldn't speak or move. Completely helpless, she listened and watched Lex, drinking in the sight of him. Tall, strong, competent and gorgeous as all get out. He would protect her. She believed in him, trusted he'd get her through this crisis. And she prayed that at some point he'd forgive her mistakes, allowing them a chance to develop something real and lasting.

"Being scrubbed from the action and relegated to a support role pissed me off. When I found out the general had done so because of you—

"I've never felt like such a fool. The betrayal cut deep, Shira."

Shira.

Lex never used her first name. Too personal. It was always Renard or during sex, baby. Damn, did it sound good though. She wanted to hear him say it again, only not in conjunction with the pain of being betrayed. She didn't care for that part.

With her eyes, she pleaded for him to understand. She had not betrayed him.

"General Hughes explained how he came to his decision. I know you didn't intend for me to be cut. Still, you and I need to have a long talk when this mess is cleaned up."

Thank goodness the general had made him understand!

"We need to clear the air between us. Talk about what happens next."

Next? Was there a next for them other than goodbye and don't let the door hit you in the ass on your way out?

"You see, I've been thinking."

Dangerous that.

His gaze darkened and for the first time she noticed his brown eyes were flecked with brilliant shards of amber. She could get lost in his eyes.

"There's something between us. Something more than intense attraction and phenomenal sex."

More than sex? Could he possibly mean...

"When I saw Weltman holding that syringe, not knowing what it contained." He growled. "Scared the hell out of me, Shira."

Okay, he'd just used her name again so it hadn't been a fluke. Her heart beat faster but her chest still rose slow and steady each time he forced air into her decompressed lungs.

"I like you, Shira."

Like was good. She could work with like.

"And my wolf...well, he has a thing for your fox."

As if on cue, her fox lifted its head and concentrated on him. She stared up at Lex, trying to let him see the strength of her feelings.

"We have this undeniable connection. I want to see if it can be more, how far we can take it. Find out if there's a chance for a future. Together. You and me."

Oh God. She never would have guessed Lex harbored this sweet, uncertain side under the hard-ass attitude.

Her heart clenched and tingling awareness started in her toes as the drugs began to wear off. The sensations grew as they spread through her body, similar to the pins-and-needles sensation of restored circulation. She coughed, choked and he stopped squeezing the bag. When her chest rose on its own, he removed the mask from her face.

There were a million things she wanted to say and do. Her fingers itched to reach out and touch his face. She floundered, staring up at him, more helpless than when the drugs had shut her body down. The paralysis from the drugs had been horrible. This was worse.

Warm fingers brushed along her neck to check her pulse. He shined a bright penlight into her eyes then he grabbed a stethoscope, rubbing the end between his hands before placing it over her heart and listening.

When he finished his examination, she struggled to sit up. A firm hand over her breastbone pushed her back down.

"Not too fast, Shira. You're going to be lightheaded and your muscles will be uncoordinated for a while."

She wanted to be anywhere other than this horrible place with that freak of nature growling at them from the desk. "Lex." Her voice cracked. She swallowed and tried again. "Get me out of here."

"Sure thing, baby."

He lifted her carefully and held her close against his chest as if she were the most precious burden. Her muscles better hurry up and get with the program because she had definite plans, things she wanted to try out with the big bad wolf.

They stepped out into the humid night. Someone had pulled the Humvee up close to the building and Lasiter stepped around the vehicle.

"Renard? What happened? Are you all right?"

She lifted her hand. "I'll be—"

"That crazy bastard shot her full of paralytics. Please tell me you got him."

Lasiter directed them to the open tail of the Humvee. Inside were all six men, cuffed at the wrist and ankle. Weltman squirmed and mumbled into the strip of duct tape covering his mouth.

Shira arched her brow and Slater shrugged. "Bastard wouldn't shut up. I got sick of listening to him."

His sharp gaze didn't miss Lex's tight hold on her or the way her head rested on his broad chest. "You okay?"

"I'm fine...now."

Wilson stepped forward, reached out toward her and froze as Lex growled.

"Not a smart idea unless you want to pull back a bloody stump," Lasiter warned.

The medic cursed under his breath and headed for the safety of the vehicle.

"I take it you're not riding back with us."

Slater's words were more statement than question but Lex answered anyway. "We've got our own transport."

Lasiter and Slater would take the suspects back to the general for questioning. She and Lex would be expected to report for debriefing too.

"Tell the general..."

What?

She had no idea what explanation would smooth over a delay in their return to base.

"We'll tell him the drugs made immediate travel impossible and McLean stayed behind to make sure you're okay," Lasiter offered. "May even take a day or so before you're up to the trip."

Damn quick for a civilian. Shira grinned.

"Still," Slater cautioned, "I wouldn't suggest being AWOL for long. The general's not the most patient man. He's going to want to see you for himself to make sure you're all right."

Lex nodded. "Thanks. I owe you one."

"No," Lasiter corrected, gripping Lex's shoulder. "Now we're even." He shot her a knowing glance. "Consider this payback for protecting my mate."

Chapter Eight

ॐ

Red taillights disappeared around a curve. Not willing to let Shira go, Lex carried her away from the lab and deep into the heart of the swamp.

"I can walk. I'm not an invalid."

"Um-hm," he agreed and continued to hold her close. Shira was a strong woman, both physically and mentally, yet in his arms she felt soft and delicate. He didn't want to ever put her down.

"Where are we going?"

"Someplace we won't be disturbed."

"Um, but you're going farther into the swamp."

"Um-hm."

She swallowed hard. "That's where the gators and snakes are."

"So."

"So," she echoed in disbelief. "Lex, they're dangerous."

"Yeah, and so am I."

That shut her up but not for long.

"I'm afraid of them."

Her whispered confession almost made him pause. He smiled down at her indulgently. "I'll protect you."

She smacked his chest and breathed a frustrated sigh. "You're such a caveman."

Ouch!

The barb stung deep. He was trying to be romantic, damn it. Find a quiet, pretty spot to sit and hold her, watch the sunrise. He wasn't that much of an ape. When he wanted to, Lex could turn on the charm. Of course, considering how he'd treated her over the past several weeks, she had every right to doubt him.

Well, he'd just have to prove her wrong. Shame he didn't have any flowers, wine or candles in his pack.

He continued to carry Shira until he discovered a small prairie bordering a shallow channel. Setting her down at the base of a large palm tree, he gathered kindling and started a fire. Not candles but it would have to do. At least it would help with the chill in the air. The idea was to get her soft and relaxed for him, not cold, tense and terrified of other predators. He was the only predator getting anywhere near her.

Sharp blue eyes watched his every move from beneath a thick sweep of dark lashes. Once he established a small blaze, Lex sat next to Shira and drew her back into his arms. "That will keep the little beasties away."

"And what about the big beastie?"

"Sorry, I'm afraid you're stuck with the wolf, Shira."

"Say it again." She spoke so softly he almost didn't hear her.

"Say what?"

"My name. I like hearing you say it."

"I've said your name before—"

"Uh-uh." She shook her head. "In bed I'm baby and out of it I'm Renard."

"Ah, back when I was being a callous dick."

"I never—"

"Called me a callous dick," he interrupted. "Not to my face, no."

Her lips clamped shut, forming a thin pale line. Shit! He was fucking this up. He sighed. "I'm sorry. I don't want to fight."

"I know. It's part of your nature to be contrary."

Damn if she didn't have him all figured out. "Can we start over? I've been a complete shit toward you. I'd like a second chance."

"You have every right to hate me after what I did —"

He placed a finger over her lips. "Let's not rehash the past. I'm sorry, baby. Will you let me make it up to you?"

Shira stared up at him with those big expressive eyes and the bottom dropped out of his stomach.

"For now, just let me hold you and know you're safe in my arms. How's that sound?"

"Heavenly."

She wiggled in his lap, stirring his randy cock, before settling with her head pillowed on his shoulder. A comfortable silence fell over them, which neither felt the need to fill with idle chatter. They simply shared the peaceful reprieve from the hectic pace of military life.

Shira had to admit that nighttime in the Everglades did hold a certain beauty. Sitting in the muted firelight with Lex as his fingertips absently traced the curve of her spine, listening to the music of the night creatures and watching stars twinkle was rather romantic.

The fox didn't share her desire to cuddle though. As the strength slowly returned to her body, the animal grew restless. After a while, so did Lex.

When the sky began to lighten, she couldn't sit still for another minute. Shira kissed the tip of his nose, jumped to her feet and started to strip. Lex watched her, his eyes darkening with lust.

"Does the big bad wolf wanna come out and play?"

He rose slowly, every inch the predator on high alert. Lex matched her movements, stripping along with her. Once bare, for the space of several long heartbeats, she couldn't move as she drank in the glorious sight of him. Her sexy blond medic.

My mate, her fox corrected.

The shift came over her fast, without conscious thought. One moment a woman stood naked in the swamp, the next a crafty red fox turned and fluttered her tail. As enticements went, it worked for the wolf. Lex shifted, tossed back his head and howled.

The chase was on.

A red fox and gray wolf were foreign to the swamp and although its natural inhabitants were curious, they stayed well away from the pair streaking across the prairie, playing hide-and-seek within tall sawgrass, yipping and barking with a pure joy for life.

Sensing a change in the air, the fox lifted her snout and caught sight of the wolf's hungry expression. Fun and games were over. The wolf wanted to finish what they'd started on the base. And this time, there would be no guards or shock collars to stop him from taking her.

Whoo-damn!

She'd dreamed about this. Hot, wet dreams that left her aching.

Instinct took over and she bolted. The fox would not just bare her belly and submit. The wolf had to prove himself worthy first. She faked right, dodged left. The wolf matched her every move.

Exhilaration electrified her senses. Anticipation made her quiver. His hot breath on her backside had her pussy clenching and cream flowing.

Sharp teeth nipped at her side then his bigger body came down over her, flattening the fox to the ground. The wolf rubbed against her until she bore his scent. Their bodies bumped together and as she rolled belly up, his long tongue slid over and around her snout. He nuzzled her neck and moved down her body, licking soft fur, gentling her.

Finding her vulva swollen, he sniffed her, taking her musky scent into him. At the first flickering caress of his tongue over her sex she whimpered with need. He continued to lick her, his tongue rasping along sensitive tissues. Sweet fluids gushed over his tongue and she writhed beneath him.

Jumping to his feet, the wolf snapped and barked, ordering his mate to stand. No sooner did she lift up on four paws before he covered her from behind. Sharp teeth sank into the scruff of her neck, holding her in place. Staking his claim. She shivered as the broad head of his cock notched at her wet, pulsing opening. The wolf filled his mate with one hard thrust and both animals howled in bliss.

Their mating was wild and uninhibited, frenzied and dominant, similar to their coupling in human form. The wolf pounded into the fox as she cried out her pleasure. He thrust into her hard and fast until her vaginal walls constricted around his shaft, gripping him tight as his cock swelled, knotting inside her.

Collapsing to the ground, they lay on their sides, remaining locked together. The wolf continued to lick the fox's snout, nuzzle her neck and gentle her after their fierce mating.

A new connection forged between them. There were no words to express his strong emotions. No need for words during the loving, post-coital glow. They shared a speaking glance and shifted while their bodies were still fused.

Lex stroked Shira's hair and held her tight until well after the last aftershocks fluttered around his shaft and the knot eased. She gazed at him with love shining in her eyes.

Two animals joining—fox and wolf—had been better than either could have imagined. And in the process, more than bodies had joined. Their hearts were now tightly intertwined.

Lex felt that elemental bond to the bottom of his soul.

* * * * *

On a bed of moss beneath the dazzling orange and red glow of sunrise, Shira experienced a sense of peace, belonging and rightness unlike anything she'd ever known. She felt complete, as if all the pieces finally connected, making her whole.

The fox and wolf had mated, forging a permanent, unbreakable bond. For her and Lex, building a lasting relationship would take time and effort. With the animals' help she figured they had a pretty good shot at it.

Rolling up on his side, Lex tucked her hair behind her ear. "Shira?"

She'd never get tired of hearing him say her name. "Hmm?"

"I know you like hard, fast, sweaty fucking."

"Um-hmm." She loved the primal way he rocked her world.

"Would you mind slow and soft? I really want to make love to you."

Her heart seized then pounded against her sternum. If she hadn't already fallen for him that would have sent her plummeting.

"No." Her voice thickened into a husky whisper. "I wouldn't mind at all. In fact, I think I'd like that."

Lex laid one of his patented mind-melting kisses on her. The kind that knocked her socks off—if she'd been wearing any. Her toes curled into the rich earth as he proceeded to reshape her idea of what making love meant.

Tender caresses and sultry kisses created a slow burn. Lex's mouth was a warm, wet haven, his tongue stroking hers. Their bodies merged as one in a slow, rocking rhythm. Filling her. Joining them.

Taking both of them to dazzling new heights of ecstasy.

With each thrust his broad crown rasped over her pleasure spot and his pelvis ground along her clit.

She loved this other side of Lex—unhurried, tender and giving. Almost as much as she craved him untamed, rough and raw.

The slow and easy buildup created a wave of bliss, the orgasm claiming her before she was ready for it to end. But Lex was right there with her, going over the edge as one then gently floating back to earth in his loving embrace.

She and Lex would face many tests, trials and adjustments in the future. Being shifters guaranteed they would live with secrecy. Shira had faith he'd be by her side, taking on whatever challenges that may come.

Also by Nicole Austin

🙟

eBooks:

Candyman

Cat's Meow

Ellora's Cavemen: Dreams of the Oasis I *(Anthology)*

Eye of the Tiger

Enough

Erotique

Flyboy

Foxy Lady

Have a Little Faith in Me

Kenna's Cowboy

Master's Thief

Passionate Realities

Rakahnja's Haven

Restless

Savannah's Vision

Tempestuous

The Boy Next Door

Trip My Switch

Print Books:

Ellora's Cavemen: Dreams of the Oasis I *(Anthology)*

Holding Out For a Hero

Passionate Realities
Savannah's Vision
The Boy Next Door

About the Author

ℰℛ

Nicole Austin lives on the sheltered Gulf Coast of Florida, where inspiration can be readily found sitting under a big shade umbrella on the beach while sipping cold margaritas. A voracious reader, she never goes anywhere without a book. All those delicious romances combined with a vivid imagination naturally created steamy fantasies and characters in her mind.

Discovering Ellora's Cave paved the path to freeing them as well as manifesting an intoxicating passion for romantica. The positive response of family and friends to her stories propelled Nicole into an incredible world where fantasy comes boldly to life. Now she stays busy working as a certified CT scan technologist, finishing her third college degree, reading, writing, and keeping up with family. Oh yeah, and did we mention all the hard work involved with research? Well, that's the fun job — certainly a labor of love.

Nicole welcomes comments from readers. You can find her website and email address on her author bio page at www.ellorascave.com.

Tell Us What You Think

We appreciate hearing reader opinions about our books. You can email us at Comments@EllorasCave.com.

Why an electronic book?

We live in the Information Age—an exciting time in the history of human civilization, in which technology rules supreme and continues to progress in leaps and bounds every minute of every day. For a multitude of reasons, more and more avid literary fans are opting to purchase e-books instead of paper books. The question from those not yet initiated into the world of electronic reading is simply: *Why?*

1. ***Price.*** An electronic title at Ellora's Cave Publishing and Cerridwen Press runs anywhere from 40% to 75% less than the cover price of the exact same title in paperback format. Why? Basic mathematics and cost. It is less expensive to publish an e-book (no paper and printing, no warehousing and shipping) than it is to publish a paperback, so the savings are passed along to the consumer.

2. ***Space.*** Running out of room in your house for your books? That is one worry you will never have with electronic books. For a low one-time cost, you can purchase a handheld device specifically designed for e-reading. Many e-readers have large, convenient screens for viewing. Better yet, hundreds of titles can be stored within your new library—on a single microchip. There are a variety of e-readers from different manufacturers. You can also read e-books on your PC or laptop computer. (Please note that Ellora's Cave does not endorse any specific brands.

You can check our websites at www.ellorascave.com or www.cerridwenpress.com for information we make available to new consumers.)

3. *Mobility.*   Because your new e-library consists of only a microchip within a small, easily transportable e-reader, your entire cache of books can be taken with you wherever you go.

4. *Personal Viewing Preferences.*   Are the words you are currently reading too small? Too large? Too… ANNOYING? Paperback books cannot be modified according to personal preferences, but e-books can.

5. *Instant Gratification.*   Is it the middle of the night and all the bookstores near you are closed? Are you tired of waiting days, sometimes weeks, for bookstores to ship the novels you bought? Ellora's Cave Publishing sells instantaneous downloads twenty-four hours a day, seven days a week, every day of the year. Our webstore is never closed. Our e-book delivery system is 100% automated, meaning your order is filled as soon as you pay for it.

Those are a few of the top reasons why electronic books are replacing paperbacks for many avid readers.

As always, Ellora's Cave and Cerridwen Press welcome your questions and comments. We invite you to email us at Comments@ellorascave.com or write to us directly at Ellora's Cave Publishing Inc., 1056 Home Avenue, Akron, OH 44310-3502.

COMING TO A BOOKSTORE NEAR YOU!

ELLORA'S CAVE

Bestselling Authors Tour

Discover for yourself why readers can't get enough
of the multiple award-winning publisher

Ellora's Cave.

Whether you prefer e-books or paperbacks,

be sure to visit EC on the web at
www.ellorascave.com

for an erotic reading experience that will leave you
breathless.